The Lost Empress

FOILED STARS
BOOK THREE

JENNIFER ASCIENZO

Stag Beetle Books

To my family:
Thank you for always believing in me and being with me every step
of the way throughout this adventure.

To my readers:
To those who see the good in everyone
and believe the villain deserves a second chance.

Prologue

THE HUMANS WOULDN'T SHUT *up*.

Ronan sat in the control seat of his destroyer with bits of cloth shoved into his ears. The humans had been at each other's throats non-stop for almost a year.

If it wasn't complaints about the quality of the food and who left hair in the sink, it was constant nagging. *Are we there yet? Are we there yet? Are we there yet?*

"No," he'd scream, throwing his hands into the air.

Not a single "thank you," or shard of gratitude had been expressed for delivering them from the slave planet of Varz.

If Ronan had the ability to travel back in time, he would've left them there to toil for all eternity. At least then, they would've been out of his hair.

He took deep controlled breaths, attempting to calm himself down, but failed miserably.

"Everyone, stop it." He ground his teeth in his mouth.

The destroyer knocked and rattled through the turbulence of space. The entire cabin thundered as he maneuvered his way through a passing asteroid shower. Pebbles skidded against the hard metal exterior of the ship. Lights from passing stars streaked across the glass of the windows.

Caleb toppled face-first over Marcela and her son Tyler, who remained huddled on the floor for much of the voyage. Their eyes bulged in their skulls with fear. They were shell-shocked and terrified.

Caleb groaned, stomping through the cabin. "I want to get the hell off this ship. When are we getting back to Earth? This is taking forever."

The only thought that kept Ronan from reaching and snapping Caleb's neck in half was that of Sean, his boyfriend who he'd met at the Castle rollerblading rink during his mission on Earth. Hopefully he'd be keen on coming back to Surge with him. He didn't want to imagine his lonely life again without him.

Two years had been far too long.

Ronan's uniform pocket vibrated. When he glanced down to see the caller, the hairs on his neck stood at perfect attention. He sighed. He had no other choice but to answer his communicator. Ronan had been dodging Dante for quite some time, unwilling to disclose his whereabouts.

"Hello," he slid the screen up and reluctantly muttered. His heart thrummed in his ears.

"You know every time you ignore my calls, a certain frequency is transmitted," Dante snapped through the communicator. "Allow me to remind you, not only are you my flesh and blood, but I am your emperor. The very least you could do is pay me the respect I deserve in accordance with my rank and pick up."

Oh no. Dante had finally given his father what he deserved. His hands sweat within the confines of his gloves.

"When did this happen?" Ronan stuttered.

"Well, if you were here, you wouldn't have to ask." Dante paused. "I know what you're thinking, and I assure you it's untrue."

No, Dante had no idea what he was thinking.

"I'm sorry. I—forgive me, the signal hasn't been the greatest," Ronan muttered the quickest excuse he could think of.

"Enough. I'm not buying your justification. I know all about your little unauthorized trip to Earth for the boy and all about the humans you removed from the slave planets without my permission."

Ronan's jaw lowered. "You do? How?"

"Of course I do. I know everything," Dante said smoothly through the communicator. It crackled against his breath. "I'm not angry, although I should be furious with you. I have a little, well, actually a huge problem, and I order you to help me."

"Okay, I'm at your disposal," he turned the control panel. The human bickering grew louder and louder by the second.

"Quiet." Ronan hissed into the cabin, waving his black-gloved hand.

"What?"

"Sorry, not you," he apologized to Dante.

Dante grumbled something incomprehensible before speaking. "Valdez knows about Earth and about my little indiscretion with Keyserike. It's only a matter of time until she informs the Grand Supreme of my betrayal if she hasn't already. I need you to collect Autumn's father and ensure his safe passage back to Surge. In the meantime, I've dispatched reinforcements to guard the planet."

"No problem at all."

"Excellent. You need to hurry up and get back here as soon as possible. There shall be no dallying. If anything happens to him, she'll never forgive me, and you're going to have a real problem on your hands."

"Yes, you have my word."

"Thank you, Ronan. I'm entrusting you with his life."

"But of course, you can always count on me."

"Don't agree with me—just obey my order. I have enough trouble on my hands. I need to find my wife."

PART ONE

A Shallow Grave

One

AUTUMN SAT in pure darkness for what seemed like forever. Her only friend was the gentle hum of the ship. Try as she might, she couldn't reach Dante through their telepathic bond, and she had no communicator to contact him with.

Armienti and Valdez had robbed her of everything. Her life, her future, her happiness.

Her own wet vomit accosted her senses. She couldn't keep any food down. Disgusting green slop was delivered to her, three square meals a day without fail. Sometimes long winding hairs stuck out of the bowl. Armienti had offered to get her better food, but she couldn't stand to eat the food of a traitor—especially one who thought she was going to marry him and rule by his side.

She gulped down the chunks greedily, desperate yet nauseated at the same time. She was too hungry to turn her meals away anymore. A fever consumed her, and delirium set in. She was far too weak to attempt to escape.

The ship stilled and the temperature in the room dropped to what felt like below zero. She shuddered, her teeth clattering together. The air was cold and dry as she inhaled. Her breath became white flowing mist.

Where were they? Had they finally landed?

She stretched her neck to peek through the windows but was unable to catch a glimpse of her surroundings. It was no longer dark and star-filled outside, but a deep murky gray.

The lights in the room flickered on and she squinted, her eyes taking a moment to focus. She'd been in the darkness for so long she'd lost track of time. She trembled as two Zexian guards approached her. Their powder-white wings sat high on their backs, twitching. Their obsidian eyes were dark and lifeless.

They keyed a code into the door of the translucent cage she occupied. They dragged her from the cell, kicking and screaming with all her might. Which wasn't much, considering she could barely stand.

She was escorted up several flights of stairs and through dark corridors. Screaming and crying echoed from the surrounding chambers. A chill skittered down the length of her spine.

Autumn was dumped on her face before a throne, sitting atop a three-stepped steel dais.

Leave it to Valdez to have a throne on her ship. How pretentious. What a bitch.

Valdez had since changed from her tattered attire. She wore a crimson toga. Her frayed hair from where Dante had burned her jade braid had been combed neatly behind her pointed ears. A sleek white mask concealed half of her face— the half he had burned to a blackened crisp. She stroked the material with her fingers.

She chuckled and crossed her legs before propping her chin with her fist. "You look terrible, human filth. Why the long face?"

Autumn struggled to stand. Her legs crumpled beneath her weight. Her energy was non-existent. It was humiliating.

Valdez yawned and picked at her red manicured talons. "What? No witty comeback? I'm rather disappointed. I prefer my game to have a little fight. This is going to be all too easy for me, and I hate to admit, rather boresome. You have it coming though. I've dreamt of this day since first we met. I can't wait to feast on your sweet, supple flesh."

Valdez snapped her fingers and two winged soldiers returned carrying the golden sunburst crown gifted to her by Dante's mother, Isidora. Autumn winced as they shoved it onto her head and the ends collided with the backs of her ears. Thick warm blood trickled over her scalp.

"Perfect," Valdez flashed a serpentine smile. "A crown fit for a fallen Empress."

The soldiers dragged Autumn to a door surrounded by Valdez's crew who heckled her on with whistles and jeers in their strange Zexian language she couldn't comprehend.

At that moment, Armienti rounded the corner and his cerulean eyes widened. "What—what are you doing? I thought we had an agreement that no further harm would come to her."

Autumn glowered before hocking saliva in her mouth and spitting on his boots.

"You said you would rough her up a little, scare her to get it out of your system, but this—"

A grin twisted across Valdez's mouth like a rabid jackal. "Well, I'm afraid I've changed my mind. And, by the way, you shall join her."

Zexian soldiers swarmed Armienti, and he struggled to break free from their grasp. They urged him onward.

Such an idiot. She rolled her eyes.

The door of the ship opened and hissed. Brisk wind blew inside shattering Autumn to the core. She'd never been this cold in her entire life. Gusts of snow whipped for as far as her eyes could see. There was nothing but violent wind and white.

"We're going to play a game. You know how I adore

games, Armienti," she held her hands against her cheeks like a giggling schoolgirl.

His eyes widened; no words left his mouth.

Valdez's blue eyes glowed with mischief. A soldier went to hand her a golden bow and arrow, but she pushed it aside.

"Never mind this useless weapon. I have a better idea."

She cracked her knuckles and tied her short hair into a ponytail. "You have five minutes. Run for your lives."

Two

AUTUMN'S HEART accelerated as she desperately searched for an escape. Wind whipped through her hair as an ice storm pelted against her frozen skin. She squinted, trying to better understand her surroundings.

With shattered ribs and diminished energy, she could barely stand. Her eyelids weighed with sickness and exhaustion.

The sunburst tiara gifted to her by the former empress on her wedding day cut against her scalp. Warm blood trickled down her ears. Her teeth chattered in her skull. She'd never been so freezing cold and miserable in her entire life.

As she surveyed the area, weighing her options, Valdez kicked her square between the shoulder blades. She stumbled face-first into the snow, wind knocked from her deflated lungs.

The white-out blizzard poured snow up to her knees, soaking her go-go booted feet to the bone. Armienti struggled to stand. His crimson cape lashed through the elements.

"Please, you don't have to do this. We can split the realm fifty-fifty like we agreed. We can join forces," hopefulness flooded through his voice.

Valdez folded her bare toned arms. "Split the realm with a weakling like you? Ha! I think not," she chuckled, along with her spiky winged entourage. "You're pathetic and useless. You've proved to me you can't be trusted. You betrayed your own family. Shame, shame." She waved a long taloned finger in his face accusatorily.

"I can't believe you betrayed Dante. How selfish and stupid can you be to trust her?" Autumn said in a low gruff voice.

They were going to die.

Valdez cocked her head to the side. Her blue eyes gleamed like two beacons in the storm. Autumn was sure it wasn't her imagination. Moments ago, Valdez was an entire foot shorter. Suddenly, her jade arms and legs bulked out with pulsating veins.

"You're wasting your breath," her voice deepened. "You're down to four more minutes. I'm counting every second. I can't wait to decorate the snow with your blood."

Sheer terror numbed Autumn to the core. As she ran, her heeled boots stuck to the snow and slush. Wind thrashed against her frozen cheeks, and bitter tears streamed from her eyes. She sprinted in slow motion, too weak to take flight.

Armienti zipped by her. She fell to her knees catching her breath. Her fists clutched the snow and ice.

"What on Earth are you doing?" Armienti's voice echoed through the elements. "We have to get out of here before she transforms. She'll kill us both."

"I don't think I can."

She laid on her side and stared at the oncoming snow as the flakes buried her alive. Her life had been one big disappointment after the next. It figured she was going to be murdered by a raging alien empress witch on some ice planet she'd never heard of.

It was the story of her life.

A few years ago, she would've thought, *what are the odds?* But now, she knew more than she ever dreamed of. She'd never see her dad or Dante again. It was all Armienti's fault.

Traitor.

In that moment, Autumn heard a loud whooshing sound as a spinning object flew through the air and landed beside her with an icy thud. She gasped at the pale decapitated head of one of Valdez's soldiers. The snow became soaked with his thick black blood and sinew. *Holy crap.*

The ground boomed and shook like an earthquake. When she turned around, a twelve-foot-tall monster with lumpy jade skin and a long slobbering tongue pursued them. Valdez's eyes grew wide and petrified in her skull. The veins in her neck protruded while her stacked muscles flexed. She closed her eyes and prepared to meet a painful end.

"Come on, Autumn. You're better than this."

Armienti grabbed her and took flight, racing against the oncoming storm. Autumn tucked her head against his chest. Behind them, Valdez jumped and soared into the air in hot pursuit.

Armienti glanced over his shoulder. "She's gaining on us."

Valdez swiped her long talons and knocked Armienti down from the sky. Autumn screamed as she went flying from his arms. Falling snow tumbled against her body at a rapid pace.

"Freeze," Valdez's low deep inhuman voice echoed through the storm.

Autumn froze mid-air, struggling to move. She was far too weak to put up a fight.

Valdez circled her, chuckling, then balled her fist and whaled her in the spine. Autumn's eyes widened as her bones crunched and ligaments separated. She bit back a scream.

Valdez snickered. "I love the sound of your bones shattering."

Snow poured from the sky. Autumn could barely see through the whiteout. Every breath she took twisted like a knife through her lungs.

"There's a certain look people get before they die. A mix of desperation and hopelessness. You're making that look right now, Autumn Martyne. How I've wished for this moment for the longest."

Valdez choked and her eyes bulged as Armienti came up behind her and wrapped his arms around her throat.

"Why you little—" She thrashed her talons at him. "You just made a fatal error, fallen emperor. Are you ready so soon to join your Empress?"

Fallen emperor, Autumn narrowed her eyes with what little energy she could muster. She couldn't believe the trouble Armienti had gotten them into.

Armienti cupped his palms against Valdez's eyes, and she shrieked. Shrill screams echoed through the snow-filled valley.

Valdez spun around in circles. "I'm blind, you blinded me!" she whimpered, body thrashing. When she opened her eyes, they were coated with a thick layer of ice.

Armienti grabbed Autumn and slung her over his shoulder. She faded fast as he took flight.

"Where are we going?" Autumn asked hoarsely, nodding off. He patted her frozen cheek, rousing her.

"You have to stay awake. Don't fall asleep on me. We need to find somewhere to hide. It's only a matter of time until her vision returns."

"But how?"

"I can generate snow and ice in addition to healing. A far less desired ability but occasionally it comes in handy," he winked.

Armienti flew through the pounding wet snow.

As he descended, he crept into a cavern, peeking over the bank.

She shuddered, closing her eyes. Her heart slowed. A cool relaxation consumed her. Bright lights danced across her vision, before she fell into the darkness.

15

Three

MEANWHILE BACK ON SURGE…

Dante couldn't stand to look at his mother. The very sight of her made him ill. Her pleading eyes tempted him to roll his own.

"I can't believe you. All these years you've been lying to me. Haven't I suffered enough?" He ground his molars together, his fists clenched with trembling ire. He struggled not to explode; no good would come from another outburst. "Between this and Father's long-standing agreement with the Grand Supreme, you two make me sick."

"Forgive me, I wanted to tell you. Really, I did. But I couldn't risk the secret getting out."

His mother glanced into the city, avoiding his eyes. She'd deceived him.

It was the same look Autumn gave him before she disappeared. Deep in his gut he knew she was up to something.

All he could think about was her excuse to go to the kitchen and thank the chef for the chocolate chip pancakes he'd made her for breakfast. Her excuse was ridiculous. He was so foolish and lovestruck to believe her. *Now, she's miss-*

ing, he brooded. Dante twisted his mouth to the side. "I suppose Armienti knows as well?"

She crossed her arms, lips trembling. "Yes."

"Despicable. Absolutely despicable. You trusted him more than me? You're *my* mother."

"I'm his too," she said in a whisper of breath, tears sparkling in the corners of her large brown eyes.

"Well, you've been mine for a year longer. I should've been privy to this information."

Dante tucked a strand of hair behind his ear, recalling the years of his life he could never get back. How he toiled under the absolute control of the Grand Supreme because of his late father's agreement. His parents never failed to disappoint him.

Thick black smoke churned through the city from his soldiers' endless searching for his wife. It had thus far produced nothing, only destruction.

"Your father wasn't a kind man. You saw for yourself. So I sought comfort elsewhere. What was I supposed to do?"

"Even still, you should've told me."

He recalled the black and blue bruises decorating his mother's skin on various occasions. Gifts from his father. He couldn't blame her for trying to escape.

Dante folded his arms. "I'll be honest, I'm not sure what I'm going to do with this information. You've proven yourself to be untrustworthy."

His mother wept in her hands. Tears streamed down her blue cheeks. "Forgive me," her voice quivered. "I'm sorry."

He paused contemplating. "I suppose Ronan is my brother as well?"

"No," she shook her head. "He isn't mine, although I've always seen him as a son. The affair I had was short-lived."

He turned his back on her, mouth twisting to the side. His mind spun a million kilometers a minute. His communicator buzzed within the confines of his pocket. His heart leapt to his throat. Dante slid his finger across the screen and answered the call.

"Hello? Yes, yes?" The communicator slid from his hand onto the shadowy ground below. It became like a speck of dust in contrast to the massive cityscape.

Nausea overtook him at the news of his soldiers recovering Autumn's grounded aircraft. He raced to the far end of the city in search of it, hoping to find a clue to her whereabouts.

Four

AS AUTUMN STRETCHED AND WOKE, her cheek rested against the frigid dusty stone. When her vision cleared, she glanced around. The cavern was cool and dark. The only sound she heard was her own breath, leaving her mouth in crisp white puffs.

Was she dead? She pinched her cheeks. They were warm and soft beneath her fingertips. *If she was dead, her skin would be cold and hard.*

She rose to a shaking stand and inhaled, taking in the brisk mountain air. Her ribs no longer ached, and her spine resumed a natural direction.

She recalled Armienti's betrayal and the fight with Valdez who was hunting them for sport like animals. She scrambled around the cave. Armienti was nowhere to be found.

Holy crap. He abandoned her on a strange planet.

"Armienti? Armienti?" She searched for him.

She sprinted to the entrance and surveyed her surroundings. In every direction, all she could see was glittering snow and ice. The storm had let up and the sun blazed in the sky which shimmered the rich cloudless hue of emerald.

Her stomach grumbled and twisted. She hadn't eaten a real meal since the day she was captured from Surge.

Armienti crept back into the cave stealthily. He held the pelt of a small animal in his black-gloved fist. "I'm glad you're awake. You look well if I might say so. I brought breakfast for us. There isn't much, but I was able to hunt this creature down."

She took a deep shuddering breath before her vision shifted to blood-red.

"You," she lunged and knocked him in the jaw with the ball of her fist. She sent him clear across the cave, slamming into the wall. His teeth cut together.

Armienti stumbled into the rocks, dropping his kill. Pebbles sprayed from the wall, misting through the air.

"What were you thinking?" she hissed, smashing her fist against his face, again and again. His blue skin shifted beneath the weight of her blows.

On the fifth swing, he caught her fist in his palm and held it taut. "Now, is this any way to thank me for saving your life? I believe it's been three times now. Haven't you wondered why you're not dead?"

"Saving my life?" Her lips curled in a snarl. "It's your fault we're here to begin with. I should've been on my way back home to Earth. It's your fault I'll never see Dante or my family again."

"I have my reasons for what I did," he folded his arms. "You would never understand."

"I don't care what your reasons are. I'm sure they're selfish just like you," Autumn said. "We have to get out of here. There has to be some way we can contact home for reinforcements. Or maybe we can try to overtake Valdez's ship," she contemplated aloud.

Armienti peeked outside into the snow-filled valley. "If you leave, Valdez will most certainly kill you. She's still hunting us as we speak. Her ship isn't too far off. Our best bet is to stick together and stay hidden for the time being."

Autumn thought long and hard for a moment about his suggestion. Her forehead pulsated. She realized he was correct. It would be suicide to leave the cave under the current conditions.

She nodded. "Agreed."

She secretly wanted to punch him in the face again. It took every ounce of energy she had in her body to unball her fists. She relaxed them at her sides. *There would be time for payback later.*

Suddenly, the entire floor of the cave vibrated. Her stomach leapt to her throat. Valdez and her soldiers were searching for them on foot.

Autumn hugged herself and then buried her face in her hands to prevent herself from screaming. Tears streamed down her cheeks from the fear rattling her to the core.

* * *

ARMIENTI STOOD NEAR AUTUMN, solemn and terrified. More than anything, he wanted to comfort her. What he did was not only reckless but irresponsible. and selfish most of all. On the exterior, he kept a neutral stance. They were in the most trouble he'd ever been in his life. Because of him, they were in danger. His former superior hunted them like frightened rats. They had nowhere to go and nowhere to hide. They were stranded on an unidentified ice world with no food, no water, and no warmth.

Escaping her wrath wouldn't be an easy feat. He knew better than anyone that once Valdez caught a whiff of their scent, she would see their demise through to the end. *Up close and personal, slowly and painfully.*

Her greatest pleasure in the world was torturing and murdering others.

It was only a matter of time until she discovered them. Although the odds were stacked against him, he was still convinced he made the right call. He wanted more than anything to claim his birthright and the girl who haunted his dreams every night.

Five

DANTE CUPPED a black-gloved hand over his mouth, then ran it through the chin length strands of his hair, tousling them. His stomach toppled with sickness.

Autumn's aircraft sat at the far end of the city with the control seat door wide open. It was like she'd abandoned it, or worse, been snatched.

As he swallowed, his throat went bone dry. He inhaled before exhaling slowly.

"Sire, this is how we discovered the Empress's aircraft." The soldier averted his eyes to the ground. His entire body quaked.

"Leave us," Dante ordered. The group of onyx-clad soldiers dispersed at his command. He fell to his knees and took a series of deep controlled breaths. He grabbed hold of the gravel as his vision blurred. This couldn't be happening.

It was like losing Maeve all over again. He tried his hardest to maintain his composure, but he was losing himself to the situation.

A gentle hand squeezed his shoulder and his muscles relaxed, then went taut.

"I know Autumn is alive," his mother's voice was

soothing and even. "She's a strong girl with a good head on her shoulders who's been through so much. She can take care of herself, my love."

He brushed her hand away and rose to his feet. His heart hollowed at his mother's betrayal as well. She was no better than his brother.

Yes, Autumn could take care of herself, but he didn't want to imagine her hurt or in danger or…no, he couldn't allow himself to think that way. If she was gone, he couldn't go on living.

He circled the aircraft, his boots falling in line, carefully weighing his options in silence when—

A twinkle of red on the seat of the aircraft caught his eye. He went over to investigate. Upon further inspection, two black velvet pouches spilled over with sparkling rubies.

What on earth? What was Autumn doing with so many rubies? Thousands of them. The same ones gifted to him by the Grand Supreme on the day of their wedding. They were stamped with his despicable headless crest.

How could she have gotten them without his knowledge?

His heart pounded and his imagination ran wild. She must've been in some sort of trouble she didn't feel comfortable enough to discuss with him.

He levitated and crossed his arms, falling into a period of deep thought. *I need to get back to the palace at once.* In an instant, he was gone.

* * *

DANTE STORMED INTO THE TREASURY, his crimson velvet cape whipping over his shoulders. His mother flanked him in complete silence. She hugged herself, clearly uncomfortable.

Treasure scattered over a long rectangular table in the

dead center of the room. Gold jewels and rubies glimmered in the light of the stained-glass windows.

The black-cloaked treasurer ambled over and fell into a deep bow, his knobby knees knocking together.

"Your Imperial Majesty, how may I be of service to you?" His eyes were affixed on Dante's boots.

"Don't 'Your Imperial Majesty' me," his jaw snapped tight, eyes thinning to slits. "You've been slacking. Provide me with a recent list of transactions effective immediately."

The treasurer ran a scan through his pad. Holographic numbers and symbols swirled through the air. Dante tapped his foot, overcome with impatience. His tolerance had been nonexistent since his wife disappeared.

Finally, anxiety got the best of him. He succumbed to a wave of panic.

"Here, give it to me," he gestured with his black-gloved hand. The treasurer obeyed, glancing away. Dante's eyes widened with disbelief as he examined the numbers. "Who authorized the removal of twelve satchels of rubies from my personal account?"

"Um, well," the treasurer stuttered between dry cracked lips. "The empress did."

His mother looked at him and shrugged.

"Forgive me sire, not the empress dowager. I mean—your wife. She told me you were aware of the transaction and used two of your credit chips to deduct the sum in full. I had a feeling something was off."

"Why didn't you bring this to my attention earlier?"

He glanced at the floor without answering.

Dante recalled entrusting her with the chips before his successful mission on Varz. Autumn had every right to access the money, but why didn't she tell him?

What was she hiding?

"Did she mention what she needed the money for?"

"No sire, and I failed to ask. Please forgive me," he

pressed his frail palms together, bones cracking. "I should've been more diligent."

Out of anger he raised his hand, conjuring a ball of crackling fire to punish the treasurer but then thought better of his inclination. He didn't want to be like Valdez, who murdered for sport, or his master, the greatest butcher of them all. Besides, Autumn, sweet innocent Autumn, would be displeased if she discovered he'd murdered one more, adding to the endless tally of bodies he'd racked up over the years.

He couldn't imagine her thinking less of him again. The thought frightened him. They'd come too far. Before this nightmare, they were finally starting to live the life he'd only dreamed of.

The treasurer slammed his eyes shut, preparing himself for certain death.

Dante lowered his palm. "On second thought, I won't waste my energy. Instead, you're relieved of your duty as treasurer effective immediately. That means *now*."

He turned on his heel and stormed from the vault. It was his good deed for the year. His lips flickered.

Anger coursed through his veins. How could the treasurer have no clue what his wife needed the money for? *What a fool.*

He stopped for a moment, stroking the cleft of his chin. His mother caught up with him. Suddenly, it dawned upon him like a spark of electricity to his brain. There were two lazy hybrid maids who could bring him closer to Autumn's disappearance.

He cracked his knuckles. He couldn't wait to *interrogate* them, and hopefully extract some answers.

Six

DANTE KICKED Autumn's bed chamber door clear in, smashing the steel against the wall across the room.

Emblem and Allegoria ducked, shielding their mops and buckets of water from spilling all over the floor and walls that they had just cleaned. Mr. Hiss hid under the bed with his large glistening eyes. His hot-pink striped tail puffed, and he released a long, deep hiss.

"You two never cease to amaze me," he crossed his arms. "You work slower than one servant on their first day of duty. You're useless." His mouth twisted to the side.

"Forgive us, we're working as fast as we can." Emblem swished the mop in the bucket, suds sloshing all over the floor.

Allegoria nodded. "Yes, we've already cleaned the windows and—"

Dante watched them, assessing. *They were a nonsensical duo.* "I think you know why I'm really here."

"I—" Allegoria stuttered.

Dante continued. "My wife is missing—"

"She promised us each a satchel of rubies in exchange for a name." Emblem blurted out, then cupped her mouth with her hands. She'd given him the information he'd hoped for. *Of course they were somehow involved*, it tempted him to roll his eyes.

"A name? Whose name?" His eyes widened.

Emblem stuttered, then hesitated.

"Tell me at once. You're holding up my investigation," he demanded, folding his arms.

When Emblem failed to answer, he sauntered over, reached out, and massaged her temples cyclically with the tips of his fingers. She trembled and her frail body fell into his arms as she drifted into a trance.

Dante's eyes fluttered closed. He saw the transaction that'd taken place. Autumn promised them each a satchel of rubies like she claimed in exchange for the name: *Treble Spriggs.*

"Treble Spriggs," he willed himself to remember the name. A long address followed. Treble resided at the far end of the city of Giarldinia—all the way out near the fields of Zym where his soldiers searched for Autumn.

He opened his eyes and cast a lazy blink at the twin maids. He laid Emblem across Autumn's bed. She'd wake up soon enough, then she could resume her duties.

"Please don't send us to Varz," Allegoria pressed her palms together, quivering. "We only did what she asked of us."

"Thank you for your cooperation," his mouth curved, and he turned on his heel, his mother following him in silence, shaking her head.

Allegoria scrambled back to her station, no further questions asked. He had an inkling of Autumn's whereabouts, but he needed to see for himself. He needed to speak with this *Treble Spriggs.*

On his way out of the room, he stopped one of the guards.

He folded his arms and his spine snapped as straight as a

rod. "And where were you yesterday? You were tasked with keeping my empress safe."

The guard stuttered before saying, "She relieved us for the day. We had her permission."

He sighed, *that's right.*

He recalled Autumn mentioning something to that effect. If he could go back in time, he would've insisted her guards remained with her at all times, or he would've accompanied her himself.

He'd failed her yet again.

He cracked his knuckles. "I see, well nonetheless, I'm displeased."

The energy in the room grew hot and static and vengeful. He struggled to remain calm under the circumstances. *This was absurd.*

"No, wait, please," the guard begged. "I have valuable information that could lead to her whereabouts."

Dante cocked his head to the side. "Well, why didn't you say so earlier? Speak, I'm listening."

"I last saw her with Prince Armienti. Yesterday morning he came to visit her in her chambers despite your instructions and when she left, well, I shouldn't say—" The guard glanced away beneath his onyx helmet.

He clenched his fists and his mind went wild. "Tell me this instant what happened between them."

The guard's teeth chattered in his mouth. "He ran his hand along her back and adjusted her bodysuit zipper."

"He touched her?"

The guard nodded. "Yes, sire, he did."

Dante was going to kill him. He was going to murder Armienti when he found him. He'd tear him apart limb from limb for putting his hands on his wife after he'd warned him to stay away.

"Thank you, you've been most useful." He continued through the hall, allowing the guard to live. His third good deed for the day.

Seven

AUTUMN SLURPED the cold meat down greedily that Armienti had brought her. It was her first meal in days, and she didn't know whether she'd be eating again. She couldn't believe she was eating meat, but it was better than starvation. The gristle slid down her throat and she choked back a wave of nausea, yet she found the food satisfying.

She was careful to keep a close watch on Armienti. She wanted nothing more than to bash his skull against the stonewall of the cave to thank him for his betrayal. Like a lady, she refrained.

Still in disbelief about their predicament, her mind raced. They were stuck on this strange ice planet with no escape, and a murderous alien witch hunted them day in and day out.

It was *all* his fault.

The rhythmic marching of Valdez's soldiers had finally stopped with the coming of night. Millions of stars twinkled through the dark sky. Rainbow ice sparkled across the ground.

"When you're finished, we should get moving," Armienti gestured to the opening of the cave. "We'll need water and warmth if we're to survive a harsh climate like this one. It makes the Earth winter seem like summer."

"Shut up," Autumn gulped down the remainder of her cold meat. She didn't want to hear his infuriating voice.

Because of him, she was separated from Dante who she never dreamed she'd miss this much, and her trip back to Earth to see her dad had been canceled. She couldn't help but worry about them. And she couldn't help but dwell on how worried they must've been for her safety.

Dante had probably destroyed Surge and all twenty-four universes searching for her.

Armienti finished the last of his meal. "Come on."

He reached for her, but she brushed his hand away. She reluctantly followed him through the passageway and into the night.

* * *

THE TERRAIN WAS barren with no trees; the sparkling ice spanned into oblivion in every direction. They walked through the frozen planet—not an easy feat in high-heeled go-go boots with frozen toes.

If only she had a pair of real shoes with some warmth, and not the always summer fashion of the Martyne court.

"Come on, pick up your feet. We have a lot of ground to cover before dawn. Valdez will be on the hunt again and we both know how relentless she is."

"Screw you," she hissed. "I can't believe you did this to us."

"I'm sorry, Autumn," his blue face hardened in the pale moonlight. His golden hair swayed in the winter wind. "I wish I could take my decision back, twenty-twenty hindsight, but I have my reasons."

"Really?" she groaned, forehead pulsating. "I bet your reasons are just as superficial as you are."

Of all the seasons, winter was her least favorite, but of all the winters, the one they spent stuck together on that miserable planet with nothing but snow and ice was her most loathed.

They walked for hours upon hours. Crisp breath caught in her lungs. Even with her untamed abilities, she grew tired and restless.

She pouted, stomping her feet. "Come on, please, we have to find shelter. I need sleep."

She was freezing through her spandex down to the depths of her bones.

As she inhaled, the sharp biting air cut against her throat. In the corner of her eye, a shadow shifted in the dead of night.

She pulled against Armienti's shoulder, not wanting to touch him but desperate to get his attention.

"Do you see that over there?"

He stopped. "Do I see what?" He turned his head, and his blue eyes bulged.

They approached the figure with stealth and precision, careful not to be seen as they advanced. Autumn winced as her feet throbbed with each step.

Someone was standing on the ice.

"Identify yourself," Armienti commanded. The figure didn't answer. Something didn't seem right. The hairs on the back of her neck stood at perfect attention. Her heart thundered in her chest. As she drew closer, she identified the torso of a headless Zexian soldier. Its thick black blood spilled over the glittering ice like tar.

She jumped and shrieked as a head rolled between her feet.

Holy crap.

A sharp pain settled in her neck. A cold steel dart pierced her skin.

Someone clapped in the distance. "Got her."

Autumn sprinted, and Armienti followed her. Her footsteps were sluggish and uncoordinated. Her vision narrowed and blurred at the corners.

Armienti passed her, never bothering to turn around and help.

"Damn him," she muttered as her legs gave out beneath her and her world faded to black.

Eight

DANTE CHECKED the coordinates of his communicator three times to ensure he reached the right location. On the third viewing, he concluded they were indeed correct. This sure was the oddest address he'd ever heard of, and being the emperor of Surge, he was surprised he'd never heard of it.

50,000th street, Building 307 million, Apartment 85.

He scrunched his nose. It amazed him how unfamiliar he was with this part of Giarldinia. Almost like the area had been omitted from the map.

Hybrid children laughed and played, rummaging through the garbage. They danced barefoot, mere centimeters from shards of glass sticking through the gravel. If they were his children, he wouldn't have allowed this behavior. It was far too dangerous.

One little girl ran up behind him and tugged on his cape. He whipped around and caught a flash of gray eyes and a mess of dark curls.

Instantly he was reminded of Autumn, and then of Maeve, although her memory faded with the passing suns and moons. He could barely recall her face anymore.

He managed to press out a smile and waved but she giggled and ran away.

"Are you going to be okay?" His mother placed a reassuring hand on his shoulder. He brushed her hand off and ignored her question.

He still wasn't ready to talk to her after her lies and deceit. He wasn't sure if he'd ever be.

"You stay with the ship, and I'll get to the bottom of this," he finally said.

She nodded mechanically, boarded the ship, and locked the doors. *Now to find this Treble Spriggs.*

* * *

THE HALLWAYS of the apartment building were an unsightly mint green. The windows were smashed to oblivion and shattered glass coated the floor. Dante sauntered, searching for apartment number eighty-five, which he discovered at the far end of the hall. It was one of the dirtiest doors he'd ever laid eyes on.

He balled his fist and knocked, not wanting to touch the filthy exterior. He waited a moment before demanding, "Open this door at once."

Whispers and shuffling came from the opposite side. "Who's there?"

"The emperor," he smoothed his hands against his vermillion cape.

Latches unlocked and chains frantically slid.

"Who do you think you are, making demands?" A boy's voice echoed through the hallway. A red bandana was tied across his brow and over his pointed ears. He ripped off the strip of fabric and his cheeks flushed. "Oh, I-I-I didn't realize you were serious." He bowed his head in submission.

Dante watched the young boy with the cloth in his hand. A supporter of the Red Cloaks, obviously. But he was too foolish to hide the symbol of rebellion. Perhaps he didn't know any better, and to be honest under the circumstances he didn't care.

He ignored the red cloth and knelt to the boy's height. "Are your parent's home perchance?"

The boy crossed his arms and stuttered. "Who wants to know?"

"Well obviously I do, that's why I asked."

The boy leaned against the door. "No, you sent them away right after I was born."

The words hit him like a gut punch.

"I'm sorry, I don't recall—" his heart accelerated, at a loss for words. "Is Treble Spriggs here then?"

"Who's there?" The door swung open. "I'm right here—" The color faded from her pallor face. She cupped her hands over her mouth and muffled a scream.

Dante rose. "I should've known it was you," he assessed her. "You're fortunate to still be alive."

He paused. "Is it all right if I come in?"

Treble nodded and winced. A dried lash mark exposed itself on her shoulder from the beating she endured.

The apartment was disgusting. Dante coughed. It hurt to breathe. Mold and mildew lined the ceilings. Baskets containing food and champagne from the palace sat on the floor. *Wait, baskets?* He did a double take.

He turned toward Treble. "Where did these containers come from?"

"Oh," she stuttered, her teeth chattering in her mouth. "Autumn, I mean the empress, brought them to me after—"

"You're forgetting about Prince Armienti. He was here too," the boy in the doorway added, his voice as gentle as a song.

Dante's stomach twisted into a cruel knot. "So, you mean to tell me they were both here *together* at the same time?"

Treble and the boy both said concurrently, "Yes."

A fury unlike any other fury Dante had ever experienced shattered him to the core. The only occasion to ever rival this sensation was the morning he lost Maeve. He silently recalled her small, delicate broken body in his arms. He inhaled, seeing shooting stars.

Autumn's good deed was unsurprising, with her kind and forgiving nature. He should've guessed; but, why was Armienti involved?

And why did she feel comfortable enough to share her plans with Armienti, but not with him? He would've gone with her. It was all his fault to begin with.

All of it.

He exhaled a deep yet desperate sigh.

They were obviously no longer on the planet. His soldiers had combed every street, avenue, and apartment in the city. They searched the endless fields of Zym and the dark surrounding forest.

Autumn was in danger and somehow Armienti had a hand in it. He was going to kill him when he found him—tear him apart with his bare hands.

"Thank you, you've both been most cooperative."

He turned on his heel to leave but then hesitated. Treble limped, following him to the door to see him out.

He faced her once more. "Those scars are going to get infected."

Treble hugged herself, running her hands over her stained light-gray smock. She stared at him strangely, brows furrowing.

"You should come back to the palace with me, and I'll see that you're fixed up."

Her mouth was agape. "Are you sur—"

"I won't extend this offer to you again," Dante could scarcely believe the words as they left his mouth.

"What about my brother?"

"Bring him as well."

"Yay, we're going to the palace," he skipped around the room.

Dante bit back a smile. He placed a hand on each of their shoulders and they teleported back to his ship. He needed to prepare for his voyage into deep space. Autumn was in danger.

Nine

WHEN AUTUMN'S eyes shot open, her hands were bound behind her back and a bit was shoved between her molars. She struggled to stand, her legs falling limp beneath her weight.

She pulled her arms apart with all her might, but she couldn't escape her bindings. Instead, an electric shock rattled through her body. In response, a muffled scream escaped her mouth. She was a prisoner.

A Zexian soldier kicked her between the shoulder blades. "Oh good, you're awake. On your feet, captive empress." He chuckled and his powder-white wings twitched against his muscular back. He spoke Ivarkian so she could understand his taunts.

She fell onto her face, cheek burning against the ice. Snowflakes fluttered from the sky coating her body, sticking to the ends of her frozen lashes. White mountains glistened in the distance partially concealed by shadows.

"I said on your feet."

When she didn't rise a second soldier approached her and slung her over his shoulder. Pale wings shivered in her face in the dead of night. She kicked and screamed, greeted by another unwelcome electric shock when she tried to separate her hands.

Terrible idea. She almost blacked out again. *Crap.*

The soldier's tiny mouth curved. His empty obsidian eyes smiled with delight.

"The more you struggle, the more it will hurt. Those bindings are designed to internalize your energy."

As she twisted, her bones burned like they were cast into an open fire. Her body fell limp over his shoulder like putty.

"Wow, what a stupid human. You'll never learn. I mean, we heard humans were dumb, but this is ridiculous." He pinched his long fingers against her cheek and her eyes bulged with fear and rage.

"What do you say we have a little fun with her?" another soldier suggested. "Empress Valdez was never specific about the condition we had to bring her back in, if we found her."

"Good idea," a second set of fingers ran through her matted glittered hair. "It's been a while since I've sampled something sweet, and I haven't eaten in days since the hunt began." He licked his colorless lips.

She frantically searched the rugged snowy terrain, but Armienti was nowhere to be found. What a jerk.

* * *

AUTUMN WAS DRAGGED kicking and struggling through a dark damp cave. She tried her best to escape Valdez's rough-handed soldiers but to no avail.

She was stupid enough to get captured and Armienti had abandoned her like a total coward.

They dumped her onto the hard stone ground. Pebbles and snow shifted beneath her weight. Her tailbone sang in agony. She could barely decipher her attackers in the darkness, but their rough clawed hands slid against her body regardless.

She shot to her feet, followed by an electric shock that coursed through her veins. *Holy crap.* She was surprised her skin didn't melt off her bones. She couldn't take any more of this torment.

Her molars ground together. The pain was indescribable.

One soldier removed her gag, and she sank her teeth into his lengthy finger. Her mouth filled with the taste of metallic blood. Black droplets rolled down her chin.

"You bit me! Why, you little—" He backhanded her against a stone wall. She slid to the ground, her vision erupting in swirls and stars. Her ears rang from the blunt force of impact.

The soldier nursed his blood-soaked finger. "If you're not sorry *now*, you will be."

He gestured to his other two counterparts. "Go build a fire, my appetite is growing fierce." They took cloth from their uniforms and zapped it with tiny metallic guns they pulled from their standard issue boots. Orange flames crackled and smoked.

He held her on the ground and her restraints sent another round of electricity coursing through her body. She screamed as his teeth elongated in his mouth, growing sharp like sabers. Drool pooled on her neck in a warm wet puddle. The points of his teeth dripped with sticky green venom. She gagged.

He was going to devour her alive.

A throat cleared and all eyes in the cave drew toward the entrance. A dark silhouette stood with his arms folded.

"This is how you choose to conduct yourselves, like a bunch of greedy pigs? Three men against one girl. And you call yourselves men? You make me sick."

Armienti's crimson cape swayed in the blistering wind. His golden hair glittered in the frozen firelight.

A wily look crossed his sapphire eyes. In a flash, he grabbed two of the soldiers by the backs of their hairless heads and slammed their faces together until all that was left of them was bone and mush. Their winged bodies fell lifelessly to the ground.

The third soldier stumbled to his feet and sprinted toward the exit. Armienti intercepted him and kicked his head so hard, his neck snapped in half. The crack of his bones echoed through the cave.

The soldier's limp body fell to the ground and convulsed. He ran a black-gloved hand through his golden hair, tousling the strands.

His murderous instincts were cruel and precise, but necessary in this situation, she hated to admit. She chewed her bottom lip, taking in the situation.

He spit on the floor. "Tough guys. Look at you now."

Her entire body trembled with relief. She wouldn't be someone's dinner. "Thank you," she breathed.

That was a close call.

The early morning sun sparkled along the snowy horizon in the distance. With Autumn's thoughts finally leveling out, she realized they were right back where they began. Bones from the small animal they consumed a few days ago were scattered along the bottom of the stone walls and lodged between the crevices.

Her heart sank. *She hated feeling this helpless. There was no worse feeling in the world.*

Armienti fell to his knees and placed a black-gloved hand on her shoulder, squeezing it. "Are you okay?" His mouth quaked.

She nodded mechanically. "Yeah, I think so." But in reality, she was petrified.

With great ease, he snapped her restraints between his fingers. She peeled them off, letting them fall to the ground as she massaged her bruised wrists.

"Next time you need to listen to me and follow directions.

Deep space is a dangerous place, especially for a young woman like yourself."

She knew he secretly wanted to say *human*, but for whatever reason he refrained. For a moment, he reminded her of Dante with his lecture.

She scrunched her nose, regarding him. He remained pompous and self-satisfied. One of his golden brows quirked.

"Wait a second. Did you let me get captured on purpose to teach me some kind of lesson?"

A sly smile crept across his lips. Anger coursed through her body, and she took her teal go-go boot and kicked him in the shin as hard as she could. He hopped up and down and winced.

She was tempted to kick him one other place as well. She knew she'd get her point across somehow.

"I can't believe you put me through this," tears welled in her eyes and poured down her cheeks. "Because of you I was almost eaten by those disgusting monsters. And it's all your fault we're in this mess to begin with."

"I wasn't going to let you get eaten," he rolled his eyes. "But I had to prove a point. If we're going to survive this ordeal, we must stick together. No more me against you. We must operate as a unit."

"I can't trust you," she folded her arms, snot rolling through her nostrils. "Not after what you did to me." *And Dante—she missed him so much her chest burned.*

"Right now, you don't have a choice. We need each other to survive. If we go our separate ways, we're dead."

When Armienti went to open his mouth again to speak, the floor rumbled, the intensity casting them both to the ground. The force was almost as strong as when Dante's ship crash landed on Earth, and she encountered him at Farrah Falls for the first time. And more forceful than Valdez's night death march.

She ran to the entrance and cupped a hand over her

mouth, biting back a scream. Valdez's conical ship soared into the sky through clouds and swirling gusts of snow. *Oh no.* They were stranded.

Stranded; her mind ran away with itself. There was no means of escape, no chance of seizing Valdez's ship and over-taking her.

"Shit," Armienti muttered.

Shit didn't even begin to cover it. They were marooned on this miserable planet. Eternal winter was their prison. They had no food, no water, no warmth, no *tampons.*

How could they possibly get through this?

Maybe it would've been better to be Valdez's next meal. At least then their demise would've been quick. They were going to freeze and starve to death.

Autumn dropped to her knees and sobbed her heart out. "Wha—what are we supposed to do now?" she stuttered between broken breaths.

She was so close to going home, so close to living the happily ever she deserved, so close to seeing her dad and her beloved husband again. Now she would never find happiness, and it was all Armienti's fault.

"I don't know," he placed a hand on her shoulder, and she shrugged it off. Her forehead pulsated, and her fists trembled, ready for impact.

It was official. They were trapped on the ice planet from hell. Her life had been ruined once again.

Ten

HOURS HAD PASSED and Armienti trudged with Autumn through the snow and ice to the location where Valdez's ship had been docked. He scoped the area, making sure it was safe.

But something didn't add up. Something was wrong, his gut screamed.

It took him mere moments to determine Valdez and her crew of Zexian soldiers were indeed gone. Judging by the smoking bones and half-drunk goblets of wine, they'd left in a hurry.

Autumn's eyes were sunken and glazed with red from crying so hard. Ice and snow crept up her calves. How he pitied her.

He'd offer to carry her, but she was proud and would decline his assistance regardless. She despised him like she'd once despised Dante, his older brother.

Probably even more after all was said and done.

This whole ordeal was all his fault. Nothing was worse than this horrifying realization. What a fool he was to trust Valdez. He should've known better, considering her reputation.

She was the biggest snake of them all.

If he allowed his emotions to get the best of him, he would've broken down and cried as well.

For the first time, he couldn't see his way out of a terrible situation. Usually he could predict the outcome, or there was light at the end of the tunnel. Some kind of hope. But this…

Even after everything they'd suffered through, he couldn't fathom why Valdez would give up her game and leave. *Why was she in such a hurry?*

His stomach churned. It wasn't like her not to win. She enjoyed beating others. Murdering was her favorite pastime, besides of course, torturing Autumn. *It was clear from the get-go she had it out for them. Autumn more so, but still…*

Something more important must've come up. Something more important than killing him and Autumn for sport.

He sighed, skin erupting in goosebumps. He was terrified to find out. The Grand Supreme was the only option he could think of.

He must have needed her for something sinister.

Growing up, he was fortunate that he never had to deal with The Grand Supreme first-hand. Dante had always been there to bear the brunt of the blows, but Armienti *had* to take responsibility—and he *wanted* to. He wanted everything to be different.

He could no longer toil in Dante's magnificent shadow. It should've been him basking in eternal sunlight all along. Dante was the true nobody. He was not emperor material.

What can I do now, and from here? Dammit.

"What are we doing? There's nothing here. I'm cold and hungry," Autumn pouted, her heeled boots skidded against the snow and ice. Poor thing was freezing to death.

"Just a moment," he knelt in the snow, searching desperately. It had to be here somewhere. *It had to be.*

He stopped when he discovered the frozen decapitated

body of one of Valdez's Zexian soldiers decorating the ice and slush with his sticky black blood.

Autumn gasped, covering her mouth and turned away. "If you think I'm going to eat that creature, you've lost your mind."

He chuckled. Apparently, she wasn't starving after all. But food wasn't what he was searching for. He reached through the pockets of the cadaver. *There had to be one here somewhere.*

Relief flooded through his bones as his fingers slid across the screen of a communicator. *Thank the gods above.*

Autumn grinned, hopping up and down. Her pure child-like happiness warmed his cheeks, even during this heinous situation.

The power bar flashed, and he hesitated for a moment. When Dante learned of his betrayal, he was going to roast him alive. But what choice did he have under the circumstances?

Oh no. His stomach tumbled. *Oh no, no, no,* the device was about to take its final breath and there was no charging station in sight.

He managed to punch in Ronan's number, fingers trembling with every character. He couldn't handle speaking to Dante. Ronan had always been easier to talk to. One ring and he picked up.

"Hello? Hello? Ronan, are you there?" He asked hopefully.

Tick, tick, tick, a beeper flashed and sounded off. Armienti dropped the communicator in the snow and took Autumn by the arm.

"What are you doing?" she gasped. "And why is the communicator making that noise?"

Armienti didn't have time to answer. Instead, he flung Autumn over his shoulder. She kicked and screamed. Her fists connected with the aching muscles of his back. He winced as he soared high into the air, and a fiery explosion of snow, debris, and ice erupted beneath them.

His ears rang with deafening silence. His heart sank in his chest.

Valdez had left them a parting gift. It was so like her to play tricks.

Eleven

RONAN'S BROWS rose as a strange frequency hummed through his communicator. He squinted as he looked at the number.

Who the heck was calling him all the way out in Universe 18?

Coordinates flashed and danced across the screen before the signal went dark again. He hadn't the slightest clue how someone had intercepted his personal line. *A wrong number,* he supposed, and he shrugged it off as such, placing the device back into the confines of his pocket.

As he glanced through the dark vastness of space, he could barely process the situation. He didn't know where to start, for before him orbited planet Earth in all its exotic glory. At least, that's how he recollected the planet when he had last laid eyes on it over a few years ago.

An invisible forcefield, put in place by his cousin, engulfed the little blue planet whole.

He'd dreamt of the moment he'd have someone to love and hold in his arms for what felt like eons. He couldn't wait to see Sean again. The apples of his cheeks warmed against his will.

Ronan hoped he'd accept his Elattion heritage. It could go either way but still—he was worth the risk.

Since Dante had been successful with his human bride, couldn't he be as well?

His short-lived excitement was interrupted by the Queen of Earth, former slave of pleasure planet Halvana.

"Are we there yet?" Misty ran around the ship in a towel. Her honey-blonde hair dripped all over the metallic floor from her shower. Steam fogged the walls and windows of the destroyer.

He rolled his eyes. This one was half naked and always yapping her mouth. How he detested the sound of her nasally voice. It pulled against his eardrums.

She stomped around, arms crossed.

"I can't wait to get off this ship and throw myself into a hot tub. I deserve it more than anyone else. This trip was brutal. It totally sucked. It would've been more exciting spending a year reading at the library."

He blinked, mouth twisted to the side, then shook his head, growing frustrated.

Misty continued. "I don't know what I did to deserve any of this. Autumn completely overreacted. Believe it or not, I never minded her."

Ronan rolled his eyes. *What a lie.* Not an ounce of gratitude was expressed on her part. When he thought back over their recent travels, none of the humans were the least bit grateful for being rescued from an awful fate.

"Save it," he muttered, recalling the cruel ways she tortured his empress in the past. She was the biggest nuisance of them all.

The others sat on the floor with their eyes closed, heads resting against the wall. Marcela ran her fingers through the strands of her son's ink-black hair.

For the life of him, Ronan couldn't fathom why Autumn forgave him. If Tyler had murdered his mother, Ronan would've dumped his body into deep space—*after* skewering it, of course. No questions asked.

Overall, the trip was long and miserable for everyone. He couldn't wait to unload the humans and be done with them forever.

The ship transmitted a silent signal to its sister vessel located at Farrah Falls.

As he waited, the breath hitched in his throat. His heart pounded in his ears as crisp white dust flowed and swirled. After a few moments, the scene cleared to reveal the emerald and blue sphere that was planet Earth—marked target of the Grand Supreme, Dante's greatest treasure, and Autumn's home world. He grinned, rubbing his black-gloved hands together.

"Finally," Caleb yawned from the floor, stretching his arms above his head. "It sure took you long enough to get us home," he muttered.

Ronan glowered. "Excuse me? You're lucky to still be alive, human. The way you behaved toward Autumn after she put her neck on the line for you was despicable. If it was up to me, you would've been the first to go." He cracked his knuckles.

Caleb opened his mouth and stuttered. "She doesn't belong here anymore. She's dangerous just like—"

Ronan folded his arms and cocked his head to the side. "Choose your next words carefully, human. Better yet, don't speak at all about the emperor and empress of Universe 13. It's in your best interest to keep your mouth shut."

Caleb's lips trembled but no words came out. He nodded in agreement.

Good, it was nice and quiet, just how he liked it.

Ronan stood up from the control seat and strode over to the humans. He escorted them to their chairs and buckled them in tight, including Caleb and Tyler, who he would have preferred to kick in the face.

The humans were almost like children, so weak and help-less. Pathetic. As infuriating as they were, he didn't want anyone to get hurt after what promised to be a rough landing.

Autumn would've wanted everyone to get home safely, despite the way they'd treated her in the past.

* * *

AFTER ROCKY TURBULENCE, lots of screaming and crying, and a bumpy landing, the ship finally went quiet.

As they exited the vessel, he surveyed the terrain, making sure the area was clear. Ronan admired the misty stardust decorating the black-cloaked sky. Farrah Falls was as he remembered it, filled with trees, small fluffy animals, and an abundance of rocks of all shapes and sizes. However, one distinct change was the barrenness after one of Dante's usual outbursts.

The humans followed him into the forest quietly, probably relieved to be back on their home planet. They talked amongst themselves and grinned into the night.

It seemed whatever Dante touched, whether he meant to or not, he destroyed. He'd always had that effect, and some-times the repercussions were worse than others.

From what he could gather though, the trees were growing back. Bits of green foliage decorated the ground on the warm summer night. Insects chirped and pale moonlight danced between the branches of the trees.

Ronan stopped and regarded the group.

"All right," he sighed. "If you each provide me with your home coordinates, I'll deliver you to your front doors safely."

Which was more than he owed any of them after the year of torture they put him through.

Of course, Misty stepped forth first, pushing the others out of her way. She played with her long golden tresses and practically shouted her address at him, like she was ordering around her own personal slave.

He rolled his eyes.

As he ran the coordinates through his communicator and typed in her address one digit at a time, he heard the crunch of fallen leaves. A figure lunged toward him in the darkness. Its silhouette was scruffy and cumbersome.

"There you are. I can't tell you how long I've been searching for you," a male voice said in a low gruff tone that meant business.

Ronan stepped aside just in time as the man went to strike him, causing him to fall knees-first into a pocket of mud. Ronan folded his arms, watching him.

He came to a shaky stand and whipped a knife out of his pants. Ronan whisked him into the air telepathically. He twisted and dangled, unable to break free. A scream erupted from his lungs before a wily expression overtook his face. He glowered beneath his silver spectacles. One frame was cracked clear in half. The tangled hairs of his beard sprayed down his neck making him appear insane.

This time, Caleb stepped forth, staring at the man with his mouth hanging wide open. He squinted.

"Mr. Ramon, what are you doing all the way out here?"

Twelve

RONAN COCKED his head to the side and looked at Caleb, before snapping his eyes back to the man.

"You mean to tell me this is Autumn's father?" Ronan assessed him from head to toe. He wasn't at all what he expected considering how innocent and doe-like Autumn was. This man was a red-hot mess. And he *stank* to high heaven.

"Yes, I'm Autumn's father," the man growled.

"I see," Ronan muttered, eyes unmoving. "I'll let you down if you promise to behave yourself."

"I can't make any promises, alien. Where's my daughter?" He ground his molars together. He could hear the enamel cracking.

Ronan released his grip and set Mr. Ramon down on the ground. His knife shook in his grasp.

"What are you doing with all these people? Are you abducting them too? And why am I not surprised that you're somehow involved, Caleb? You never had my daughter's best interest in mind," he glowered. "I'll ask you again, where's my daughter? And where's Dante? When I find him, I'm going to give him a piece of my mind."

Caleb stared at his palms as if ashamed.

Ronan crossed his arms, spine snapping straight. "I'm not at liberty to tell you, but I can say that you're coming with me."

"She's in outer space," Marcela blurted.

Ronan whipped around and glared at her. He was practically ready to scream. He'd had enough of the drama. The clock was ticking, and he needed to find Sean and get off this planet and back home to his own world.

"I don't give a damn," Marcela continued. "Tell the man where his daughter is, or I will. I know what it's like to be a parent. We invest everything into our children only for them to go out and disappoint us."

Tyler glanced away. His deep brown eyes wavered on the verge of tears.

"Autumn would never disappoint me," Mr. Ramon countered. "She's a fine young lady. Now tell me where she is."

"It's a long story that I don't have time for right now," Ronan insisted, checking the clock on his communicator.

Mr. Ramon held the knife again. "Then make time. I've waited long enough to see her."

His mouth curved. "You know what? You're right. Follow me, I'll bring you to her at once."

He led Mr. Ramon back to the destroyer, still hidden in the dead of night. He disengaged the forcefield. The door opened and steam seeped into the humid forest. He gestured for Mr. Ramon to enter. At the last second, he sealed the spacecraft airtight, leaving him trapped and with no choice but to wait patiently for his return.

Mr. Ramon kicked and pounded against the door. With a wave of his hand, Ronan concealed the spacecraft from plain sight. The trees swayed in the warm summer breeze.

It was good enough for the time being.

"Is everybody ready to get going? My time *and* patience wear thin," Ronan checked his communicator again. Dante and Autumn were counting on him to come through. *At least he had her father in tow.* It would save him a trip.

Everyone in the group nodded. For the first time, nobody bickered or protested. He put his human disguise into place and grabbed hold of his charge. Misty rode piggy-back, Marcela and Tyler sat in his arms, and Caleb dangled from his boots.

Four more stops, he reassured himself. Four more stops until he could see Sean again and wipe his hands clean of this situation. He'd deal with Mr. Ramon when he returned.

Ronan raced into the skittering stars. This was going to be a long night.

Thirteen

IT WASN'T OFTEN Dante dreamed of Maeve as of late. He thought of her so seldom, he could barely recall her face, but her eyes were forever etched into his memory. Those eyes, gray like milky starlight, moonglow, and space dust combined.

She shouldn't have been in Universe 10 that day, but he was a fool. He never should've allowed her to accompany him, but he wanted to make her happy. *It was his job to make her happy, after all.*

She always got her way, one way or another.

Against his better judgment, he brought her on a mission at her request.

Her first and *last.*

It was the final mission he tried to convince himself he enjoyed, although he never truly had a choice.

His gut wrenched at the phantom silhouette of her broken body dying in his arms, drowning in her own blood. Her charred skin, brittle bones, and long winding tresses smoldered to dust. Her silver-gray eyes were red and listless.

How had she been caught in the crossfire? He was sure she

was sleeping in her quarters. It was the last place he remembered seeing her.

She died not long after. How foolish he was. How *very* foolish.

And with Autumn missing... He removed his glove and subconsciously chewed a nail as the gem-hued buildings of Giarldinia raced by the windows of his destroyer. He'd picked up one of his wife's bad habits. He cracked his knuckles before pulling his onyx glove back on.

Treble and her younger brother snapped him from his tortured thoughts, which had been punishing him more as of late. He could never forgive himself.

His mother spoke with Treble who hunched over slightly from the beating she endured at his command. Her brother leaned against the back of the control seat, excited for a trip to the palace.

The boy spoke a little too loudly and jumped up and down in a hyper sort of way. He was only a child. Little more than the age he was when he became a captive and was forced to conquer planets for monetary gain.

He sighed. If only he'd pardoned Treble like he'd planned and stood up to Valdez sooner, none of this would've happened, and Autumn would still be here. He'd proved himself to be just as cowardly and heartless as his late father. One of his worst fears.

The destroyer came upon Sanguis with its crystal obsidian exterior sparkling in the rising sunlight. Stars from the night before vanished into the clear blue cloudless sky.

"We're here, we're here, we're here!" Kittlen cheered as he bounced around. Dante bit back a smile that quickly turned to a frown. "Does Kyo live here as well? Is that why he never came home?"

Treble's eyes snapped to him, but she didn't dare utter a word. Rage burned behind her blue pupils; rage she couldn't contain. He knew that feeling all too well.

Dante opened his mouth to speak, but his mother interjected. "He's away on holiday, dear." For the first time after the disaster that'd taken place, he was thankful to have her with him for damage control.

"Oh." Disappointment hummed through the boy's voice. "I wish he invited us to come with him. It's not fair."

"Stop asking so many questions, Kittlen," Treble hissed. "The emperor was kind enough to invite us to his home, and you're being rude."

"Sorry," Kittlen's eyes fell to his hands.

"It's quite all right. No need to apologize." Dante ran a hand through his hair, tousling the dark strands.

The ship hummed as the underbelly docked onto the roof of the palace. Pebbles sprayed and the vessel landed on X marks the spot.

Dante unbuckled his harness and rose from his seat. His crimson cape fluttered over his shoulders. He ushered the hybrid siblings to the door of the ship, and his mother followed, graceful like a shadow.

* * *

DANTE TRANSPORTED Treble to the medical bay. As she was lowered into the rejuvenation tank, blue liquid consumed her body and seeped into her open wounds. She was placed in a coma-like state. A mask was affixed over her nose and mouth to ensure she received enough oxygen. Kittlen pressed his hands and face against the glass, fogging it with his breath.

"How long until she's healed?" Kitten tilted his head to the side, blinking his large innocent eyes.

He watched for a moment, then glanced away. Guilt crept through his subconscious. "A few hours. You're more than welcome to wait with her."

"Thanks, I think I will," Kittlen smiled, his cheeks shifting to pink. "And thanks again for bringing us here. You're not as bad as they—"

At that moment, Emblem and Allegoria ambled into the room. When their clear blue eyes fell upon Kittlen, Treble, and *himself*, their skin paled to the whitest shade imaginable. They quivered, staring at the floor, before smoothing their palms against their light-gray smocks.

He sighed. He'd grown accustomed to this reaction from *everyone*, and their encounter earlier didn't help.

"Aunt Emblem, Aunt Allegoria, what are you doing here?" Kittlen ran over and hugged them.

Dante stared between them; his mouth twisted to the side. *It figured they were somehow related; they all looked alike.* "You know what, I don't even want to know. And I don't have time for this." He threw his hands up in surrender.

He turned on his heel and left the bay. His mother continued to converse with the hybrid family. He was wasting time and had one more stop to make before embarking on a treacherous mission into deep space to find his wife.

* * *

DANTE SPRINTED into Autumn's chambers, cape fluttering in the warm afternoon breeze. *He had to be around here somewhere.* Heart pounding, he knelt on all fours and searched underneath her bed.

"Here kitty, kitty," he moved his hand around.

A growl followed by a hiss splintered from the shadows. A pair of sapphire eyes blinked, glistening through the darkness with claws unsheathed, fangs bared, and a magenta and onyx tail puffed.

"There you are," his mouth curved.

As he reached, a spiral of blue energy shot from beneath the bed.

With a wave of his hand, he deflected the rays and they disintegrated against the wall with a zap. "Mr. Hiss, I don't have time for this. Do you want to help me find your mother or not?"

Dante splayed his fingers, and Mr. Hiss yowled as he scruffed him by the hot-pink striped fur of his neck. The ling twisted and bared his teeth in his grasp, shooting energy around the room, hitting the ceiling and walls. Stone crumbled and sprayed through the air.

For the life of him, Dante couldn't figure out why this beast hated him so much, especially since he was only trying to help.

He scratched him behind his ear, and he stopped in his tracks. He purred and nuzzled him with his soft pink snout. His claws retracted and his defenses dropped. He was just a baby acting out.

Dante hated to admit it, but the creature was actually kind of sweet when he wasn't trying to blast his head off.

"You're coming with me. I'm sure your mother is worried sick about you. I'm going to find her, no matter the cost."

Mr. Hiss watched him and blinked his large indigo eyes. For a moment, Dante was sure the baby ling could understand him. Maybe he wasn't a dumb animal after all.

He meant every word of what he said. He was going to crack skulls, destroy planets, and break his enemies' kneecaps until Autumn was safe and back home with him again. He knew precisely where to start his search.

Fourteen

AUTUMN BURIED her face in her knees, trembling and out of breath from Valdez's parting gift.

Evil witch—setting them up like that.

The worst part was the brief sense of hope she experienced only to have the feeling ripped out from under her once more. They were officially stranded with no chance of escape from this remote world.

Warm blood and snow trickled down her sleeve. She shivered as Armienti held a ball of ice against his bleeding scalp. Red droplets streaked his golden tresses.

As she closed her eyes and tried to relax for a moment, she heard the flow of water. From what she could gather based on the crashing sound, there was a lot of it.

She spotted a stream filled with misting green water flowing in the distance. Her time on this planet had been so distressing she had failed to notice it earlier. She jumped to her feet and raced over with what little strength she had left.

The water was warm to the touch. A welcome change from frostbitten fingers, toes, and the icicles matting down her long curly hair. She frantically pulled off her ice encrusted bodysuit and go-go boots, desperate to experience a sense of warmth again, but suddenly she stopped.

She eyed Armienti. He cast her an appreciative glance but then looked away. Her face flushed. This was probably a dream come true for him.

"Don't watch me," she said as she finished pulling off the remainder of her teal bodysuit. Her bare feet slid against the frigid elements.

Armienti chuckled, running a hand through his golden tousled hair. He had since rejuvenated himself. "Believe me, Autumn Martyne, despite what you may think, the world doesn't revolve around you. We have much bigger troubles than me watching you bathe, which by the way, is the most unimpressive sight I've ever beheld." His mouth curved.

He *had* to be trying to save face.

Her cheeks set on fire, and she placed a hand on the fullest part of her hip. Her spine straightened. "Just do as you're told; I'm still your empress," she sounded like Dante as the words left her mouth. "This mess is all your fault, and I won't hesitate to tell Dante what you've done when I see him again. We could be back on Surge warm and full, or I could've traveled home to Earth by now."

Armienti winked a brilliant blue eye. "I'm not worried about Dante. There's a good chance we'll never see him again so save your idle threats. Out here, you're nothing more than a lost empress."

Her forehead pulsated as she lowered herself into the water. The frigid wind bit against her cheeks, but for the first time in a while, she was warm.

She hugged her knees to her chest as the water flowed against her body in ripples and waves. She never wanted to climb out. If time allowed, she could stay here forever.

In the corner of her vision, Armienti undressed himself. His blue defined muscles shifted in the winter elements. Only this time, his bottom half wasn't concealed by a white fluffy towel, like he tended to traipse around the palace in.

She turned her head, cheeks setting on fire as he climbed in, and she got the entire picture.

What a picture it turned out to be. The water settled around them.

Armienti rested his back against the icy bank. "You see, that wasn't so bad. Now, was it?"

She shrugged and closed her eyes. "I don't care."

Autumn tried her hardest to envision her husband's face. The high peaks of his cheekbones, the cleft of his chin, his piercing amber eyes, and his tousled midnight hair. Even the scars on his chest he never wanted to talk about.

Not Armienti.

He had to be worried sick. Hopefully he wasn't being too destructive in her absence. That was probably more than she should hope for, knowing his *tendencies*.

Armienti closed his eyes. "I find it rather humorous that you think he can protect you. First of all, he'd have to find us, which is highly unlikely. And second of all, Valdez isn't the best at keeping secrets, and believe me when I say she knows *everything*."

"Everything?" Autumn gulped and a wave of panic crashed through her body interrupting her soothing bath.

"*Everything*," Armienti reiterated.

"When the Grand Supreme learns of his treachery, I'm sure he'll want him dead. Perhaps he'll name a new successor to his territories—" Armienti's chest puffed.

She stared at him at a loss for words, unwilling to imagine Dante being in any sort of danger. The thought induced nausea.

A slithering sensation passed between her calves. Sharp scales scraped against her skin.

She jumped onto Armienti's lap, and he snorted. "If you wanted to sit by me, you should've just asked from the beginning. I don't bite, I promise. Unless you want me to, that is." He winked.

She ignored his stupid remark, pointing to the water with a trembling finger. "We're not alone."

Armienti glanced, then reached into the streaming water and pulled out a fish the size of her. The creature twitched its rainbow whiskers and its two heads tried to swim in opposite directions.

"Good job, Autumn, you found our dinner. I knew there had to be more food on this planet somewhere."

He tossed the beast onto the bank, flopping against the ice. As the emerald sky grew dark and cloudy, hail began pelting their heads, interrupting their soak.

Armienti climbed out and extended his hand. "Come on now, don't be bashful. We need to find shelter before another storm breaks out."

Autumn twisted her mouth to the side, reluctantly accepting his help. When she climbed out, she didn't bother to conceal herself.

He made one of the stupidest faces she'd ever seen in her life. It was like he'd never seen a naked girl before, which was impossible.

* * *

ARMIENTI'S STOMACH twisted and turned from Autumn's threat, but he refused to let her see how terrified he was. Dante would indeed kill him for not only conspiring like a fool with Valdez, but for endangering his wife's life.

Mostly the latter.

On the other hand, however, the Grand Supreme would perhaps reward him for bringing forth a traitor. It was high time Dante was knocked down a peg and he received what he was entitled to.

Emperor, he shook his head. *Must be nice.*

"Will you come on already?!" Autumn shouted, suddenly taking charge of the expedition. How easy it was for her to hurry him along when she wasn't the one with a heavy double-headed beast slung over her back.

His eyes grazed the slope of her hips and the way her wet bodysuit clung to her legs, but he looked away, face flushed. It was the warmest part of his body in the impending storm. He'd never forget how beautiful her body looked when she exited the stream moments earlier.

Autumn was still Dante's wife, all things considered. Perhaps if he begged for forgiveness on his hands and knees, he would show him mercy.

No, he couldn't allow himself to be such a pushover. Couldn't allow himself to stoop to such a humiliating level.

Plus, there was a good chance he'd never find out. They were stranded on this cruel ice world with no hope of escape.

As they entered their usual cave, he experienced a wave of panic upon the realization that this could be their *permanent* home. *No, please no*, he pleaded to the gods.

He set the fish down on the floor and Autumn rubbed her hands together for warmth.

"So, how are we going to cook this thing?" He heard her stomach grumble.

"Well, um, we're not. As you know, I don't have the ability to—"

"Generate fire," she muttered. "That's right. It Figures."

A wave of heat simmered over Armienti's face and neck. Another reminder that his ability was essentially useless. *It Figures.* Embarrassment rattled him to the core.

"Well, that was rude," he peeled back the skin of the fish and took a bite. "Although you spotted it, I caught the damn thing for us to share. If it wasn't for me, we'd starve for another night."

Autumn folded her arms. "I don't care. I'm not here to be nice and I'm not here to be your friend. You're lucky I'm a fan of sushi," she sat cross legged, skinning a section of the fish and took a bite. "It's actually not that bad."

Together, they carved the fish dry. Neither one of them uttered a word to one another. He was secretly mortified.

What Autumn had said hit a nerve, because it was the *truth*.

He'd been overlooked and underappreciated his entire life. It wasn't fair. Somehow it hurt more coming from her. She was one of the nicest people he'd ever known, even after everything she'd been through.

What *he* put her through…

He couldn't help but watch her, staring into her eyes, haunted by two silver ghosts. *Maeve.* He'd never be good enough for anyone, no matter how hard he tried. He was born to be first but treated like the dust at the bottom of everyone's boots.

Fifteen

"ARE WE THERE YET? Seriously, are we there?" Misty's bottom lip protruded as she batted her large cerulean eyes.

Not again, Ronan sighed.

The sound of Misty's voice pierced through his sensitive Elattion ears. Her incessant questioning made him crave a goblet of wine. Of course, he would never drink and fly.

"Has it really been that long that you've forgotten where your own dwelling is located?" He stared at her, forehead twitching.

He was at his wits' end. In two seconds, he would drop all of them to their deaths and be done with this mess. Then he could finally be with Sean and take him and Autumn's father on their way back home. *If only his emperor and empress weren't counting on him.*

"Don't be ridiculous," Misty crossed her arms, "Of course I know where I live. You need to fly faster to Mansion Ridge. You hear me? Mansion Ridge!"

Her eyes narrowed at him as he typed the location into his communicator again. His fingers trembled with ire. The device clicked and beeped before bearing the coordinates 41°17'35.5"N, 74°10'46.9"W.

Caleb glowered. "Misty, stop it, we all want to go home and put this disaster behind us. Why are your needs always first? You and your stupid mansion—"

"Shut up, Caleb," Misty hissed. "I didn't do anything wrong—Autumn did. This is all her fault for putting us through this and conspiring with that monster, Dante."

Marcela rolled her eyes. "You stupid kids with your stupid problems. I've missed an impossible amount of work. I'm probably out of a job by now—and the state of my mortgage. I shudder when I think about it. If anyone has a right to be pissed off, I do."

Tyler buried his face in his hands, not joining in on the conversation. Ronan supposed he had the most to be ashamed of. He'd struck Autumn's mother and left her for dead in a hit and run car accident. The offense was unforgivable, but somehow Autumn had managed to pardon him as well. Forgiveness for such a crime was unfathomable where he was from. Tyler would've been executed.

"Will everyone please be quiet for just a second?" Ronan snapped. "I can't find your homes if I can't think straight."

His temples throbbed as he searched the poorly lit ground below.

In reality, all he could think about was Sean and what he'd say once he found out he wasn't human. What if he wasn't interested? What if he didn't want him anymore after he'd traveled all this way? And what would he say to Autumn's father once he returned to his ship?

That should've been Dante's job. If only he offered her father a mature and proper explanation for his intentions or invited him to come along in the first place. He was so selfish.

Ronan descended from the sky, desperate to return Misty before the others. She was the loudest and most distracting human he'd ever dealt with, and he wanted her out of his hair.

He landed on the steps of her so-called "mansion," which

was a below-average-size dwelling back on Surge. Some of the hybrids had better living arrangements.

"It's about time," Misty crossed her arms, breasts puffed. "There's so much I need to catch up on. Shopping, groceries, gossip, my socials haven't been updated in forever. I'm probably hemorrhaging followers."

Ronan rolled his eyes so far back it surprised him they didn't get stuck in his head.

Misty pounded her fist against the door. Lights flickered on from the surrounding garden and the dwelling itself. A woman walked out with waist-length blonde hair, wearing a short fluffy pink robe. She froze, blue eyes widening. She released a piercing scream before colliding with the gray. Her legs wobbled and she passed out cold.

"Mommy," Misty knelt and shook her. "Mom, it's okay I'm home. I hope you didn't clean out my room and sell my Range Rover. I'm going to need both. And what about my phone—"

Ronan tugged on her ponytail and Misty winced. "Don't ever forget the great kindness bestowed upon this night. You have Autumn to thank and no one else. Never forget it. If it was up to me, I would've left you on planet Halvana to serve out the remainder of your sentence."

She deserved to suffer for being one of the most annoying people he'd ever met in his life.

"I—" Misty's pink lips quivered. Her eyes teared up.

"Just remember that. If the empress ever changes her mind, you'll be transported back to Halvana in a heartbeat with no questions asked."

Misty gasped before nodding mechanically. His point was well received.

"Th—thank you," she stared at her hands. "If it wasn't for you I—"

Ronan turned on his heel, ignoring her impending speech. *Okay, one human down, three to go,* he reassured himself.

Already this mission promised to be one of the longest nights of his life.

He bit back a smile, to finally be rid of her. Her incessant whining and complaining was outrageous. A year with her was enough for a lifetime and he didn't have any more time to waste.

He needed to get Sean along with Autumn's father and get the hell off this planet.

Sixteen

AUTUMN SAT cross-legged in the corner of the cave. Her new *permanent* dwelling. Her teeth chattered as she blew warm air against her palms. With her stomach full, she grew exhausted and frozen to the core. Every time she closed her eyes, a cold cruel wind whipped by the entrance rattling her bones raw. *I'll never sleep at this rate.*

Meanwhile, Armienti lounged at the far end of the cavern. His bare blue chest and muscles glowed in the dancing firelight. *Of course* he'd discover a minigun in one of the pockets of Valdez's dead Zexian soldiers *after* they'd eaten. To be fair, she didn't remember to check either. She was too busy almost becoming dinner.

He laid down, resting his head against his makeshift pillow.

The scarlet cape he'd stolen from Dante.

"You know, Autumn, you're more than welcome to join me. There's enough fire and warmth for both of us to share." His lips tugged toward a smile in a pretty sort of way.

"Don't worry about me," she glared. "I'm fine over here."

Even though she couldn't convince herself she would be okay as white mist flowed from her mouth.

"Are you sure?" His long lashes grazed his prominent blue cheekbones, while his lips drooped into a pout. *Like she was supposed to feel sorry for him or something.*

"Seriously, Armienti, how can you be so calm considering we're stranded here for all eternity? This is all your fault. To think I trusted you. I thought you were my friend."

"Well, I have my reasons," he picked at his nails, appearing disinterested.

"I'd love to hear them," she muttered. "It's not like I have any other choice or anyone else to talk to."

"You'd never understand."

"Just try me."

Armienti's lips moved. "Do you know what it's like to live your life as a shadow? To never be enough, no matter how hard you try? To toil in the glory and magnificence of everyone around you?"

"Actually, yes, I do," her teeth chattered, her breath escaping in thick white puffs. "I've never been popular at school. I've always been delightfully average, taking it day by day, caring for my family, always ending up two steps behind everyone else. I'm not perfect, but I give my all, then something like this happens and I get hit with a shitstorm. Unlike you, however, I know how to make the best of a bad situation. To always be hopeful. I'd never sell anyone out, especially not my own family."

"Well then you understand why I made the decision I did. I had a glimmering chance to be something more than average and now here we are, back at square one again."

She folded her arms. "Wait, you can't be serious. Do you really expect me to feel bad for you after your little plan to overtake Dante with Valdez went awry?"

"I knew I shouldn't have trusted her. My gut screamed no, but I didn't have a choice. Working with her was the only way I could've gotten what I wanted. What's rightfully mine."

"Wait…what do you mean?" She couldn't believe she was asking. She didn't care about his answer, but boredom got the best of her.

"I'm the true crown prince. My father was murdered by the former emperor because he was jealous of his station and the weaker of the two siblings, although he was the first born. The Martyne dynasty should've been my inheritance. I should've been appointed by the Grand Supreme to hail through the universes as the Great Conqueror."

She crossed her arms tighter as goosebumps consumed her body. "How is any of this Dante's fault?"

"Well, it's not actually, but it doesn't mean I'm any less thrilled about the situation. Wouldn't you want something that was rightfully yours from birth?"

"To think his own cousin has been conspiring against him the whole time." Her eyes thinned to slits. "Whatever happened to blood is thicker than water?"

Armienti shook his head. "We're not cousins actually. We share the same mother, but Dante isn't aware. I overheard one of her infamous fights with the emperor in passing when I was younger. To think I could've had you instead of him."

Her heart accelerated. A lump fastened itself in her throat. "*Had* me? How can you be so sure I would've fallen for you?"

The apples of his blue cheeks shifted to pink. Fire danced through the strands of his golden hair. "Trust me, you would've, if I'd gotten to you first. But Dante always takes whatever he wants with complete disregard for everyone else. You know that by now, don't you?"

"Well don't get any ideas," she scoffed. "Just because we're stranded here, it won't change how I feel about you."

"Trust me, I've had plenty of ideas," he winked. "The thought of you excites me to no end. But I understand, I owe you respect."

The wind howled through the cave. Bits of ice fell from her wet, matted hair. As annoyed as she was and as much as she didn't want to admit, he was right. She'd freeze to death if she didn't comply.

Although she'd developed and fostered her own set of abilities, generating warmth *wasn't* in her skill set.

She got to her feet and marched over to him. Her hand rested on her hip. "Move over and keep your hands and thoughts to yourself."

Armienti raised his palms in the air, surrendering to her wish. "I'll be on my best behavior, I promise. Although I'm just saying, it would be much warmer if we slept in each other's arms. Preferably nude. But only for survival purposes." He chewed his bottom lip into a smile.

"I'm sleeping with my clothes on, thank you very much, storm or no storm," she grumbled. "And you'd better not shed even a sock, *or else*."

She stretched and yawned shivering from head to toe. Goosebumps prickled over her skin. She was beyond freezing. Autumn crawled next to him rolling onto her side. His hot peppermint breath flowed against her exposed throat.

He wrapped a well-defined arm around her waist. As she laid there in silence, his golden locks tickled the frozen skin of her cheek sending shivers ripping across her limbs.

Autumn closed her eyes. The gentle heaving of his breast relaxed her. She drifted off, all the while pretending he was Dante. She couldn't help but wonder how he was doing in her absence.

Seventeen

AUTUMN HAD *to be here somewhere.*

Dante tapped a nervous finger against the back of the pilot's seat of his destroyer. An endless maze of stars flickered and whipped by the cockpit windows.

Sweat slicked the back of the pilot's neck from the heat of the fireballs he generated then retracted out of sheer frustration, but mostly anxiety. The warmth of his flame fogged the windows of the ship.

His wife was in danger. He had a terrible feeling in the pit of his stomach.

He attempted again and again to reach her through their bond, but there was no answer, only still darkness.

As he ran a hand roughly through his obsidian hair, he hoped she was okay. She had to be. He couldn't handle life without her.

He planned to murder whoever was responsible for her disappearance.

No, he couldn't deal with the agony of loss a second time. *Maeve, it's happening all over again.* History had a way of repeating itself.

He suspected Valdez, after he'd thrown her love admission in her face. She had reason to despise him and exact revenge. Deep in his gut, he had a feeling she took her wrath out on Autumn instead; the most important person in his life.

Valdez's greatest joy in the universes was hurting others.

His communicator buzzed and his heart leapt to his throat. *Autumn.* But when he went to check—*oh no, please, no,* he begged anyone who would listen. It couldn't be.

The Grand Supreme.

Receiving a personal call from him could only mean one outcome. A summons to Universe 24. *Had Valdez revealed his indiscretion about sparing Earth and murdering General Keyserike? A chill rattled down the length of his spine. Was there a price on his head?*

He slid his finger against the ignore button and continued his journey. Answering for his crimes could wait. Conquering more planets could wait. Lord Izzo could wait. Everything and anything interrupting him could wait.

He didn't care about the consequences. All that mattered to him was finding his wife and making sure she was safe.

He cracked his knuckles and a smirk curled over his lips.

He was arriving on Diode in mere minutes. He was going to make Valdez pay for her treachery with her life.

* * *

DANTE and his crew docked their destroyers on the desert planet of Diode. The always-bright amethyst sky twinkled in the sunlight. Endless stars sparkled from the depths of space.

White sand ran beneath his heavy black boots. He gestured to the sky and soared through the thick overcast clouds. His crew of elite soldiers flanked him.

When they arrived on the vast grounds of Gypsum Palace it was pitch quiet outside. The gigantic white cube with thousands of black arch ways remained deathly still. A smoky scent drifted through the air. Nobody greeted them in a formal capacity. *Why was he not surprised?*

He folded his arms and shifted his weight from side to side, assessing the situation. It was as he expected.

A blue sparkle of energy zapped by his ear. Fiery heat singed his skin. A moment later, they were swarmed by Zexian soldiers. Their crooked powder wings twitched high against their backs. Flat silver blasters sat in their palms, twisting around their long bony fingers.

"What's all this?" Dante's smile widened. Bloodlust flowed through his veins. He closed his eyes, reveling in the thought of connecting his fist with someone's unsuspecting face.

"By order of Empress Valdez Aventura, you're no longer welcome on planet Diode or in any of her territories. You have five seconds to vacate the premises or suffer the consequences."

He cocked his head to the side. "Is that so? Who's going to make us leave, you? Don't make me laugh. By now you should know I take whatever I want. They don't call me the Great Conqueror for nothing."

Violent streams of energy flowed from the zappers. With a wave of his hand, he deflected the beams away from himself and his soldiers, causing explosions in the garden and along the palace walls.

In the blink of an eye, he unleashed hellfire onto the Zexian army, burning every last soldier alive. Screams echoed as their bodies disintegrated into fine black dust.

One soldier attempted to lift his head, but it thudded against the cobalt grass.

He knelt and scruffed him by the collar. "Where's my wife?"

The soldier trembled. His charcoal eyes rolled back into his head before refocusing on him. "I don't know."

"Don't you dare lie to me," Dante's fist tightened. "Tell me where she is, or you die."

"Sire, forgive me. I never meant to challenge your authority. Please have mercy—"

"A lesson learned too late," he raised a hand, casting a fireball into his face, the embers of his flame swallowing the soldier alive. He'd slipped up and lost his temper. Not his finest moment.

He rose and hocked a ball of saliva in his mouth before spitting on the ground. "Search the palace grounds. Harm no female, child, or beast in the process." He threw in the beast order as he thought of Mr. Hiss who waited for him back on the ship. Autumn would have wanted the animals to stay safe.

"Sire."

He led his soldiers through the premises. Screams and smoke erupted from the palace. Residents took flight, their wings twitching and flapping in a frenzy through the air. Marble pillars crumbled to soot, and vines singed along the ceiling.

He raced around the palace with his crew until he passed one room in particular. He'd ignored its existence during his last trip to Diode, but the chamber beckoned to him. It was all that was left of her.

When he walked inside, to his surprise, the room remained unchanged. The bed was made, neat as always. Silky purple sheets were tucked in and folded to perfection. Vines twisted and swung from the ceiling. And the open marble pillars allowed a beautiful view of the city. Although much of the metropolis was on fire after his arrival.

He walked over to the chest of drawers. Everything was as he remembered, including a brush with traces of Maeve's long winding black hair. Her faint floral scent consumed him.

He couldn't believe this was all that was left of her. No, he couldn't allow the strange coincidence. He left her room solemn but furious. For a moment, he could've sworn the ghost of his dead lover giggled and grabbed his arm.

* * *

AFTER A FEW HOURS, the chaos finally settled. A hole burned in his chest when his warriors brought forth the surviving members of the palace, but Autumn was *nowhere* in sight.

They'd checked every room, corridor, and crevice of the palace and failed to find her.

He gritted his teeth, fists clenched. Dante ran a hand over his face and through his chin-length tousled hair. He huffed a deep shuddering breath.

A soldier ran up to him and fell into a bow. "There's no sign of the empress or of Empress Valdez. What should we do with the captives?"

The prisoners stood there shaking. Tears streaked their pale cheeks as they hugged each other, preparing for death.

Dante folded his arms before turning on heel and levitating. "Spare them. We've wasted enough time here."

After he spoke, a drone drifted in front of his face. He was being watched like always. He disintegrated the device with his fingers.

* * *

ARMIENTI LAID beside Autumn and caressed her hair while she slept. He twirled the long strands of her dark curls around his fingertips. Yet another storm erupted outside the walls of the cave. Snow and ice pounded to the ground as the wind howled and gusted.

He couldn't believe the mess he'd gotten them into,

couldn't believe they were stranded forever on an uncharted ice world all because he was an idiot who trusted the infamous Valdez Aventura. She was known to be untrustworthy.

What on earth was wrong with him?

He sighed, eyes gravitating toward the stone ceiling. Icicles dropped and shattered from the entrance of the cavern.

Autumn stirred, her gray gaze meeting his sleep deprived stare. Her eyes narrowed to slits as she yawned and pulled away. Embarrassment warmed his face after the story he'd told her earlier about wishing they could be together. Not that any of it mattered anymore.

She sat up and tied her hair into a high ponytail. A few strands matted to her forehead. They hadn't had a proper bath in a period of time. Oh, how he missed his luxurious suite back on Surge. He could never return, though, even if they did manage to get out of there one day.

"How long will you hate me?" His voice was low and gruff. He admired her through the dancing shadows.

Her lips parted. "I really don't need this first thing in the morning."

"Oh," he glanced away. "I'm sorry, but to be honest, it's all I can think about."

She rolled her eyes. "I don't hate you, but you do annoy me. And you're selfish. Not as selfish as other people I know, but still selfish nonetheless."

"What if I were to find a way off this planet? Could you forgive me?"

"I can't make any promises," she stretched. "Right now, I'm starving. I'm going out to find some more food." She came to a stand and pulled on her boots.

"I don't think that's a very good idea. We should wait until the storm passes." Heavy flakes danced from the gray sky in waves.

"Try and stop me," she challenged him, crossing her arms.

He hesitated, his mouth twisting to the side.

"That's what I thought, wimp."

He found himself scrambling to dress as Autumn disappeared into the whiteout snowstorm.

"Hey, wait for me," he waved at her, trotting behind like a desperate fool.

Eighteen

AUTUMN'S STOMACH groaned as she trudged through the snow and ice. The heels of her go-go boots slipped through the elements. It was her greatest regret that she didn't have something warmer to wear. How she missed her light-blue puffer jacket and duck boots that she'd sported back on Earth during the winter season. She relished the memory.

Armienti jogged after her. His crimson cape lashed through the harsh wind. Sleet pelted his golden flowing tresses.

"I knew you'd come to your senses. If we don't act quickly, we're going to starve," she scoured the terrain. She hoped, upon hope, she could find another fish in the stream. If not, they were screwed.

When they arrived at the stream, her stomach twisted and tied itself in a hungry knot. A thick sheet of ice coated the water. The temperature was so cold outside that the water had frozen overnight. Her teeth chattered as she climbed down the bank, feet skidding over the elements. If she could somehow make a hole, they'd have a fighting chance at eating another meal and staying alive for another day.

Her fists trembled as she punched at the ice repeatedly. Stress cracks formed along the ice but at the speed she worked, the barrier reformulated in seconds.

"Crap," she muttered underneath her breath. At this rate, they'd starve to death.

Armienti came up behind her and with the full force of his body, rammed his heavy black boot through the barrier. The ice shattered, particles scattering everywhere; creating just enough room to slide a fish through the gap.

She grinned. *That should do it.*

"I bet you're glad I came along," he ran a hand through his golden tousled tresses and smiled.

Although she was weak, she mustered the energy to roll her eyes. He was beyond infuriating, making light of a situation like this.

She reached through the cavity and swept her fingers through the steamy, pulsing water. Her vision was impaired as the storm continued to rage.

She sucked in a deep shuddering breath and dunked her head into the water, desperate to find a fish. It was clear and warm and calm, a welcome change from the raging storm above. She admired the stream floor as rainbow plants danced and swayed with the moving water.

A dark figure swam her way and her eyes snapped toward the shadow. Her adrenaline pumped with excitement. A fish, or at least, she thought. When she went to grab hold, she was pulled in and her entire body was submerged. Long twisting fingers dug through her frozen scalp. Her face and body burned as the creature latched on and slid her beneath the ice. She swallowed water as she twisted and turned trying to escape its grasp, but the creature was too strong.

She kicked and screamed, bubbles erupting from her mouth. She clawed her nails into its scaly hands. No matter how hard she tried, she couldn't escape, couldn't get the beast to stop. When her head collided with a rock, she saw red and tasted the metallic flavor of blood.

Her vision faded around the edges as the creature's dead, inhuman eyes stared back at her. She inhaled and water shot up her mouth and through her nostrils. The cool pull of darkness began to overtake her. Lights danced before her eyes as water filled her lungs. Her limbs slackened as she faded from consciousness.

* * *

ARMIENTI RACED ALONG THE ICE, his heart thundering in his chest. Snow piled, impairing his vision, but he was able to make out the dark outline of Autumn's body as she was pulled beneath the ice and dragged away. Whatever had taken hold of her was fast, even for him. His boots skidded, as he jumped through the elements doing his best to outrun the creature, but it was no use.

To catch up, he had to be two steps ahead.

Screw it, he thought. He was wasting time. *At this rate, Autumn's going to drown.*

He flew into the air and dove, fists first, shattering through the ice. Warm water consumed his body as he raced after the beast. A long slippery tail swished back and forth in a rhythmic wave. Autumn's limp body hung tangled in its tentacles. She no longer moved or struggled.

He grabbed hold of the tail and dug his nails deep into the scales, stopping the creature in its tracks. A high-pitched shriek echoed from its mouth. Armienti let go to cover his ears. The sound was so loud that his teeth vibrated through to his brain.

The creature continued to swim. *Oh, no, no, no.* It was getting away, and he was running out of breath.

He swam up and inhaled, then exhaled through a pocket in the ice before continuing his pursuit. This time he swam deep down below. His boots hit the muddy stream floor. With all his might, he charged the beast, ramming the creature in the gut. Its body shattered through the ice and flopped onto the bank with a *BOOM*.

He raced over, desperately searching for her. *Please let her be alive, please let her be alive.*

But when he found her, her body was cold and wet and ensnared, and her golden-olive skin shifted to a pale pasty gray. He removed his glove and pressed his fingers to her throat. She didn't have a pulse.

Nineteen

AUTUMN BENT over in her closet digging through mounds of unfolded clothes she should have tended to a long time ago. The central air droned overhead. Light spilled through her window and into her room on a brilliant late spring day.

"So, what are you going to wear to prom?" Lauren batted her large cerulean eyes, twirling a golden strand of hair around her finger.

"Yeah, Autumn," Ellie chimed in as she used her selfie phone camera to apply a layer of pink lip gloss. When she finished, she slid her phone into her back shorts pocket. She combed her fingers through her long umber-brown hair before fastening the strands into a sleek, high ponytail.

Autumn looked up from a paperback she found at the bottom of her closet while searching for a pair of heels she had in there somewhere, buried beneath one of her many piles of laundry.

Lauren chuckled as she reached over her head and pulled the book from her hands. She groaned. "Seriously, girl, you're not acting like senior prom is the day after tomorrow. You need to stay focused. You never know what might happen between you and Caleb," she winked. "You've been together for four years and maybe he's finally ready to seal the deal prom night."

Her cheeks set on fire, and she nodded. "Yeah, you're right. I'm probably worrying for nothing."

Ellie knelt beside her and tilted her head to the side. "What do you mean?"

"He's just been so distant lately, and weird. He's been spending a lot of time studying with Misty of all people. They were assigned some 'project' together."

Ellie gasped. "Oh no, that hoe! She's probably putting her moves on him. I hate to say it's not his first time. I heard from a reliable source he was flirting with—"

Lauren kicked her in the butt, and she fell forward, softening her fall with her hands.

"Seriously, Lauren? Ouch!"

"We don't need your negativity and gossip column right now. Autumn is trying to focus," Lauren threw her hands up in the air.

A knock came to the door, interrupting their conversation. Her mom entered with her golden highlighted curly hair fastened in a high bun. Tendrils framed her heart-shaped face. Her large brown eyes sparkled, crinkles forming. A plate of peanut butter and jelly sandwiches sat in her hands.

"I thought you girls might be hungry," her mom smiled, placing the tray on her bed.

She chewed her bottom lip then continued, "And *mija*, I overheard you were having a little trouble," she winked.

"Yeah, I think I am," she admitted. "I don't know if I want to go through with this prom thing." She twiddled her fingers.

"You see, moms know everything," she placed a hand against her hip, grinning.

Her mom turned and left the room then reemerged with a

white satin garment bag and passed it to her. The bag was weighty and fluffy with air.

"Mom, seriously, what did you do?"

Her mom shrugged. "Just go try it on."

Worry seeped through every pore in her body. *What if it was something frilly? Or something her grandma would wear? Eww, no. She didn't want to be seen looking like a little grandma at prom.*

But she didn't want to hurt her mom's feelings, so she took the garment bag and went into the bathroom to change. As she pulled down the zipper, she was far from disappointed. When she reemerged, she wore a dress of tulle with golden foiled stars. It was the most beautiful dress she'd ever seen.

She grinned, and her mom took her by the hand and spun her around in a circle. She stumbled over her feet, but her mom caught her before she hit the wall. *Crap.* "We can work on your dancing skills later," she chuckled. "You need to move your hips more like this." Her mom danced around the room and her friends giggled.

"Yeah," she ran a hand through her hair, shrugging off her embarrassment.

"Now that's what I'm talking about." Lauren ran up and hugged her tight.

Ellie clapped her hands. "You look amazing."

"Thanks," her cheeks warmed as she glanced into her floor-length mirror. She really did.

"We'll go shopping for your accessories tomorrow," her mom raised a brow. If you don't get this kind of reception from Caleb, he isn't worth your time. I don't care how long you've been together, four years or a lifetime. You want a guy who always puts you first and puts your needs before his own. He should be willing to take a bullet for you if it comes down to it."

Ellie snorted. "I don't think any guy like that exists,

they're all so selfish and stupid, and they only want one thing."

Her mom smiled, tucking a coiled strand of hair behind her ear. "Believe me, he's out there. You just have to be ready for him when he comes around. He may show his love in unconventional ways, but it doesn't mean he loves you any less, and sometimes that's the best kind of love. A love that sets you ablaze."

Twenty

ARMIENTI SHOOK AUTUMN, then ran his fingers over her frozen cheek. Her eyes were closed, and her body felt limp and lifeless.

"Oh, no, no, no, please, no, Autumn, you have to wake up," he shook her again a little bit harder. "Wake up."

He removed his gloves and gently slid his fingers over her temples cyclically.

His heart accelerated as he transferred his life force to her. It'd worked twice before, so why not again?

He watched her hopefully, but she didn't stir. She lay in his arms, quiet and unmoving.

Panic overwhelmed his senses.

"Autumn, come on, Autumn, wake up. Please, you have to wake up," his tone grew frantic as he laid her flat on the icy ground.

If she died, he'd *never* forgive himself. If she died, he'd rather go with her than stay here.

He lifted the shirt portion of her bodysuit and quickly glanced away. His face warmed at the sight of her breasts. He placed his bare hands on her chest, applying pressure a few times before lowering his mouth to hers and trying to breathe life back into her.

After the thirtieth or so push, she laid there. Still and silent. Tears threatened to roll from the corners of his eyes. As he blinked, they burned. He couldn't believe this. Why couldn't he heal her? *Dammit.*

And worst of all, this was all his fault.

Armienti continued pumping her chest, each push more frantic than the last. Snow and sleet fell from the sky from the storm, skidding over her body and through the long strands of his hair.

The next time he pushed, she stirred, so he pumped her chest harder, offering her more breath. Finally, her body convulsed, and water poured from her mouth. She spit up all over the ice, coughing and choking everywhere. A wave of relief flooded through his limbs.

"Are you all right?" He held her close, her body trembled against his.

"Yeah," she said between coughs. "I think so."

"I'm sorry, this is all my fault. I should've been the one to go in. I should've insisted."

"And I should've listened," she admitted, placing her hand on his cheek. She closed her eyes. Shivers trickled down his spine from her gentle touch.

"Well, the good news is you're alive, and we won't have to hunt for food anytime soon. This fish should last us a lifetime."

* * *

DANTE APPROACHED his destroyer as thick black smoke consumed the amethyst sky of Diode. He and his soldiers had searched every last kilometer of the planet to no avail.

Autumn was nowhere to be found. They'd searched for days

and nights and their efforts yielded nothing. *Absolutely nothing.*

Rage simmered through his veins. Another wasted trip, and one more day Autumn wasn't back home safe with him. Flames welled in his palms with an unimaginable fury. An explosion of fire ripped through the sky. Crackling orange flames exploded before shifting to blue. Clouds evaporated as the wave of heat made its way through the atmosphere and into outer space. His team of elite soldiers ducked, and others ran for cover.

He fell to his knees balling up white sand with his pitch-black gloves. He couldn't believe this. He knew she was here. She had to be. It made no sense. Where else would Valdez have taken her, unless—*no, it couldn't be.*

Dante turned his head as a snout and a soft ball of fur ran up against his leg again and again. Mr. Hiss purred and rolled through the sand. His muzzle upturned and a sense of calm overtook him as if he was smiling.

"Mr. Hiss, not now. I'm not in the mood," he moved his leg away, but Mr. Hiss persisted.

The cub rolled on his back and blinked his brilliant sapphire eyes. Dante sighed and reached down to stroke his soft underbelly. His tail swayed. *Mr. Hiss wasn't worried, so why should he be?*

He inhaled a deep shuddering breath before exhaling. Everything was going to be okay. Everything was going to be okay. *It had to be.*

His moment of relaxation was interrupted by the buzz of his communicator within the confines of his pants. He whipped the device out of his back pocket and slid up the screen. His heart thundered.

"Why hello, Dante."

Valdez.

"Where is she?" He ran a hand roughly through his hair

and waited on her every word. He could barely breathe. Desperation crashed through his body.

She chuckled. "Nice to hear from you too. I know you probably thought you'd never hear from me again, but you're all I ever think about."

A long awkward silence ensued.

"Tell me where she is or else—"

"Or else what? What can you possibly do? I hold all the cards. I'm the only one who knows where your precious little human is. And I know your dirty little secret to boot," her seductive voice crackled through the speaker. Scrambling whispers echoed in the background. She wasn't alone.

The hairs on the back of his neck bristled. "Name your price. What is it you want from me?"

"Unfortunately for you, there's no price on revenge. The revenge is payment enough," she snorted before going silent again.

He balled his fist furiously. He didn't expect anything less from her. She was like a feline toying with its prey. Everything to her was a game.

"Okay, how about I agree to a hint? It's more fun for me this way since I can't stay and play much longer. I have some pressing business to attend to."

"Fine, what is it?" he asked, desperate for a hint though he despised having no choice in the matter.

"I'm not going to give up the information that easily, you have to beg me on your knees."

He could tell she was smiling on the other end based on the sound of her voice.

"And believe me, I'll know if you do, I'm watching you." Another drone zipped by his face, hovering in front of his eyes before flying back into the smoky sky.

He was all out of options. He chose to appease her and swallowed his pride for the sake of the woman he loved.

He fell to his knees, bowing his head in submission. "Please tell me."

She snorted. "Please what?"

"Please, Mistress Valdez."

"Very well then, although I don't even owe you this considering you invaded and ransacked my home planet. I mean, how dare you," the poisonous words dripped off her razor-sharp tongue. "And what you did to my beautiful face, I should repay ten—"

"Out with it already," he demanded. "I've done what you asked. I'm sick and tired of your nonsense."

"All right, all right," she hissed. "And you're going to love this. I'm surprised I thought of it on such short notice. Originally, I was going to take her home and bring her on a little hunting expedition, and you would've been right to check here first, but I had a far better idea," she paused for a long moment. "She's stranded on a planet in Universe 18, and if she isn't already dead, she will be soon enough."

"What do you mean?"

"The air quality is breathable, but not for long. I would say she has another fourteen suns and moons before her lungs collapse and her brain suffocates from lack of oxygen. Good luck searching all five hundred and fifty planets for your great love," she laughed.

"You—"

"This shouldn't come as any surprise," she said nonchalantly. "If you're not with me, you're against me, and it's clear you've gone rogue for quite some time. I can only imagine what the Grand Supreme will say when he learns of your betrayal. Who knows? He might already be privy."

Valdez hung up her communicator and the contents of Dante's stomach rose and splattered all over the sand. He wiped his mouth against his glove and jumped to his feet, Mr. Hiss in hand. He was wasting time feeling sorry for himself and the clock was ticking on Autumn's life. Only fourteen suns and moons remained, and he didn't have another second to waste.

PART TWO

Shades of Earth

Twenty-One

THE WARM SUMMER air blew through Ronan's hair as he soared over the small township of Monroe. Marcela and Tyler sat patiently in his arms while Caleb clutched his heavy black boots for dear life, dangling as he zipped through the starlit sky.

A wave of excitement and relief rushed through his body to finally be rid of Misty. She was the most annoying person he'd ever encountered, human or otherwise.

A great weight had been lifted from his shoulders as the phantom sound of her nasally voice echoed through his ears then disappeared. Next, he had to focus on getting the other three humans home so he could go to speak with Sean. If all went according to plan, he could leave with him and Autumn's father to embark on the long journey home to Surge.

Caleb lived close to Misty. Ronan's communicator beeped, revealing coordinates 41°18′8.728″N, 74°10′31.227″W.

The rectangular structure he resided in was much smaller than Misty's home and surrounded by a dark, dense forest of trees.

Ronan lowered Caleb to the ground before landing. Unlike

Misty, nobody came outside to greet him. His home remained dark, like he lived by himself.

"Well, I guess this is goodbye," Caleb turned to leave. Thank you for the ride—"

Ronan twisted his mouth to the side. "You're such a disappointment. The hate you demonstrated toward Autumn was unforgivable and rather disgusting if I may say so myself. Despicable for a former lover with no cause."

Caleb's cheeks flushed and lips moved as if he wanted to speak.

"Choose your next words wisely, human. I'm in no mood for retaliation," He tightened his fists. Marcela and her son took a few steps in retreat, eyes growing wide.

Caleb took a deep breath, settling himself. "Honestly, I've had time to think about my behavior and I'm sorry for the way I treated her. She didn't deserve the hate I gave. But I'm more sorry she got tangled up with someone like Dante. He destroyed her life and any chance we ever had of being happy together."

"Contrary to popular belief, he saved all of you actually," Ronan ran a hand through his hair, tousling the short spiky strands. "It's all thanks to him that your planet is still in existence, even if the way he handled it was rather foolish and reckless. And you never deserved Autumn. She was never your first choice. Am I right?"

Caleb's lips moved. "How did you—"

Ronan's mouth flattened. "Don't answer, just think about it. She's nothing but a memory to you anyway. Now run along, home before I change my mind."

He ushered him away, waving his hands. Caleb paused and looked over his shoulder one last time before knocking on his door. The lights turned on and voices spoke from inside the dwelling. He was allowed inside, and once again, the body of a parent fainted on the floor.

He sighed a deep regretful sigh at how much this idiot

had hurt Autumn, but he didn't have time to fixate. He grabbed hold of Marcela and Tyler, and they made their way off into the starry night. All he could think about was how he was going to explain this situation to Sean and if he would consider them endgame.

Twenty-Two

AUTUMN TRUDGED with Armienti through the ongoing snow and ice storm. She leaned against his body for support. Their boots slipped through the elements. The sun had lowered itself in the distance, and the stars beyond the clouds shimmered through the rich emerald-green sky. It was twilight in this frigid alien world.

The enormous fish was slung over Armienti's back. *The fish that'd almost killed her.*

Her stomach grumbled as they walked together. She couldn't wait to sink her teeth into its scaled flesh, to have her hunger curbed. Her mouth watered at the thought of filling her empty stomach to the brim.

"Are you feeling any better?" He glanced over at her, golden hair swaying against his back. Sleet clung to his uniform and scarlet cape as they walked.

"Yes, I think so," she offered him a small smile. In reality, she was beyond *embarrassed*. Her cheeks warmed. She'd put them through so much trouble and had almost paid with her life.

Her temples throbbed. After they ate, all she wanted to do was laze by the fire and watch the shadows dance against the golden rocks of the cave. She stretched and yawned, muscles aching.

When they arrived at their cavern dwelling, Armienti tossed the fish at the entrance. Its heavy body and tangled tentacles laid still and lifeless. They proceeded inside and started a fire with the minigun Armienti had found on the person of one of Valdez's dead Zexian soldiers.

Her teeth chattered as she removed her gloves and held her hands by the fire for warmth.

She couldn't help but wonder what Dante was up to at that moment and how much he missed her. Had he lost his mind searching for her and worried she was dead? He must've gone insane. As insane as her dad after she'd been taken.

When she closed her eyes, she could still smell his spicy cinnamon scent. She shivered at the recollection of his calloused hands sliding across her naked skin and over her hips as they made love.

"Oh Dante," she sighed, imagining him. His brilliant amber eyes, the cleft of his chin, and his solid arms holding her tight on a cold night like this one. Her face warmed and her body ached for him.

Armienti fiddled with the fire. "I'm sorry, did you say something?" He glanced at her, his blue eyes sparkling with intrigue.

She shrugged, pushing Dante from her mind. He was a fantasy nothing more. A hole punched through her chest, leaving her dizzy.

"I didn't say anything," she watched her hands as the red-orange fire flickered and danced in the background. She so wasn't in the mood to talk about him with his brother. The situation proved more than she could bear.

* * *

DANTE SAUNTERED BACK onto his destroyer, Mr. Hiss in hand. He couldn't believe Valdez. *How could she do this to him?*

His mistress had always been cruel to a fault, but this was unfathomable. Cunning *shrew*. She'd managed to outsmart him, which he found infuriating, all because he declined her "generous" offer.

He stood by his decision; she was not his wife.

His body shook with the weight of his stride. Fire threatened to rise from his hands once more, but he didn't have time to waste on another fruitless outburst. Autumn was counting on him. If he couldn't save her, nobody could.

He had fourteen suns and moons to find her among a gathering of five hundred and fifty planets. Life was so unfair.

"Pilot, change course to Universe 18," he commanded as he buckled in his harness. Mr. Hiss yawned and purred in his arms, tail swaying. He refused to admit it, but this animal was growing on him as well.

They ascended through the rainbow atmosphere and into the endless sea of stars.

* * *

NOT LONG INTO THE VOYAGE, Dante pulled out his communicator and conducted a search.

"Show me planets in Universe 18 with non-habitable air quality," he muttered.

A hologram swirled from his screen, yielding instant results. Mr. Hiss's indigo eyes widened, and he clawed through the air, playing with the translucent 3D images. Dante caught his paw with his black-gloved hand and stroked behind his ear. He rolled over and fell asleep on his lap. At least one of them was comfortable.

If they visited 3.6 planets a day or fifty planets divided by fourteen days, it was possible to save her. But it meant *no* rest, *no* sleep, *no* meals, and *no* distractions until he found her.

Fifty planets were non-habitable. Relief flooded through his limbs. The number was far better than the five hundred planets Valdez had boasted.

They appeared to be scattered throughout Universe 18. Some of the planets were prison planets, while others were barren ice worlds.

Autumn meant everything to him. He vowed to love her for all eternity until every star, sun, planet, and moon was no longer in existence. Until the universes ceased to be. He had to find her. He couldn't let her suffer this way, couldn't let her meet the same terrible fate as Maeve.

Oh Maeve, it was happening all over again. He refused to deal with another loss. A loss of this magnitude would *destroy* him.

His first stop was the prison planet of Joule.

Twenty-Three

PLANET JOULE WAS a step above the slave planet of Varz, but not by much. It was an unsightly little world that bore the wicked scent of salt and despair.

The terrain was rugged and rough. Snow fell from the sky in a tornado of gray soot and charred bones, and the air was the nauseating shade of hazy yellow.

Dante pulled on a helmet and adjusted the oxygen levels so as not to inhale any of the smog. He smoothed the visor over his eyes and tucked the wisps of his hair inside the hard material. He sealed his helmet airtight. He prayed Autumn hadn't been made to suffer here. What a miserable place to be stranded.

Although the outskirts were barren, the majority of Planet Joule was occupied by maximum security cells in a monstrosity of a prison called *Revolving Sight.* Only the worst of the worst criminals were transported here from around the universes to serve out their sentences, paying for their crimes with their miserable lives.

The Grand Supreme found it more amusing to leave the prisoners alive rather than dispose of them upfront. He decided the dates of their executions at random. In many ways, it was worse to be sent here than to be made a slave.

Most never saw the light of day again after entering the facility walls and their suffering never ended. There was no escape but death.

Although he hoped it unlikely, if there was any chance Autumn was on this planet, he had to search for her.

Dante dispatched his men to scour the outskirts while he teleported into the windowless obsidian dome of the facility. He stepped lightly. There were still forty-nine other planets to search if this one yielded no results.

* * *

INSIDE OF THE building was eerily quiet and clinically white. Not a single body occupied the hallway. The building consisted of fifteen floors of numbered windowless doors that circled the structure in straight lines, coming to a head like a hive.

His heavy black boots clicked against the metallic tiles with crisp precision as he surveyed his surroundings.

Okay, where to start?

In an instant, he was swarmed by a team of guards who pointed their silver blasters at his head.

"Easy," he held his hands up in mock surrender. A smile twisted over his mouth from beneath his helmet. His blood boiled with vengeance, secretly he hoped one of them fired so he could act upon their attempt.

He was approached by the captain of the guard as identified by the words embroidered into the left breast of his uniform.

"Identify yourself." He cocked his metallic blaster. His fiery orange hair framed his emerald-hued face. Long fingers hovered over the trigger.

Dante removed his helmet, holding the protective gear in

the crook of his arm, his spine straight. Everyone gasped and fell to one knee. He didn't need an introduction.

"Forgive us," the captain stuttered. "There was no formal announce—"

He held up a hand to silence him. "Save your excuses. I don't have time for them. I'm searching for my wife. Where is she?" he demanded.

Whispers erupted among the guards. "Why would the empress be here?" the captain finally asked, lips trembling.

He ignored his foolish question. "If I find out you're lying or playing dumb, you're all dead men. You have one minute —empty the cells."

"But we—"

"Fifty-nine seconds," he folded his arms. "Trust me, if I get down to zero, you're not going to like what happens next."

The guards jumped to their feet at his threat. They scrambled from cell to cell, unlocking them. Doors sprang ajar and white puffs of steam poured into the hallway.

Dante followed the guards, glancing inside of each chamber. The conditions appeared miserable. There were no windows and blinding white lights with barely enough room to stand. The prisoners were shackled to the wall by their ankles. Hope had long since left their eyes.

He searched through hundreds upon hundreds of cells. The one trait all the occupants trapped inside possessed was they had defied the Grand Supreme in some way or another and waited for their execution date.

At the end of his rounds, he determined Autumn wasn't there.

"Thank you, gentlemen, you've been most cooperative," he turned on his heel to leave and then paused.

Wait, someone is missing. His heart hammered in his chest.

He turned back around, his mouth curving. "Take me to the hole."

Twenty-Four

AUTUMN RESTED on the floor of the cave. The glow from the fire danced along the ceiling in spirals and swirls. Her appetite was finally sated, but she still hadn't recovered from the day's catastrophe.

How embarrassing to be resuscitated by her captor, she cringed.

She was more exhausted than usual, and it took longer to catch her breath. Her muscles screamed in pain and a headache threatened to conquer her. If only she hadn't been so eager and had taken the time to strategize, she wouldn't be suffering.

Armienti stood in the snow with the shirt of his uniform off. His defined blue muscles gleamed in the pale moonlight as he cleaned and prepped the fish for tomorrow's meal. He wiped the sweat from his brow with the side of his arm before their eyes locked for a moment too long. He smiled, white teeth sparkling in the evening light, before looking away.

Her cheeks warmed against her will. Her heart raced. As much as she hated him for putting them in this situation, he'd saved her life many times. And despite her better judgment, he looked handsome tonight. Although he briefly crossed her mind, she snapped back to reality. He was a traitor, and she had a husband who she adored out there somewhere searching for her.

She closed her eyes and rerouted her thoughts to Dante. His smiling face and arrogant swagger. His amber eyes flecked with green when the light played off them the right way. Would they ever see each other again? Or would she spend the rest of her life wondering what could've been?

* * *

DANTE STRODE down several flights of stairs hastily. The captain of the guard raced after him. His standard issue boots clicked against the steps, weapons wavering in his holster. He had to be sure, had to see for himself. If there was any possibility of Autumn being down here, he had to at least check so he could cross Planet Joule off his list.

"The hole is to your right, sire," the captain's shaky voice echoed through the corridor. They approached a large steel door. Shadows danced across the ceiling and over the pristine white walls. The breath caught in his throat.

He turned toward the captain, pulling his communicator from his back pocket. He stared at the time. At this rate he was going to be behind schedule.

"Open the door at once, or I'll rip the hinges off."

The captain quaked, sliding his fingers over the digital keypad. Red buttons clicked and beeped and blinked. They were granted access and the door slid open. Inside was pitch dark.

He ignited a flame in his palm to use as a torch and sauntered inside. Mildewy water covered the floor. There was no bed to speak of and no facilities. The foul stench of excrement assaulted his senses. Dante choked on the disgusting smell.

Autumn wasn't there, and this time, he was thankful.

In the far corner, the prisoner he'd been wanting to see sat cross-legged against the wall, face buried in his hands.

Dante hesitated for a moment, then approached. A lump formed in his throat. This was all his fault. He was solely responsible for his misery.

"You're coming with me." He knelt to help the prisoner to a stand, wrapping an arm over his shoulder. He steadied him on his feet.

A gun cocked, and a set of ragged wings flashed across the wall. "I'm afraid neither of you are going anywhere."

Twenty~Five

DANTE'S SENSES were excellent in the dark, perhaps better than in the daylight. Despite this fact, he worried for the safety of the prisoner. If the stream of energy ricocheted off the wall and struck him, he'd be done for. He was too weak to withstand the attack.

Dante's mouth twisted to the side as he cracked his knuckles.

The Zexian aimed the blaster straight between his eyes. His wings sat high on his back as he crouched, ready to pounce.

"Are you sure you want to go through with this?" Dante's smile grew wide and eager. His blood pumped through his ears, his desire to spill blood in that moment insatiable.

"As you know, it's not a matter of choice," he winked a lifeless black eye. "My empress has covered all her bases. She sends her kindest regards."

The Zexian fired his weapon and a swirl of blue energy zapped through the air. Dante shielded the prisoner with his body, causing the rays to spark against the wall.

He raised his hand, folding his thumb across his palm.

"I'm afraid nobody ever learns— I'm not one to be trifled with."

Dante released a massive ball of fire, engulfing the Zexian captain whole. Blood curdling screams filled the room as his body disintegrated from the heat, melting all over the floor of the cell. Dante watched in silence as one of Valdez's lackeys lost his life in a foolish attempt to stop him.

He'd wasted enough time. He had to get out of here. He removed his helmet and pulled it over the prisoner's head.

"You're going to need this more than I do," he reassured him. In the blink of an eye, they teleported from the hole and onto the outskirts of the building.

Dante held his breath as they sprinted toward the destroyer. He opened the door, and they entered the ship, sealing the entrance airtight.

He fell to his knees, gasping. Mr. Hiss yawned and stretched on the control seat. He cast a lazy glimpse, before drifting back off to sleep, his tail puffed as it hung over the edge of the seat.

Dante rose to his feet brushing the snow from his uniform. "Are you okay?" he asked the prisoner.

The prisoner hesitated. "Yes; is it all right if I take this helmet off?" He asked in little more than a whisper.

"Of course," Dante reached and helped him remove the protective gear. Kyo stared back at him, trembling. His wide eyes wavered with confusion.

Twenty-Six

"WILL this night ever come to an end?" Ronan groaned beneath his breath.

He sighed as he carried Marcela and Tyler in his arms, careful not to drop them. They soared over the township of Monroe. Evening lights flickered and blinked. The trees swayed in the warm post-midnight summer breeze.

One more stop, just one more stop, he kept reminding himself, before he could see Sean again. He hoped their meeting would go well. His hands sweated within his gloves. He'd traveled far and wide across the universes for him.

Finally, he exhaled a deep sigh of relief. They arrived at coordinates 41.3652778°N, -74.1822222°W. His communicator beeped and buzzed in his palm, indicating the correct location.

Ronan lowered the remaining humans from the sky to the same dwelling where he had attended the party a day after the crash-landing when he had first come to Earth. It turned out Sean had been there as well, but they hadn't met until a few suns and moons later. It had to be destiny.

His boots touched down on the green. He placed Marcela and Tyler upright on their feet.

"Wait, you can't be serious," Marcela's eyes scoured the premises. "My ex lives here with his new wife. I don't want to see him ever—"

"Save it—not my problem," Ronan said matter-of-factly, a smile tilted on his lips. As far as he was concerned, he'd completed his task and then some. Autumn would be pleased.

Marcela groaned and crossed her arms. It was ridiculous how little gratitude anyone expressed. No human had told him thank you or otherwise for the elaborate rescue mission and year-long trip to bring them home he'd organized.

Ronan turned toward Tyler. "I'm not sure why Autumn allowed you to breathe, but for whatever reason, you have her to thank for your second chance at life."

"Once again, I am so, so, sorry," Tyler's bottom lip quivered. Tears spilled from his deep brown eyes as he inhaled a shuddering breath, "I didn't mean to kill—"

Ronan turned on his heel and levitated in the air. "Unfortunately, sorry doesn't fix the situation. Sorry can't bring her mother back to life. Be more responsible in the future."

Tyler hugged himself and glanced away.

Marcela crossed her arms and scowled at her son. "If you're not sorry now, you will be, for putting us through all this misery and for hurting that poor girl. As much as I don't care for her, she deserved better," she paused. "After we wake up from this horrible dream, we're going to the authorities. You can explain to them what occurred."

Tyler nodded mechanically.

At least he'd finally get what he deserved. Ronan jumped into the air and soared off into the night. He'd had enough of the humans and their drama for a lifetime.

* * *

DANTE CLOSED HIS EYES, resting his chin on the ball of his fist. Stars whistled by the windows and miniature comets scraped against the steel exterior of the destroyer. He tried his hardest to get some rest. Planet Joule was a fruitless mission, and he'd worked himself to the bone. He was no closer to finding his wife and still had forty-nine more planets to conquer—in less than thirteen days' time.

His nap, if he could even call it that, was interrupted by a warm wet sensation that formed on his lap. He glanced down. *Drat.*

Mr. Hiss.

"You can't be serious," he said to the baby ling.

Mr. Hiss purred, rubbing his head against his ribcage. His hot-pink striped tail slid across the wet spot on his leg, puffing.

Dante sighed, coming to stand, cradling the baby ling in his arms, then sauntered over to a side compartment and grabbed a cloth from the cabinet. He blotted Mr. Hiss's soft underbelly before wiping the wetness from his pants.

Autumn would've wanted him to be taken care of.

He stroked Mr. Hiss's head with his finger before pouring him a bowl of water. *Probably not the best idea considering his track record.* Afterwards, he crumbled and laid out bits of freeze-dried meat for him to eat.

"When we find your mom and return home, you're getting trained," he scratched behind his ear. Mr. Hiss purred and he could've sworn he smiled at him beneath his fluffy muzzle.

A lump formed in his throat after he spoke. If *he found her.* No, he couldn't allow himself to think negatively. Everything would be all right, it had to be. He inhaled and exhaled slowly.

"You'd make a good father," Kyo said as he lounged against the wall staring out into space. The stars flew by in streaks and waves. A strand of his moonglow mohawk fell over his eye. His neck tattoos flexed in the shadows.

"Come again?" Dante's eyes met Kyo's, who watched him from the darkness.

"Sorry, I hope you don't mind me saying so. The way you take care of that animal—"

"Mind your own business," Dante crossed his arms. "Don't be so familiar—I'm still your emperor."

"Geez, sorry I said something nice," Kyo rolled his eyes. "You don't know how to take a compliment, I guess."

Dante huffed a breath and took Mr. Hiss back to his seat. He closed his eyes, attempting to resume his nap.

Kyo cleared his throat. "I didn't get a chance to say thank you for freeing me. That place was beyond terrible. But I can't help but wonder why you changed your mind? I committed high treason."

Dante's eyes shot open, and he sighed. He'd never get to sleep at this rate. *The questions from this guy. Why couldn't he be thankful in silence?*

"I don't owe you an explanation. A simple thank you will suffice. Unless you'd prefer I return you to Planet Joule," he threatened, although it was a lie. He had more pressing matters to attend to, mainly finding Autumn. Traveling back would put him off schedule.

He continued. "The only reason you're still alive is because of the love I bear for my sister, although I have no idea what she sees in you."

Kyo's face paled and he turned away.

Dante sighed. "Don't worry, I won't send you back to the cells. I promise."

"Your promises are worthless, you're an elitist pig," the words slipped from Kyo's lips, and he threw a hand over his mouth.

"Your pardon?" His eyes widened.

"Sorry, I don't know what I was thinking. I didn't mean to be—"

"So honest?"

Kyo stared at him strangely. "Yes."

He had a new insult to add to the long list of slights that had been spewed at him throughout the years. *Elitist pig*, he chewed his cheeks. He had to admit the name was rather creative.

He sighed, refocusing on his current situation. He didn't have time for this. He needed to get some sleep so he could be ready for the challenges ahead. Autumn needed him more than ever. Determination singed through him to make matters right. He couldn't deal with the burning agony of another loss and could never imagine life without her.

Twenty-Seven

AUTUMN LAID on the floor of the cave as the makeshift fire crackled and blazed inches from her body. Slow shadows drifted along the ceiling and over the walls. Snow fluttered to the ground outside in pitch silence.

The marmalade embers of the fire warmed her golden-olive skin as she rolled on her side. For the first time in a long time, her stomach was full and satisfied.

But she was exhausted. So exhausted she could sleep all day. As she turned and yawned, she bumped into Armienti. He lay slumbering, chest gently rising and falling. Strands of his shoulder-length golden hair tousled about his face, falling over his blue pointed ears.

What an idiot he was for getting them into this situation, for kidnapping her and trusting Valdez. The murderous bitch. How she wished she could give her a taste of her own medicine. She balled up her fists, wanting to throttle them both.

But still, being with him was better than being alone on this planet, she supposed. And maybe, just maybe, he wasn't all that bad. Foolish and selfish, yes, but not a bad person. Not really. He had a chip on his shoulder like most everyone else she knew.

Armienti stirred and she closed her eyes, pretending to sleep. She rolled toward the warmth of the fire.

"I know you're awake, Autumn," his gruff voice played off his lips. His warm soothing peppermint breath caressed her neck. "You're not snoring, so you're not fooling anyone."

She turned and looked into his brilliant sapphire eyes. "I do *not* snore."

He chuckled, running a hand through his gilded hair. "No, you don't. I'm only kidding. But if you did, it would be kind of cute."

Her eyes widened and her face flushed. *Cute.*

He shifted his head to the side. "You know, I dreamed of this moment for a long, long time—just you and me alone together—and I can't believe I'm telling you this," he glanced away before meeting her gaze. "It used to give me hope and help me get through the days when we were stranded on Earth. Days where I felt I could no longer carry on. Every time I close my eyes, I dream of you and what it would've been like if I had met you first. I wish you were mine."

She opened her mouth to speak but then hesitated. Her entire body trembled. *What did he expect her to say, laying this on her first thing in the morning? She could barely see straight.*

"You don't have to reply or say anything at all, and you don't have to pity me. Gods, I pity myself most days. I'm such a fool for putting us through this. Can you ever forgive me?"

She watched him. She'd heard it all before.

"What about Dante?" she finally asked through quivering lips.

He shrugged. "What about him? It's not like we'll ever see him again," he said matter-of-factly.

The words hit her like a gut punch. Tears threatened to spill from her eyes. There was so much truth in what he said whether she wanted to admit it or not.

She remained quiet for a moment and then spoke. "I can try."

"That's good enough for me," his lips curved. "Can we please start over? Can we at least be friends?"

"I guess," she said, because what choice did she have? They needed each other to survive. "But friends don't do what you did. How do I know I can trust you again? Trust is earned and not given."

"I know and I'm sorry," he leaned over and hugged her tight. His solid arms held her close to his warm body. Her eyes fluttered closed. "I know you've been through so much. I promise I'll spend the rest of my life trying to make this up to you and trying to win back your trust."

She rose, her stomach trying itself into knots. This conversation was getting *way* too intense. And under the circumstances she couldn't deal.

She went to leave the cave to get some fresh air and clear her head, but the snow was starting to pick up. Rather than wet her go-go boots for the hundredth time, she focused her energy on flying.

She went to levitate over an ice bank, but instead, the tall heels of her go-go boots slipped against the slick pile of elements. Armienti jumped up from the ground and caught her before she hit the rocks.

What happened? She was sure she channeled her energy correctly; she'd done this so many times before.

"That was weird," she turned toward Armienti. He placed her on the ground, feet first. "I tried to float over the ice, but my abilities didn't work."

He twisted his mouth to the side, contemplating. "How peculiar. Now that you mention it, after you were pulled under the ice I tried to heal you and for the first time in my life, I was unsuccessful. I thought maybe my energy was low because we hadn't eaten for a period, but this doesn't make any sense. Our energy levels should be back to normal by now."

A cool chill trickled down her spine. Something was very, very wrong on this planet. She could feel it deep in her gut.

"There's only one way to test this theory," Armienti's mouth twisted to the side before he flashed a dazzling grin. "Go freshen up and meet me outside."

Twenty-Eight

AFTER AUTUMN RELIEVED herself and washed the sleep from her eyes with loose snow, she left the cave to go meet Armienti. As she walked through the field of ice, her go-go boots skated with each step. *Why couldn't she fly anymore? A lump formed in her throat; her heart sped. Was there something wrong with her? Was she sick?*

She had a vague idea of what Armienti wanted her to do and she hoped she wasn't out of practice. It'd been a few months, and she didn't want to embarrass herself in front of him. Her cheeks suddenly became the warmest part of her body.

Armienti sat cross-legged in the snow. The shirt portion of his uniform was off, and he assumed a deep state of meditation. Wind and flurries drifted through the long golden strands of his hair. His blue muscles gleamed in the muted sunlight.

She cleared her throat and her hand slid down to the fullest part of her hip. "Seriously, can we get this over with?" Her teeth chattered. She was dying to go back inside where it was warm and dry.

She was so cold and tired and desperate for another nap.

She yawned as a second round of sleep clouded her eyes. *Why was she so exhausted after a full night of rest?*

Armienti came to a graceful stand, feline-like and beautiful all at once. He ran a hand through his gilded hair. "Just because we're friends again doesn't mean I'll take it easy on you, Autumn Ramon-Martyne."

She rolled her eyes. "Let's get this over with." She meant every word.

His mouth tilted to the side, and he assumed a fighting stance. She crouched and took one as well, fingers flexed. Her unused muscles trembled, head spinning with anticipation. Her heart pounded through her throat.

Armienti lunged at her and launched a kick. She stepped to the side as his heavy black boots skidded against the ice.

"Great reflexes," he winked.

She grinned suddenly, overwhelmed with the urge to fight. Her non-human half took control. She couldn't help herself. Blood pumped in her ears. She wanted to connect her fist with bone. "Are my reflexes great, or are you getting rusty?"

His pretty face contorted, eyes narrowing to razor-thin slits. "There she is."

He circled her. Her eyes locked with his.

"How about we up the stakes a little?" The frigid wind howled through his gilded hair. Amusement graced his charming face. "If you win our match, I'll wait on you hand and foot. I'll prepare your meals and fetch your water. I'll clean up after you and essentially be your slave. But if I win, I get to kiss you," the corners of his mouth flickered with excitement.

Autumn stared at him in silence. The thought of kissing Armienti and not Dante made her heart shatter into a million pieces.

"No."

"Aww, you're no fun," he winked. "Suit yourself. Perhaps I'll be your slave regardless."

After he spoke, she made a fist and thrust it toward his chin. Armienti caught the ball of her fist, chuckling—until she took her leg and kneed him in the gut. He doubled over and sputtered backwards, spitting up bile all over the ice.

She covered her mouth, biting back a smile as he glanced at her, coughing. Fighting was the best feeling in the world. Uncontrollable bloodlust pulsated through her veins. A few years back she couldn't imagine anything feeling so satisfying.

"What did you think Dante and I did all day every day, make out?" She laughed.

He came to a stand, catching his breath. "You're going to be sorry for that."

Armienti charged at her, knocking her from her feet and onto her back. The wind escaped her lungs as she hit the cold cruel ice. They skidded and rolled together, their bodies covered in powdered snow, limbs entwined. The white world spun around and around and around until—she heard a crack and a groan.

They stopped rolling and she climbed off him. He lay in the snow, white puffs of breath seeping from his mouth. His hair covered his face, and his right wrist bent the wrong way. Bits of muscle and bone pierced his skin. Droplets of blood seeped into the pant leg of his uniform. She cupped her hand over her mouth. *Oh, no, no, no. Please no.*

"I am so, so sorry, Armienti. Are you okay?" she asked as her body quaked all over. She snapped out of her daze. "Here, let me help you." She reached down and pulled him to a seated position. His eyes shot open.

"I'm okay." He went to move his hand, but it fell limp in his lap.

"No, you're not," her brows furrowed. "You're hurt."

And it was all her fault.

He held his arm out before flashing a crooked smile. "Don't worry, this isn't the first time I've broken a bone. I'll just rejuvenate myself."

He focused on healing his bent wrist. Nothing changed. The bone remained dislodged. Her stomach twisted.

Armienti's jaw dropped. "I don't understand what's going on. Why can't I rejuvenate? What the hell?" Sweat beaded along his brow as he examined his hand.

"I don't know." She shuddered. "It's like this planet is draining our abilities."

"Or slowly killing us," his eyes widened, face paling.

Twenty-Nine

RONAN HELD his breath as he stood before Sean's dwelling located at 41.362574, -74.293859.

He took a quick glimpse into his communicator to ensure his human disguise was still in place. Everything was as it should be; relief flooded through him.

His heart accelerated as he raised his fist to the door. Before he made contact, his communicator beeped and buzzed within the confines of his pocket.

He slid the device out and glanced at the message. *Sean.* His face warmed against his will.

":)"

…

…

"Are you still coming tonight?" Sean typed.

"I'm here actually, at your front door," Ronan was quick to respond, biting his cheeks. He couldn't contain his excitement.

A few moments passed and a tap came to his shoulder. He whirled around, caught off guard, considering he was always ready for anything.

Sean stood before him with a smile on his face. Dimples

crinkled against the apples of his cheeks. Ginger-blonde bangs with dark roots cascaded over his large brown eyes.

"I can't believe you're here," he rolled into him. Ronan glanced at his feet—he wore skates. Sean pulled him in for a warm embrace, running his fingers against his back.

Ronan's body tensed then relaxed. He wasn't so used to being held this way. Humans were more affectionate than higher life-forms and that was a fact.

"Me neither," he finally replied. Seeing him after all this time was like a dream.

Sean pointed at his skates. "I have an extra pair in my garage. If you want, we can get out of here. Sorry, I know it's lame that I invited you to my parent's house on summer break, my car is still at the mechanic's—"

He ran a hand through his short spiky hair. "No, it's perfect actually. And no worries, I don't have a car."

Sean cupped a hand over his mouth. "Oh, I shouldn't complain. Sorry, I didn't mean anything by that. How did you get to my house then? Did you take an Uber?"

"Something like that," Ronan tilted his head to the side.

"Here, let me pay half," Sean reached into his pocket.

"Don't worry about it, your money's no good here."

Sean smiled and rolled away into a dark side entrance of his home and reemerged with a pair of skates. They had four horizontal wheels and a series of straps and clips. He handed him a pair of grips and frayed knee pads, not that he needed them, but the thought was still kind.

Ronan removed his heavy black boots and secured his feet into the skates. A perfect fit. He pulled on the safety gear, to be polite, then placed his shoes by the side of the house, before they rolled off into the night.

Stars sparkled overhead and a warm breeze flowed against his body as they zipped over the hills. Shadows swayed between the lush green trees.

After several laps over the black rubbly ground, longing

glances, and shy smiles, they arrived at a series of wooden benches surrounded by a field of green. Half-lit two-story houses sparkled all around them. Ronan sat down with Sean who rested his head against his shoulder. His hair had a sweet scent he couldn't quite place. The loose strands tickled his jaw.

"So how are you? It's been a long time." Sean ran his fingers along his arm.

"Fine, I guess," Ronan stared at the stars before looking over to him. He wished this moment could last forever, but it was impossible. Nothing lasts forever and he knew that better than anyone.

"Just fine?"

"Well, I've been traveling a lot. I only just landed a few hours ago."

"That's so awesome that you get to travel all over the world for work. I wish I could do that. How long are you planning to stay in the area for?"

"I'm only here for tonight," the words left his mouth in slow motion, and he couldn't take them back.

Sean turned his head, his voice lowered to a whisper. "I was afraid you'd say that."

Ronan hesitated. "Well, that's kind of what I wanted to talk to you about."

"Okay?" Sean's eyes met his. "I'm all ears. What's up?"

"Maybe, if you want, you could come with me."

A pause came to their conversation and Ronan's heart leapt to his throat. He could scarcely breathe.

"For how long?" Sean finally asked, excitement flooded through his voice. "The rest of the summer? I just finished up my second semester and I don't have any vacations planned. I saved a bit of money from work—"

"How long is summer?" Ronan asked as his face warmed. He couldn't remember the length of the human seasons.

Sean chuckled. "I didn't think you'd been out of school *that* long. I'm off for the next three months."

He sat there for a moment at a loss for words. Three months, ninety suns and moons. That was no time at all. He still had to transport Autumn's father safely back to Surge. *Dammit.* Would that be enough time to get Sean back to school? Probably not but he'd do the best he could under the circumstances.

To make matters more complicated, Sean still had no idea he wasn't human, and he only had one night to tell him the truth.

"Well, I'd love to come with you," Sean squeezed his hand reassuringly. "I just need to tell my folks."

Thirty

AUTUMN LED Armienti back to the cave. He winced and shivered with each trembling step. As he clutched his broken wrist, dread and shame overtook her. She couldn't believe she'd hurt him.

Why had their abilities vanished without a trace?

She guided him over to the fire. Tiny embers crackled and blazed from earlier that morning. She blew on them, causing the flame to reignite. Flames spread through the ashes and orange glowed across the ceiling as the fire warmed their bodies.

"I'm going to set the bone, but first, I need something to stabilize your arm," she raced outside to where the giant alien fish lay, searching for supplies. Armienti remained inside the cave in silence.

Blood pulsed through her ears. Sure, she was pre-med at one point and had two semesters under her belt at Rockland Community College, but this was real life. How she wished she had been able to resume her studies.

Was she ready for this? She shook her head. *Toughen up, Autumn,* she scolded herself. She had to be strong, although she was terrified. Armienti needed her help.

She knelt and snapped two rib bones from the fish's enormous chest cavity. Calcium and minerals disintegrated in her gloves as she held the pieces in her palm. She raced back into the cave and fell to her knees beside Armienti as he sat on the floor. Sweat beaded against his brow.

She placed the bones on the ground. Her fingers shook. "Brace yourself, this is really going to hurt." She could only imagine the agony he was in.

She removed her teal glove and rolled the fabric up before placing it between his teeth.

"You can bite down on this if the pain becomes too much."

Deep in her gut she had a feeling it would be. They had no anesthesia and nothing to numb the sensation.

Armienti's golden hair swayed over his well-built shoulders. He closed his clear blue eyes. The cave grew as silent as death.

She continued. "Okay, on the count of three I'm going to shift the pieces together. One, two, three."

As she reached the end of her countdown, she straightened his wrist with a *CRACK*. Armienti bit down hard on the fabric in his mouth and groaned in agony. She took the severed bone and connected the pieces. Fortunately, it hadn't splintered. With her other hand she placed the fish bone supports on either side and held them steady.

Crap, her heart accelerated. She needed to hold the makeshift splint in place. Her eyes fell upon his crimson cape she'd been using as a blanket on the coldest of nights. She ripped off a few pieces and tied them in tight bows along the splint. She used a larger piece of fabric to create a sling for his arm.

Armienti sat on the floor and exhaled. The roll fell from his mouth.

"Thank you. I bet this is what it feels like to be human," he released a weak chuckle. His face began to resume its normal blue hue.

"Yeah, something like that. We're fragile creatures, remember?" She rolled her eyes. She was so tired of everyone giving their unwarranted opinions about humans.

She went to the entrance of the cave and grabbed a handful of snow. Flurries and sleet began to pour from the sky. Big surprise. The storms on this planet were never-ending.

When she returned, she blotted the snow against the corner of his cape, melting the ice and snow by the fire. She cleaned the blood from his face and off his uniform, then washed her hands.

"Okay, I'm going to prepare dinner for us," she announced.

When she went to stand up, he caught her by the arm with his uninjured hand. "Thank you, Autumn. Really. You didn't have to help me after everything I put us through, but you did anyway. I'm so stupid and you have such a kind heart. How can you be so kind?"

"I—" she stuttered as he stared into her eyes intently.

"You're such a good person, I don't even deserve to be in your presence," his voice jumped as he spoke, and his lips quivered. He ran his fingers along her frozen cheek. Her body trembled from his touch.

He leaned in close, so close she could feel his heartbeat against her own. Rays of light from the crackling fire danced against the dark ceiling of the cave. The warmth of his breath caressed her neck, sending shivers down her spine. She shook as he tilted her head to the side with his good hand and pressed his cold lips and desperate tongue against hers, sliding it into her mouth. He ran his fingers through her hair, catching them between her curls, then moved lower, kissing down the length of her throat.

She pulled away suddenly, jumping to her feet. He watched her in silence. His mouth moved as if he wanted to speak.

"I—I have to make dinner," she stuttered.

"Forgive me," he said.

* * *

DANTE'S FINGERS trembled within the confines of his gloves. He'd searched twenty more planets in Universe 18 for a total of twenty-one, but he was unsuccessful in locating Autumn.

This couldn't be happening.

The clock was ticking, and his wife was suffocating on some remote world with each passing day. He couldn't find her, no matter how hard he tried. Every breath could be her last.

He was useless. Shame shattered him to the core. No matter how hard he searched, he couldn't seem to find her, and he couldn't move fast enough. He'd had no food, no sleep, and he hadn't been able to rest for the last seven suns and moons. Every time he tried to close his eyes, he had nightmares of her smiling face disintegrating into ash.

The Grand Supreme had reached out to him several times, and each time he ignored his calls. Dante couldn't deal with him under the circumstances but wondered if he summoned him for a mission or if Valdez had spilled the truth about what he'd done? At this rate, he didn't want to find out.

Maeve—he couldn't deal with the pain of loss for a second time. It was too much to bear. Failure was *not* an option.

Every planet he had visited spelled death and destruction, whether intentional or not. Smoke poured from the ice city of Nilak. He cracked his knuckles, then crossed his arms as yet another soldier bowed and brought him unwelcome news. He couldn't stand being disappointed anymore.

Exhaustion from searching consumed him, his vision became unfocused and blurred at the corners. His legs wobbled with weakness as he turned on his heel and headed back to his destroyer. Snowflakes fluttered from the sky. White puffs of breath escaped from his mouth.

He didn't have time to dwell on his failure. Only seven days remained until Autumn's death. Only seven days until she suffocated on an uninhabitable world. No, he refused to let that happen.

As he entered his ship, he was greeted by Mr. Hiss. He trotted up to him, fluffy striped tail swaying through the air. Hopefulness filled his oversized cerulean eyes.

"Meow."

Dante couldn't bear to look at him either. He was a failure and all Mr. Hiss wanted was his mother.

Mr. Hiss followed him over to his seat, paws padding against the metallic floor the only break in the silence. After he strapped himself in, the ling jumped on his lap and nuzzled his snout against his ribs.

"Meow."

Dante scratched behind Autumn's pet's ear, unable to keep his head up. They had to get going. Twenty-nine more planets beckoned to be explored.

Kyo lounged against the wall, arms crossed. Shadows played through the strands of his moonglow mohawk. Dark tattoos swirled along his neck.

"You look exhausted, sir—I mean, sire," Kyo corrected himself.

Dante's eyes snapped to him. "Please, just stop. I don't need this right now."

"I was only trying to say that if you need help, I can offer my assistance."

His mouth twisted to the side. "Please, how could you possibly offer your assistance to someone like me? You're too—"

"Weak? Too much of a hybrid?" Kyo spat back at him. His eyes narrowed to razor-thin slits. Kyo's reaction was well deserved after the suffering he'd put him through.

"No, sorry," he shook his head. "That's not what I meant. What I meant to say was, you're too inexperienced on a mission like this one."

Kyo drew closer and Mr. Hiss studied his movements. He smiled beneath his hot-pink snout. His tail curled in Dante's lap.

Kyo cleared his throat. "While that may be true, as I've only been trained in the food delivery service industry, I'm no stranger to losing someone and going above and beyond to help my family."

"I see," Dante checked the time on his sleek black communicator. *Where on Earth was the pilot?* He was taking too long, and they needed to get going. *What was he doing, sightseeing?*

"What I mean to say is that, if you need someone to talk to, I'm here for you."

He stared at him at a complete and utter loss for words. Nobody besides Autumn and Maeve had ever cared what he thought and how he felt before. He had to admit he didn't quite know how to handle this offer. Kyo had to have an angle.

"Thank you, I think," Dante finally muttered at Kyo's thoughtful gesture. He struggled with what to make of his offer, especially after how poorly he'd treated him in the recent past—publicly kicking his ass, then sending him to Planet Joule for high treason. "But I don't need anyone." Besides Autumn, he left unsaid.

Dante's thoughts raced. He couldn't wait another second. They were officially *five* minutes behind schedule. His fists trembled with fury. The pilot would have to find his own way home. He couldn't afford to waste another second lingering on this fruitless planet.

He exhaled. "If you want something done right, you have to do it yourself."

He unbuckled his harness and held Mr. Hiss in the crook of his arm, then sauntered over to the control seat.

"If you want, I can fly while you sleep. You look like living hell," Kyo offered.

Dante turned around. They'd be late for sure. "Come again?"

"Iris and I—I mean Princess Leyla," Kyo corrected himself, "used to sneak out in your destroyers late at night. We would fly around the city and sometimes we orbited Surge and made love—"

"Enough." Dante's jaw lowered at this horrifying tidbit of information. His ears burned from the words that'd left Kyo's mouth. He wished he could unhear the admission of what he and his sister were *really* up to in their spare time.

His eyes gravitated toward the control console. The bright colors, flickering lights, and levers all seemed to meld together into one. His sleep debt was far too great to continue this way.

He blinked hard and yawned, covering his mouth with his black-gloved hand. "I'm going to pretend that I didn't just hear that."

He continued. "Why are you helping me after the way I treated you? Also, it's common knowledge around the city that you hate me, and you hate my family."

"You've been through a lot, and you look like you could use someone to talk to. And you released me from the cells when you didn't have to."

Dante's head lowered before he raised it again. He didn't have time for this, he was ready to collapse from exhaustion.

"I think I'll take you up on your offer. The job is yours." He gestured toward the control seat, changing the subject. "And like I said before, I don't need anyone."

Dante turned around and ambled back to the passenger seat. He buckled his harness. Mr. Hiss rolled over and slumbered in his arms. He rested his cheek on the ball of his fist and closed his eyes.

"Great, I promise you won't be disappointed, and I'll do

my best to help you find your empress," were the last words Dante heard before he drifted into the cool, quiet darkness. Secretly he was flattered by Kyo's kind gesture. But Autumn's face and *those eyes* continued to haunt him through his subconscious.

Thirty-One

ARMIENTI SAT BY THE WARM, crackling fire as Autumn prepared their supper. He clutched his broken wrist in the makeshift sling she'd created for him out of the cape he'd stolen from Dante.

He deserved the symbol of status—not Dante, his brother. So, in his eyes, it wasn't stealing but taking back what should've always been his.

Embarrassment swelled through his body. He struggled to breathe as his thoughts raced to the issue at hand.

Their abilities had suddenly vanished, and he couldn't believe he'd kissed Autumn. It was forbidden on so many different levels. But he couldn't help himself. He found her irresistible.

Since the *incident*, she hadn't uttered a single word or looked his way for hours on end. Her eyes seemed to skip around the cave, avoiding him.

"Are you seriously never going to talk to me again?" he asked as she held two pieces of fish to the fire, cooking them on both sides. Water melted between a hole in the ice she'd carved near the exit of the cave.

He continued when she didn't answer. He wasn't

surprised. "I mean, come on, you're a pretty, young woman. I can't imagine this is your first time being kissed. Caleb, Dante, and what was that human coward's name, Iain—"

"I don't want to talk about this right now," her eyes rolled as she rested a hand on her hip. "But dinner is ready, so go wash up."

"Are you serious?" he asked. When she didn't answer, he groaned, trudging his boots to the door of the cavern and wiping his good hand in the snow. He smeared snow over his mouth and wiped flakes against his black skin-tight sleeve.

When he returned, she walked over and handed him his fish, staring at him for a moment too long as if she wanted to speak.

"I can't believe you've been keeping count of the guys I've kissed. It's kind of creepy."

She sat on the opposite side of the fire and ate her piece of fish. His ears and neck burned with shame. *Yes, he'd been counting out of jealousy.*

"It's not that I've been keeping count, it's just—"

"You know there's a human phrase for a situation like this one," she chewed and swallowed her piece of fish.

"And what's that?" His ears perked up.

"It's complicated. So please, can we just leave it at that?"

"I guess," his chest welled with an agonizing emptiness. Once again, he royally screwed up. He wished he could take everything back, but it was too late. He was such a fool to trust Valdez and get them into this horrible situation.

A long awkward period of silence followed.

"You know, I've kissed a few females in my day, but none of the kisses I've ever had in my life were as satisfying as the one I shared with you," he admitted. "I wish I could erase them all. None of them truly mattered and none of them compared. I love you, Autumn."

She choked on the piece of fish in her mouth before swallowing. Her eyes grew wide as she rose to her feet and tossed the bones into the fire, causing the flames to spray.

"I'm sorry, I don't know what you expect me to say," she hugged herself. "You're laying this on me after a horrible day where I broke your arm and our abilities vanished into thin air. I'm so confused."

"You don't have to say anything. I just want you to know the truth about my feelings for you. I can't help the way I feel, and I want to know that I at least tried."

She crossed her arms, racing toward the door. He grabbed her hand and slid his fingers through hers, but she pulled away.

"I'm sorry, I need to be alone. I can't handle this tonight."

* * *

AUTUMN WALKED INTO THE DARKNESS, her go-go boots sliding against the elements. She hugged herself, running her arms along the length of her body for warmth. Stars sparkled in the sky and the triple moons cast long liquid shadows over the snow. The storm had let up a bit, but knowing its track record, it wouldn't be for long.

She couldn't believe Armienti's admission, although she'd always suspected he had feelings for her, even when they were back on Earth.

The silver-spired snow globe he'd handcrafted for her birthday said it all. His longing glances and the way he always went out of his way so they could cross paths was so *not* a coincidence. And he'd saved her life more than once.

But what did he expect from her?

She loved Dante, although the chances she'd see him again grew slimmer by the day. Maybe she was fooling herself into thinking he'd be able to find them. Maybe it was a fantasy that they would end up together again. Maybe she was just being plain stupid. Or maybe she was lonely.

Yes, the kiss was nice, but she refused to entertain the possibility of there being another one. Her heart ached for her husband.

The sky began to pelt snow and ice. *Walk officially over,* she shivered. She headed back to the cave to find Armienti lounging by the fire, cradling his broken wrist in the makeshift sling she'd created for him. He glanced at her with his brilliant sapphire eyes.

"You know, if it was up to me, I would've let you finish school, if that's what you wanted. You could have followed your dreams."

"Some dreams aren't meant to come true," goosebumps prickled along her arms. She was so tired of being cold and miserable all the time. The weather on this planet was unbearable.

"I would've made sure yours did," he came to a stand and drew closer to her. His boots slipped over the rocks. "I had so many plans for us. We'd travel and see foreign worlds, we'd eat exotic foods, and you wouldn't have to deal with being a royal if you didn't want to. It would've been your choice. Your life would've belonged to you. The reason I trusted Valdez is because I knew it would get me closer to you. I was willing to take that chance, no matter how impossible it seemed."

Armienti continued. "I didn't want to see the same thing that happened to Maeve happen to you. I knew eventually it would. Eventually our lifestyle would put your life in danger and swallow you alive."

A chill skidded down her spine. Her frozen lips moved. "What do you mean?"

He shook his head. "Why am I not surprised Dante omitted the finer details of what occurred?"

Thirty-Two

AUTUMN STOOD in silence as the firelight flickered off Armienti's brilliant blue eyes. Shadows played against the angles of his high cheekbones. His expression grew drawn and solemn in the yellow-orange glow.

After she asked about Maeve, she wasn't sure she wanted to know. Her mouth grew dry, but curiosity got the best of her.

Armienti cleared his throat, tucking a golden strand of hair behind his blue pointed ear. "Well, where do I begin? I'll start at the beginning I suppose. Princess Maeve always had a thirst for adventure, and believe me when I tell you, she always got her way." A small smile crept across his lips. Autumn listened intently.

He continued. "She caught Dante's eye at a palace function, and it was love at first sight. He was smitten. She could get any guy to fall in love with her without even trying. They were inseparable when he was around, and when he was sent away on missions, they were always in frequent communication—but that was never good enough for her. She always wanted more. But what she desired more than anything was to be part of the mix and to prove she could be one of us. Unfortunately, or fortunately, I should say rather, she wasn't built that way. She was kind and innocent, unlike the rest of her family who always had their own selfish agenda."

Autumn twisted her mouth to the side, wringing her fingers together behind her back. She didn't like where this story was headed.

"So, there was one mission that she really wanted to go on and Dante was desperate to make her happy, although he should've said no. Any sane individual would've said no. Ronan wasn't even old enough to go. But he let her come along with us regardless because she always had her way. Everything was fine at first until it wasn't."

Autumn's bottom lip trembled. "What happened to her?"

"Well, on this particular mission, there were to be no slaves and no survivors left behind. The Grand Supreme ordered the entire planet eradicated, just like Earth was supposed to be after he utilized your fellow humans to rebuild according to his plans. For whatever reason he wanted both races dead, but that's beside the point. Anyway, somehow, she got caught in the crossfire. Dante was the one who issued the order. She was fifteen years old."

Autumn remained quiet, scarcely able to believe what she'd just heard. *Maeve was caught in Dante's crossfire?* But he was young; too young to be put in such a terrible situation, being forced to conquer worlds for some monster. The Grand Supreme. Dante was too young to bear this shame.

Anger, intense fear, and extreme sadness welled deep in her chest. A hole hollowed through her heart.

"Why tell me this here? Why now?" Her eyes blurred, tears streaming down her frozen cheeks. The salt water turned to ice before the droplets hit the ground. "Are you trying to score points with me by making him look bad? Is that your angle to try and win me over?"

"No, I would never do that," he stuttered, his eyes going

wide. "I love you. I thought you should know the truth about who you're dealing with and the monster that he truly is."

"You're no better," she crossed her arms, eyes thinning to slits. "From here I can see more than one monster."

"You don't mean that, do you?"

"I don't know what I mean anymore," she looked at her hands before staring into his eyes.

He walked over slowly and tucked a stray strand of hair behind her ear before lowering his mouth to hers. He kissed her, caressing his strong arm along the length of her back. He breathed against her throat, lips grazing. He hung his head, the strands of his golden hair tickling her cheek.

She pulled away, stumbling over the heel of her boot. "I'm sorry, I can't do this," she said in little more than a whisper. Her mind continued to race. All she could think of was Dante and how he was too young to bear the burden of Maeve's death.

"I was hoping I could change your mind, but I see now it's impossible," he glanced at his gloves. "What does he have that I don't?"

"He—"

She began to speak when a vibration knocked them off their feet, clear into the ground. Rubble spilled from the ceiling of the cave. Golden-orange embers from the fire rose then shrank. They fell into each other's arms, belly to belly, legs tangled. Autumn trembled then came to a shaking stand. She reached down and helped Armienti to his feet as well.

"What was that?" she asked, staring at him. He shrugged, eyes bulging.

They walked to the entrance of the cave. Her heart leapt to the cusp of her throat. In the not so far off distance sat an obsidian ship in the snow with blinking lights, swirling in a kaleidoscope of color through the stormy night.

A wave of panic crashed through her limbs. Dizziness set in. Valdez had come to finish what she started.

Thirty-Three

RONAN SAT on Sean's bed as he packed almost every item he owned into two large rolling bags. Clothes, books, his skates, *of course*, even some odd silver instrument he could blow in that made a series of high-pitched notes.

He looked forward to hearing Sean play for him, but he still had so much on his mind. He needed to subdue Autumn's father and explain his situation to Sean before heading back to Surge.

The emperor and empress were counting on him. But worse still, he hadn't told Sean he wasn't of this world and needed to figure out the right time.

Planets from the Earth's solar system hung from the ceiling, surrounded by rainbow glow in the dark stars. Sean had never mentioned he had a fascination with outer space, but it was apparent upon first glance around his bedchamber.

A positive sign, or at least he hoped.

Sean stood on his bed to grab some of the stars from the ceiling. "I know you're going to think this is silly, but I can't sleep without these. I count them over and over again until I fall asleep every night. I even stuck them around my dorm room. My roommate thought I was crazy." He chuckled.

"I don't think it's silly, but you won't need them. There are plenty of stars for you to count where we're going."

"Come again?" Sean glanced at him, mouth tilting to a grin.

Ronan's face warmed against his will as he ran a hand through his hair.

Sean continued. "Oh, and I don't want to forget this." He raced over to the shelf and pulled out a large black leather-bound book with silver edges.

"What's this?" Ronan cocked his head to the side.

"My sketchbook."

"Oh, you never mentioned you liked to draw."

"That's because it's kind of a secret," Sean shrugged and flipped through the pages, searching through his sketches. "But I enjoy it so much, I'm actually thinking of changing my major from event planning. Do you want to take a look? I've never shown it to anyone else before."

"I'd be honored." He took the book from his boyfriend and examined the drawings. He was pleasantly surprised at how life-like they appeared. Some were in black and white, while others were in full color.

The opening pages featured Earth's magnificent scenery—farm landscapes, beautiful night skies filled with a full moon and whistling stars, the vast woodland. Ronan could've sworn he was looking at a picture of Farrah Falls.

"These are exquisite," he glanced up from the book, smiling.

"Thank you. I'm so glad you like them."

As he continued to flip, the images grew darker—some of monsters covered with full body fur and fangs, while one was coated from head to toe with iridescent black scales with long twisted talons popping from his fingertips. His slit-eyes were a lifeless yellow like golden butterscotch that seemed to shift to deep purple as he flipped through the pages. A razor-sharp lethal tail hung above his buttocks dripping in crimson blood.

Its eyes watched Ronan no matter what angle he positioned the book. Goosebumps ran down his spine. Sean had a wild imagination.

Ronan struggled to pull his eyes away from the scaled monster. He continued to turn the pages but stopped dead when he reached an image of a flying saucer in a field surrounded by little green men with large obsidian eyes and four fingers on each hand. He bit his cheeks so hard as not to laugh and hurt his boyfriend's feelings. This one was ridiculous.

"Wait, is this what you think aliens look like?" Ronan quirked a brow. Never in any of his travels had encountered any creature who appeared so primitive.

At that moment, Sean's mother burst into the room holding two brown paper bags and cold orange drinks that read *Fanta*. Her brown curly hair sat in a mid-length ponytail, and her large brown eyes smiled at them.

Sean pressed the book closed, hiding it behind his back.

"Here, I packed you both some snacks for the trip. Are you sure you can't stay a little longer? Your father and I would love to talk more with you and your friend. Thank you again for your service, Ronan. It isn't every day we have a handsome man in uniform come and visit our home." She batted her eyes.

"Um, you're welcome," Ronan's face burned from the compliment.

"Where did you say you two are going again?" Sean's mother asked.

Ronan opened his mouth to speak but Sean interrupted. "Please, Mom, stop, you're embarrassing me. I'll text you when we get there. We promise we'll check in."

"Okay," Sean's mother ambled over and hugged him, kissing his cheek and leaving a red lip imprint. He groaned, pulling away.

"We should get going," Ronan glanced into his pocket at

the time on his communicator. The screen read 22:00 hours. "We're going to be late."

"Well, you sure packed enough, didn't you mijo? It's hard to believe only the two of you are going on this trip."

"It's three of us," Ronan corrected her.

"Mom, please stop, I got this," Sean's face flushed a deep crimson.

She winked. "I know you do, and I know you'll make us proud."

Ronan's heart sped. They needed to leave *immediately* in order to maintain his schedule and come through for Autumn and Dante.

Sean struggled to carry the bags he packed. His belongings spilled from the sides and fell to the floor. Ronan took them from him and slung them over his shoulders.

Sean's mother gasped. "Not only is he cute, he's strong too." She fanned her face.

Sean rolled his eyes as they made their way through the door and down the steps.

* * *

RONAN MADE his way outside with Sean. Lights sparkled through the windows of Sean's house and into the night. His parents stood in the doorway waving goodbye, and his mother blew kisses at them.

"I'm sorry about her, she's a bit extra," Sean glanced his way, shaking his head. His ginger-blonde hair shifted over his eyes.

He chuckled. "It's okay." Secretly Ronan wished his own parents would have cared more about him.

They approached a midnight-blue land craft parked along the black.

"I ordered an Uber so we could get going as soon as possible. I know you have to get back to work."

They climbed inside with Sean's numerous bags tumbling over their laps. The pilot of the vehicle turned around and addressed them. "Where are you headed?"

Sean shrugged and glanced at Ronan.

"Take us to Farrah Falls."

"You got it."

Sean tilted his head. "By the way, who's the third person coming with us?"

Ronan pressed out an uneasy smile. "You'll meet him soon enough."

Thirty-Four

AUTUMN LEANED against the wall of the cave all day and all night, watching the ship in the distance. It was their one and only chance to get off this miserable ice planet and back to civilization. Stars sparkled until dawn in the emerald sky. The storm had ceased for a few hours, allowing her clear sight of the rugged snowy terrain, not that there was much to look at anyway.

Armienti paced the room, staring at her often, but she ignored his longing gazes. The memories of him pressing his lips to hers and his passionate embrace haunted her. She could still taste the peppermint on her tongue and see the yearning in his clear blue eyes. She could feel his heart shatter into a million pieces when she rejected him. Rejection was never easy for anyone, but it was a necessary part of life.

However, she reminded herself there were bigger issues at hand and their futures depended on their success.

"So what's the plan?" she asked him, and he stopped dead in his tracks. He ran his good hand through his golden waves. The sling holding his broken arm shifted. His eyes met hers.

"Well, I—" he stuttered. "I haven't been able to think of one. I can only think of you."

She rolled her eyes, throwing her hands into the air. "We need to stay focused here. This opportunity may not come again. What are the chances we could sneak on board or over-power Valdez and her crew?"

"Valdez is a force to be reckoned with. She's never lost a fight. I haven't seen the full extent of her true power and I've known her for most of my life. She keeps it under lock and key, only releasing it in the most dire of situations."

Autumn shook her head. "I hope you're not giving up on me. We at least have to try and fight. It's better than staying here week after week, month after month, for who knows how long?" Her temples throbbed, and she fell to her knees grabbing her head. Her breathing grew shallow as she groaned.

He ran up to her, palming her back, "Are you okay?"

She trembled, staring at him. "I don't know anymore. My head hurts so badly. I'm constantly in pain, and our abilities—"

"Same," he admitted. "My head has been bothering me for a few days now, since I broke my wrist. I'm not sure if it's related." He shrugged.

She stumbled to her feet. "That's exactly my point. I'm afraid there's something wrong with this place and I can't take it anymore. I want to go home."

The ship door lowered in the distance, and she crouched on the ground. Armienti followed suit. Guards spilled out wearing obsidian uniforms, carrying their metallic rocket launchers. They raced on foot through the snow. Her heart sped. She had to get closer, undetected. She had to do every-thing she could to take the ship from Valdez.

She crawled out on all fours, belly down on the ground against the snow. "Well, aren't you coming with me?" she hissed at Armienti, gesturing toward the ship.

He exhaled, falling beside her. "Yeah, I suppose so," he said, quietly.

"Then let's get going."

* * *

RONAN PULLED up with Sean in the Uber to Farrah Falls. Shadows swept through the dense treetops. The crescent moon offered a sliver of pale light in the darkness. The stars glimmered in the pitch-black sky.

"Are you sure this is the right place?" Sean's large brown eyes sparkled in the blackness of the landcraft.

"I'm positive," Ronan offered him a reassuring smile.

Sean followed him outside as he held onto his numerous travel bags. He waved the land craft pilot off into the night.

Finally, they could be alone again. Ronan's heart accelerated.

There was a moment of pure silence followed by an awkward laugh. "So where do we go from here?"

"I'm taking you to my vehicle to get you settled. We'll be departing for our destination soon enough."

"Great." Sean's eyes scanned the long stretch of black. "But I thought you said you don't have a car?" He stared at him strangely, brows furrowed.

"I don't," Ronan pointed into the vast woodland of Farrah Falls. "My transportation is located in the woods though."

Sean's mouth lowered. "Oh, do you have an ATV? Were you off-roading?"

He chuckled. "Something like that."

Sean hesitated before taking a step back, wringing his hands.

"Don't worry, you have nothing to fear. You have the stars above and me as your guide. We'll reach our destination soon enough." Ronan offered him his hand. When Sean grabbed hold, droplets of perspiration slid against his black gloves. For a moment, Ronan pitied him for being so nervous without cause.

"There's no need to be afraid. I promise I'll protect you no matter what monsters we encounter."

Sean nodded, offering him a warm smile. "Okay, you're right. I'm being silly. I've never liked the dark, but I've always loved this place."

They headed into the woods, hand in hand, each carrying a bag over their shoulders. Insects chirped and glowed as they flitted through the forest trees. Brown animals with large innocent black eyes and white tails pranced gracefully through the night. Water babbled and the ground crunched beneath their footsteps.

Sean tilted his head to the side, the strands of his ginger-blonde hair grazed his ears. "It's a shame about the fire that took place a few years back, but I'm glad to see the forest is finally healing."

"It is a shame, isn't it?" Ronan recalled his cousin destroying the forest in a fit of rage after Autumn broke up with him and then falling into a deep state of depression about ruining one of her favorite places in the world.

Dante had come a long way since then, and he was glad for him.

They walked further still, passing by the pouring falls. Water crashed against the slick mossy rocks.

Sean stopped and hunched over to catch his breath.

"How much further?" he rasped, sweat slicking his brow.

"It won't be long now," Ronan reassured him, but inside, his heart did acrobatics.

How could he breach the subject of not being human? Ronan's mouth grew as dry as desert sand. His hands sweated within the confines of his gloves. *What would he do if Sean freaked out and rejected him?* No, he couldn't handle rejection—he'd be devastated. He needed to be more positive about the entire ordeal.

They arrived at the crash site where Dante ordered a few trusted guards to remain behind and monitor the force field emanating from his stranded ship. The destroyer wasn't too far off. He stopped dead in his tracks and turned around.

Sean panted, fanning his face. He stopped as well.

"Is everything okay?" Sean wiped an arm across his brow. "Do you need to rest for a minute? I think I do—"

"Yes, and there's something I need to talk to you about."

"Okay?" Sean placed his bag next to his feet before taking a seat on a rock. He crossed his legs. "I'm all ears."

"There's something I've been meaning to tell you, but I'm not exactly sure how and now I'm afraid I've waited too long," the words left his mouth in slow motion. His bottom lip quivered.

"You know you can talk to me about anything, right?" Sean offered him a smile.

"I do," Ronan's face and neck warmed. His adrenaline crushed his senses. He only had this moment to confess the truth. "Okay, um, well I know we've been in a long-distance relationship for a few years, but I haven't been entirely truthful with you."

"What do you mean, Ronan? Is there someone else?"

A long awkward pause followed. He shook his head. "No, of course not. There's no one I'd rather be with than you."

Sean's mouth curved; his cheeks flushed pink.

"You see—I'm not from Earth."

"Huh?" Sean's brows furrowed. What are you talking about?"

"I'm not from Earth," Ronan repeated, unable to imagine a clearer way to spell the situation out.

"I'm sorry, I'm not sure what you're trying to say." Sean shrugged.

In that instant, the bushes rustled. Twigs snapped and cracked from their limbs. Autumn's father charged full force at him, feet scraping against the rocks and fallen twigs. Ronan's eyes widened. In all his haste, he must've forgotten to lock his ship.

Thirty-Five

RONAN BLOCKED Sean with his body as Mr. Ramon lunged at him again, arms swinging through the warm night air. His knife sat in his hand. Long tangled hairs prickled down his neck. His cracked spectacles sat askew on his face; mouth curled in an angry scowl. Clearly, he hadn't learned his lesson earlier.

"So you're at it again? Abducting my daughter wasn't enough?"

As Mr. Ramon came dangerously close to him and Sean, Ronan raised a palm and swept him through the air telepathically. Autumn's father twisted and groaned as he attempted to escape. Ronan bent his knife with his mind, throwing the weapon into a nearby patch of green.

Sean gasped and slid backwards from the rock and onto the ground. His eyes followed Ronan's every move. He glanced at Sean before looking at Mr. Ramon. He'd imagined this moment going a little more smoothly. *For shame.*

Ronan crossed his arms. "You need to start behaving yourself, it's going to be a long ride to where we're going."

"How are you doing that?" Sean's teeth chattered but

Ronan remained still and focused. Unfortunately, he would have to wait to continue their conversation later.

"Everyone told me I was insane, but clearly I'm not," Mr. Ramon growled. "I've been waiting here all day and all night every day for the better part of a year for the chance to confront one of you *aliens*. Now tell me, where's my daughter?"

Ronan cocked his head to the side. "I shall bring you to her soon enough."

"I know Dante has her locked away out here somewhere doing who knows what. I've seen your mothership, but I can never get onboard before it disappears, kind of like the ship you forgot to seal me inside of when you left to go and gather your next victim. When I get my hands on that punk—"

Ronan stared at him, flabbergasted. "I'm not abducting anyone; this is my boyfriend. He's out here of his own free will," he blinked. "If I set you down on the ground, do you promise to control yourself?"

"I can't make any promises," Mr. Ramon's fists shook at his sides. "But I can try for the sake of my daughter."

"Very well then, you had better try hard. I'm your one and only chance of ever seeing her again," he lowered her father to his feet. "I know Autumn, but she's not here. She's been gone from Earth for years."

"What do you mean gone?" Mr. Ramon's mouth quivered with rage. "Did he—"

Ronan felt like he was speaking in circles. The man didn't understand, no matter how many ways he tried to explain the situation, so he decided to spell it out. "Dante took her with him to Universe 13 to be his wife."

Mr. Ramon threw his hands into the air. "Oh no. No, no, no, I don't believe you. That's impossible. She has to be here. She just *has* to. There's no such place as Universe 13. There's only one universe. What do you think I am, stupid? Take me to her before I call the cops."

An awkward silence followed.

"We both know they don't listen to you anymore, they haven't for a while," Ronan shifted his weight. "And I'm afraid you're mistaken, there are twenty-four universes, not one like you humans are groomed to believe, but I will take you to her. I was sent to fetch you by my emperor, Dante."

Her father rolled his eyes. "*Emperor Dante.* That's fine, I don't care what you want to call him. I'm going to give that boy a piece of my mind he'll never forget. How dare that wanted criminal marry my daughter without my permission."

"You can take that up with him personally, but I'm afraid we must step lightly. I'm on a tight schedule. We need to go back to my ship."

Mr. Ramon walked past them grumbling obscenities beneath his breath. He turned around. "Well, what are we waiting for? Let's go, alien."

"My name is Ronan actually," he corrected. *Wow, what a rude man.*

He remained behind for a moment with Sean. Bits of pink sunlight sparkled through the treetops. Dawn rapidly approached.

"I'm sorry you had to find out about me this way. I should've told you sooner, but I didn't know how. I understand if you don't want to be with me anymore. I'm not sure I would want to be with me at this point," his face and neck burned with shame.

Sean reached and tucked a stray strand of hair behind his ear. "It's okay, I wouldn't have believed you until I saw for myself. I don't like that you lied to me, but at the same time I can understand why."

Ronan nodded slowly. His heart raced in his chest. He was so kind.

"Yes, I want to be with you, and I still want to come with

you on our trip," Sean squeezed his hand reassuringly. "Just don't lie to me again."

"I won't, I promise." Cool relief flooded through his limbs.

Sean lowered his voice to a whisper. "And you need to tell me what was up with that guy. That was just plain *weird*."

"Of course, I'll tell you anything you want to know. All you need do is ask."

Sean waited in silence.

He continued. "Two words, family drama."

Sean's eyes grew wide and curious. "Oh, we have plenty of that going on in my family too—one of my cousins just eloped."

They began to follow Autumn's father through the long stretch of trees when Sean stopped in his tracks abruptly.

"I have one more question. You might think it's kind of cliché, but I have to ask." His cheeks pinkened.

"Okay?"

"Do you come in peace?"

Ronan hesitated for a few moments before his mouth curled. "Yes, this time I do." And for the first time in his life, it was the truth—and it felt good.

Thirty-Six

AUTUMN CRAWLED ON ALL FOURS, drawing closer to the ship. Her throat ran dry, and her body trembled with each unnatural movement. She inhaled, struggling to catch her breath. The corners of her vision shattered with stars.

She slowed down, resting on her belly for a moment before pushing herself up and continuing along her slushy path.

What choice did she have but to challenge Valdez? It was either fight her or be stranded on this miserable planet *forever.*

Armienti crawled beside her. The elbow of his injured arm propped up his weight, sliding against the snow and ice. His blue complexion shifted suspiciously off color. He stopped for a moment cupping his mouth. He gulped, shaking his head. A thin layer of ice sparkled, coating his long golden tresses.

"I'm not sure what's wrong," he admitted quietly. "I feel so very—"

"Don't you dare chicken out on me," she hissed. "We both feel like crap. You need to back me up. I can't take her on alone."

He nodded as they drew closer. They came upon a dense pile of rocks covered with snow. Flurries trickled from the sky. Autumn stopped and rested her back against the stones, catching her breath. Armienti joined her, sky-blue eyes closing before glancing at her.

He inhaled. "Maybe we don't have to do this. Maybe we could stay here forever and live out the rest of our lives in peace. We could have a fam—"

"Please don't do this right now, I need you to focus," she reached out and weakly squeezed his hand. "I know you're scared and so am I, but we have to try. There's no backing out. It's fight her or die."

As she inhaled, a sharp pain welled in her chest. She winced as it became more difficult to catch her breath. *What was happening to her? It was like she was suffocating a little more with each passing day.*

She hesitated. As she glanced around the corner of the rocks, she heard music whistling through the wintery terrain. Figures dressed in black wispy clothes skipped and danced around in circles. Guards cocked their oversized metallic guns and stood around them in silence. Laughter and merriment ensued. *What the heck? How could they be celebrating at a time like this?*

But what really sent her over the edge was the smell of fresh food sizzling through the air. *Mmmm.* Her gut tied itself in a million knots. She salivated before swallowing. All that sat in her stomach was weeks and weeks of ice world fish.

Yuck.

How she missed eating a freshly prepared meal. Gooey chocolate chip pancakes, her dad's arroz con gandules, cheese fries. Heck, she'd even eat meat if it was in front of her. Desperation rattled her to the core.

It had to be some kind of trap.

She turned back to Armienti, who sat beside her with his eyes closed. "It's our last chance, Autumn. We could go back to the cave and be safe until—"

She inhaled before exhaling slowly. Her vision fogged.

"Until what? We die? You see what's happening to us, don't you? Our abilities are gone. We can barely function—"

He rested his head on her shoulder. "This time I've spent with you has been the happiest in my entire life. I feel so connected to you out here, and I never want this feeling to end."

She paused. "I'm sorry but there's no *we*, Armienti. And right now, we need to focus on staying alive, not your ridiculous fantasies."

He ran his good hand through his matted golden hair. His face fell in a way she'd never witnessed before. His broad shoulders slumped. "I know," he said quietly. "I can dream though, can't I? Dreams are the one luxury we have in this life."

She sighed, pitying him for a moment. "I don't want to hurt your feelings, and I don't want you to think that I haven't thought at all about what could've been. Because believe me, I have. Maybe if I had met you first or if Dante's wasn't in the picture things could've been different," she paused. "But the fact of the matter is, he's my husband and I love him more than any—"

Before she could finish her sentence, he crushed his mouth to hers, running his hand through her frozen tangled coils. He kissed her deeply, setting her on his lap. The side of her body scraped against the pile of rocks. His tongue swirled in her mouth, tasting of fresh peppermint.

He hadn't been listening to a word she said. He was as dense as a log. Frustration and anger rattled through her. When she pulled away to scold him again for disregarding her wishes, his leg buzzed and vibrated.

Her stomach dropped into the great unknown and his eyes widened.

"What is that?" She reached into his pocket, splaying her fingers. He tried to move away but she was too fast. She slid out a sleek black communicator.

"Wait, Autumn, please—I can explain."

Her fists clenched with fury as she examined the device. The charge was full, and the signal was strong.

"How long have you had this?"

He glanced away.

She grabbed the cleft of his chin and forced him to look into her eyes. "How long, Armienti?"

"Well, you see," he stuttered. "I suppose since the incident in the cave with Valdez's soldiers. I discovered it amongst the bodies with the mini blaster we've been utilizing for fire. I meant to—"

"I can't freaking believe you. You mean to tell me we could've been rescued by now? How could you do this? How selfish are you? What were you trying to do, get me to fall in love with you?"

"Well, I—"

Armienti sprang to his feet and threw her behind him, blocking her with his body. She winced as her back smashed against the sharp rocks. When she opened her eyes, they were surrounded by onyx clad soldiers with cocked metallic guns. *Crap.*

Thirty-Seven

AUTUMN SCANNED HER SURROUNDINGS, anxiety rattling her to the core. At least thirty guards encircled them with no escape in sight. The sentries closed in on them in one fluid movement, their weapons aimed square between her and Armienti's eyes.

"Look what we got here, a couple of trespassers," one of the sentries chortled. "You both look like corpses rotting in the ground."

She exhaled a breath, eager to defend herself. She wasn't going down without a fight. Her fists quivered with fury, ready to smash them through one of the guards' helmeted faces.

At the same time, tears welled in the corners of her eyes. She was so terrified she couldn't function.

"I wouldn't get any ideas if I were you little girl," another guard chimed in, cocking his head to the side. "We're taking you to our emp—"

"Well, I'm full of ideas," she glowered. "So screw you."

With all her might she raised her go-go boot and rammed him in the shin. He stumbled backwards skidding across the ice. His navy-blue uniform shredded.

The guards swarmed them, and shots were fired, blasting through the rocks and ice. In the distance the music had stopped, and the dancers scattered. She needed to keep her wits about her. Valdez was bound to show up at any time to finish what she started.

Armienti dodged the blue streams of energy, clutching his broken wrist, following close behind her. She could barely breathe, could barely see straight. Her legs wobbled beneath her weight as she ran for her life.

They raced through the commotion, the guards hot on their tails. As they entered the belly of the ship, the premises were far more crowded than she remembered. *Holy crap*, they couldn't make their way through the halls without disrupting the food and the festivities. The foot traffic was too dense. A wave of hunger consumed her, leaving her nauseous. The food smelled too delicious.

Colors swirled and melded together as one. Creatures screamed and scattered, making way for them.

When she turned her head, the hairs on the back of her neck stood at perfect attention. They passed by the throne room. She saw flashes of short, braided hair and a long wispy violet gown. *Empress Valdez.*

She gulped, then gasped as a glove roughly grabbed her hair, pulling her backwards. She landed on her backside with a thud. What little air left in her body escaped her lungs as she was dragged kicking and twisting along the cold metallic floor. She fought with all the strength that she had. Everyone stared, wide eyed.

A heavy boot crushed her chest. Her ribs crunched. A metallic gun cocked and aimed at her head. The heat and smoke from the weapon caused her brow to bead in a cold sweat.

"Any last words, trespasser?" The guard's fingers slid over the trigger of his gun. A scream erupted, followed by the scamper of footsteps.

"Get off of her, get off. Keep your filthy hands off my sister." Leyla shouted.

The sentry's eyes widened with fear beneath the visor of his helmet. He sputtered backwards. "Forgive me, I didn't know."

Autumn's eyes fluttered closed and she collapsed on the ground, fading into the darkness.

* * *

DANTE KNELT, tracing his black-gloved fingers through the snow and ice. He'd searched forty-five planets for Autumn. His chest hollowed as he wiped away a stray tear lingering in the corner of his eye. This was the most humiliating failure he'd suffered in his life—since Maeve. Heaven help her.

It seemed no matter how hard he prayed the gods never cast favor upon him. To be honest, he didn't blame them. He didn't deserve their mercy, for he seldom showed any.

He was out of time. Another fruitless mission had come and gone.

Thirteen suns and moons had passed in the blink of an eye and the present day drifted into the fourteenth day, which was the final day Autumn would be alive if what Valdez had told him was true. Despite his efforts, he'd failed her.

He clenched his fists and his soldiers stumbled backwards, gasping. He would make Valdez pay with her life.

He ran a hand roughly through his hair before pulling his helmet back over his head. He couldn't stand to be seen this way. Weak, pathetic, and heartbroken. What kind of emperor was he if he couldn't lead by example?

None of his warriors had uttered a word, keeping their distance, and Kyo had been careful to stay out of his way. He remained seated at the control panel of his new station; eyes averted in silence.

Mr. Hiss meowed, and meowed, and meowed. Dante was sure he could sense his sadness as well. He remained curled on his side on the floor, tail flickering back and forth along the cold metallic tiles. His cerulean eyes blinked slowly.

He was all he had left of her.

As Dante reached to pick him up, his pocket vibrated. His stomach flipped. He pulled his communicator from his pants then released an aching sigh. *Ronan, drat.* He slid up the screen.

"Hello," he said dryly.

"It's nice to talk to you too," sarcasm dripped from his cousin's voice. "All the trouble I went through for—"

"Don't you dare give me sass. I'm not in the mood for your attitude. You and I both know you have your own agenda." He went to hang up his communicator, barely able to formulate a sentence. The agony of loss crippled him to the core.

"Wait," Ronan said. "I have him, just like you asked."

Dante's throat grew dry. How he dreaded having a conversation with Autumn's father more than anything in the universes. What would he tell him? He'd murdered one of his fellow humans, abducted his daughter, loved her, then no… he couldn't bear to have the conversation with him. It was far too shameful. He'd failed them both and an apology wouldn't suffice.

"Thank you. I'll see you soon." He hung up, temples throbbing with an impending migraine.

He sat on the ground and Mr. Hiss climbed onto his lap, purring. He nuzzled his head against Dante's ribs.

His communicator buzzed a second time. He muttered obscenities under his breath. If the caller turned out to be the Grand Supreme again, he was going to lose his mind. Whatever he needed from him no longer mattered. Life no longer mattered. Damn him.

The characters turned out to be a sequence of numbers he

didn't recognize. His communicator buzzed and buzzed and buzzed. Finally, he sighed, giving in to his curiosity. If it turned out to be the Grand Supreme, they would get "disconnected," he decided.

He answered. "What?"

His eyes widened as the other party spoke.

"Yes, yes, thank you. I'll be there at once. Wait—*what?*" He couldn't believe the last part.

The other party repeated the information.

"Thank you." He hung up his communicator for the second time.

He stumbled to a stand and raced to his seat on the destroyer so fast his feet didn't touch the ground. A wave of dizzying joy flooded through his limbs that Autumn was found safe. However, red-hot rage boiled through his blood at who she was discovered with. Armienti.

PART THREE

The Ice Princess

Thirty-Eight

AUTUMN SAT ON HER BED, her smartphone trembling in her grasp. Her chest ached—to the point where she couldn't function. She hadn't slept in days. Not since Caleb cheated on her and Misty plastered it all over social media like a bitch. As usual she was the last one to find out although she suspected him of being unfaithful.

How she wished she'd listened to her gut. It wasn't his first time cheating on her.

As she looked at a picture of them kissing, her vision fogged, then reddened. She took her phone and smashed the device against her night table, causing the battery to fall out of the back. She instantly regretted her decision. *Crap.*

A knock came to her door, and she jumped to her feet searching through her night table. She discovered a roll of packing tape and a package of butterfly stickers in her drawer to hold the battery in place with.

She sucked in a breath as the door opened and her mom peeked inside. Her highlighted hair sat in a curly bun. Her mouth straightened.

"I thought I heard a noise, are you okay?"

"Yes," she stuttered, tossing her phone onto her bed.

Her mom walked into her room. "What happened to your phone?"

"I—" she started, but it was too late. Her mom ambled over, seeing the photo of Misty and Caleb that remained on the screen covered with cracks. Autumn struggled to lock her phone as the screen froze with their glowing faces in place.

She sighed, sitting next to her on the bed, lacing her fingers together. "He doesn't deserve you."

Autumn glanced at her hands. "I know, but I can't help but love him."

Her mom shook her head. "He's not worth your time. You shouldn't have to work this hard for love. It should happen naturally."

"But we've known each other since—"

"It doesn't matter how long you've known him, and it doesn't make it okay for you to destroy your property. You should cherish what's yours. What you have one day isn't guaranteed for the next."

Autumn nodded in silence.

"Your father and I work hard to keep a roof over your head and to give you the best life we can. What's he going to say when he sees what happened to your phone and when he finds out you destroyed it over a guy?"

"Um," her fingers twitched. She'd never thought of that.

Her mom ran a hand through her hair.

"Sorry," she muttered. It was all she could think to say under the circumstances.

The door slammed shut downstairs. "Hello, is anyone home?" Her dad yelled through the hall. He'd been under a lot of stress at work, and she was mad at herself for adding to the mix.

When her mom went to move her foot, she kicked a paper bag under her bed.

"What's this?" Her mom knelt, reaching beneath her comforter skirt.

Oh, no, Autumn cringed as she tried to take the bag first, but her mom was too fast. The paper crinkled in her hands as she pulled out a brand-new flat iron.

Her mom's brows rose. "Since when do you straighten your hair?"

She crossed her arms, twisting her mouth to the side. "Since now."

Her mom sighed. "I hope you're not doing this for some *guy* to look like some *girl*."

Autumn took the bag from her. "No, I'm not. I'm doing this because I want to." An outright lie.

Her mom hugged her tight. "You're beautiful just the way you are, and you don't need to do this to prove it to anyone. Especially someone who doesn't deserve you."

Autumn remained quiet.

"I'll tell you what, let's go downstairs and have breakfast with your father. Afterwards, I'll go out on my run and see about getting you a new phone, so he doesn't get suspicious," her mom winked. "He doesn't need to know about this, he's under enough pressure at work as it is. The catch is, you have to pay me back when you can. You can't go around destroying your property like this. Do we have a deal?"

She nodded. "Yes, I'm sorry, Mom. It won't happen again."

"I know," her mom hugged her tight, perfume smelling of lavender. "I promise everything will get better with time. Time heals all wounds."

Autumn wished she'd never let go.

* * *

AUTUMN YAWNED and stretched as her body slid against deep-purple satin sheets and a warm comforter. A gentle hum thrummed in the background. The air smelled of hot cacao. As she sat up, her head pounded. *Ouch.* It took a moment for her foggy vision to sharpen and for the colors to settle against her weary eyes.

The room she occupied was beautiful with rainbow twinkling lights dancing across the silver ceiling in a flickering stream. Clothes in many vibrant hues spilled from a side closet. Stars and planets whizzed by the long rectangular windows at an impossible speed.

When she went to sit up, the sound of utensils and cups stirred in the corner of the room.

"Wait, don't get up too fast. You took quite the beating," a familiar voice said to her, soothing and even.

She did a double take, followed by a deep wave of relief coursing through her limbs. Leyla stood in the room, dressed in the strangest clothes. Her cascading light-brown hair was arranged in two braids like a milkmaid across a central part. She wore a long silver dress with bell sleeves trimmed with white fur. The ensemble highlighted her glowing blue features.

Autumn bit back a smile.

Leyla rolled her eyes. "I know I look utterly ridiculous, but it's the traditional Zambarian custom for the winter festival of illa lunam deam. And to think, I thought Earth's fashion was subpar. I guess the jest is on me."

She stared at her in silence and Leyla shrugged, cheeks shifting pink. "You know what I mean. Here, drink this, you'll feel better."

She ambled over with a silver tray and two steaming hot beverages, then handed Autumn one. The metal mug warmed her frozen hands. A dollop of cream floated in a sea of bubbling hot chocolate. She sipped her beverage, and the liquid heated her throat. Suddenly, she froze. The hairs on the back of her neck raised at perfect attention.

"Where's Valdez?" Her eyes bulged.

Leyla blinked, then shrugged. "I don't know. I'm assuming she's still back at the palace wreaking havoc.

Everyone saw how she tortured Kyo's younger sister, ordering her lashed. I hate her guts." Her eyes welled with tears, but she wiped them away before they could fall. "She deserved so much better."

A wave of relief coursed through Autumn's body. At least Valdez wasn't here. Her imagination had played tricks on her earlier.

Leyla continued. "And Dante, I never want to see him again. After what he did to me and Kyo's family," she grew quiet for a moment. "I'm sorry to complain so much, it's so very selfish of me. What about you? How are you feeling, and what were you and Armienti doing all the way out here in Universe 18 on planet First?"

Autumn took a long sip of her refreshment, answering between gulps. "We were stranded there by Valdez. She tried to kill us."

Leyla gasped. "That shrew. You were lucky we stumbled upon you when we did. We happened to land to gather more ice for sculptures to continue the celebration of the winter festival. The oxygen levels on First are low, rendering it uninhabitable for elongated periods of time. If you remained there any longer, you could've died, which is probably what she wanted in the first place."

It all made perfect sense considering how awful she felt and how her and Armienti's abilities vanished without a trace. Hopefully after she rested up, they would return. *Damn Valdez Aventura.* She tightened her fists, trembling. How she despised her.

"When Dante finds out, he'll wage a war," Leyla shook her head. "He's never been one to forgive or forget, especially when it comes to someone he loves as much as he loves you. But you already know that."

Autumn twisted her mouth to the side then hesitated. "That's not all, Armienti was in on my kidnapping. It's his fault we were stranded on planet First and almost died."

Leyla sipped her drink as steam poured over the metal mug. "What do you mean?"

"He was planning to overthrow Dante, something about his birthright and them being brothers. He believes he's entitled to the throne."

"Oh no," Leyla shot to her feet. "I've always suspected, with the way my mother treated him and the frequent fights she had with my father. Sometimes I would hear—never mind, it's not important. We must warn him. Dante is on his way as we speak. Although I think Armenti's actions were idiotic and unwarranted, I don't want to see him executed for treason."

She didn't want to see him executed either. Armienti had made a foolish mistake, but she didn't want him to die for it. Everyone deserved a second chance, or at least that's what she believed.

Leyla grabbed her hand and set down her drink on the tray. Autumn wobbled to a trembling stand. Her energy was low but gradually coming back. She held onto Leyla's arm.

"Here, let's get you changed," Leyla brought her over to the closet and pulled out an equally horrifying gown for her to wear. The fabric was ruby metallic red with long bell sleeves trimmed with thick white fur.

It was an outfit Mrs. Claus would wear. She was sorry she laughed earlier.

"I'm sorry, the fashion here is atrocious," Leyla rolled her eyes. "I can call for help—"

"No, it's fine." Autumn pulled off her dingy teal bodysuit, tossing it to the ground, then took the most hideous dress she'd ever seen in her life and pulled the fabric over her head. Leyla laced up the back. Her long dark curly hair cascaded over her shoulders. She sighed as she pulled on a pair of black sparkling booties. It couldn't get any worse than this.

They walked toward a steel door. It slid open and they entered the bustling hallway.

This time around, *everyone* noticed her. She had an *inkling* as to why. They curtseyed and bowed as she made her way through the crowd with Leyla, who held her head high. Her feet seemed to float as her gown dragged against the heated metallic floor.

This species of alien appeared different from the Elattions with silver skin and hair that was either jet-black or a stark white against their striking metallic complexions. Their long, pointed ears pierced through the strands. Many were tall and lean with elongated arms and fingers. Others were built as well as Dante and Armienti, with toned muscles bulging against their skin-tight navy-blue uniforms.

Autumn bit her bottom lip as her thoughts drifted to Dante and how she couldn't wait to see him again. But as soon as the thoughts arrived, she pushed them out of her mind. She needed to focus on the task at hand.

She followed Leyla down a series of winding steps and into an open corridor lined with countless doors on either side. The hallway was empty, save for a few servants carrying trays of steaming hot food. Her stomach grumbled but she willed away the sensation. She couldn't wait to have a real meal again.

They stopped mid-way in the hallway. Leyla raised her fist and knocked hard. Autumn flinched as the sound of hollow banging steel echoed against her eardrums.

"Armienti, Armienti, I know you're in here," Leyla demanded. "Don't tell me you're in there screwing around with some Zambarian girl. Gross, you've only been here for a few hours' time."

The door slid open and Armienti stood there dressed in a navy-blue bodysuit like the silver-skinned aliens she'd seen moments ago. His golden, wavy hair was affixed in a sleek low ponytail. His arm was slingless as he pulled on a pair of elbow-length gloves. Knee-high boots of the same hue concealed his feet.

"No, I assure you I'm perfectly by myself," his chiseled features straightened. "What on earth are you both wearing?"

Autumn's face heated as she glanced down at her garish outfit.

His eyes drew to hers. "Never mind, I need to talk to Autumn. Preferably alone."

She looked at Leyla. "I'll be okay, just give us a moment."

Thirty-Nine

AUTUMN'S HEART pounded in her ears as she followed Armienti into his room. Leyla remained in the hallway, arms crossed, and eyes rolled in the back of her head. She could only imagine what Leyla was thinking and why Armienti desperately needed to speak with her—

Alone.

Her hands shook as the door slid closed behind her. She sucked in a breath.

The room was sparse with an obsidian comforter thrown over a circular bed. Armienti's tattered uniform was tossed in a ball in the corner of the room. Endless stars skittered past the long rectangular windows as they made their way through space.

She glimpsed at her reflection before staring into his crystal blue eyes. "I can't believe you lied to me. All this time, we could've gone home. You almost killed us. You created a real mess, Armienti. Do you have anything to say for yourself?"

He picked at his gloves before looking into her eyes. "I know, I'm sorry. I don't know what to say," his boot brushed against hers and she stepped away, avoiding physical contact. "I really fucked up. What else is new?"

"Dante's on his way," she breathed.

Armienti shrugged. "I figured as much."

He moved close to her, so close her back pressed against the smooth metallic wall. The breath hitched in her throat. He leaned his hand by her head. Apparently, it'd healed. Hopefully that meant her abilities would return as well. The rich scent of peppermint consumed her senses. Her lips parted.

"I want you to come with me."

She glanced away. "I can't."

"Just think about it. No more court and foolish protocol. No more conquering, and no more Grand Supreme. We could run away and be free to live the lives we've always dreamed."

She remained silent as he stared into her eyes. "I spoke to Ronan. He has your father, so you know. We could meet them halfway and Dante would be none the wiser. We'd all be one big happy family. It would be a golden world if only you'd agree."

Her knees knocked together. She couldn't stand up straight. Her eyes spilled with warm salty tears. "Wait, are you serious? How is he? Is he okay? I—"

His lashes grazed his prominent cheekbones. "He's fine and he's healthy. He's desperate to see you."

She nodded mechanically. Her dad was on his way.

"This is your last chance, Autumn. All you have to do is say yes, and I can handle the rest."

She hesitated as her mind scrambled a million miles an hour. All she could think about was seeing her dad and Dante again. She rested her palm against the high plane of his cheek before she turned away.

"I'm sorry, I can't. I love Dante."

* * *

THE WORDS TRICKLED from Autumn's lips like a sucker punch. He stared into her wavering gray eyes. Time had repeated itself. Maeve. The same words poured from her full pink lips when he attempted to win her over as well.

I love Dante.

No matter how hard he tried, he could never measure up to his brother. He was never enough.

Dante always got whatever he wanted. All the girls he fancied, the power, and the riches that should've belonged to *Armienti*. He was always left to pick up the pieces and forced to live off the scraps of his brother's glory. He was tired of dwelling in the shadows.

Autumn's rejection was living proof of this, and somehow it hurt more than when Maeve rejected his advances.

A hollow sensation pierced his chest. Full body weakness threatened. His vision blurred for a moment before he blinked away the sensation. Warm fury settled in his bones.

"Are you sure?" he asked again, hoping her answer would change. He knew better, but he couldn't help himself. He had to try one more time. He had to hear her response to believe it wasn't some kind of mistake.

Her eyes grew large and glassy. "Yes, I'm sure. But I'm more than happy to speak to him on your behalf. I can ask him to par—"

"No, that isn't necessary. Suit yourself," he moved away from her, folding his arms. His demeanor grew as cold as ice. "If Dante wasn't in the picture—"

"Please don't say that."

A loud knock came at the door, startling him. His heart collided with his throat. Autumn stared at him, lips parted. His time was up.

KNOCK, KNOCK, KNOCK. The knocking continued, the pounding of the hollow steel door rattling him to the core.

He released an aching sigh, readying himself. He pressed

a button beside the door, and it glided open swiftly and silently.

A team of twenty or so guards held their sonic blasters straight at him. Leyla watched him from the opposite wall. Her palms covered her mouth as her body trembled with fear.

He quirked a brow. "What's this about?"

"By order of Emperor Dante II, you're not to leave this ship," one of the guards offered. "We're taking you into our custody."

He twisted his mouth, smirking. "Who's going to stop me?"

As the sentry went to fire the sonic blaster, he cupped his hand over the muzzle of the gun. A thick layer of ice sprayed from his palm, consuming the weapon before spreading all over the guard's body. His eyes bulged beneath his helmet before the ice engulfed him, suffocating him alive, freezing his organs to glass. Armienti kicked him in the gut as hard as he could, and his body shattered against the cold metallic tiles, the guard's severed head rolling between his legs.

He glanced at Autumn one last time before sprinting through the hallway. He'd never forget the disappointed expression on her face. He'd failed her yet again.

The guards chased after him, firing their weapons but missing often. They were no match for his superior speed. He teleported several times, landing in various places around the ship, finally settling on the docking bay. He discovered an obsidian vessel, ready to be launched into space.

A Zambarian pilot scrubbed the ship clean with a cloth. His long, gloved fingers wiped handprints from the glass.

Armienti ran up to the pilot, catching his breath. "I'm taking this ship. Open the loading bay at once."

"Who gave you clearance?" the pilot stopped working and asked, folding his arms. His snow-white hair fell over his pointed ears in wisps.

Armienti held a palm before his silver face. The man's

teeth chattered together. "Open the bay or you die. Do you understand?"

The Zambarian nodded slowly, eyes bulging in his skull, and approached the bay switch like he'd asked. Armienti climbed inside the ship, strapping himself into the control seat. His heart raced. He shook his head, haunted by memories of Autumn's rejection. She despised him.

It was fine though—she didn't deserve him anyway, he attempted to convince himself. *She was only a human.*

As the door opened, the ship hovered and slipped through a gathering of Elattion destroyers zooming inside the bay.

He ducked his head down so as not to be seen, catching a glimpse of his brother who he'd never measure up to before disappearing into the vastness of space.

Forty

COMMOTION RATTLED through the hallways of the ship. Guards sprinted around searching for Armienti, holding silver metallic guns in hand. Steel doors opened and slid closed as they searched countless rooms for him.

Autumn's stomach flipped as she stepped over the dead body of the guard Armienti froze to death, then shattered before her eyes.

He'd created some mess.

She shook her head—another needless death. Nobody in space had any respect for life whatsoever. *How could he do this?*

She approached Leyla and hugged her tightly. "Are you okay?"

Leyla nodded before brushing off her long silver dress. "Yeah, I think so. What was that all about? What did he say to you in there?"

"Nothing," Autumn lied, crossing her arms over her cardinal-hued metallic dress. Leyla didn't need to know what'd transpired between her and Armienti. It was too much to process. "He just wanted to know if Dante would pardon him for his mistake."

She couldn't tell Leyla the truth. She'd never understand how much Armienti cared for her and how she broke his heart.

Leyla stared at her hands. "There's no way my brother is going to pardon him after this fiasco. I'm sure he'll want him dead. He's inconvenienced him too much."

Autumn watched her in silence. Her stomach twisted in a hard knot. She didn't want to think about the consequences.

"Come on," Leyla gestured toward the opposite end of the hallway. "We should go back to my room. I'm worried Emperor Brumha will check in on me after all the commotion, and I want to pretend I'm indisposed."

"Isn't it good that he cares if you're all right?" Autumn blinked.

Leyla's face contorted in disgust, and she stuck her tongue out. "Oh, gods no, although his brother is quite handsome. The rumors are true in that department. It's hard to believe they're related. But still, he's no Kyo." Her mouth fell flat, eyes wavering with tears. "You'll meet him soon enough."

As she began to walk back to the room with Leyla, footsteps pattered across the metallic tiles.

"My lady, my lady," a disembodied voice echoed through the hall.

Autumn turned around as a silver-skinned servant girl wiped a long slender arm over her beading brow. She curtseyed, struggling to catch her breath.

"Emperor Dante II is here. He's searching everywhere for you." Autumn inhaled and a wave of dizzying excitement consumed her. Her legs wobbled beneath her, and it wasn't because of her heavy dress. She couldn't wait to see him.

"Are you coming?" she asked Leyla, who grew silent in response to the news.

"No, I never ever want to see him again. But you go ahead. I'll catch up with you later," she waved.

Autumn respected her wishes. Leyla turned on her heel,

making her way through the winding corridor. Her silver dress glided across the floor until she disappeared into the shadows.

She inhaled. She'd check in on her later. She was suffering so much.

Autumn followed the girl through the hallway, unable to breathe. They descended many flights of winding steps. The train of her gaudy dress trailed along the floor behind her.

Crap, if only she'd looked the least bit decent, but it was too late to change.

They arrived at a remote door on the far end of the ship. She pressed frizzy strands of hair behind her ears. The servant punched the code into the keypad beside the entrance and she was granted access. She wrung her hands behind her back as she walked into the room. Her heart pounded in her chest so fast she feared she might faint.

Forty-One

THE ROOM WAS pitch black apart from a long rectangular window displaying the whizzing stars of the galaxy they traveled through at lightning speed. Rays of sparkling light glittered across the glass. The door slid closed behind her. All Autumn could hear was the sound of her breath and the droning of the ship as it traveled through the vastness of space.

When she went to take a step further to explore her surroundings, a warm body brushed behind her. Goosebumps rose over her skin. Her lips parted.

"I missed you so much." Dante rested his chin on her shoulder. His black-gloved hands slid down her body and over the slope of her hips, pulling her closer to him. She could feel the beat of his heart.

She turned around, running her fingers through the dark fallen stands of his hair. His brilliant amber eyes twinkled in the shadows. He leaned down and kissed her. Her fingers played against the hard muscles of his back as his tongue brushed against hers in gentle strokes.

He touched his warm soft lips to hers once more before pulling away. She trembled, melting into his rich amber gaze.

"You were right, and I was wrong," he pressed her body against his. "I should've sent Valdez home as soon as you asked. I never should've allowed her to come to Surge to begin with. This is all my fault. I'm so glad you're alive and safe with me again."

As she went to speak, her dress lifted slightly, and a ball of fur rubbed against her ankles. A puffy tail swirled around her leg. She knelt and picked her pet up. Mr. Hiss purred, rubbing his head against her neck.

"I can't believe you brought Mr. Hiss with you," she grinned so hard her cheeks hurt. Her eyes began to well with warm salty tears. Pure happiness consumed her.

"He missed you as much as I did," he took her hand in his. "We kind of bonded, I guess you could say. I see why you enjoy his company so much." His mouth tilted.

"Is that your way of saying that you like him, and he isn't just some animal?"

He shrugged, mouth curving. "Perhaps."

He led her to a daybed in the far corner of the room. She took a seat, holding Mr. Hiss in her lap. Dante pulled over a chair from a nearby table. Planets and stars shimmered against the glass of the lone window. The reflection of her silver-gray eyes stared back at her in the darkness.

He rested his hands on her knees and gazed into her eyes. His lips moved as if he wanted to speak. He glanced away for a moment before meeting her gaze.

"Did Valdez hurt you?" he outright asked. His eyes narrowed with smoldering intensity. Her body grew rigid.

"Yes, she did," she looked away, recalling her stay on her ship and being hunted like an animal. She treated her like she was less than human, because to her, she was. "In ways you can't even imagine."

He cracked his knuckles. "When I get my hands on her, and I swear to you I shall, I'm going to make her suffer for what she did to you. I'm going to make her beg for her life."

The air in the room grew hot and thick with energetic rage. A long silence followed. He continued. "She knows about Earth, and she knows what I've done. It's only a matter of time until the Grand Supreme finds out—if she hasn't already told him."

Her heart slammed against her rib cage. "What are we going to do? What's going to happen to Earth?"

She squeezed his hand, waiting for an answer.

"I promise I will protect your planet until my dying breath. The forcefield is still in place. In the meantime, I'm having Ronan transport your father here—"

"So it's true?" She set Mr. Hiss down on the bed. He rolled onto his back, tail swaying against the comforter. "Armienti told me, but I wasn't sure whether to believe him."

Dante cocked his head to the side. "What about Armienti? I'm assuming he was in on this too?"

She twisted her mouth. "He made a mistake. A big one."

That was putting it lightly. He'd colossally screwed up.

"What a coward," he folded his arms. "He couldn't even face me like a man. Couldn't hear what I had to say. He proved his own guilt by running away with his tail between his legs. He failed my test." A long silence followed. "My soldiers are pursuing him as we speak. I swear he'll answer for the part he played in this."

"I want you to pardon him," she laced her fingers in her lap, straightening her spine. "He's family."

"I'm not sure I can pardon a crime of this magnitude even if he is my flesh and blood. Did he hurt you too?" he asked as he tucked a strand of hair behind her ear. Her mind raced a million miles an hour, recalling all their interactions. If Dante found out that he kissed her and tried to turn her against him, he'd destroy the universes.

"Did he?" he asked again through their bond. Goosebumps prickled against her skin. She chewed her bottom lip as his voice caressed her mind.

She finally answered. "No, he didn't, honestly." *But she'd hurt him. She'd broken his heart, which proved to be disastrous. Who knew what he was capable of?*

There was so much she couldn't tell Dante about what transpired on planet First. She didn't want to add more fuel to the fire and create more bad blood between the two brothers.

Dante ran a hand through his hair and changed the subject. "When your father arrives, I promise everything will be different. I'll try harder to be respectful. I'll prove myself to him like I should've from the start. We're going to be happy together as a family if you'll still have me after all the mistakes that I've made. I can't seem to stop making them, no matter how hard I try."

"We all make mistakes," she stroked his cheek with her fingers. "Some are bigger than others, but we can't let them define us. We should learn from our mistakes and grow from them."

He kissed her, then a smile flickered across his lips. He moved his hands up her thighs to where she wanted him, then snorted.

"What on Earth do these Zambarians have you wearing? This is the most ridiculous ensemble I've ever seen." He rubbed the tacky fabric of her dress between his fingers. *She was surprised it took him so long to notice the ugliest dress in existence.*

She shrugged. Warm embarrassment spread across her face and neck. He was right though, she definitely looked foolish.

"It's no matter," he moved closer, pressing his lips to her lobe. Her core tightened, aching for him. Her toes curled in her boots. *How she missed him. His touch. His scent. But most of all, being with him.* "You won't be wearing it much longer." His mouth fell crooked.

She tilted her head to the side as he nipped at her throat. "Is that so?"

She slid backwards on the daybed. He climbed beside her, kicking off his knee-high boots. He reached and undid the laces on the back of her dress, freeing her from her gaudy outfit. The dress slipped onto the floor in a heap of metallic fabric and fur. She removed the shirt of his uniform, brushing her fingers over his muscles and the scars of his blue chest. She still wondered how he'd gotten the deep, cruel, twisted marks, but didn't dare broach the sensitive topic again. His pants slid low on his hips, and he ran his hand over the tattered corset that she'd worn as she suffered on planet First. He inhaled, closing his eyes, pressing his nose to the fabric.

"This has to go. I don't like how it no longer bears my scent. It smells like *him*. You're *my* wife."

She gasped as he unlaced the worn undergarment and tossed it onto the floor, leaving her uncovered. She stared up into his eyes, wrapping her legs around his waist. Her fingers slid through the fallen strands of his midnight hair, over the high planes of his cheeks and his eager lips. Every pore on her body was set on fire. She trembled beneath him.

"I don't care what anyone thinks, and I don't care what mistakes you've made. I just want to be with you." Her entire body quivered as they melted in each other's arms. Toes curled, limbs tangled, rolling between the sheets as they made love.

Forty-Two

DANTE TREMBLED, staring into Autumn's silver-gray eyes. He tilted her head, pressing his lips to hers. His tongue explored the sweet crevice of her mouth. His face heated from the love they shared together only moments before. No matter how hard he tried, he couldn't convince himself he wasn't dreaming. *The joys of being with his wife.*

He rested his head against her shoulder, breathing against her neck. He wound a curl around his fingertip, bringing it to his nose, soaking in her rich floral scent. He traced his finger from her jaw to her breastbone.

He was so grateful she was alive after everything that'd transpired. But at the same time, the blood boiled in his veins with vengeance. He planned to repay the pain and suffering Autumn had been caused ten-fold. He swore it on his life.

"So, before we go home, I have to take care of some pressing business," the words played off his lips. He waited for her response.

Autumn glanced over to him, tracing her fingertips along his chest. "What kind of business?" she asked.

"Well—" he ran a hand through his hair, tousling the strands.

She stopped and brought her lips to his ear, kissing his lobe. "You promised me, no more secrets," she whispered into his ear.

Shivers covered his entire body. If she wasn't careful, he'd start up with her all over again. He might start up with her regardless, she looked so beautiful. His eyes fluttered closed then reopened before he rerouted the conversation. "How's my sister? I know you've seen her."

She crossed her arms, twisting her mouth to the side. "She's really, *really* pissed at you."

"Is that so?"

She nodded, rosy cheeks blossoming through the darkness.

A great sadness settled over him. He never meant to create a rift between himself and his sister. He thought he was doing what was best for her. *But who knew what was best for anyone anymore? And what right did he have to make that determination?*

"I don't blame her. She has every right to be angry." He'd be furious if he had been in her place—powerless, and unable to make his own decisions. That's when he recalled they were in the exact same situation. *The Grand Supreme.*

Autumn snorted. "You think? It's always your way or the highway, what did you expect? You never listen to anyone else's point of view."

He stared at Autumn, sensing a slight tone in her voice, but was unsure of what she meant by the expression. He remained quiet, inhaling a breath. Damn the human phrases he'd yet to grasp in the few years they'd been together. He was sure at this point he would never learn them all. It was a hopeless cause.

When he opened his mouth to respond, her voice whispered through his mind. *"It means you give everyone no choice but to do what you want them to."*

He nodded slowly. How right she was. She was always

right about everything it seemed. But he was too proud, and it'd taken him this long to admit his fault.

"I'm aware it's something I need to work on," he crossed his arms, staring at the ceiling. He watched the lights from the stars race over the silver finish. He paused, an inkling of guilt rattling through him. "I think I'll go and pay my sister a visit."

Dante jumped up from the daybed and prepared to teleport to Leyla's room.

Autumn cleared her throat and pointed to his uniform rolled up on the floor. She snorted. "Wait, aren't you forgetting something?"

His entire body warmed. She was right again, but when he grabbed his uniform to get dressed, he stopped dead in his tracks. The pocket of his pants vibrated. He reached inside and grabbed his communicator, and his heart sank to the floor. *Please, no.* A missed call from the Grand Supreme and one from Valdez Aventura.

"Who is it?" Autumn asked, head tilted to the side.

"Nobody important." He declined both frequencies. He'd do without them both. They only spelled trouble. He tossed his communicator into his pile of fallen clothes.

He chewed his bottom lip into a smile and made his way back over to her as she still lay in the daybed. He leaned down and kissed her as he pulled the sheet away from her naked body. He'd never tire of being with her.

"I knew somehow you'd get me started again. By being so thoughtful and beautiful and completely yourself."

She giggled, pulling him back into the daybed. At that moment, nothing else in the universes mattered to him more than Autumn, and he was going to make sure she felt loved.

AFTER THEY FINISHED for the second time, Dante dressed in a rosy daze determined to stay focused. He cast Autumn a lazy smile as she lay in bed playing with Mr. Hiss.

"I'll be back shortly," he reassured her. She nodded, resting her cheek against the pillow.

He teleported through time and space, seeing a swirl of colors and blurred faces of inhabitants of the ship before finally locating Leyla's bedchamber.

As his heavy black boots hit the ground, he sensed her great sadness. It seeped through the air that she breathed like death. He glanced around the room and discovered her lying on her stomach on the bed in a dress as hideous as the one Autumn wore with a silver bodice and white fur-trimmed sleeves. *These Zambarians.* He rolled his eyes. *They had no fashion sense.* He bit his cheeks to stop himself from laughing.

She kicked her feet back and forth, with pods in her blue pointed ears, listening to some music he could've sworn his late father banned on threat of death.

He sauntered over and grabbed a pod from her ear and stuck it into his own. *Yep.* She whirled around with an expression of combined shock, horror, and disgust.

She rolled off the bed and came to a stand. She crossed her arms, breast puffed. "Get out of here."

He chuckled, shaking his head. He quirked a brow. "Is that any way to talk to your emperor?" He leaned over to kiss her cheek, and she pushed him away. He stumbled backwards, resuming his stance gracefully. He straightened his spine, smoothing his crimson cape in his black-gloved hands.

Her blue face shifted the deepest shade of scarlet. "You really have some nerve, coming here. And with that smile you're so famous for. Why is it you're the only one who's ever happy?"

He shrugged, sauntering over to the bed. He took a seat, crossing his legs. Leyla fled to the far end of the room and folded her arms. The window behind her sparkled with comets and passing stars.

Dante laced his fingers around his knee, bouncing it. "So, how have you been?" As soon as he spoke, a boot flew through the air straight at his head. He caught it with one hand before it made an impact.

"If you've come here to gloat and make small talk, then I must kindly ask you to leave. You know where the door is." She folded her arms, staring out the window. He placed the boot onto the floor.

"Hm, an interesting proposition," he mused. "But that's not why I'm here."

She turned around, resting a hand on the fullest part of her hip. "What are you talking about?"

He shrugged. "Now I guess you'll never know." He came to a stand, pretending to get ready to leave.

She moved closer. He could tell she was intrigued by the expression on her face. Her demeanor changed. "Out with it then."

"What if I'm here to tell you that you can come home?"

Her mouth twisted to the side. "I'd say, what's in it for you? We both know you always have some kind of angle, Dante the Great Conqueror."

"Wow, Leyla, can't I do something nice for you?" He threw his hands into the air in surrender. "Do I always have to be a monster?"

"You brought that name on yourself. Look at the horrific things you've done over the years."

"I had no choice," he said quietly. "And you know that."

"That's what you say," she glanced away, crossing her arms again. "But we both know the truth."

The room stilled and she continued. "Even if I come home, you ruined my life and it'll never be the same."

He ran a hand through his midnight hair, tousling the

chin-length strands. "Is it because of Kyo? Okay, I'll admit I got a little carried away."

Her deep-brown eyes thinned to slits. "Hold the *little*. Of course it's because of Kyo. Look at what you did to him and his family. They were nice and hardworking. They cared about me as much as I cared about them. You always have to ruin everything. I know you only wreaked havoc because they're hybrids and you think everyone who isn't pureblood is beneath you."

His chest ached and his stomach twisted at what she thought of him. He tried his hardest to conceal the hurt. He *had* thought this way once.

"First of all, that's not true. I sent him away to protect you because you can't protect yourself."

From Valdez and the Grand Supreme, it tempted him to add. But it no longer mattered, the situation had escalated.

Leyla rolled her eyes. "You're such a liar."

He continued. "Well, let's see how much of a liar I am then. What if I was to tell you that Kyo is here and he's downstairs waiting for you?"

"I—I'd say," her legs wobbled, and her blue skin grew pallor. He'd caught her off guard. Dante rushed over to catch her before she hit the ground. He knelt, setting her against the wall. She trembled with tears beading in her eyes. He handed her a goblet of water from a nearby table. She sipped from the contents slowly.

"Relax, everything is going to be all right."

He reached into his pocket for his communicator and sent Kyo a text. "Come upstairs. I'm in room 313. I need to speak with you."

In a matter of moments, a hollow knock came to the steel door. Dante rose and walked over to the door, sliding it open. Sure enough, Kyo stood outside with his arms folded.

"You asked to see me?"

"Ah, yes." He made space for Kyo to come inside the bed chamber. The door closed behind him.

"What's this about?" Kyo asked. His eyes grew wide, and his tattooed neck tensed as his attention settled on Leyla sitting against the wall. Kyo froze, looking back and forth between them.

"I—" he stuttered.

Dante crossed his arms. "You're not in trouble, and this isn't an attack. I figured you two have a lot to catch up on. You have my blessing if you want to be together."

Leyla covered her mouth, and tears fell from her eyes.

"But I don't understand," Kyo began. "I thought—"

Dante brushed past him and left the room. He didn't have an answer they'd both comprehend. Even he didn't understand his own decision. A smile crept across his mouth at the realization he'd done something kind for once.

Forty-Three

AS ARMIENTI RACED through the vastness of space, stars and meteors glittered against the glass of the destroyer he'd stolen from the Zambarian royal vessel. His heart bled from the pain Autumn had caused him. The agony of being rejected *again*. He'd never be enough for anyone, no matter how hard he tried.

Nobody cared if he lived or died.

The constant transmissions humming through the ship indicated Dante had several destroyers out searching for him. The order was given as soon as he'd departed, and when Dante wanted something, *he was relentless*.

But what his brother didn't count on was the invisible mode his ship traveled on. The destroyers sped by him in an obsidian streak giving him plenty of time to escape as he melded into the darkness of the stars.

For the first time, he'd outsmarted him. His pompous and self-centered older brother. His lips flickered with self-satisfaction. Perhaps Dante wasn't as intelligent as he believed himself to be.

He had no one left in the universes to confide in except for Ronan. He was desperate to find him.

Once again, Autumn's words haunted him, stripping him bare. A twinge of humiliation rattled through his bones, burning his core. If his brother was out of the picture, then *maybe* she would've chosen him. *Maybe.* Although *maybe* was a long shot, it was still a possibility.

Anything was possible. *Wasn't it?*

He pulled a sleek black communicator out of his pocket. The same device he'd hidden from Autumn on planet First after discovering it on the body of one of Valdez's dead Zexian soldiers in a failed attempt to get her to fall for him.

What an idiot he was.

She no longer wanted anything to do with him. *Dammit.*

His navy-blue-gloved fingers trembled as they slid over Ronan's number. The frequency transmitted and after a few moments Ronan answered. Relief flooded through his limbs.

"Hello," Armienti said, his voice tremulous. "Where are you?"

"It's nice to hear from you again." Ronan sounded happier than he had in a long while. Armienti rolled his eyes. *It figured.* Even his younger brother found love before he did. Life was so unfair. The speaker crackled and popped as Ronan breathed, then he continued. "We're coming up through Universe 8."

"I see," Armienti placed the communicator on speaker, sitting the device in his lap. He re-fastened his long, gilded tresses into a low ponytail and inhaled a deep shuddering breath. "Any chance we could meet up?"

Ronan snorted. "I thought that was the plan all along. I can't wait to introduce you to Sean." Armienti heard laughter and merriment in the background. He experienced a twinge of jealousy. His chest ached, gut twisting. "Autumn's father isn't bad either, he's just worried about Autumn. By the way, how is she?"

"She's fine," Armienti lied through his teeth. He couldn't

bear to talk about her, couldn't bear to hear the sound of her name. "So where are we meeting?"

"I'm sorry I asked. Are you fighting with her or something?"

"Of course not," he snapped. Ronan didn't know the half of it. The situation was far worse than anything he could've ever possibly imagined.

"Is it Dante then? Is he being a pain in the ass? Shall I call and smooth him out? Ever since he was crowned emperor—"

Armienti's stomach flipped. "No, no, that isn't necessary."

"Very well then. Are you sure you're okay?"

"Yes, yes, of course I am."

Phew, that was close, he wiped the sweat beading on his brow. Armienti was so glad he'd spoken Ronan off a cliff. One wrong move and he could've been busted, or worse, executed for treason.

"Let's meet in Universe 10, Sector 86," Ronan suggested. "That way we can catch up before heading—"

"Perfect, I'll see you there." Armienti clicked off his communicator. His entire body trembled right down to the tips of his toes. He had to be careful how he handled this next situation. His very life depended on his success.

* * *

RONAN SHOOK his head as he flew the destroyer through the vastness of space. Stars zipped by the vessel in sparks and waves, their tails lighting the way. Armienti was acting *weirder* than usual. He hoped his older brother wasn't in some kind of trouble, but knowing him, anything was possible. He'd pulled some stupid stunts over the years.

His attention drifted to Sean. His ears and neck warmed as he admired his boyfriend sketching everything he saw in his notepad. Stars, suns, planets, even his natural form which he'd slipped up and shown him right after they boarded the ship—with zero notice.

For a moment, he thought their relationship was over.

Lucky for him, Sean thought it was the coolest thing he'd ever seen in his life. As he sat beside him, copying his likeness, he'd managed to shade his skin the correct hue of blue and portray the vibrant green of his eyes. A perfect resemblance. His mouth curved. He couldn't help but smile. His boyfriend was so talented.

Autumn's father, *not* so much.

He sat in the corner all by himself sipping a hot beverage. His back pressed against the wall. Steam fogged his cracked spectacles as he watched them in silence, his eyes narrowed.

"Do your parents know you're out here?" he asked between sips. Droplets of water settled in his facial hair. He wiped them with his hand.

"Yes," Sean glanced up from a sketch. He pushed his ginger-blonde hair behind an ear. His deep brown eyes smiled, glowing against his golden complexion. "They know we're going on a trip."

"I see, but do they know about—"

Sean shook his head. "No, not yet, but when the time is right, I'm sure we'll have that conversation with them." He reached over and squeezed Ronan's black-gloved hand. He melted, cheeks turning pink.

"And you?" Mr. Ramon addressed Ronan. "I know we got off to kind of a rough start, but I can't imagine your parents would be okay with you traveling so far away from home picking up humans all by yourself."

"My parents are dead. They died a long time ago." Ronan offered. Honestly, he couldn't recall their faces. He was too young. The only parents he'd ever known were the former emperor and empress and his older brother and cousin who kept him in line.

"I'm very sorry for your loss," Autumn's father lowered his voice.

"It's okay," Ronan glanced out the window. "What does it matter now?"

"I'm sure they loved you very much. I know what it's like to lose a family member."

Ronan nodded slowly, crossing his arms.

"My wife passed away a few years ago and I miss her more and more every day."

Mr. Ramon came to a stand and walked over to them. He held his cup close to his chest. Horizontal lines swept across his brow. His mouth moved as he prepared to speak. "How is my daughter really? Is she okay? Is she hurt? Is she scared?"

Ronan sighed. This had to be the fifth time today he'd asked. The answer never changed.

"I assure you, she's fine." Although she was slightly *different* from how he remembered her back on Earth, it tempted him to add. He couldn't deal with the backlash. Her father was too fragile.

His cup shook in his hand. Sean gasped. "When I get my hands on Dante, I'm going to give him a piece of my mind he'll never forget. That punk, taking my only daughter, my little girl, from behind my back. Alien or not, he has to learn some respect." He paused. "You know he's wanted, don't you?"

Ronan bit his cheeks concealing a smile. "Of course I do." Her father didn't know the half of Dante's capabilities.

"Then you understand. I won't put up with his shenanigans. I don't care if he's emperor—he's going to answer to me. I plan to give him a wake-up call he'll never forget. You never ever mess with someone else's family and expect to get away with it." His hands shook, and he smashed the cup against the wall.

Forty~Four

AUTUMN BLUSHED as she walked hand-in-hand with Dante through the halls of the Zambarian ship. They passed by countless silver-skinned aliens. The women donned hideous dresses almost as ugly as her own. It seemed they saved the worst for royalty, with poofy skirts, tons of fur, and outlandish colors. The men wore simple bodysuits of indigo. *Lucky them.*

She cringed, then sighed. For the first time she couldn't wait to go back to Surge. She wanted to be in the warmth and the sunlight of eternal summer and best of all, get ready for her dad's arrival. She couldn't wait to see him again. Her heart skipped a beat. This all felt like a dream.

As she grinned to herself like a fool, Dante glanced at her and flashed a spectacular smile. She melted at the sight of his handsomeness before snapping back to reality. *Crap.*

She wanted, no *needed*, to get this meeting over with. She recalled what Leyla told her about the emperor and his grossness. She couldn't help but wonder what she meant.

If only she didn't insist on knowing what Dante was up to earlier. But curiosity got the best of her. And because she was an empress, she had to start acting like one, and that meant dealing with the current issue at hand.

Whatever it was.

As she fidgeted with her hands, Dante took her fingers and brought them to his soft blue lips. He leaned down and whispered into her ear. His soft-spoken voice caressed her. She couldn't stop thinking about what they'd shared earlier after so much time had passed. And how much she enjoyed being with him. She couldn't wait to be alone with him again. The memory of their interactions made her face flush.

"I apologize in advance about what we're about to walk into," Dante scrunched his nose, disgust clear on his face. He sighed.

"Huh?" She looked up at him. *What the heck was he talking about?*

They turned a corner and entered a room lined on either side with rows of steel chairs topped with ink-blue velvet pillows. Long rectangular windows offered a spectacular view of outer space, glimmering with countless planets and stars.

As her eyes gravitated away from the beautiful view she covered her mouth in shock. The bile rose from her gut, singing her esophagus.

Holy Crap. Was this who she thought it was?

A silvery man stood before a glowing raw-crystal throne addressing a fellow Zambarian. He stood a foot above her head with a rounded belly, stark white hair, and eyes like two beady black magnets. But there was a softness about him, a gentleness. Not like the rumors she'd heard about him devouring his victims. And not like the other murderers she'd encountered in space, her husband included.

The interaction seemed normal enough at first, filled with laughter and talking in their strange alien language. However, upon further inspection, globs of spit rolled down his mouth and over his chin as he spoke. They soaked and sprayed the neckline of his uniform. *Eww gross,* she gagged.

She took two steps in retreat, but Dante urged her onward, placing his hand on the small of her back. She could see why he'd threatened Leyla with marriage to Emperor Brumha. Anyone would be on their best behavior after witnessing this horrific sight.

She inhaled a deep breath trying her best not to be rude. Dante made a brief face of disgust that he managed to conceal, pressing a hand over his mouth.

He straightened his spine as she held onto his arm, fingers digging into his bicep. He spoke in a weird language she didn't understand, and the silver alien replied with clicks of his tongue and more spit than she'd ever seen in her life.

* * *

DANTE FIXATED on the dribble hanging off the edge of Emperor Brumha's lip in disbelief it'd come to this. He was positively revolting. His gut churned as he cleared his throat.

"Thank you for seeing us on such short notice," the words ran smoothly off his tongue.

"The pleasure is all mine," droplets of saliva sprayed from Emperor Brumha's mouth, covering Dante's extended hand. He stepped aside, wiping his black glove against his pants. Autumn moved closer to him, wide-eyed. He could only imagine what she thought of this slob. He had to get this meeting over with.

"First of all, I'd like to offer you my condolences about your father. It seems we have some sadness in common."

"Thank you for your kind words," the emperor said, then changed the subject, eyes flickering toward his wife. "This must be your beautiful bride, the delightful Autumn Martyne. I've heard so much about her." He took her hand and brought it to his slobbery mouth. Autumn's face paled and she gulped, but she managed to push out a polite smile handling the situation like a true empress. Once the interaction was through, she took her hand and subtly wiped it on Dante's cape. "If you like we can speak in your native tongue so she can be included in our conversation."

"I'd like to have a word with you in private first," Dante crossed his arms. "I need to practice my Zambarian and she doesn't need any more stress, she's been through enough, but surely you know that. Don't think I haven't heard how she was welcomed by your sentries on planet First."

Emperor Brumha twisted his wet silver lips. "There are no words to express how embarrassed I am about the way she was treated. If I had been present, it never would've happened."

Dante cocked his head to the side. "I demand retribution for her suffering."

"As you should, and that's why I've taken the liberty of rounding up the guards who were involved in the incident and you may do whatever you like with them."

He stroked the cleft of his chin. "Hmm…an interesting proposition and a good start, but I'm afraid it's not satisfying enough. Not only did they put their hands on my empress under your jurisdiction, but you allowed a traitor to escape. What kind of shit show are you running here, Emperor?"

Emperor Brumha nodded in silence, not offering a defense. He remained calm on the outside, contemplating.

He cracked his knuckles, straightening his spine. "I propose a different solution. I'll have a long hard word with the guards, and believe me it shall be a conversation they'll never forget. The princess is coming home with me, and I want half of your fleet at my disposal." He watched and waited for the emperor's response. His mouth curved, self-satisfied.

The emperor sucked in a breath, spit spraying in globs.

Dante took a step back. He'd had just about enough of his repulsiveness. Brumha opened his mouth to speak.

"Think carefully about how you answer," Dante added. "It's been a few years since I've conquered a world but I'm itching to expand my territories. It's what I live for. Deny me and yours becomes next on my carefully curated list."

Dante prepared himself for the backlash as a long awkward silence followed.

"You're taking the princess too?" he finally asked. "I was hoping that if she didn't take a liking to my brother that—"

"I'm afraid you're not her type," Dante said matter-of-factly. "Your brother either." Although for the life of him, he was surprised Leyla hadn't fallen for the younger prince. He was one to watch. Dazzling, handsome, and full of life—kind of like himself. But what was done was done and there was no turning back.

Brumha crossed his arms. "We don't want a war. We haven't had one for the last four hundred years. We're a peaceful nation and I intend to keep it that way. I don't want bad blood between you and I or myself and the Grand Supreme. We both know how that ends."

"Is that a yes? Is our deal done then?"

Emperor Brumha inhaled, spraying another round of spit. He inwardly cringed. "Half of my fleet will remain on call, if need be, for your purposes."

"A wise decision on your part," Dante switched back to Ivarkian so Autumn could understand. "Thank you very much for your hospitality. My lady and I shall make our leave back to Surge."

Dante took Autumn by the hand and led her out of the room. Gusts of snow and ice followed them, sprinkling against their hair and backs in glittering swirls. Emperor Brumha must've been pissed from losing to him, but he didn't care. He'd gotten everything he wanted like always.

He only needed to summon the courage to make the first move.

Forty-Five

AUTUMN GAGGED as they left Emperor Brumha's throne room. That was one of the most disgusting sights she'd ever seen in her life. The drool and saliva that came out of that alien's mouth was unbelievable. She felt like she'd just been bathed in spit. She cringed, wiping her hands against her dress in case she'd missed a drop.

As she made her way through the hallway to the departure bay with Dante, he flashed a self-satisfied smirk, his chest puffed.

Something was definitely up.

He practically skipped through the hallway; his head held high. His crimson cape swayed over his shoulders in rhythmic waves, almost like he'd won a fight.

"What was that all about?" She finally asked, assessing his mood from head to toe.

He flashed her a too-white smile, then shrugged. "Oh nothing. He thanked us for our visit. It isn't everyday one gets the extreme honor of having Martyne royalty ride aboard their ship.

"That was a whole lot of words for *nothing*," she muttered, folding her arms. *He was full of crap.* She glowered at him.

He stopped dead in his tracks and took her hands in his. His warm body brushed up against her own. Her lips parted as he kissed her forehead. His gentle voice sifted through the secret corridors of her mind. *"You need to trust me more. Everything I've done and everything I continue to do is to protect you."*

She sighed. She'd heard it all before. She hoped he wasn't in some kind of trouble. But her gut screamed otherwise.

At that moment, Leyla came prancing down the hallway wearing her shimmering silver dress with white trimmed fur sleeves. Kyo walked behind her carting her heavy trunks of clothes. The ceiling lights played off his moonglow mohawk and the tattoos of his neck stretched as he smiled. Leyla spun around on her toes before placing her fingers around his long arm, pulling him in close.

She did a double take. *Wait, Kyo?*

"What's he doing here?" She glanced over at Dante. His lips coiled. "You're just full of surprises, aren't you?" He shrugged then winked at her.

"Are we ready to get going?" Leyla grinned, her blue cheeks flushing pink. Autumn hadn't seen her this happy since *ever.*

Dante's midnight hair swayed against his jaw. "Yes, I handled everything. There's nothing to worry about. Let's go home."

They made their way to the loading bay where the destroyers were located. Mr. Hiss trotted out of the open ship to greet them. His pink and black tail wavered with each padded step. He rubbed his head against the trim of her dress before Dante scruffed him by the neck and carried him purring in his arms.

When they went to enter the ship, a silver Zambarian waved them down. He was tall, well-built, and handsome, with raven-black hair that fell over his head in soft curls. A ruby and sapphire crest sparkled over the right breast of his dark-blue uniform. A floor-length white velvet cape rested over her shoulders.

Autumn's jaw dropped as she beheld the younger prince, second in command. He was *nothing* like his slovenly older brother.

Leyla froze and turned around. "I'll be right back." She sauntered over to him. They had a conversation that lasted a few minutes. Autumn stretched her neck, desperate to eavesdrop, but they spoke so low it was impossible to hear the details, even with the abilities she hoped to fully regain after she recovered from this nightmare.

Their exchange ended with her kissing him on the cheek. As she walked away, he watched her for a moment too long before disappearing around the corner, shoulders slumped.

"Okay, now we can go," Leyla smoothed her hands over her dress as she returned. Her deep brown eyes were glassy. Kyo wrapped his arm around her shoulder as they boarded the ship. Autumn followed close behind with Dante and Mr. Hiss.

They took their seats, and he buckled her harness in place. For the first time in a long time, she didn't protest. She missed him too much. For all she cared, he could buckle her in all day every day, *forever*. She rested her head against his solid shoulder. Mr. Hiss rolled in her lap, nuzzling her ribs.

Kyo and Leyla sat side by side in the control seat. "Okay, everyone, next stop: Surge."

For the first time in a long time, Autumn was at peace. Her eyes fluttered closed, breath slowing. As she drifted off to sleep, she thought only of seeing her dad again. *How could she explain everything to him in a way he would understand?* Hopefully, he could find a way to love her and wouldn't react like her friends when he found out she was no longer human.

* * *

RONAN INHALED a deep shuddering breath as he landed his destroyer on planet Olm located in Universe 10, Sector 86. His gut screamed to get far away from this place. Every pore on his body prickled up at perfect attention.

This place creeped him out to no end.

Wind whipped against the exterior of the ship, sending up gusts of red pebbles and swirling dust. The sky sparkled the color of rich maroon. Three full, blood moons glowed into the foggy night.

Sean sat beside him with his rollerblades on, legs crossed, sketching the triplicate moons. He was blissfully unaware of his surroundings, enjoying their trip to outer space, or so Ronan believed. He wished he could adopt such a carefree attitude toward life. But he felt responsible for Sean, and vowed to protect him from harm, especially this deep out in space where he needed it the most—as a human.

Mr. Ramon paced the floor, his tangled whiskered mouth twisting to the side. "Is Autumn here? Is this where my daughter has been staying?" The light reflected off the glass of his cracked spectacles. A wiliness crept through his eyes.

"No, not exactly," Ronan glanced over at him. "But we'll see her soon enough, I promise."

A ship simmered through the red sky, followed by a long crackling fiery tail. The vessel landed in the sand with a *BOOM* that made the entire ship vibrate, spraying debris everywhere.

Finally, he breathed a deep sigh of relief.

He came to a stand, sauntering over to the door. "I'll be right back," he said to both Sean and Autumn's father. They nodded.

As he exited the ship, the wind howled through the strands of his short spiky hair. Thick desert heat warmed the fabric of his uniform.

He approached the circular pod one step at a time. His boots slid against the ruddy sand. The door whistled and opened, steam pouring through the air. Out stepped Armienti with a twisted grin. His golden hair fluttered over his shoulders, obsidian uniform appearing sharp and precise.

Armienti folded his arms. "Where's Autumn's father?" he asked, getting straight to the point.

"On the ship," Ronan offered. "Where else would he be? Are you sure you're okay? You're acting kind of odd. Did Dante get under your skin or something?"

Armienti's sky-blue eyes flickered with annoyance. "No, why would he?"

Ronan shrugged. "No reason, but you know as well as I do that he has that abrasive way about him whether he means to or not—"

"I can take it from here," Armienti said. "Really, you're worrying too much."

He fell into a deep state of thought, contemplating his brother's offer. "Well actually, it would save me a trip. I must get Sean back to Earth so he can continue with his studies. Luckily, he took what the humans call fall semester off, so we don't have to rush back right away. I'd like to show him more places around the univer—"

"I see," Armienti's eyes widened with intrigue. "How fascinating. What was the state of Earth when you visited?"

He shrugged. "The same as always, I suppose. Are you sure you're okay? You know you can tell me anything, don't you? If you're in some kind of trouble I can help you. That's what brothers are for."

Armienti pressed out a smile, the corners of his eyes crinkling with delight. "I'm fine, really. I just want to be of assistance."

Ronan gestured. "Okay, follow me."

As they walked back to the ship, he attempted to slip into his brother's mind, but all was quiet. *He knew him all too well and probably anticipated this move. Older brothers...* He rolled his eyes.

When they entered the destroyer, Ronan cleared his throat. "I'd like to introduce you to someone."

Both Sean and Mr. Ramon glanced over. "This is my older brother, Armienti."

Sean put his sketchbook down on the chair and rollerbladed over, extending a hand. "Nice to meet you." He offered him a warm smile. Armienti complied, but his eyes focused on Mr. Ramon the entire time.

"Nice to meet you too," Armienti turned toward Mr. Ramon, regarding him. "You're the father of Empress Autumn Ramon-Martyne?"

Mr. Ramon's skin paled, his fists balled at his sides. "Empress? Nobody ever mentioned anything about her being an empress. What's going on here? And why am I the only adult on this trip? I need to see my daughter right now."

Ronan hadn't mentioned this fine detail, fearing this sort of response.

Armienti crossed his arms. "It's a simple yes or no question. Answer it."

His deep-brown eyes thinned to slits beneath his spectacles. "Yes, I'm Autumn's father. And if you don't bring me to her this instant—"

"You knew that, Armienti," Ronan interjected. "I think all of this space travel has melted your brain."

His brother shrugged nonchalantly. "Perhaps."

Armienti approached Mr. Ramon and extended a black-gloved hand. "You can come with me—I'll take you to her."

Mr. Ramon followed his older brother without question. As they went to leave, Ronan blocked the door with his body. "Wait a second, I forgot to ask you something, Armienti."

The room stilled, falling eerily quiet. His heart raced as he glanced at Sean. His palms erupted in a cold sweat.

Armienti blinked then smiled. "Yes?" The word played off his lips with a sly coolness.

"What name does Leyla go by when she sneaks around Giarldinia after dark?"

Armienti's mouth fell crooked on his face, eyes shifting in his skull. "Come again?"

"What name does Leyla go by when she sneaks around Giarldinia after dark?" Ronan spoke slowly and clearly, repeating his simple question.

When he blinked, Armienti's teeth twisted and elongated, snapping shut. As Ronan went to strike him, puffs of dark-purple smoke flooded the ship. He released deep dragging coughs as did Sean and Mr. Ramon. The muscles in his body became weak and uncoordinated. Fragments of light blurred before his burning eyes.

Oh no, please no, Mr. Ramon and Sean, his mind scrambled with confusion and panic.

Ronan crawled toward the imposter, trembling on all fours still trying to fight before collapsing into the darkness.

PART FOUR

In Her Eyes

Forty-Six

DANTE STOOD in his bed chamber, head held high. He smoothed his black-gloved hands over his freshly pressed obsidian uniform, running his fingers over the crest. His ship had landed, causing a commotion outside. Through the windows he watched as alien inhabitants ran and screamed for their lives. Outdated military forces prepared to defend the planet with their useless rickety ships. His mouth curved as he prepared to solidify a name for himself once and for all.

Maeve walked up behind him. Bringing her soft lips to his ear, she whispered, "Dante the Great Conqueror. It has a ring to it, doesn't it?"

Although he enjoyed when others called him this name, he didn't like the way it sounded coming from her. The words caused his stomach to twist. She shouldn't be here, his gut screamed.

He should've said no, should've insisted. But here they were. She always got what she wanted from him one way or another.

His proud smile faded as he turned around. She stared up at him with her large sparkling gray eyes, too innocent for a life such as this.

"I'm leaving in a few minutes to go and perform my duty as instructed by the Grand Supreme." He smoothed the fallen strands of his hair behind his ears.

She chewed her bottom lip and twirled a dark curl around her finger. "Oh, what does he know anyway?" She rolled her eyes. "He's just a heartless power-hungry creature in need of a good kick."

He bit his cheeks, shaking his head, then continued. "I need you to wait here until I'm finished. Under no circumstances are you to leave this ship. Don't come looking for me. It's too dangerous. If you need to reach me, you can—"

"I know," she brought her lips to his to silence his command. Warmth flooded through his body as she ran her soft hands down his back. His tail wound around her waist. She pulled away. "You told me seven times this morning alone."

"I need to make sure you understand, if anything were to happen to you—"

"What could possibly go wrong?" She spun around on the ball of her toes before falling onto his bed. She grinned looking up at him through piles of curls. Her long lashes fanned her rosy cheeks. "I'll be here waiting for you until you come back. I promise."

* * *

AUTUMN HAD NEVER BEEN SO happy to go home to Surge. As they landed in the destroyer on top of Sanguis on X marks the spot, excitement flooded through her body. The sky sparkled a cloudless blue and the heat from the dual suns warmed her skin through the ship's glass windows.

She combed her fingers through Dante's hair as he rested his head on her shoulder. Mr. Hiss hopped down from her lap and meowed, his pink and black striped tail puffed. Dante then yawned and stretched, his amber eyes blinking before meeting hers. She leaned over and kissed his hollow blue cheek. His lips flickered then curled into a grin.

"Welcome home," Dante whispered into her ear, nipping her lobe. He rested his hand on her upper thigh. Goosebumps trailed the length of her spine.

A throat cleared distracting her from thoughts of him. Leyla stood up from the control seat with a hand on her hip. Kyo turned to face them, running his fingers through his moonglow mohawk.

A reminder they weren't alone.

"We're not going to stay," Leyla crossed her arms, shifting her weight. "We need to check on Kyo's family. They've been alone for all this time—"

"Oh, there's no need for that," Dante came to a stand, grabbing Autumn's hand with his. Her face warmed from his touch. "They're here. I had them taken care of while you were away."

Leyla scrunched her nose. "Wait, are you serious?"

Dante nodded.

"Th-thank you," Kyo stuttered. "You didn't have to do that." Dante remained quiet as Leyla led Kyo out of the ship. They raced into the palace.

Autumn batted her eyes. "You're just full of surprises, aren't you?"

He shrugged, then flashed a lazy smile. As they made their way outside and onto the rooftop, the jewel-toned buildings of Giraldinia glittered in the sunlight. Aircraft whipped through the skyway like fireflies.

The surprises didn't stop there. As they made their way through the door, heavy construction took place. Servants applied fresh coats of paint over black burn marks on the walls and ceilings. A thick smoky scent churned through the air. Steel furniture was melted along the crimson carpeted floors, sticking to the velvet fibers.

Her forehead pulsated. Somehow, she knew he was responsible for this mess.

"After you disappeared, I left no stone unturned while I was searching for you," he ran a hand through his hair. "I'll admit, I lost my temper on several occasions. I was worried I'd lost you forever, and that's something I could never forgive myself for. This isn't even the worst of it. I ransacked a couple of planets in the process—"

The room stilled as she walked through the wrecked hallways, stepping over shards of metal and debris. She sighed, *this had to stop.*

"This can't happen again."

"It's a flaw I'm actively working on. I can't make any promises, but I'll do my best."

She wrapped her arm around his waist and kissed him.

* * *

WHEN THEY ARRIVED in the medical bay, Autumn found Isidora seated in a chair reading a story to Kittlen who hopped up and down on the floor. From the handheld device the words swirled through the air in a tornado of glowing hieroglyphic-like symbols. Although she was fluent in Ivarkian, she still couldn't read the language.

Treble sat on a metal table, swinging her legs. A doctor examined her back, which was finally free of the twisted scars she'd suffered from the mistake Dante had made ordering her punishment for stealing food from one of his royal supply ships. Another medical professional wiped blue gel from her ice-blonde hair and face. Leyla and Kyo arrived out of breath, racing into the room.

She could only imagine why they were late, her eyes rolled.

Treble hopped down from the table and ran over to Kyo, Kittlen following suit. They jumped into his arms.

"Are you okay?" Treble asked.

"We missed you so much," Kittlen buried his head against his chest.

"I'm fine," Kyo said. "But more importantly, how are you after—"

Treble's eyes widened, tears welling against her lashes, but she remained quiet. She glanced at Leyla. "Iris? But I don't understand. How did you change—"

"My name isn't Iris, it's Leyla," she said. "We have a lot to discuss."

Isidora rose gracefully from the chair, smoothing her golden tulle floor-length gown beneath her palms. She threw her arms around Autumn, practically smothering her as she gave her a hug. "I'm so glad you got home safely." She reached for her son, but his stance hardened. "Can I ask what happened?"

"Armienti," Dante offered a single word.

"You didn't hurt him, did you?" Isidora's dark brown eyes wavered. "I pled for mercy on his behalf—"

Dante turned on his heel mid-conversation and exited the room. Autumn pulled away from his mom, who had tears streaking her cheeks, and ran after him. A lump formed in her throat.

She caught up with Dante, catching her breath. "What are you planning to do with him when you find him?"

"If I'm honest, I'm not sure yet," Dante crossed his arms. She stared into his brilliant amber eyes flecked with droplets of green.

"I know he made a mistake, but—"

"There's no buts, he endangered your life and betrayed our family. He shall pay dearly for his indiscretion. But I haven't decided how."

They walked side-by-side through the crimson-carpeted hallway.

"To be honest I don't want him near you ever again. He's always had this fascination with you, and I can't say I don't blame him, but I think his inclinations have the potential to be dangerous." A long awkward pause followed. "Are you sure nothing happened while you were on planet First? He didn't try anything, did he?"

She froze, her stomach twisting with nausea. She didn't need to add more fuel to the fire, especially because he'd kissed her on a few different occasions against her will. Dante was under enough stress and didn't need the gory details of their stranded stay.

"Nothing happened. We survived, that's all," she laced her fingers behind her back.

His midnight hair brushed against his sharp features. "Good, I just want to put this nightmare behind us. Your father is on his way, and we have enough to deal with as it is. I want to focus on rebuilding our family."

A loud buzz came to Dante's pocket. He slid out his communicator and swiped the ignore button. She stretched her neck trying to see who had called him, but he shoved the device back into his pocket with lightning speed, his expression hardening to stone.

"Who was that?" She finally asked.

"Nobody," his muscles flexed beneath his obsidian uniform.

"You're acting kind of weird for nobody," she countered.

"I have to go." He vanished into thin air, and Autumn stood in the hallway, forehead pulsating, wondering what kind of trouble he was in.

Forty-Seven

DANTE SAUNTERED through the bottom floor of the palace, his temples throbbing with an impending migraine. He growled as he whipped out his communicator. The damn thing wouldn't stop buzzing and his wife was on to him.

How he hated worrying her after all she'd been through—because of him. And they'd only arrived home *hours* ago.

He checked the missed calls. The Grand Supreme *again* and one missed call from Valdez. His stomach tied itself in a hard knot, inducing nausea.

His molars ground in his mouth as he returned Valdez's call, fingers quaking with rage over the screen. The communicator rang and connected in a heartbeat.

"I never thought I'd hear from you again," her voice caressed him through the speaker in a way he found infuriating. His eyes rolled to the back of his head. Screams and explosions erupted in the background, crackling against his eardrum. *She was up to her old tricks. Someone was suffering for her amusement.*

"What the hell do you want?" he hissed. "You're lucky I didn't break your neck for what you did to Autumn."

"Why the insolent tone?" she chuckled but he didn't laugh. His black-gloved fist tightened.

She continued. "I called to congratulate you on saving your precious human filth. If it wasn't for you, she'd be long dead, frozen bones rotting in the ground, which I must admit I was hoping for, but there's always time for that later. I still owe you for scarring my beautiful face as well."

"I'd hardly call you beautiful." Her soul was as black as death, kind of like his own. "You're rotten to the core." Dante could hear the scraping of her taloned fingers as they tightened against her communicator.

She huffed a breath.

"You waste my time with your idle threats?" he added, his finger hovering over the disconnect symbol as red flashed across his vision.

A long silence followed.

"You and I both know that's not an idle threat."

Dante ran a hand roughly through his hair. "When I see you again, I'll kill you."

She snorted. "You kill me? Don't make me laugh. We both know which of us is stronger. Sure, we've had our scuffles over the years, but my strength far surpasses your own. Keyserike was nothing but a weak—"

"Until then," he clicked his communicator off, hanging up on her mid-sentence. He exhaled slowly, calming himself down. He couldn't catch a break.

She had some nerve.

His lips flickered with amusement. Little did she know, he tracked her exact coordinates during the call. For once, the jest was on her. She'd pay for hurting Autumn with her life. He swore it.

She was in for the rudest of awakenings.

He cracked his knuckles and continued making his way to the only place he could find solace in a stressful time such as this.

* * *

DANTE ENTERED the gravity chamber and tossed his shirt to the ground. He limbered up, preparing himself for a hard, sweaty training session. His eyes snapped to the corner of the room at the Zambarian guard shaking, knees knocking together. A wet spot between his legs soiled his navy uniform. Dante chuckled, enjoying the impression he made on his foes.

As he approached him, preparing to teach him a lesson he'd never forget for putting his hands on his wife back on Emperor Brumha's ship, a throat cleared, catching him off guard. He whipped around. *Drat.* He laced his fingers behind his back.

Autumn folded her arms. Her hair was tied in a knot atop her head, and she wore a traditional obsidian Elattion uniform rather than the ridiculous Zambarian attire she'd traveled in. *Thank the gods*, he'd never seen an uglier dress.

Her silver-gray eyes assessed him. "How did I know I'd find you here up to no good?"

He froze as she approached him, unable to formulate a sentence. His mind raced. *Busted.* She gestured at the cowering Zambarian guard in the corner.

"Tell him he's free to go. I arranged transportation for him back to Universe 18. The ship is waiting for him on the rooftop."

He nodded and before he could protest, he did as she asked. She had a way about her he couldn't deny and couldn't resist. The Zambarian guard slid across the room with his back to the wall, eyes wide, staring at them unwaveringly before making a clear run for it.

She traced a finger down his back, and his body erupted in goosebumps down to the tips of his toes. She chewed her bottom lip. "What am I going to do with you?"

"He put his hands on you—"

"I don't want to waste any more time thinking about him.

I just want to think about us," she stood on her tip toes and kissed the cleft of his chin. His face and body warmed.

"What do you have in mind?" His imagination ran away with itself. All he could think about was her trembling body pressed up against his, his mouth and tongue on her neck, and her hands grasping the hard muscles of his back as he took his time on her.

"Close your eyes." He did as she asked, standing there with red-hot anticipation. He could only imagine what she had in mind. Buttons clicked and his vision grew darker although his eyes remained closed. Metal clanged together. The weight of the air pushed his bare feet into the ground.

"Okay, now open them."

He opened his eyes slowly and she stood before him in a fighting stance.

He ran a hand through his hair, tousling the strands. "Oh, I thought. Never mind—"

She chewed her bottom lip. "There's time for that later. Right now, we need to train. I don't ever want to feel helpless again."

"You need to rest—you've been through a lot. You've suffered a serious trauma—"

"There's no time to rest," she said. "Valdez is out there somewhere, and she wants me dead. There's no telling when she'll strike again. And the Grand Supreme, doesn't he know—"

"I'll protect you—"

"You can only protect me so much. I have to be able to defend myself."

He watched her, knowing deep down she was right. He'd failed her thus far despite his best efforts. He couldn't afford to fail her again or else he feared she'd wind up like Maeve. And that was the most frightening thought he could ever imagine.

"Very well then," he slid into a fighting stance, balancing

his weight over his crouched legs. There was no reasoning with her. He decided to give her what she asked for but take it easy on her regardless.

She lunged at him with the full force of her body. Her fist and bent elbow flew over her shoulder through the air. She went to crack him across the jaw, but he moved his arm blocking her attempt. He refused to strike her back, although a fight called for that action.

"I know you're holding back on me," she moved her arm wiping the sweat from her brow against her sleeve. Ten times normal gravity wore on her body. It was clear to him she needed to rest and not complete a training session. "Armienti fought me for real when we were stranded. He—"

His forehead pulsated. "Wait, are you serious?" Armienti would have enjoyed the pleasure of fighting with her, he was sure. His molars ground together. "What if he hurt you?" He made a mental note to check in with his soldiers about his brother's whereabouts. There was no telling what he was up to, and he refused to let this error slide, more so than the others. He'd endangered Autumn's life for the last time.

"He didn't though. I hurt him by mistake. Our abilities were waning. I didn't mean to—"

"Okay, I'll fight you for real just this once, but don't say I didn't warn you. One hit is all you get from me." He finally caved.

"Agreed."

He cracked his knuckles, watching, waiting for her next move.

His brother had some nerve fighting her.

Her brow crinkled. She lunged at him, and he teleported behind her, hoping to give her a good scare. She jumped and whirled around, but this time he caught her fist in his hand as she went to hit him. He took his leg and kicked her in the ribs, sending her clear across the room. She went flying, slamming her chest into the wall. His heart stopped as he raced over to her, and she fell face-first on the floor. *Perhaps he'd taken matters too far. He never should've agreed to fighting her.* She pushed herself up to a shaking stand and he helped her to her feet.

"Autumn, Autumn, I'm so sorry. Are you okay? Did I hurt you?" Panic and shame erupted through his body. He should've never agreed to this.

"I'm okay," she reassured him, her voice sounding weak. She dusted herself off. "Let's try this again. This time you can stop coddling me."

"I agreed to fight you one time and one time only. Clearly, you're not—"

"What are you scared or something?" She winked. "Fine, I'll go and find someone else to train with—"

"Okay, one more time then," he reluctantly agreed, but he was positive she'd be sorry.

This time he clenched his fist, sending the ball straight at her rosy cheek, without warning. She caught it in her hand and raised her knee, hitting him in the gut. He sputtered backwards, inhaling a breath. After he regained his composure, he launched a roundhouse kick and she ducked, sliding to the floor, taking out his other foot with her boot. He stumbled before flying into the air. She was on him in a heartbeat.

She threw her leg into a kick, and he blocked it before she disappeared into thin air. *What the devil?* He searched for her spinning around in circles but to no avail. Suddenly, a heeled boot collided between his shoulder blades, sending him flying and crashing headfirst into the metallic tiled floor. He groaned, pushing himself up. He wiped his thumb against the corner of his mouth, smearing a droplet of blood.

He slid his tongue across his teeth, making sure they were still intact. "Impressive, I stand corrected." He brushed himself off. "Where did you learn that move from?"

She shrugged. "I've been practicing, I guess."

"You guess?"

She shrugged again, mouth curving.

She walked over to the wall, killing the gravity. She grabbed two steaming hot towels from the table and handed him one. He wiped the sweat from his face. When she turned to leave, he grabbed her hand, twining her fingers in his. He pulled her in close. He could feel the warmth of her body and her racing heartbeat up against his.

Dante stared down into her moonlit eyes, running his hand across her cheek and over her full pink lips. "You are so very beautiful my Little Moonlight."

She smiled, her cheeks flushing pink.

He brought his mouth to hers. tasting her. He'd never grow sick of her sweetness, her innocence. Her purity. She trembled as he pushed her back up against the wall, staring into his eyes. She removed her shirt, legs straddling his waist. His pants fell to the ground in a heap of spandex. She buried her fingers in the strands of his midnight hair, moving them over the nape of his neck. Goosebumps covered his body as she brought her lips to his. How he loved her and wanted nothing more than for her to be safe in his arms. To protect her from harm. To have her this way always and forever. Together they shattered the stars.

Forty~Eight

THERE WAS no rest after being crowned Emperor of Nine Hundred and Eighty Skies, and Dante knew this better than anyone else. As he sauntered down the hallway, his crimson cape fluttering over his shoulders, his mind remained on Autumn. She'd gotten so much stronger since last he saw her, taking him by surprise.

His cheeks melted every time his thoughts drifted to her. Her dark coiled hair, large moonlit eyes, and soft pink lips—he could still taste traces of her sweetness on his mouth. Shivers trailed down the length of his spine. He could barely focus on the task at hand, but under the circumstances, he didn't have a choice.

Business needed to be handled.

When he entered the conference room, all his high-level advisors rose to their feet and fell into bows. He made his way to the front of the room through the cool darkness. The 3D map of the 24 Universes twinkled along the center table. Everyone watched and waited as they sat in the shadows.

His eyes roved among the attendees. Armienti and Ronan's absence was apparent. *Oh, Armienti*, he shook his head. *What was he thinking?* One advisor rose to his feet and cleared his throat. Dante's eyes rested on his dark silhouette.

"Permission to speak, sire."

"Permission granted," he gestured with his black-gloved hand.

"There are unsettling reports of the Grand Supreme repossessing some of our more prominent crystal mines, particularly the one on Varz, threatening a crystal liquid fuel shortage. How do you plan to address this matter?"

A single drop of sweat rolled down his back, between his shoulder blades, disappearing into the spandex of his uniform. He puffed his chest, so as not to display any sort of weakness. *He refused to look weak, being placed in such an inconvenient position, yet again.*

Ultimately it didn't matter what the Grand Supreme did with the crystal mines for what Dante had in his possession was priceless. He'd gotten to the object before his master could catch a whiff. Its existence had been whispered about throughout the Universes for the last four hundred years. He had discovered the secret worth killing for was not just an ancient legend.

"Unfortunately, we have little control over what he chooses to repossess. I propose we set up a bigger mine, a better one right here in Universe 13," he suggested. "Planet Current is rumored to have unfathomable wealth and is ripe for the picking. It's one of the few planets in this universe I don't have in my collection."

"But there's a treaty in place protecting it," another advisor offered. "We're supposed to honor the treaty."

Dante's mouth curled. "Treaties are made to be broken, my lord."

He pointed to the bright green sphere on the glowing map, stars twinkled through the surrounding area.

The first advisor nodded, seemingly satisfied with his answer. The second advisor shook his head but didn't dare challenge him on the matter. He knew better. It was impossible to please everyone.

"For good measure, we could set up a mine on planet Burd as well. It's located on the edge of Universe 14."

As he went to point to the glowing yellow sphere, a violent frequency pierced through the air. Everyone groaned, throwing their fingers in their ears to block out the noise. The sound was so loud, his teeth stung and vibrated in his mouth. He could taste the pain.

As he glanced down, a red button flashed. One lone call awaited. His heart stopped in his chest.

"Answer it, Your Imperial Majesty," advisors shrieked through the room, pleading with him. There was no way around it. He was cornered.

He inhaled a breath, allowing the call to go through. The pain instantly subsided. Everyone exhaled a sigh of relief.

Neon green and blue lights swirled through the room, lighting up the shadows for a brief moment until the Grand Supreme appeared. His thin black slit-eyes, oil-slicked scaly complexion, and a twisted crown of horns, pierced through the jagged skin of his head. He stood the size of a child or smaller in his stupid little black uniform with a red and gold crest of a decapitated man with his head in the crook of his arm. The bastard.

His expression was serious and his long, pointed tail thrashed back and forth, whipping against the ground. He held a silver goblet in his hand and, taking a lingering sip, his long talons scraped against the metal. His mouth was tinted with the shade of blood.

Everyone in the room fell to one knee, lowering their eyes. Dante ground his teeth in his mouth, fists quivering at his sides before following suit. He refused to break eye contact with his master and refused to be intimidated.

He rose to a stand, head held high, smoothing his crimson cape beneath his black-gloved hands.

"You're a hard man to get in contact with," the Grand Supreme lisped, cracked lips curling. "I've been reaching out to you for quite some time, and I have a sneaking suspicion you've been ignoring me. Am I correct?"

Dante watched him, his jaw tightening. He had to choose his next words wisely.

He raised his head. "Sire, I—"

"Don't you dare interrupt me," the Grand Supreme snapped. Everyone in the room stared at him, wide-eyed and cowering. "After all I've done for you, this is how you choose to repay me? You were like a son to me. I took you under my wing and welcomed you into my home."

More like a slave forced to fulfill his every whim. Dante lived to serve him—to conquer at his will.

The Grand Supreme stretched his neck, searching the room. The holographic image crackled. "Where's your human? I wish to speak with her as well."

His mouth dropped open, and a wave of dizziness overcame him. *What did he need Autumn for?* It was his worst nightmare realized. He hoped to never have to subject her to his master in this lifetime.

"She's—"

"Fetch her at once," the Grand Supreme snapped his taloned fingers. "I shan't ask you again." He took another long sip from his goblet.

Fury seethed through his body as he was forced to obey him without question. A fireball raged in his palm behind his back, growing then retracting over and over again. How he wanted to smash the flame in Emperor Izzo's face and teach him a lesson he'd never forget.

He ordered an advisor to go and fetch Autumn like he had been commanded.

Forty~Nine

AUTUMN SAT in the central courtyard with former Empress Isidora. The dual suns shone high in the clear blue cloudless sky, illuminating the swirls and stars of the mosaic-tiled ground. Oversized butterflies fluttered through the air in vibrant hues of magenta, emerald, and marmalade. The scent of fresh lavender reminded her of home. Her chest swelled with warmth.

Finally, she was happy.

Kittlen ran in circles around the courtyard playing hide-and-seek with Emblem and Allegoria. He spun around on his toes, giggling as they counted to ten, pretending to search for him. He crouched behind a column, peeking around the corner. A sly smile crept across his lips.

A tall Elattion advisor came running through the door, arms flailing. The blue skin of his face grew pale. He hunched before her, palms on his knees, catching his breath.

Kittlen took one look at him, his mouth quivering, then he burst into tears. Autumn walked over, picked him up, and hugged him.

"What's wrong?" she asked, holding Kittlen close to her, rocking him back and forth to comfort him.

The man fell into a bow. "Your Imperial Majesty, your presence is required in the conference room."

Her brows furrowed. "Why?"

"Please just hurry."

"I'll come with you," Isidora interjected, the white tulle of her gown blowing in the forever summer breeze.

"I don't think that's a good idea," the advisor folded his arms. Isidora stared at him strangely before nodding.

Sensing the seriousness of the situation, she handed off Kittlen to the former empress. Kittlen finally stopped crying and they continued their game of hide and seek.

* * *

WHEN SHE ARRIVED, the cool darkness summoned her into the room. Her stomach twisted with anxiety. Thirty sets of vibrant inhuman eyes stared up at her from their seats. Everyone seemed frozen in time. With one hand, Dante motioned for her to join him at the front of the room. With the other, he continuously grew and retracted a sizzling flame in his palm.

She gulped, not wanting to be the center of attention but had no choice. She wondered what was going on. As she approached him her eyes drew to a frightening creature—one she'd never seen before and hoped to never see again. Uneasiness crept through her bones, but she maintained her composure so as not to appear scared.

Her eyes drew to Dante. "What's this all about?"

"Ah, if it isn't Empress Autumn Martyne," the monster's forked tongue flickered through his dry cracked lips. He stared at her through the glow of the hologram with his beady black eyes. "The rumors of your beauty haven't been exaggerated."

"Thanks, I think," she crossed her arms, shifting her weight from side to side. *Gross.*

"You don't know who I am do you?"

"Why? Should I?"

Gulps erupted around the room, and advisors threw hands over their mouths. Dante remained serious and still by her side.

"Perhaps you should. I'm Emperor Izzo, reigning sovereign of Universe 24. Destroyer of Worlds, Lord of the Universes, the Grand Supreme."

"Is that something you're proud of?" she asked. A moment of eerie silence followed.

Izzo stroked his talons against his black scaly chin. He swirled his goblet before taking a lingering sip. "Nobody has ever asked me that before, but I suppose the answer is *yes*."

"Well, I think you should be ashamed of yourself," her heart hammered in her chest. Her throat grew as dry as desert sand. "Stealing planets that aren't yours and enlisting others to do your dirty work. You've ruined countless lives. It's disgusting."

"Well, that's not my concern."

She placed a hand on her hip. "It should be."

Her mind tingled with a whisper from Dante. "*Autumn please, stop. Let me handle this.*" But she ignored his plea.

"You really have some nerve, human, speaking to me with such an insolent tone." Izzo shot to his short stubby feet, throwing his goblet against the floor, clanging. He pointed a finger at a viridescent alien man passing by in the background. He was swept into the air, twisting and squirming in his invisible grasp. His eyes bulged before his body expanded then exploded into fine space dust.

Autumn cupped her hands against her mouth to muffle a scream.

Emperor Izzo's mouth twisted into a grin. His yellow jagged teeth sparkled in the 3D light. "Okay, let's get down to business, shall we? It seems you haven't been entirely honest with me, Dante. *Tsk, tsk.* I know you've been dodging me." He waved his taloned finger back and forth.

Dante cocked his head to the side, remaining calm and collected. "How so, sire?"

"Even still, you lie," neon purple specks of energy swirled around his body glowing in an extraordinary light. His aura simmered against his toxic-waste complexion. "You stand here, and you look me in the eye and take me for a fool. I know about Earth and how you spared it over a girl. How you defied my orders." His mouth twisted with strange delight. His black eyes grew vacant. "Well, you won't be able to ignore this. I have something that belongs to you."

Izzo motioned for someone off the projection to approach. Two hideous scaled alien creatures dragged over a man and threw him onto the floor. Autumn's stomach churned with sickness. The bile rose in her gut. Her legs grew weak, she could barely stand up. Dante steadied her weight, resting his arm around her waist.

"Judging by your reaction, I gather you know this human?"

"No," she lied because she didn't want him to be hurt. "I mean, yes," she admitted when she stared into his large brown eyes wavering beneath his silver frames. His expression lit up just like she remembered. Warm and kind.

"Autumn, it's you," he raised a hand through the projection, trying to touch her. She reached to embrace him, but the ghost-like glow of his fingers faded against her arm, disintegrating through the air. His cracked glasses sat askew on his face. His wild, tangled beard ran down his neck. He looked like he'd been through hell and beyond. "I'm so glad you're alive."

His eyes snapped to Dante. "And you, this is all *your* doing. You kidnapped my little girl. My only child. When I get my hands on you, I swear you're going to regret it, murderer. I told you, Autumn, he's no good for you. Fathers always know best."

Dante glanced at the ground. He didn't answer him as if he was ashamed.

Her dad's eyes roved around the room.

"What the heck is going on here? Why is everyone dressed like it's a Halloween party? Why am I here and not with you?"

The Grand Supreme snorted. "It sounds like you have quite a bit to unpack, former princeling. But I'm not here for your family drama. You have a debt that's owed to me, and I intend to collect what's mine."

A dark latent anger inside of her swelled. Red flashed across her vision. Her body quivered with rage. "You'd better let him go, you scaly disgusting despicable creature."

Dante held her arm. "Autumn please." But she ripped away from his grasp.

"And what will you do if I don't? What can you possibly do to me, human? I'm a living god. Lord of all you see—even your precious emperor."

She gritted her teeth, slamming her fist against the table. The 3D map of the 24 Universes vibrated upon impact. Everyone flinched, watching and waiting for her answer with bated breath.

"We're going to raise the largest fleet you've ever seen to take him back, and then—I'm going to kill you," Autumn's lips quivered.

Izzo stared at her in silence before bursting into a fit of laughter, slapping his knee. Dante stared between them, the expression on his face was solemn and worn. The energy in the conference room grew torrid and unpredictable, swirling against her body.

"You'd better get a hold of your wife," Izzo flashed a jagged-toothed grin at Dante before turning back to her. His black, forked tongue flickered through his lips. "I shall remember your feisty words when I come to reclaim Universe 13. I hope you're ready for me. I'll torture you both within a thread of your worthless lives. I prefer to take my time with my prey. Dante knows that better than anyone else."

He took his razor-sharp talon and ran it down her dad's cheek, splitting open his skin. He let out a wide-eyed shriek that rattled her to the bone. Izzo's tongue snapped out of his mouth as he slurped up droplets of her father's blood. Crimson coated his lips. She threw a hand over her mouth, shaking.

"Until then, I'll be waiting. Try not to miss me too much. Hopefully I don't get hungry in the meantime." Her dad's shrieks assaulted her senses as the image faded into darkness, flickering off. A hole hollowed in her chest.

"Everyone out," Dante addressed the advisors who rose and scurried out of the conference room like frightened mice. The steel door slid closed behind them. He held her tight as she cried in his arms. Her warm salty tears dripped down her face and onto the obsidian fabric of his uniform.

He wiped his fingers under her eyes, smearing the tears against her cheeks. "I can't believe you did that Autumn. What in the world were you thinking? You just waged a war."

"What do you mean, what was I thinking? This is all your fault. You told me he was safe and assured me he would be here soon enough," she lowered her face into her palms, sobbing until it hurt to breathe.

He remained quiet and she continued. "You just stood there, and you didn't try to stop him or negotiate. I know you don't get along with my dad, and you've made some mistakes, but you could've at least tried—"

"You didn't give me a chance."

She remained quiet.

"I'm sorry," he squeezed her tight.

"Well sorry isn't good enough." She went to leave but he pulled her back into his arms.

"I'll make everything better, you'll see," his black-gloved hands visibly quaked. His words said one thing, but his body language betrayed him.

She'd never seen him afraid before and didn't know how to process his reaction. Her skin prickled with uneasiness. Clearly, he was as terrified as she was.

He smoothed his onyx-gloved hand against her cheeks and lowered his warm blue lips to hers. He pulled away, staring into her eyes. "I promise I'll get him back no matter the cost. I'll bring him home safely to you and make everything right."

Fifty

RONAN'S TEMPLES throbbed as he came to a shaking stand. His eyes burned, tears rolling onto his cheeks. His heart raced as he searched around the destroyer. Hints of dark purple smoke lingered in the air.

How long had he been asleep?

A wave of panic consumed him. *Where's Sean?* He stumbled over his own two feet searching as his vision focused. He raced over finding his body crumpled on the floor.

He knelt in a frenzy and attempted to rouse him. "Sean! Sean!" He shook him gently, to no avail.

He slid his black glove from his hand and pressed his index and middle finger against his throat. Thankfully, a pulse remained. He was alive.

Sean groaned then let out a haggard cough. His bloodshot eyes opened, and he cast him a lazy glimpse. Ronan leaned over and brought him up to a seated position. He held him in his arms, resting his head against his shoulder.

"Are you all right?" he dared ask, waiting for his response with bated breath.

Sean's lips moved. "Yes, I think so." He attempted to rise to his feet, but his body gave out, landing back in Ronan's lap.

The sedative effects of the gas wore off, but he still needed to rest.

"I'm glad you're okay," Ronan gently lowered his mouth to his, catching his hand in his soft hair.

When he pulled away, through the corner of his eye, he watched as an orb-shaped spacecraft burned its way through the atmosphere trailed by sparkles and embers, landing into the ruby-red dirt. Particles spewed everywhere, scattering against the exterior of the destroyer. Adrenaline seeped through his veins; he could barely breathe. *Had the imposter returned?* He rested Sean's slouched back and head against the passenger seat and made his way outside the ship.

This time he was ready to defend himself and his boyfriend with every ounce of strength he had. He wouldn't be taken by surprise, nor would he be deceived. Not again. He waited before the door, his arms crossed. His mouth twisted to the side.

The door opened and smoke seeped out in thick white puffs.

Armienti exited the craft wearing a navy-blue uniform, alien in nature. A white velvet cape hung over his shoulders.

He scrutinized him. "Identify yourself."

Armienti stopped dead in his tracks, golden eyebrows furrowed against his rich blue complexion.

"I don't have time for this, Ronan. Where is Autumn's father? I need to collect him at once, it may be my one and only chan—"

Ronan blocked him with his body, heart racing. He refused to fall for the same trick twice.

"Identify yourself," he repeated, fists trembling.

Armienti rolled his brilliant blue eyes. "Are you drunk or something?" he demanded, but Ronan refused to let up. He was prepared to fight to the death to keep Sean safe.

"Tell me one thing only you would know." Ronan assumed a fighting stance.

Armienti sighed, running a hand through his golden hair, tousling the strands. "Very well then, if you're going to make me say it then so be it. I kidnapped Autumn, suffered betrayal at Valdez's hands, and got us stranded on planet First at the far end of Universe 18. I confessed my feelings to Autumn several times—kissed her even, and it was wonderful," he mused, his mouth tilting. "I know now what I did was wrong, but the fact of the matter remains that I still love her and this is my only way back into her good graces. So please, let me through, I don't have another second to waste."

His eyes widened. *Come again?* "I'm sorry did I hear you correctly?"

"Yes, every word of it."

Ronan withdrew his stance. It was indeed his brother; only Armienti would get himself into a mess as ridiculous as this one. *Unfreakingbelievable.*

Dante was going to be furious.

Ronan turned on his heel and raced back onto the destroyer. He had to tell Dante Autumn's father had been abducted as unpleasant as the conversation promised to be.

Armienti sprinted after him. "Wait, where are you going?"

When he entered the ship, Sean had taken a seat. He sipped on a glass of water. The color had returned to his face and his brown eyes grew lively again. He jumped as Armienti entered the destroyer, his glass of water shattering against the cold metallic tiled floor—splattering water in every which direction. He moved back in his chair as far as he could go, teeth chattering in his mouth.

"It's okay," Ronan assured him. "This is my brother for real this time."

Sean extended a hand. "Nice to meet you."

"Pleasure, although we've already met," Armienti winked. "I *never* forget a face."

Ronan grabbed hold of his sleek black communicator. His throat grew dry. He punched Dante's number into the device in slow motion. It rang and connected. He placed it on speaker so his brother could hear their conversation.

"When were you going to tell me about the kidnapping?" Dante spoke in little more than a whisper. Ronan supposed Autumn was within earshot.

"I—" Ronan began.

"The Grand Supreme has him. It's been a nightmare."

Adrenaline pumped through Ronan's body. *That was the worst news he could ever possibly hope to hear.*

"It doesn't matter anymore. I have to get him back." Dante seemed cold and distant like always. "When are you coming home?"

"I'll be there as soon as possible," Ronan reassured him.

"Not if I get to him first, brother," Armienti interjected.

Ronan placed a hand over his mouth and gasped, eyes widening. A long moment of silence followed. *Brother*, he thought. *But how was that even possible?*

"You dare speak to me after the stunt you pulled?" Dante hissed. "You're no longer welcome here. There's a price on your head—"

"We'll see about that," Armienti smirked, pushing a golden strand of hair behind his blue pointed ear.

"You'd better be prepared for me if our paths ever cross again—"

Armienti grabbed the communicator and clicked off the signal mid-sentence.

Ronan shook his head. Armienti was in a world of trouble, *as usual.* He had to figure out a way to bail him out.

Again.

A gasp erupted from across the cabin. Ronan whirled around and raced over to Sean, who covered his mouth, eyes wide with shock. His sketchbook flipped by itself through the pictures of the monsters he drew and settled on the image of the creature with inky scales and lifeless purple eyes. Then the pages erupted in flames, evaporating to dust.

Fifty-One

ANGER QUELLED deep inside of Autumn's gut as she watched Dante whispering in the corner on his communicator. She couldn't believe whatever he was planning, he didn't think enough to include her. More secrets and lies she supposed.

It was *her* dad who was kidnapped by the Grand Supreme. The most evil badass alien around. *What a disgusting little creature.* She threw a nail in her mouth, chewing the cuticle down to a nub. There was no telling what that monster was up to. She could still hear her dad's phantom screams and see the pure terror in his eyes no matter how hard she tried to forget.

When he hung up, she marched over to him, folding her arms. The golden light from the setting suns played through the windows of the conference room, shattering through his midnight hair. The map of the 24 Universes illuminated through the shadows.

"What was that all about?"

"Nothing, I have the situation under control," he said, matter-of-factly.

Funny, it didn't sound like *nothing*. She stared at him strangely. He wasn't fooling anyone, least of all her.

"I depart at first light for Universe 24."

"I think you mean *we* depart," her voice jumped.

He crossed his arms and his expression straightened. His crimson cape swayed against his well-defined back. "Absolutely not, you're too distracting and I won't be able to do what needs to be done. But more importantly, I need you here in case—"

Her heart accelerated. "In case of what?"

"In case everything doesn't go according to plan," he looked to the side before meeting her gaze. There was a sadness about him, a desperateness she couldn't quite place. She'd never get used to seeing him this way. Broken and terrified.

"I'm sorry, no matter what you say, you can't stop me. I'm going with you, whether you like it or not."

As she went to leave, he took her by the hand and pulled her against his warm body. He cocooned her within his cape, creating a safe space. He held her close, resting his head on her shoulder. "Autumn, please don't make me. You represent everything that's good and pure in my life. If something were to happen to you, I don't think I could carry on. I don't think I'd have the strength."

"I'm sorry, but my mind is made up," she pulled away from him and didn't dare turn back around as she left him standing alone in the conference room. Her heart shattered into a million pieces thinking about how she disappointed Dante and how much her dad needed her.

* * *

WHEN SHE ARRIVED in her room, she was greeted by Mr. Hiss, who yawned and stretched making his way out from beneath the bed. He slowly blinked his oversized indigo eyes her way. He followed her over to the fireplace, hot-pink and onyx tail swishing. She sat on the white fuzzy carpet burying her face against her knees. Warm bitter tears erupted from her eyes, spilling onto her cheeks. She couldn't believe the predicament her dad was in.

The Grand Supreme.

As she wallowed in misery, her bedroom door slid open. Emblem and Allegoria raced over to her and threw their arms around her in a warm embrace.

"We're so sorry about your father," they said concurrently. Their clover green eyes quaked with concern, and their melodic voices lowered to a sympathetic whisper.

"Thank you," she muttered. But nobody was as sorry as she was.

A pair of heavy boots landed on the floor behind her. She sighed.

The fact that Emblem and Allegoria still wavered in his presence was a dead giveaway.

"You're free to leave."

She turned around and shot him a look, her eyes thinned to slits.

He shrugged. "What I meant to say is that if you'd like to leave and spend some time with your family, now is the perfect time to do so."

Autumn bit her cheeks. "They're your family now too, you know." Ever since Leyla was permitted to be with Kyo their families had united.

He massaged his fingertips against the bridge of his nose. His forehead twitched. "Please, don't remind me."

Emblem and Allegoria gave her one last hug before exiting her bedroom. The steel door slid closed behind them.

She glanced away as he knelt, lighting the fireplace with embers from his palm. The fire crackled and smoldered creating warmth in the room. A dark blanket of stars shimmered through the sky. The twin moons illuminated a pale white glow. A cool breeze drifted through the open French doors of her private balcony.

"I'm sorry, but you can't change my mind." She picked up her transcribed book collection that he gave her and began to read a fascinating tale about an ancient space battle and a secret portal.

He remained quiet as he took a seat beside her, stretching his neck to see what she was reading. "This story is one of my favorites. The mighty emperor wins the war in an over-whelming victory." He winked.

She rolled her eyes as he spoiled the ending. *How annoying,* she huffed. She turned off the device and stared into the flames, hypnotized by their radiance. "No matter what you say, you can't stop me from wanting to save my dad. After all this time, you owe me."

"I wish you'd let me handle the situation," he rested his hand on hers. He cocked his beautiful head to the side. His brilliant amber eyes twinkled against the flames. "I grew up around him. I know the horrors he's capable of. You can't even imagine what I've seen, and I never want you to do so—"

"Is this about Maeve? Do you feel responsible for what happened to her?" She regretted her words as soon as they slipped out. His face fell. Thanks to Armienti, she knew everything.

"Every day, and it never gets easier. Her final moments continue to replay through my mind, and I can't figure out where I went wrong. I should've known better, but I was such a fool back then."

"I'm sure you did everything you could to help her."

"I did," he glanced away. "But it still hurts like hell."

A long awkward silence followed, and Mr. Hiss rolled on the floor purring, lightening the mood.

He tucked a stray strand of hair behind her ear. "I need you here to watch over my family and to rule in my stead in case I don't come back. I'm leaving you emergency instructions. If he gets through me, he won't stop until he finds you and the rest of our family. I want to make it impossible for him to hurt you—"

"Don't think like that," her heart ached. She couldn't imagine what her life would be like without him. She loved him despite his countless flaws. They were as numerous as the stars in the sky, but deep down he was just like her—in pain. They needed each other more than ever.

She leaned over, bringing her lips to his, tasting his spiciness. Her fingers wandered, exploring the hard lines of his jaw. His eyes smoldered through her, truly seeing her for who she was. For the first time in her life, she felt seen and desired. She pulled off his shirt running her hands along the twisted scars of his chest, against his rippled abs, and around the band of his pants, pulling them lower on his hips. They rolled over in each other's arms eager and desperate, melting together by the crackling fireplace. Embers danced through the strands of his raven hair. Shadows flickered as they became one. Their entire bodies were beaded with sweat and goosebumps.

Aircraft sped in the distance, muffling their noises and the city lights of Giarldinia twinkled through the night. Deep down she was afraid but would never admit it aloud—terrified that after that night, they'd never see each other again.

Fifty-Two

THE FOLLOWING morning when Autumn woke, she stretched her hand across the width of the bed searching for Dante, but the linen was cold beneath her palm. Destroyers whizzed by the balcony window vanishing through the cloudless atmosphere. The metropolis glittered in the distance. A faint smog settled above the city.

Her forehead pulsated and she tried her hardest not to be angry because, not only did he leave without her, he left without saying goodbye.

As she went to stand, her body shook beneath her weight. Droplets of sweat trickled down her forehead followed by chills. She rubbed her arms over her shoulders as her teeth chattered together. A wave of dizzying illness hit her like a brick wall. She covered her mouth taking deep controlled breaths, willing away the sensation. Her head hit the pillow once more and she pulled up the blanket to keep herself warm.

When she closed her eyes, she felt the springs pop. Her heart skipped a beat. But when she glanced, a pink snout followed by a rough tongue licked her across the face, leaving a wet streak. Mr. Hiss settled beside her, purring. She combed her fingers gently through his hot-pink and onyx striped fur.

"Are you unwell?" a voice asked from across the room. She shivered, glancing. Dante. She tried to press out a smile, but she was too weak.

He approached the bed wearing his blood-red armor, appropriate for battle. His frightening horned helmet sat in the crook of his arm.

He removed his glove, pressing the back of his hand to her forehead. Lines crept across his blue brow.

"You have a fever."

"I'm fine," she reassured him, waving her hand. "I guess all that time on First finally caught up with me. I haven't had a good night's sleep in months."

He set his terrifying helmet down on the edge of the bed and walked over to the bathroom. He reemerged with a damp cloth. With his fingers he blotted it against the skin of her face, cooling her body temperature down. Relief trickled through her.

"I know you thought I would leave without saying good-bye. I would never—"

"I'm still coming with you," she said between chattering teeth, too weak to sit up but defiant nonetheless.

"You're sick and you need to rest," he kissed her dry, chapped lips.

Suddenly, another bout of sickness wreaked havoc through her stomach. She covered her mouth as he swept her up, running into the bathroom and placed her in front of the toilet where she vomited up her guts.

She groaned, wiping her mouth against her arm. Embarrassment swept through her. She didn't want him to see her like this. Weak, sick, and disgusting.

"Here, I'll help you get cleaned up." He held her by the sink, where she gargled repeatedly. Her golden-olive complexion paled, and her matted curly hair stuck to the back of her neck. She looked awful.

He carried her back to the bed, where she collapsed into the sheets, groaning. Her white camisole and satin cloud shorts were sweat-soaked.

"Do you look this bad when you get sick?" she asked.

"I've never been sick, not once," he winked. *It figured, Mr. Invincible.*

He reached into his pocket and pulled out a scroll tied with a red satin bow, placing the parchment in her hand. She stared at it and began to undo the ends.

"Wait," he raised his palm, stopping her in her tracks. "Don't open that unless there's an emergency."

She rolled her eyes and continued, disregarding his warning. She needed to know what was inside.

"I'm serious," he stopped her again. "And if you must open it, and I pray that you don't, keep the contents to yourself. Don't share it with anyone and don't call or text the information or it risks being compromised."

She nodded slowly, rolling over onto her side. She could barely function in this state. She held the scroll in her palm, staring at it, wondering about the details it contained.

Her vision began to fade and her eyes fluttered closed. A pair of lips hit her cheek. When she opened her eyes again, he was gone.

* * *

DANTE ENTERED the cockpit of his destroyer, pulling his horned battle helmet onto his head. His hands quaked, sweating within the confines of his gloves as he took the control seat and buckled his harness in place. This mission was far too dangerous, so he preferred to travel alone. He refused to risk Autumn and couldn't imagine what would happen to her if she fell into the wrong hands *again*.

The Grand Supreme—sickness wrecked Dante's gut. His fists quaked. Why him?

His chest burned. He hated leaving his wife while she was ill, but he had no other choice. Her father was in very real danger, more danger than he could let her know—lest he cause her more worry in her weakened state and risk her coming along.

Whether he liked him or not, he had to help. *And he most certainly did not care for her father,* his eyes thinned to slits. Not after their interactions on Earth.

The destroyer hovered and rose from the docks in pure silence. All he could hear was the sound of his own breath gently pulling from his throat. As he navigated his way through the clear blue cloudless sky, he admired his home city of Giarldinia for what promised to be the last time.

No, don't think that way, he scolded himself. *You're the Emperor of Nine Hundred and Eighty Skies. You're the mightiest warrior the 24 Universes has ever seen. You're undefeated.* Too bad he couldn't get himself to believe it.

The Grand Supreme was untested in battle and for good reason.

The gem-hued buildings shimmered in the early morning sunlight. He closed his eyes for a long moment, inhaling after taking in the magnificent sight. He'd try to remember his home world this way, always.

When he passed through the rainbow layers of the atmosphere, his ears popped as he ascended higher and higher into the great unknown. Finally, he entered the lonely darkness of deep space. Shadows pulled against his blood-shade armor, cloaking him whole. Coolness settled against his skin.

Surge turned slowly in a cobalt-blue ball beneath his ship. He clicked a few buttons and pulled a few switches, transmitting a silent signal. The forcefield faded his home world to darkness, protecting it from plain sight as he'd done with Earth.

When he turned the ship, the rest of the destroyers were precisely where he instructed them to wait. He zipped through the stars passing them by. They followed him wherever he commanded, navigating his way through the vastness of space.

While he traveled, a great sadness consumed him before his lips flickered into an uncontrollable smile. He burst into laughter on the verge of hysteria. Bloodlust consumed him. Someone was in for a rude awakening.

PART FIVE

Into the Shadows

Fifty-Three

THE TEMPTATION WAS TOO strong as Dante navigated his way through Universe 17 toward Universe 24 where Emperor Izzo resided. He hoped Autumn's father was still alive. There was no telling what type of condition he was living in. Or if Izzo had gotten bored of him, which was always a possibility.

What he did know is that if he didn't bring him back unharmed, Autumn would *never* forgive him.

This was different from stealing a car, murdering a foe, conquering a planet, or abducting her ex. No, he'd messed up countless times before, but this time there was no coming back if he failed.

He'd been traveling for a little over thirty suns and moons according to his calculations. During his voyage, he could only focus on one thought besides keeping Autumn safe and rescuing her father—

Cold-blooded *revenge*.

He itched to repay a favor, one that was long since overdue. It kept him up into the wee hours of the night, kept him focused, kept him obsessed. And thanks to his superior's stupidity, he knew her exact coordinates. *Valdez.*

His fists trembled against the control panel. Try as he might, he couldn't let this one slip.

What she'd done to his wife was unforgivable.

It would take him a few days off course, but the satisfaction he'd enjoy was worth the trouble. She'd never hurt anyone else again, he'd see to that. Autumn would finally be safe from her reign of terror. He grinned a wicked grin.

Deep down he hoped she hadn't opened the parchment he'd given her. She wasn't ready for the contents.

* * *

A FEW SUNS and moons later Dante arrived with his warriors at a substantial emerald planet in the center of Universe 17. Valdez was still present judging by the streaks of exploding fire visible from space ripping in lines through the terrain and the static frequencies.

He instructed his soldiers to wait for him off planet. This was one task he preferred to indulge in alone.

His body boiled with bloodlust as he descended through the viridescent atmosphere. He gripped the steering panel with intense ferocity as he soared through the lime green sky.

He couldn't wait to see Valdez again, couldn't wait to thank her for all she put him through and for the way she made Autumn suffer. His fists clenched against the steering panel.

His destroyer landed amidst a demolished city. Buildings crumbled to the ground, dark smoke churned through the air in thick gusts, and glass crunched beneath the weight of his ship as it settled on the dusty ground.

He unbuckled his harness and stretched his weary limbs. It felt good to finally be free of his traveling constraints. As the door whooshed open, he walked outside, surveying the area. The planet had all the evidence of a sloppy conquering mission. He shook his head in disgust.

Half crumbled buildings heaped in piles of twisted metal, dead bodies laid haphazardly all over the demolished structures, abandoned spacecraft smoked, and screaming persisted in the distance. It was an utterly pathetic sight.

He shook his head. *Tsk, tsk. Where did Valdez learn how to conquer a planet? Obviously, she hadn't been paying attention during training.* What a shame she couldn't get this right.

Suddenly, a shriek erupted louder than all the others combined. He knew the sound of suffering all too well. The cries of panic and despair assaulted his senses. Someone's life was in grave danger.

She must be close. He cracked his crimson-gloved knuckles. *Excellent.*

Dante took flight, traveling above the demolished metropolis, surveying the terrain. He was sure to stay low and quiet so as not to be detected by his former mistress or any of her half-brained posse.

They followed her everywhere; it was such a sickening sight.

He arrived at a hill where he came to a dead stop, lowering himself to the mossy ground, arms and belly first. He slid on his stomach, peeking over the steep rise.

Debris and shattered buildings littered the ground. Thick smog wafted through the chemical-tinged air. Amidst the chaos, Valdez's soldiers kicked around a group of green alien children. Their parents begged and screamed for their lives.

Valdez sat on the edge of a silver wall with her legs crossed swirling a golden goblet of wine in her sadistic palm. She took lingering sips of her beverage as if she was amused by the sight. Half of her mouth curled with cruel satisfaction.

The right side of her face was concealed by a sleek white mask, disguising the parting gift he left her with. He could still recollect the scent of her burning flesh from the ball of fire he tossed against her cheek, crisping her smooth skin.

Her formerly long jade braid was quartered at its length

and pushed behind her ears in wisping strands, the ends frayed. She wore a suit of gilded armor, and her gloves were rainbow crystal encrusted. Her jagged wings twitched high on her back.

Dante perked up and his fingers dug into the dirt as one of her Zexian soldiers aimed his blaster between one of the parent's eyes—or so he assumed based on the way he screamed. His knees buckled beneath his weight. As he went to press the trigger, he soared down with lethal precision and connected his heavy boot with the side of the soldier's face. Bones cracked as his neck turned in an unnatural direction before snapping in half. His head hung limp as his body went airborne and slammed into the dirt in a twisted heap of wings and elongated limbs.

Valdez jumped up from her seat, spilling her wine into the sand. The red droplets faded and evaporated.

Her dirty blue eyes widened as they connected with his before thinning to slits. Her mouth fell slack.

He chuckled, crossing his arms. He shifted his weight from side to side. "What's the matter, surprised to see me?"

She flashed a wicked grin that was only half visible beneath her mask.

After a few moments she said, "So at long last we meet again."

A blaster cocked behind him. The heat from the lethal weapon radiated against his back. In an instant, a ball of crackling fire shot through his palm and singed the soldier to ash.

The remainder of the Zexians stopped in their tracks. As they turned around to flee, Valdez raised a hand, freezing them in place.

"Who are you running from? Him? I don't have room for cowards on my crew."

She raised them into the air, dangling like flies. Their large black eyes widened with terror, their pale-white limbs crunched and splayed before they exploded to dust. Their screams erupted as soon as they disappeared into the afterlife, remaining for a few moments after they were gone. The wind howled, sweeping away their remains. Ashes blew against his armor.

The alien inhabitants watched them, their bodies quivering. Dante removed his horned helmet, placing it in the sand. As he rose, he swept a hand through the chin-length strands of his hair, tousling them. He cocked his head to the side.

"I want to get a clear picture of you as you die. I want to see the light fading from your eyes," he mused. "I'm going to repay every ounce of suffering you've ever caused. I'm going to make you beg for your miserable life, you shrew." He assumed a fighting stance, knees bent, fingers locked in place.

She chuckled, placing a hand over her mouth. She crossed her arms, straightening her neck. "Is that all? You bore me, Dante. I'm sure you used the same little speech on Keyserike before he met his end. Well, it's not going to work on me," her voice fell dead tone. "He was a weakling, and everyone knows it."

She stopped for a second, then continued, "When did you become so high and moral? Like you're not guilty of all the same crimes as we are. Like you're exempt from the pain we've inflicted over the years. Your human filth sure did a number on you for the worst. No matter how hard you pretend, you'll never be—"

"Just shut up and fight me, unless you're afraid I'll win," he smirked. "You claim you're stronger, let's settle this once and for all, unless you're as cowardly as your soldiers. Never once have I seen you train. You sit back and relax while I'm out working my hands raw."

She paused for a long moment before assuming a fighting stance.

Her lips curled. "Very well—have it your way, Great Conqueror."

* * *

AUTUMN COULDN'T BELIEVE she fell for his tricks—again. Dante had managed to leave without her all because she was sick. She could've come along, could've recovered on the ship, or even been part of the negotiations with Emperor Izzo.

Her fists trembled as they connected with a punching bag in the gravity chamber that she pretended was his face. She hit it repeatedly as sweat dripped down her back. She collapsed on the floor out of breath as a dizzy spell overtook her. She fanned her face with her hand. She still didn't feel like herself, not for the last month or so.

It must be the stress of having her dad captured by the Grand Supreme and not being there to see him, and of Dante being so far away again. She hoped he was okay; she couldn't handle losing another parent. Her eyes teared up. At least not yet. No, she had to be more positive.

She was stuck on Surge to worry and watch over the planet. *The empress.* She supposed she had to get to work, although she dreaded doing it alone. She wished Dante and her dad would come home safely, sooner rather than later.

Autumn sighed a long aching sigh as she dug into the skintight pocket of her pants and held the scroll Dante had given her. She fiddled the parchment in her hand, fingers sliding over the red bow. She imagined what it contained. She started opening it again. *No,* she scolded herself, resisting temptation. She promised she would wait and intended to keep her word for everyone's safety.

Fifty-Four

THE BREEZE SWAYED through Dante's chin-length hair as he stared into Valdez's frosty hate-filled eyes. His fingers and entire body tensed as he summed her up, anticipating her first move. Her lips pursed, her dead stare flickering to his. Her mouth twitched beneath her halved mask.

Suddenly, she jumped into the air, flying up, up, up high above the demolished metropolis. He was on her in a heartbeat. The world spun beneath their feet. The golden sunlight illuminated the lime green sky, sparkling against her gilded armor. He raised his fist to strike her in the face.

"Freeze." He was frozen in place, teeth gritted together. His eyes bulged with rage. He struggled to move, twisting and trembling, trying to break free from her telepathic grasp. *Dammit.*

She chuckled, flying up behind him, wrapping her toned arms around his neck. Her gloved talons sank deep into the skin of his throat. She squeezed him with all her might, cutting off his oxygen supply. He gasped, elbowing her once, twice, three times in the gut. Valdez flipped him around and turned him upside down. She charged him into the earth headfirst, and he collided with the terrain sending debris and rubble spraying everywhere.

He rose to his feet and flashed a taunting smile, tucking a fallen strand of hair behind his ear. Dirt tumbled down his armor. "Is that all you've got? If I traveled all the way out here for that cheap trick, I'm rather disappointed."

She gasped as he turned and punched her square in the chin, knocking her veil higher onto her face. He caught a glimpse of the crusty damaged skin he'd given her as a parting gift. She went airborne, landing into a nearby building, crumbling the structure to the ground. He lit a ball of fire in his hand, tossing the flame after her. The sphere ignited, exploding against her fallen body. Embers fluttered to the ground.

As she pushed herself to a shaking stand, he heard the sound of whimpering. Distracted, he stared at the alien family cowering beside the wreckage. The frightened children buried their faces against their parents' arms.

"Everything is going to be okay," he mouthed to them.

When he looked at Valdez again, she'd grown two heads taller over the course of a few seconds. The hard muscles in her legs and arms bulked out sporting pulsating veins. Her neck thickened like a tree trunk. Her voice deepened as she growled, charging at him. The ground vibrated and cracked beneath her monstrous stride.

At the last possible moment, he grabbed her by the arm and sent her flying straight toward a steel wall. She turned on her heel with precision and grace, whipping around, facing him.

"Freeze," she bellowed in a deep unnatural voice. From her tone, she wasn't messing around.

He struggled again to move, trying his best to maneuver his limbs. *Why couldn't he break her hold with as much strength as he possessed?* He had to admit she was a formidable opponent. A wave of sparkling energy shot from her hand, engulfing him whole, rattling him to the core. Waves zapped through his teeth and bones sending him tumbling through the sky. The thick taste of metallic blood filled his mouth as he collided with a building, shattering clear through a glass window.

He pushed himself to a shaking stand, catching his breath in long quaking attempts.

"It didn't have to end this way, Dante," he heard her shout from outside. Her voice echoed through the destroyed metropolis. "If only you had cooperated. You could've had everything you've ever wanted and so much more."

"I already have everything I want," he reassured her. "If you're referring to yourself, don't make me laugh. You disgust me, always have."

He flew outside, passing over the shards of glass and through the demolished window when from out of nowhere her body slammed him against the building, pinning him in place. The breath ripped from his lungs as he stared at her revolting face. Her bloodshot eyes tore through him like sabers. Her pointed teeth gritted.

"I'm serious," her voice caressed him, causing bile to rise from his gut. "I'm not referring to your human or our history. You could've been immortal—a god."

He rolled his eyes. "Why would I want to be immortal? So I could be a slave to the Grand Supreme for all eternity and take orders from the likes of you?" He spit the blood from his mouth, running his tongue against his teeth.

He paused for a moment as a wave of shock and horror simmered through him. His eyes bulged. *Wait, oh no.* "Is Izzo—"

"No," her cracked jade lips curled. "But he will be soon enough, as will I after we receive the missing piece to the puzzle."

She continued, tightening her grasp around his throat. His vision darkened at the corners. "I can't believe how much you sound like Maeve—it's sickening. She was nothing but a sweet little liability. She made you soft and weak like a baby ling suckling from its mother's breast."

His mind scrambled with rage. His molars ground in his mouth.

"Why do you bring her up? Why now?" he choked out. *She never did care for her and made no secret of her feelings.*

"I have a little secret to tell you." She brought her vile lips close to his ear. Her warm breath poured against his skin as he gagged into her hand. "She always trusted me more than anyone else, even more than she trusted you. But I think you already know that. The way she looked up to me, after all, what are big sisters for?" She winked her left eye on the unscathed side of her face. A cruel smile widened across her lips.

He squirmed in her grasp, trying in vain to free himself, but he'd underestimated her strength.

"On that fateful day, she called to check up on me to make sure I was okay—like she tended to do—and to see that you were safe during our mission. I told her yes, I was okay, but that you had been injured in the crossfire. In blind stupidity, she trusted me, and why wouldn't she? I'd never given her a reason not to," she chuckled. "With the help of Keyserike, who had nothing better to do at the time, I lured her off the ship, and guess what happened next?" Valdez pulled a long, pointed arrow out of her gilded armor, twirling it between her fingers. Dante stared on in horror.

She continued. "I'll never forget the look in her eyes as I fatally wounded her and dumped her body in the sector I knew you were working on. The look of, not only shock, but cold-blooded betrayal. She deserved to die. What a weakling. I'll never understand what you saw in her and why you couldn't see the same in me. And when I'm done with you, sweet little Autumn will be my very next kill."

Dante could still feel the pain in his ribs and chest as

Maeve ripped against his skin with the dagger he'd given her to protect herself in a panicked, dying state. The fear and hysteria in her eyes when he discovered her burnt body. His insides quaked with sickness. As he reminisced, Valdez took the arrow between her meaty taloned fingers and twisted the weapon into his gut, cutting him through. He wheezed, doubling over in pain.

He looked up at her slowly, his eyes unwavering. "Is that true? What you said about Maeve?"

"Every word of it."

He took his knee and rammed her in the stomach, sending her sputtering through the air. He flew after her, taking his fists high above his head, striking her and thrusting her into the earth. Rubble crumbled from the fallen buildings as she collided with them.

He flew down after her, his stomach dripping with blood. Dizziness frayed his sight. Valdez scrambled to her feet and raced over to the alien family cowering on the sidelines. They had nowhere to run, nowhere to hide.

She grabbed the youngest by the back of his neck and he screamed, kicking. Dante approached her, fire burning in his palm. His legs straightened. He remained steady and focused.

"If you come any closer. He dies. We both know how weak you've become," her mouth sat crooked on the good side of her face as the child squirmed.

The ball of fire in his hand swelled larger in size. "I'm calling your bluff."

He took a step closer, and she tightened her grasp around the whimpering child, then threw him in front of her like a shield.

"I'm serious," her teeth chattered before her eyes grew wide and desperate. "Wait, please don't. You—you need me. You'll never be able to defeat the Grand Supreme on your own. Trust me, I've thought about it myself many times. We can team up." She paused, her eyes wavering with fear.

"Please, let's join forces. I never ever mentioned what tran-spired between you and Keyserike. I kept your dirty little secret. And Earth—"

"Save yourself the groveling, it's pathetic. We both know you never did me any favors. You only think about yourself. The way you worked me to the bone—you're a monster."

Her face contorted as she raised the child high in the air. Her tattered wings shifted. A ball of fire ripped and swirled from his palm, striking her square in the heart. The wave traveled clear through her body as she slammed into the metal wall. Black blood oozed over her golden armor. Her mouth moved but her whisper grew faint. Her head fell to the side, wings collapsing. The light faded from her eyes.

Dante shuddered, his fingers running over his own injured abdomen. Blood stained his dark-red gloves. He fell to his knees and collapsed before everything went dark.

Fifty-Five

ARMIENTI RACED THROUGH UNIVERSE 17, past twinkling stars and alien planets of the solar system, determined to beat Dante to the Grand Supreme. He'd seen the signal of his brother's destroyer flicker through several sectors before fading into the radar grid. He had to be around here somewhere. *But where?* He hoped that their paths didn't cross again.

It would spell disaster or even death for one or *both* of them.

A price had been placed on his head for treason, but he had plans to negotiate Mr. Ramon's freedom with the Grand Supreme. He was determined to get him back. It was the only way Autumn would forgive him for acting like an idiot and for being such a fool to trust Valdez.

At the time, he was desperate. Desperate to be number one, desperate for his birthright, and desperate for the girl who could change his life.

How he hoped Valdez wasn't there either. He couldn't stand to face her. Shame rattled him to the core. He wished he could withdraw his actions, but he'd dug his own grave. He hated to admit it wasn't the first time he'd gotten himself into trouble.

He shuddered at the recollection of the way he behaved on First. *What was he thinking?* He shouldn't have kissed her. His face and neck warmed at the not-so-distant memory of his lips pressed against hers, and how badly he wished she was his.

Although, since the day he had kissed her, she was all he could think about—no matter how hard he tried to dismiss his feelings for her. She was the first person he thought about in the morning and the last person he thought about before he closed his eyes at night.

His chest hollowed. He needed her in his life—no matter the cost.

Armienti's heart slammed against his ribcage as his ship beeped with approaching vessels on the radar. Anxiety crippled him to the core. His body tensed as he made his way through Universe 17.

He did a double take. Dante's fleet surrounded an alien planet. He slipped his own ship into invisible mode, melding with the stars and hiding the vessel from plain sight. *What were they doing?* He stared at the ships in formation, unmoving. He supposed Dante had gotten greedy and decided to add another planet to his collection on the way to Universe 24. How selfish, when Autumn's father was in danger. It was like him to always want more.

He wasn't surprised. His brother only ever thought about himself.

His mouth curved. This spelled good news he supposed. While Dante was distracted, he'd sweep through and play hero.

Wonderful.

Armienti sped through the end of the universe, making his way through the beginning of Universe 18. This was Dante's loss and his gain; he'd personally see to it. He'd arrive in Universe 24 in ten more suns and moons, rescue her father, then Autumn would have no choice but to love him back and leave Dante. *For good.* Or at least that's how the situation played out in his mind. Hopefully she'd see his true colors. His plan was perfect. His lips curved.

Dante would finally be the one to lose out. He would personally see to his misery. He was unworthy and Armienti would finally be the one to come out triumphant.

* * *

AUTUMN SAT atop Dante's steel throne that belonged to his late father. A red bubbling liquid pulsated through the veins, stemming along the arms and legs of the seat. *What an eyesore.* Her stomach turned as she wondered if the liquid was in fact blood. It was a good possibility, knowing his history.

Eww, gross. A wave of queasiness hit her. She placed a black-gloved hand over her mouth, easing the sensation. She took a few deep controlled breaths.

A heeled go-go boot gently kicked the side of her shoe. Her attention shot over to Leyla who sat next her, brown eyes wide.

"He asked you a question," she whispered. Autumn glanced over at the salt and pepper haired lord down on one knee before the dais. His hazel eyes watched her in silence. He was probably getting a leg cramp from how long she made him wait for an answer.

This meeting sure was boring.

"I'm so sorry," she snapped out of her thoughts. The entire court stared at her waiting for a reply. Even the servants stopped pouring wine. Her mouth grew dry, and her palms sweated in her lap. How she hated this part of being the empress.

"What was the question again?" she asked.

Leyla snorted silently. Her face warmed with embarrassment. She needed to pay better attention. These were her people, and they needed her help.

"Is there any news of the emperor, Your Imperial Majesty?"

Her heart sank in her chest. How she wished she had heard from him. For the time being they weren't communicating for his safety. The scroll burned a hole in her pocket. Curiosity ate away at her. She wished she could open it and read the contents. But she resisted the urge.

"Um, yes," she straightened her spine, holding her head high, desperately trying to recall the lessons she'd learned in speech class and from Dante. Public speaking was the worst.

"He's doing well," she lied through her teeth. "He should be arriving at Universe 24 any day now to recover my father. And then he'll be home in no time at all."

"How do we know he'll be successful in the negotiations?"

"Why wouldn't he?" she countered.

The lord shuddered. Sweat beaded along his blue brow, dripping down his cheeks. "Forgive me, my lady, I meant no disrespect. Nor did I mean to question your answer."

She stared at him, taken aback. He was clearly terrified. At this point she figured Dante would send a fireball his way to send some kind of "message." But instead, she tried a lighter approach.

"Don't let it happen again."

He nodded mechanically and rose to his feet. His legs swayed as he walked back into the crowd.

"Does anyone else require my attention?" She looked around the room, but nobody made a sound other than a cough and a sniff.

"Very well then." She rose to her feet with Leyla, and they made their way out of the throne room. Everyone fell into bows. She was tempted to make a run for it.

Finally, they were free from the hot seat.

Leyla pulled her aside, lowering her voice. "How many times are we going to tell them that before they realize something is wrong. He would've reached out by now, don't you think?"

"Not this time," Autumn said. This time everything felt different. She'd been having dreams of Dante where he came to visit her as a ghost in the dead of night. He hovered over her while she slept, features wisping, followed by fire raining from the sky. But she didn't dare tell Leyla. She didn't dare tell anyone.

She took her sister by the hands and pushed out the most convincing smile she could muster. After all, she was the empress and it was her job to keep everyone safe and calm. Her lies hurt more than anything.

"I promise everything is going to be fine."

Fifty-Six

DANTE SAUNTERED around the twin watering holes as Autumn skipped along the gray rubbly ground. The sky twinkled with billions of stars. The pale crescent moon shimmered over the town of Monroe, illuminating the trees and structures. Long shadows danced across the green. How grateful he was that the phase wasn't full. He didn't want to risk frightening her with his transformation. One he never enjoyed and one he couldn't control.

Did she know the truth about him? No, she couldn't. He didn't suspect she did. She was innocent and trusting.

Suddenly, she quickened her pace and his heart leapt to his throat as she approached a crater he'd created out of pure anger—

Anger he couldn't be closer to her. Why was he always so quick to snap? It was something he needed to work on.

Fearing for her safety, he raced after her, sweeping her into his arms. She giggled and his insides smoldered. It hurt to be around her. Deep down he knew he'd wind up hurting her even if he didn't mean to.

"Thanks, I missed that," she pointed to the damage on the ground as he placed her back onto her delicate feet. She was so sweet and helpless and beautiful all at the same time.

He ran a hand through the hair of his human disguise. "Not a problem."

She hugged him, burying her soft cheek against his chest. His body grew rigid. Nobody had ever hugged him like this before. Nobody had ever hugged him, period. Not since Maeve.

A star skipped across the sky; she smiled and pointed at the stream of light, following it with her large gray eyes.

She tilted her head to the side, her dark curls falling over her shoulder. She stared up at him with her mesmerizing moonlit eyes. "You have to make a wish."

"A wish? But why?" He asked.

She snorted. "They don't have stars where you're from? Or wishes?"

He went dead silent, and she shook her head. "I'm just kidding. I'm sorry. I'm surprised you haven't heard of this before."

He shrugged. "No, I haven't, but I'll make a wish."

It sounded simple enough to him.

"I made mine already," she twined her fingers in his. "Make sure you keep it a secret or it won't come true."

He quirked a brow. "Okay, I'll never tell a soul."

He inhaled, holding her close to his body. He could feel her heartbeat quicken as he leaned over and rested his chin on her soft curls. He made a wish like she asked. Just one.

He wished Maeve would forgive him, because although he loved her and always would, he loved Autumn more.

* * *

BRIGHT ORANGE LIGHTS played off Dante's eyelids as they fluttered open slowly. He squinted and tensed, as his vision cleared. He surveyed his surroundings. The room was dark. Cracks spanned along the walls and floor. A sliver of light from the setting sun shone through the long, fractured windows.

Where was he? He tried to sit up, but a sharp pain crashed through his abdomen, causing him to grit his teeth. Bandages were wrapped tightly around his stomach. He made a fist, laying back down on the makeshift cot, tensing his fingers against the fabric. He groaned.

He couldn't believe the damage one of Valdez's arrows had inflicted. It must've been laced with acid.

He had to get out of there.

Although Valdez would never pose a problem to anyone ever again, he needed to rescue Autumn's father. She was counting on him.

How he missed her. He'd really messed up, but the temptation was too strong. He didn't regret his decision to take Valdez out. She more than deserved her end but especially so after what she confessed. She was pure evil, murdering her own flesh and blood and making him feel responsible for her sister's death for all these years. Maeve deserved better and so did he.

Autumn was probably worried sick about him. He hoped her father was still alive or else she'd never forgive him.

He could never look her in the eyes again. There'd be no redeeming himself.

Dante did a double take, snapping himself from his panicked thoughts as an alien woman entered the room. Her green skin shimmered in the setting sun. Her long dark hair was secured in a low neat ponytail.

He tried to sit up again, but she raised her palm, willing him to stay in bed. "Please don't get up, you're injured. It took hours to dislodge the arrow and stop the bleeding."

His hand covered his stomach; the arrow had indeed been removed. He recognized her as the mother inhabitant from earlier, trying in vain to protect her helpless children. She was gentle and soft spoken like a whisper floating on a breeze. She moved like grace itself in a simple floor-length gray smock. She appeared to float along the stone floor with each step she took.

She pulled up a chair beside him, holding a damp cloth in her hand. She blotted it along his forehead.

"Do you know who I am?" he asked.

She stopped, her dark brown eyes flickering towards him with uncertainty. "Of course I do. Everyone knows who you are, Dante the Great Conqueror."

"Then why are you helping me?" His voice was dry and hoarse as he assessed her from a lying position. "Aren't you afraid of me like everyone else?"

She squeezed the water from the cloth in her hands into a metal bucket on the floor. Droplets trickled down the sides. "Yes, of course I am, but you looked like you needed help. And I wanted to thank you for saving me and my family from that monster." Tears welled in the corners of her dark brown eyes, but she blinked them away.

"How do you know I'm not a monster too?" He tilted his head toward her, straightening his features. "How do you know I won't do the same to you once I recover?"

"I think it's always a possibility," she glanced at her small hands. "But I think you would've done it by now. I think you're different than she was, better somehow."

A fair assumption, he watched her in silence.

He sat up in bed and sighed. "You don't have to worry, no harm will come to you or your family, at least not while I'm around. You have my word. Do you have a name?"

"Luz," she said quietly.

"Well, Luz, thank you for your hospitality, but I must be leaving."

He slid his legs to the side of the bunk and every single muscle in his body screamed in agony. Cold sweat beaded against his brow as he came to an unsteady stand. He struggled to breathe. Nausea racked his stomach. He had to get out of there, had to continue his mission. He couldn't let his soldiers see him this way, weak and pathetic. Victorious but at the same time defeated.

Autumn was counting on him to come through for her.

As he went to walk, his knees buckled beneath his weight, and he stumbled. *Drat*, he was still too drained to go anywhere in this condition.

Luz shot to her feet, ambling after him. "Here, let me help you, please."

She wrapped his arm over her shoulder and propped him up. His face heated, *how humiliating*. He'd never taken such a beating in his life. But he accepted her assistance nonetheless, despite his panic as the time he had remaining dwindled.

They made their way together in slow steady steps. His legs wavered so much he could scarcely stand. Valdez had really done a number on him.

* * *

WHEN THEY ARRIVED OUTSIDE, dark smoke churned through the crisp night air. A rich burning scent drifted every-where. Demolished buildings laid to rest under the black starry sky. Not a soul could be seen anywhere. His eyes drew to Valdez's dead body, propped up against the steel wall. Shadows dulled her glorious golden armor. Her head hung forward; her mask still affixed to the left side of her face. Her choppy hair frayed in strands.

Vermin festered through the hole in her chest, squeaking and biting away at her remains. Who would've thought that not so long before she was the second mightiest warrior in the universes; a title that would fall upon him with her gone. His lips flickered with self-satisfaction as he admired his handi-work before he winced.

She deserved every bit of pain she experienced and so

much worse. One issue remained. He couldn't stop dwelling on it. Valdez had mentioned immortality for not only herself but the Grand Supreme. It was clear she wasn't immortal, but was he? Dante shivered with fear.

"Which way is your ship?" Luz glanced at him.

He hesitated, body shaking. His mind spun with a better idea than going straight to his destroyer. Valdez's ship had to be nearby. He could take her weapons and supplies and tactical plans. She no longer needed them where she'd gone.

Dante scanned the area for any sign of the vessel. Valdez wasn't known for traveling light. She always made a dramatic entrance.

In the distance he spied one of her luxury cruisers.

Excellent, his face lifted.

As he approached, his chest sank as another ship crash-landed through the city. The vessel was mighty in size, causing debris to swirl in thick heavy puffs. From where he stood, the origin was unrecognizable.

Please no, he clung to Luz for support. He was in no condition for another fight. He could barely walk let alone defend himself.

He was in a world of trouble.

Fifty-Seven

RONAN SAT in the cockpit of his destroyer as he zipped through the endless stars with Sean by his side. His boyfriend was still shaken up, and for good reason, unable to sleep for the last few suns and moons. The call with one of the Grand Supreme's lackeys was way too close for comfort, and Mr. Ramon was missing—

Because of him.

How could he stand to look her in the face again? He'd let Autumn down on so many different levels. *He was a complete and total failure.*

Guilt wracked his twisting insides as they entered Universe 13, Sector 1, right on schedule. They approached Surge at a rapid speed. When they arrived, the planet was hidden from plain sight, thanks to an invisible forcefield. After he sent a silent signal from the cockpit of his ship that he was waiting, a small circular pathway cleared for him to enter. The planet underneath glimmered the brilliant shade of cobalt blue.

Although he was home and should be happy to be here with Sean after all this time, he felt responsible for the kidnapping.

What was wrong with him? How could he not recognize his own brother? What an idiot he was. And worst of all, Armienti was headed to Universe 24 to sort matters out.

Whatever that meant.

He hoped he was okay and wouldn't get himself into any more trouble, or worse, *killed.*

They descended through the rainbow atmosphere, shooting through the vibrant layers of sky. Giarldinia was as he remembered it: brilliant, robust, and full of life.

His stomach toppled as he lowered the destroyer onto the rooftop landing pad marked with a simple white X.

In a matter of minutes, he'd have to face his empress. The ship stirred before going quiet and he turned to Sean who stared out the window eyes wide.

"This is where you live?" Sean turned to him and asked.

"Yes," he nodded slowly. "But before I give you a tour of the grounds, I have to speak with the empress about what happened."

How he dreaded the conversation. He cringed. Autumn was going to be so furious with him.

Sean's mouth twisted to the side. Clearly, he sensed the severity of the situation. He didn't mean to worry him.

Ronan unclicked his harness and Sean followed suit. They walked onto the granulated rooftop. The golden rays of the sun warmed his skin through his bodysuit. He inhaled the rich floral scent. There was no place like home.

"This is amazing," Sean's brown eyes sparkled as he admired the massive cityscape. "I want to take a second semester off college so I can stay a bit longer. If that's okay?" He squeezed his hand. His reddish-brown hair brushed against his cheeks.

"Sounds good," his mouth curved into a deceptive smile although he was a nervous wreck. His hands perspired inside his gloves. All he could focus on was how Autumn would react.

* * *

THEY ENTERED THE THRONE ROOM, and nobody was there to greet them. *Unsurprising.* The hairs on the back of his neck rose. He was in for a shitstorm no doubt.

A pair of footsteps came up behind him. He whirled around. An obsidian clothed guard stood there with his blaster cocked in his hands. Sean clung to Ronan's arm for dear life as he fell into a bow.

"The empress will see you in the gravity chamber, Your Imperial Highness," he said in the monotone voice the guards of the palace tended to have. They were like robots. He rolled his eyes.

Fine.

Why there? He wondered, but he followed the guard nonetheless. Was Autumn going to fight him? Was she going to try to kick his ass?

When they arrived, the steel door of the gravity chamber was sealed airtight. A training session was in progress.

He gulped and raised his fist to the door and knocked a few times. The commotion inside stopped followed by a high-pitched hum cutting the gravity off.

He braced himself for impact.

A pair of heeled boots stomped against the floor, and he blocked Sean with his body just in case. All his boyfriend could do was watch in silence.

The door slid open, and Leyla stood there with her hand resting on her hip. She rasped, catching her breath. The sun from the skylight sparkled along the fibers of her hot-pink bodysuit. Her long wavy hair was bound in a high ponytail.

He bit his cheeks. *Was she actually training for the first time in her life? It appeared so.*

"You'd better wipe that smug smile off your face this instant, Ronan Martyne." She slammed her boot against the ground. "Where have you been?" Her shrill voice echoed through the hallway. The guard who accompanied them took two steps in retreat, quivering against the wall. The guards lined up on either side of the door followed suit. *What a loudmouth.*

She continued. "You sneak off like a bandit in the night and tell nobody where you're going, and I have to find out from a secondary source. *What* were you thinking? And somehow in the process you managed to get Autumn's father kidnapped. Absolutely pathetic. I could've done a better job. And by the way, everyone in the universes knows what happened to him and that it's all your fault," she stretched her neck, peeking behind him. "Who the heck is this? Your lover boy? Unfreakingbelievable."

Like brother, like sister. He shuddered to think how Dante would react if Leyla was this pissed. It would be ten times worse to face him.

Ronan stared at her in silence, feeling more foolish than he'd ever felt in his life. He'd really messed up this time.

Leyla's brown eyes thinned to slits, as she leaned against the doorframe. "You're lucky I didn't speak in human so your boyfriend could understand. Autumn and I have been practicing," she said matter-of-factly.

"Leyla, stop," Autumn walked up behind her wiping the sweat from her brow against her arm. She appeared thinner than usual. Her full rosy cheeks became gaunt and worry lines crept across her forehead. Leyla stood to the side, arms crossed, glowering at Ronan.

"I'm so sorry, Autumn, truly I am. I never meant—"

"I know; accidents happen, and I don't blame you for this. No matter what I do, I'll always be a target because of who I'm married to," she stared at him, her gray eyes becoming glassy with impending tears. He'd never been so sorry in his life. She sniffed. "Thank you for bringing everyone back home safely though. I really appreciate your effort after the mess Dante made." She shook her head.

She turned to walk back into the chamber, and he grabbed her hand, stopping her in her tracks. "How can I make things right? Should I go to Universe 24? Your wish is my comm—"

Autumn folded her arms, her soft features straightening. "There's no need, Dante is already on his way to negotiate."

"And she hasn't heard from him since," Leyla hissed in a lowered voice. "Nobody has. You've done enough damage, cousin."

His stomach twisted and turned with dread, but he figured he needed to tell everyone one other detail regardless of their reaction.

"Armienti is also on his way to Universe 24 to speak with the Grand Supreme," he blurted.

Autumn's jaw lowered; her gray eyes widened. "What? Are you serious? When did you see him?"

"Not too long ago," he paused for a moment. "He's trying to make things up to you. He's so very sorry about what transpired."

After he spoke, Autumn's knees buckled beneath her weight. He rushed over and caught her before her backside hit the ground. Leyla knelt and held her in her arms.

Autumn sighed. "Sorry, I haven't been feeling well and I haven't been sleeping much either. I'm too stressed out. Training is the only thing that relaxes me anymore. Reading doesn't even help. All I want is for my dad and Dante to come home safely."

Sean knelt as well. Leyla's eyes flickered to him, and Autumn flashed him a small smile. "I remember you from the Castle, welcome," she extended a hand. "I'm Autumn, the empress of Universe 13."

"My name is Sean. Thank you. It's nice to meet you. I remember you too." He stuttered as he shook her hand in a form of human greeting. They helped her back to a stand and she brushed her palms along her black spandex uniform.

"How can you be the empress if you're a human like me?"

She tilted her head to the side. "It's a long story for another time."

She turned toward Ronan and sighed. "I can't say that I'm happy about this. To be honest I'm angrier than ever," her fists tightened. Ronan could sense her change of energy zap through the air. It was staticky, frustrated, and rageful. But she stayed calm and poised on the outside, maintaining perfect composure. Her face remained painfully neutral. "Regardless of what's happened, we're family now, and family sticks together no matter what. I need you here with me, especially now."

Ronan glanced to the side before looking her in the eyes. He was determined to make things right. "I won't let you down again."

She leaned against the doorframe. "I know I can count on you."

Fifty-Eight

DANTE'S HEART raced as Luz helped him walk through the yard. He limped with one hand nursing his injured stomach, the other wrapped over her shoulder. He clung to her for dear life. Every pore on his body broke out in a cold sweat.

The foreign vessel sat in the distance. He struggled to identify its origin through the buildings and debris. He stopped in his tracks as he passed Valdez's corpse. It lay rotting against the wall. *Good riddance*, he spit on the ground. The universes would be better off without her. She'd caused too much destruction.

As he went to climb the divider with Luz, several blasters cocked, emitting a high-pitched frequency. He turned around scarcely able to catch his breath. He crouched hunched over with his hand on his stomach. Pain radiated through his torso.

"Emperor Dante, is that you?" a familiar slobbery voice asked. *Oh no, please not him,* he begged the gods above. *Anyone but him.* He couldn't bear the humiliation.

He tilted his head up slightly and Luz stood behind him, cowering.

"Emperor Brumha, I presume." His legs gave out and he

rested his head back against the wall. His body broke out in a cold nauseous sweat.

Emperor Brumha approached him, arms folded. The Zambarian soldiers remained in formation. His eyes gravitated between him and Valdez's deceased form. Drool dribbled down his pronounced chin.

Dante made a face against his will.

"We received an SOS signal from outer space, and I decided to investigate. Is this your handiwork, Martyne?" He pointed to the city smoking in the background. Screams and cries echoed through the rubble.

He shook his head. "Not this time."

The emperor examined him. "You're bleeding."

"You're an observant one, aren't you?" Embarrassment rattled through him as he pressed his hand against his stomach. Wetness stained his red glove. He was indeed bleeding again.

"You've been a nuisance for many years around the universes. Stealing worlds and enslaving entire civilizations to meet your ends. I know you have your orders, but it's still despicable."

He glanced to the side. Sometimes the truth was hard to swallow. "Tell me something I don't already know. You're boring me." He yawned, then winced.

"And you're still defiant even while knocking on death's door." A drop of saliva rolled down his chin. Dante couldn't handle any more of this. How disgusting. Was this the last sight he would ever hope to see?

"If you've come to kill me, just get it over with already. What are you waiting for? I'm tired of this conversation—but please let her go." He gestured to Luz who shuddered so hard her teeth chattered. He pitied her.

"I could waste you here and now, put an end to your reign of terror. You have zero respect for others. You come into Universe 18 demanding my fleet and threatening to invade if I don't comply. What gives you the right?" He cocked a brow.

Dante glowered with what little strength he had left. "I think you're a pushover."

"I didn't want to embarrass you in front of your bride."

He stared at him in silence.

The emperor continued, "You didn't even bother to invite me to your wedding. I guess my invitation was lost in transmission. And you dissolved our royal alliance over a hybrid. My brother is still upset—"

"My sister's happiness is more important than your brother's feelings. He'll get over it."

Brumha went quiet. His mouth fell into a tight flat line.

Dante closed his eyes, leaning his head against the wall. He focused on the sound of his breath and visualized Autumn. Her rosy cheeks, her smiling face, the warmth of her embrace and the light in her eyes. How he loved her his heart ached.

He wondered what she was doing, and if she was thinking of him. He hoped she hadn't opened the scroll yet. She was the one good thing to ever happen to him. At that moment, he died inside. He'd never see her again.

"If you're looking to hear me beg for my life, I won't give you the satisfaction, neither will I issue an apology."

When he opened his eyes again, Emperor Brumha stood right over him. He supposed he wanted to make his death up close and personal. After all, the bragging rights would be his forever. Everyone would want to know how he killed him. His death would be legendary.

The emperor crouched down, staring him in the eyes. His silver skin sparkled in the firelight. Stars glittered through the smoke churning in the sky.

"What if I choose to believe you? That you didn't create this mess and it was all Valdez's fault." His eyes drifted to her sunken form.

Dante stuttered. "I—"

"Regardless of what you've done and the endless sins you've committed, you're an impressive warrior, and it would be a shame to lose you. I've always admired you, even now staring death in the eyes. I know there's only one logical reason you'd be out here. I heard all about the unfortunate series of events."

Dante didn't know what to say. His vision faded black in the corners. His entire body trembled before he succumbed to the darkness again. All he could see this time were stars swirling from space and Autumn's gray eyes staring back at him.

Fifty-Nine

AUTUMN SHOT up from her bed in the dead of night, sweat soaking her plain white cotton cami and satin cloud shorts. Her long, coiled hair matted to the back of her neck. She inhaled and exhaled, followed by a dizzy spell. Her heart raced as she jumped to the floor and sped to the bathroom, vomiting up her guts into the toilet. She knelt, resting her head against her arm, laying along the cool metal bowl.

Something was wrong; she could feel it deep in her bones. Dante was in trouble, and her dad—she hadn't heard from either of them in months. Every time she was tempted to text Dante on his communicator, she stopped herself for his safety.

Leyla came sprinting into the room, her features drawn and solemn. Mr. Hiss trotted after her. He nuzzled her ribs with his wet velvet nose, before sitting in her lap, purring. His hot-pink and black striped tail swayed against her leg.

"I shouldn't have let him go alone. I should've insisted on coming with him," she groaned before flushing the toilet. The contents swirled and disappeared. *Why did she have to be sick on his departure date? Life wasn't fair.*

Leyla knelt beside her, pressing the back of her hand to

her forehead. "You don't look so good—you feel warm. You need to rest. You've been pushing yourself too hard."

Leyla helped her to a trembling stand, and she walked over to the sink to gargle and brush her teeth before climbing back into the warmth and comfort of her bed. Aircraft zipped and twinkled through the city, their lights sparkling along the glass of her French doors leading to the balcony.

Leyla sat cross-legged beside her on the floor. She'd been sleeping on the couch for weeks, although she insisted it wasn't necessary. Mr. Hiss climbed onto the covers rolling against her side.

"I know the wait has been long, but we need you here. I need you, Autumn," she squeezed her hand. "I'm sure my brother is okay. He knows what he's doing, and he always has a plan to succeed. I know your father is okay as well, so please don't worry. Everything is going to work out."

"I hope so," Autumn yawned, her eyes fluttering closed before staring back at Leyla through the darkness.

Her sister's large brown eyes widened. Her pink lips twisted to the side. "If anything, I'm worried for Armienti. I mean, what is he thinking, trying to play the hero after what he did to you?"

Autumn gulped. She was officially going to be awake all night. *What was he thinking? Was he going to Universe 24 to try to win her over? Did he think if he rescued her father, she'd choose him over Dante?* She couldn't help but dwell on the gory details of their last conversation.

He wanted her by his side more than anything, to be his empress.

Another bout of sickness rattled through her, but she managed to will the sensation away. *Great, now she had to worry about him too.*

* * *

ARMIENTI'S SPACECRAFT rattled with an SOS signal that he promptly ignored. As soon as the frequency started bleeping through the cabin, he hit the silencer on the control panel. His lips flickered with amusement. The message emitted from the planet Dante occupied. He wondered if he'd gotten himself into some kind of trouble.

What a shame that would be if he died. It would serve him right.

He shrugged, biting back a smile. How he hoped so. If that was the case, then it was his lucky day. He'd be the one to retrieve Mr. Ramon and return home victorious. He'd be the hero in her eyes, and she'd have no choice but to love him back. *How he desired her.*

He touched his navy-gloved fingers to his lips; he wanted her more than life itself. If only he could stop screwing up. If only he could get this right, for the first time in his life.

He deserved her more.

Stars flashed across the glass of his vessel as he entered Universe 23. It wouldn't be long. He'd go straight to the Palace of Despair and request an audience with the Grand Supreme.

He'd only been this far out in space a handful of times, and he'd been to the palace maybe once—if he remembered correctly.

One time was all he needed to forge a relationship. The Grand Supreme couldn't be as bad as everyone claimed. Could he? A hard lump formed in his throat.

Poor Dante was forced to serve out his formative years in this miserable place. For a fleeting moment he pitied him, but then he came to his senses.

His brother always won, but not this time. This time he was determined to come out on top no matter the cost.

Sixty

IS *this what death felt like?* Dante wondered. At this point, he'd rather be dead. The embarrassment he'd suffered thus far had been indescribable. Of all the species to discover his defeat, why did it have to be the Zambarians? He shuddered with shame.

Is this what it felt like to be weak like everyone else? To be completely and utterly average? To be helpless?

His eyes flitted open and an oxygen mask was attached to his face, wrapping around the back of his head. A cool blue liquid encased his body whole. His hand hovered over his abdomen. The puncture wound had healed. A smile crossed his mouth that instantly flattened when his eyes connected with Emperor Brumha's, who stared back at him through the other side of the glass.

He was on display for all to see. Medics scurried in the background, monitoring his vitals.

Brumha's arms crossed as he leaned against a steel table in the medical bay. He sighed through his mask. *Dammit.*

Dante could only imagine what he'd ask of him for this favor. He owed him his life.

The liquid began to drain, although he wished he could stay in the tank forever to avoid having a conversation with his inferior.

He glanced down, he was naked to boot. As he climbed out, his feet collided with the smooth metallic tiled floor. Emperor Brumha ambled over and handed him a white fluffy towel, which he ran over his body before wrapping it around his waist.

He crossed his arms, staring back at him.

"You look well," the emperor spittled as he spoke. *Why did he have to be so gross?*

Dante remained silent, regarding him.

"I think a thank you is in order. While you were out, I carried you here myself," the emperor's chest puffed.

He scowled. "A thank you? I don't think so. I defeated Valdez with my bare hands. I watched the hellfire fade from her eyes. It's not like I lost the fight against her. She nicked me. I would've recovered eventually without your help," he lied through his teeth. Dante had been knocking at death's door. It was the worst feeling he'd ever experienced in his life, besides being separated from his wife.

Brumha shrugged. His snow-white hair fell over the silver points of his ears in wisps. "Believe whatever you want to believe, emperor. You're lucky I found you when I did. Any longer and you'd be hunched against the wall beside your superior with insects and vermin devouring your remains."

"Where's the inhabitant I was with?" His fist shook.

"She and her family are being taken care of. You'll see her in due time."

His mouth flattened. "Where's my armor?" He scanned the room. Having made a full recovery, he needed to search Valdez's ship for supplies before going on his way. Universe 24 promised to be a treacherous journey.

Brumha walked to the opposite side of the room and

grabbed a pile of blues. He handed them to Dante, who made a face he couldn't control.

"Don't think for one second that I'll be wearing your Zambarian garb. Where's my handcrafted armor? Give it to me at once. I need to be on my way."

"It had to be destroyed in the process of stripping you. The material was pretty far gone and had no hope of being repaired." Emperor Brumha stared at his navy-gloved hands.

Great, just great. He sighed a long, agonizing sigh. He had no choice but to comply. He'd failed to pack a second set of armor. It was either wear this foreign uniform or travel in the nude. He mumbled obscenities beneath the warmth of his breath. He was all out of options.

Dante grabbed the pile of clothing from the emperor's hands and began to dress himself, pulling on his navy-blue bodysuit, gloves, and knee-high boots. A circular emblem of silver snowflakes and mountains sat over his right breast. It didn't so much matter what he was wearing, he supposed. But this wasn't the ensemble he envisioned murdering the Grand Supreme in. He wanted to wear the armor from his house. So he'd never forget it was he who had defeated him and broken the four-hundred-year treaty.

In the meantime, he needed to rescue his wife's father and get home to her. His entire body ached for her presence.

Dante smoothed a navy-gloved hand through his midnight hair. He brushed past Emperor Brumha and didn't utter a word.

Emperor Brumha folded his arms, head held high. "My fleet."

Dante stopped dead in his tracks, his fists clenched at his sides as he turned around. "What about your fleet?" His interest piqued, but he tried his best to hide it.

"I know you're on a rescue mission to the furthest universe on the map. I'm sure you could use some help. The Grand Supreme—"

Dante turned again to leave. "You know nothing of him. You haven't seen the half of it, so don't pretend for a second that you have," he paused. "I could kill you right here and now and take your ships from you. I don't need your permission to command your fleet."

"Even still, I offer you my hand, and you don't have an ounce of gratitude in your body. It's not a sign of weakness to ask for help. We could all use help sometimes."

He sighed and turned back around, folding his arms. Brumha was right, he could use all the help he could get, although he refused to admit it aloud. He couldn't believe he was going through with his ridiculous offer.

"Fine, what do you have in mind?" he finally asked.

"I propose an exchange," the emperor's silver cheeks lifted.

He cocked his head to the side. "My sister is off limits as I indicated earlier—"

"I was thinking more along the lines of becoming allies or friends."

Dante's jaw dropped, his mind spinning in circles. He didn't have time for this nonsense. Autumn's father was waiting. He hoped he was still alive, or he'd never be able to face her again.

"You want to be my friend? But why? Why would you want to be friends with someone like me? Don't you know the horrible things that I've done throughout the years? I'm a monster."

"I'm well aware," Emperor Brumha smoothed his hands against his velvet white cape. "Like I said, I've always admired you, Dante. You always made the best out of a bad situation that was out of your control. Nobody is perfect, but you handled yourself so well. We're both different in our own ways, and I feel we have so much to learn from one another."

He turned on his heel and left the medical bay. "I'll think about it." Was all he said.

Deep down he was jumping for joy. Nobody had ever wanted to be his friend before. And as strange as the emperor was, he wanted to take him up on his offer. He'd always wondered what it would be like to have a friend.

Sixty-One

AS ARMIENTI APPROACHED planet One in the beginning of Universe 24, his stomach fastened itself into a hard knot. The stars ended and darkness followed from there on out, consuming his ship in shadows. He shivered, rubbing his hands against his arms. *What was he in for? He didn't remember Universe 24 being this cold.*

The brief glacial spell was followed by an intense sweltering heat. Four suns surrounded the gigantic lush green planet. He descended through the rainbow atmosphere at top speed before soaring through the emerald sky and landing in a tangle of jungle weeds.

He sat for a moment in silence, listening to the sound of his own heartbeat. The ship stilled. He had to get this right. There was no room for error.

He only had one chance to succeed or *die*. Autumn was worth the risk and so much more.

His fingers slid over his harness, unbuckling his restraints. He came to a stand.

He planned to travel to the Palace of Despair and request an audience with the Grand Supreme. It was there he'd make his case for Autumn's father's freedom.

Everything would be perfect, or at least he assured himself.

As the door of his vessel opened, he squinted as the rays from the suns shone into his eyes. He didn't remember planet One being this bright. He didn't remember any of this. *Had he ever been here, or was it a place that'd only existed in his nightmares?*

He inhaled, but as soon as the oxygen entered his lungs a wave of sickness wracked his insides. Armienti fell onto his knees and threw up in the mud. The putrid smell of rotting corpses and warm blood filled the air. Displaced whispers of laughter swept through the tangle of swaying trees. Even the foliage mocked him.

He pushed himself to a stand. *Not a problem*, he assured himself. He went back inside and grabbed his helmet, placing it onto his head, tucking his golden hair away. He regulated the oxygen levels and blocked out the scent of death. *Thank goodness.*

These disgusting cannibals wouldn't stop him from completing his mission.

Sweat stained his back and pits as he made his way through the jungle one pace at a time. He stepped over the occasional half-eaten body and decapitated head, but he didn't let fear stop him. Nothing could stop him.

Autumn was counting on him. The fear of losing her again kept him motivated like no other.

In the distance sat the monstrous palace that nobody dared enter. Those who ventured inside came out *different.* They were never the same again.

The Palace of Despair was what nightmares were made of. They lived there but never escaped.

* * *

WHEN DANTE STEPPED out of Emperor Brumha's ship, the sun rose in the sky. Pink and golden rays of twilight sparkled over the metropolis ruins. Valdez had done a number on this planet. Her handiwork made his molars clench. He was frustrated he was left to clean up another one of her messes.

Fortunately, it was for the last time.

When he passed through a formation of Zambarian soldiers who cleared the way for him, he spotted Luz standing with her family. Her children rough-housed and played, giggling in the morning light.

Her eyes lit up when she beheld him, and she approached him one graceful step at a time. Her light-gray tunic swept across the rubble ground. The pointed tips of her ears peaked from beneath her dark cascading hair.

"I'm glad to see you're doing well," her eyes brightened like two shooting stars. A cordial smile flashed across her green lips. "The gods have been kind."

"They have," he admitted, staring down at her a foot below his chin. "But I must be on my way. My wife is counting on me."

"Wait," she dug deep inside her pocket and pulled out two blue metal vials of liquid that glittered in her hand. She placed them in his palm.

He scanned the containers. "What are these?"

"It's what she was after. I discovered them on her person. It's liquid from our sacred stream—she drained the contents for her own selfish gain."

"Immortality?" He recalled Valdez's words to him, his eyes widened with fascination as he examined the bottles.

"No. Instant rejuvenation. You had one life—now you have two."

Dante placed the containers into the pocket of his Zambarian uniform. "Thank you."

She bowed and returned to her family. He made a mental note to send reinforcements to help rebuild the planet once this ordeal was done and over with. It was the least he could do.

He stood there for a moment in disbelief he was thinking about helping someone other than himself with no gain involved. *What was happening to him?* He truly was soft. He must've been closer to death than he thought. Or else, Autumn had rubbed off on him.

For better or for worse. His lips curved then flattened. How he missed her.

He took flight, soaring over the ruins. Wind whipped through the strands of his raven hair. A glimmer of obsidian caught his attention in the distance. The arrogant murderess didn't bother to conceal her own ship. His lips flickered with amusement. What a fool.

Dante descended from the sky feet first, landing on the roof of the vessel. Taking his fist, he struck the top of the angular spacecraft creating a large enough crater to climb through.

He lowered himself inside and scanned his surroundings. All was still and quiet. Valdez's Zexian crew must've made a run for it after her demise. All that remained of them was tattered uniforms and half-melted helmets. Freeze-dried food crumbled across the silver metallic tiles of the floor.

He sauntered through the long hollow stretch of steel. The lights flickered above his head as if her ship was somehow drained of its power. His eyes rolled at the makeshift throne and dais she'd erected. *It was so like her to create something that ridiculous to stroke her own ego.*

When he went to pass through the room, his navy boot collided with a projector unit on the floor. A hologram swirled before his eyes of Autumn being dragged inside by soldiers and thrown before Valdez's gilded boots when she was first kidnapped from Surge and transported to Planet First. The fear in her eyes, combined with her weakened state, was more than he could bear. He should've known better. He should've been there to protect her. But he failed, all because he was scared.

He wouldn't fail her again.

His blood boiled with rage as he witnessed the abuse she suffered first-hand. A shadow of gold crossed the hologram. Armienti stood in the corner and made nothing but pathetic excuses, trying to weasel his way out of the situation.

When he found him, he was as good as dead. He closed his eyes, envisioning punching him in his pretty face. But more so Dante was frustrated because at one point in time, he behaved like Valdez. He never wanted to act like her again. He turned off the projector, shaking with fury, and continued on his way to the control room. He didn't have time to waste.

Dante arrived at the cockpit, searching for signs of military secrets and blueprints for weapons. They had to be around here somewhere. He hit gauges, buttons, and switches but to no avail. He swept the room, probing through crevices and pockets in the ceiling. He lifted tiles from the floor, peeking underneath.

Where could the information be? It had to be around here somewhere.

Still furious from his earlier discovery, he slammed his knuckles into the back of the pilot's seat. The arm bent, colliding with the dashboard and turning on a radar. A drawer opened, and out popped a series of silver crystal data chips. His mouth flickered, then coiled as he palmed what he was looking for, placing the chips in his pocket. It was his lucky day.

Excellent, he rubbed his hands together.

In a heartbeat, his excitement shifted. A wave of pure panic whipped through his body. His eyes widened, limbs going numb. *No, no, no, it couldn't be.* Dizziness overtook him. Sweat stained his brow.

A radar flashed displaying vessels shifting from invisible mode, swarming together like insects. Thousands upon thousands of ships gathered in the lower universes, surrounding his home planet. A massive ship, sweeping shadows through the galaxy, led the way.

Universe 13 was under attack. The Grand Supreme had outsmarted him.

"You fell for our little diversion, foolish emperor," the heat of a blaster scalded his right temple. He turned and stared into the black lifeless eyes of one of Valdez's Zexian soldiers. His powered wings twitched high on his back as his long bony finger hovered over the trigger. His bald head cocked to the side, neck cracking. "She knew you couldn't resist a fight. She knew you'd come for her. And she was correct. Long live—"

"She's dead, and so are you," he spat.

The Zexian's eyes widened. Dante crackled a swirling ball of fire in his palm before he could push the trigger. A radiant stream of light passed through his hand, cutting clear through the soldier's chest cavity. The blaster melted. He stumbled over his own two feet and landed onto his back, unable to rise.

The soldier wheezed, taking an unsteady breath. "You don't stand a chance against the Grand Supreme. He's been undefeated for centuries."

He sent a second fiery ball his way. The Zexian fell back as the flame ripped through his body.

The Zexian's entire form shuddered. His white, cracked lips curved into a smile. "By now I'm sure he's close to achieving immortality. You're wasting time."

Dante's eyes bulged in his skull. "What do you mean?"

The soldier's mouth continued to move before he succumbed to death, eyes rolling back in his head. His body stilled.

Dante leapt over him and raced out of the room in a frenzy. He had to get back home at once. Everyone he knew and loved faced extermination, and it was all because of his stupidity. If he hadn't been so hell bent on revenge, he would've picked up on the legion traveling through to the lower universes. He could've been better prepared.

He could've stopped him. How he hoped the Grand Supreme wasn't immortal, or he was going to have bigger problems than he could ever possibly imagined.

Sixty-Two

AFTER WALKING through a long stretch of jungle for hours on end, Armienti reached a clearing. He arrived at the front steps of the Palace of Despair, or at least he hoped they were the front steps. The structure was hideous and confusing, composed of a series of brown cubes with tinted rectangular windows. They were stacked haphazardly, every which way, in a horizontal direction along the ground.

He raised his navy-gloved fist and knocked on the steel front door. Dead heat from the suns rained down on his body, scorching him to the core. He fanned his face with his hand; it was impossible to cool down no matter how hard he tried.

And he'd been trying harder than anything.

The thick jungle weeds surrounding the palace seemed to close in on him. They made the hair on the back of his neck stand at perfect attention. The smell became more and more offensive, although he had the oxygen in his helmet turned up on high.

Disgusting cannibals, he'd stepped over more dead bodies than he could count on his way here. More than he'd seen in a while.

Where the heck was everybody? There wasn't a single

guard patrolling the grounds. The palace appeared almost abandoned. Beneath his helmet all he could hear was the sound of his own heartbeat, followed by the heat of his breath, fogging against the visor.

As he turned away to leave and explore a different option of entering the facility, the massive door slid open a crack. Cold air poured over his body in puffs, drifting along the gray crumbled steps.

Finally, he sighed.

A black-scaled creature half his height ambled out. His eyes were brown, appearing gold in the sunlight, and his long, pointed tail swept along the ground in gentle strokes. He wore armor of obsidian. His talons were black as midnight. Twisted horns danced in a circle around his head.

He stared down at the creature. His lips trembled, but he willed his spine to straighten. He had to put on a fearless front. He owed Autumn this for the way he made her suffer.

"I'm here for—"

"I know why you're here, Armienti. We've been expecting you," he gestured with his long taloned fingers, coated with inky scales. "Please, do come in."

At his request, Armienti stepped inside the palace. He could scarcely breathe as the blood in his veins froze over. He had to be strong for Autumn and her father. If he couldn't help them, nobody could. Especially *not* Dante.

The door slid closed behind him. Cold darkness followed. He removed his helmet, still able to make out the creature's dark silhouette.

"How do you know my name?" he asked.

The being's tongue flickered through his lips before he offered a cracked smile. "We met a long time ago. You wouldn't remember me, but I remember you."

A chill rippled down the length of his spine. "I'm pleased to make your acquaintance again," he said in the politest voice he could muster under the circumstances. He tried his hardest to conceal his uneasiness.

His iridescent eyes never left him.

"I'd like to request an audience with the Grand Supreme. I know he's very busy." *Conquering planets and enslaving civilizations,* it tempted him to say—*exterminating lower life forms for pleasure. Destroying worlds.* "But I really need to speak with him."

"The waiting list to see him in the flesh extends into the following year," he lisped, chuckling. His black forked tongue flickered against his lips.

Armienti's mouth fell wide open. "Wait, are you serious?"

"Deathly."

He glanced at the ground. "Oh, okay."

He turned around to leave. What a wasted trip. But then he realized the door was still closed. He turned back around, hands shaking. His mouth opened as if to speak.

"Can you—"

"Double check with him," the little beast offered. "Sure, why not." He shrugged.

It wasn't what he planned to ask, but he was pleased, nonetheless.

"I'll be but a moment, Elattion prince."

In the blink of an eye, the creature had disappeared. Armienti's fingers sweated inside of the confines of his gloves. What if he agreed? He hadn't practiced what he would ask him if that was the case. He should've written down his speech. What was he thinking?

What an idiot he was.

He was so nervous his teeth chattered in his mouth. *Focus, Armienti, focus,* he scolded himself.

The monster returned, popping up behind him. He gasped, and the little beast chortled, flashing a mouth of jagged yellow teeth. "You're so easily frightened. Why don't you relax and stay a while? Have a drink—unwind."

He walked over to a side table and picked up a vase filled with blood-red liquid and poured it into two titanium goblets littered with onyx crystals.

He hoped it was wine. *Please let it be wine and not*—he couldn't stand to think about it. His insides toppled. Vomit threatened to rise.

He swirled the beverage in his hand before taking a lingering sip. Armienti stared into the liquid void.

"What's the matter?"

He glanced up and remained silent. Every instinct in his body told him to leave the palace at once, yet he remained.

"Don't be rude—it's wine. Do you think I'm some kind of barbarian?" His lips flickered into a smile before flattening.

From the looks of the palace and surrounding jungle, yes, he did.

He closed his eyes, lowering his mouth to the goblet. He couldn't believe he was going through with this.

When he inhaled, the liquid smelled rich and salty. He took a sip, and to his surprise the beverage tasted fruity like sugar cane. Armienti consumed his drink in a few gulps, wiping his glove over his mouth.

The beast took his empty cup and placed it onto the table.

"The Grand Supreme will see you now."

Armienti gulped. Sometimes he had to be careful what he wished for because his wishes occasionally came true.

He followed the creature through the long winding hall, trying his best not to be phased by the body count and putrid stench.

He could see the white puffs of his breath as they traveled deeper into the heart of the palace. How much longer would they have to go?

Armienti's head grew heavy, and he yawned, willing himself to stay awake. His limbs slackened. Although it was scorching outside, the icy weather made him drowsy.

Or—no, it couldn't be.

They arrived at a set of vermillion doors, extending in points toward the ceiling. *Here goes nothing.* He was determined to straighten up this mess. Perhaps he could offer his service in exchange for Autumn's father's freedom.

After all, the Grand Supreme probably needed help leading his missions.

The doors opened, and when he glanced, the creature had gone. His hands ran down his stomach, resting at his hips. His vision tilted as he stepped inside the room.

The chamber was dark. The doors closed behind them. He stood there in the Great Hall. Nobody was present. A chill rattled through his body.

Armienti jumped as his eyes fell upon elongated shadows. They swept across the ceiling whispering in languages he didn't understand. Cool darkness swirled around him. In an instant, he could see the faces of everyone he'd hurt throughout the years.

Maeve, Autumn, countless inhabitants of conquered worlds. Ronan. But for whatever reason, looking back at Dante hurt him most of all. It was like looking at everything he could never have, even if he deserved it more than he did. He saw red.

He was reminded of every painful memory he'd ever experienced. His knees knocked together, and his body weakened as he fell onto the floor. When he opened his eyes, the lifeless shadows stared down at him, pulling him into the black void.

He screamed as everything went dark.

$$Sixty\text{-}Three$$

THE DAY WAS like any other day on planet Surge as Autumn meandered through the central courtyard garden. The dual suns sparkled in the clear blue cloudless sky, warming her golden-olive skin. Giraldinia hummed with life beyond the palace walls of Sanguis. Aircraft zipped through the skyway like specks of light at five thousand kilometers per hour.

Her muscles ached from her afternoon training session with Leyla. Her go-go boots slid against the starry mosaic tiled ground as she paced back and forth dressed in an obsidian bodysuit with a gilded asymmetrical stripe. Training was the only activity that calmed her nerves as of late. She hadn't slept in weeks.

She yawned, clapping a hand over her mouth as she read from the translated hologram story collection Dante had gifted her with.

She struggled to focus as her mind raced in circles, unable to comprehend the text. Tears welled in the corners of her eyes that she attempted to blink away when her thoughts drifted to Dante. All communication had gone radio silent. She couldn't help but wonder what he was up to and if he thought of her as much as she thought of him. She refrained from contacting him for his own safety as painful as it was dealing with his absence.

The Grand Supreme, she shuddered. There was no telling what he was capable of with his disgusting lizard-like features and taste for pain.

She rested her cheek on the ball of her fist. She missed Dante more than the countless stars in the sky. She hoped he and her dad were okay and coming home safely to her soon. She didn't know what she'd do without them.

She couldn't survive.

As her thoughts scrambled in a million different directions with what ifs and gut-wrenching guilt, hundreds of shadows swept across the sky, hovering in formation. She tore her attention away from her hologram book. *Crap*. She lost her place just when the story was getting good. The images sputtered then closed in a frenzy, disappearing before her eyes.

She tilted her head up, squinting into the light of the fiery dual suns. *What the heck was going on? Maybe an oncoming storm?* She wondered. *Weird*.

As far as she could remember, there had only been one storm on Surge to date.

Rain. And it came on a day when she was as sad as this one.

At that instant, Sean rollerbladed by her in a flash and she stumbled a step backwards, fumbling the device in her hands. Even with her heightened senses, she couldn't detect his human movements because she was too distracted.

"Sorry," he waved, rollerblading around the garden on one foot, flashing her a warm smile. She returned his gesture.

A ball of soft hot-pink and black fur passed between her legs. Mr. Hiss trotted after him, tail swaying and white muzzle curling. He loved to play and had taken a liking to Ronan's boyfriend.

She tore her eyes away from the happy scene and glanced

back into the sky, tracing the dots with her eyes. She shook her head. At least Ronan was happy, even if she was miserable.

"Hey, wait for me," Kittlen yelled, sputtering after them, wearing his signature red scarf fastened around his brow and pointed ears. The symbol of dreams and freedom fluttered in the warm afternoon breeze.

Everyone deserved to be free, to live the life of their choice and not be a slave forced to serve.

Kyo raced after them, the strands of his moonglow mohawk illuminated in the sunlight.

"Sorry about him, Your Imperial Majesty," Kyo yelled, waving a hand. "He had way too much candy this morning and the sugar went straight to his head. You know how that is." He chuckled. "Kids."

"It's okay," she nodded, envious that everyone else was happy except for her. She never seemed to find happiness for longer than a few seconds.

She sighed, turning on her heel, and taking one last look at the sky before she walked into the palace. How she dreaded the upcoming task. She wished she could hide.

* * *

WHEN SHE ARRIVED LATE for the afternoon meeting, she was scheduled to conduct, the conference room was packed to the brim. As she entered the cool darkness, she was greeted by dozens of sets of vibrant inhuman eyes. Elattion officials stood up from their seats, watching as she made her way to the front of the room.

The table glowed with a 3D map of the 24 Universes. Planets and stars blinked and rotated. The breath caught in her throat, but her nerves softened when she spotted Ronan with Leyla among the crowd. Leyla offered her a reassuring smile and Ronan winked.

Everyone took their seats, and she resumed her place at the head of the table. A throat cleared and her attention drew to the group of advisors. How she dreaded their *thorough* questions after her husband's departure. She never had the answers they hoped for no matter how hard she tried.

"Permission to speak, Your Imperial Majesty."

A long awkward silence followed; she wanted to hide under the table.

"Go ahead," she said, anticipating more questions about Dante. She could scarcely breathe as all eyes drew to her. Her fingers perspired within her gloves as she inhaled.

"Is there any news about the emperor? It's rumored—"

BOOM.

A loud noise rattled through the conference room followed by thunder ripping through the sky. The ground shook beneath her feet and everyone stumbled to a stand staring at each other, mouths agape.

Ronan and Leyla ran up to her, eyes widening.

"Are you okay?" Leyla hugged her tight. "What was that?"

"Yeah, I think so—"

BOOM.

A second vibration rattled through the room. This time a few advisors fell to the ground while others landed into their seats. Their faces contorted with fear, eyes bulging. Autumn raced over to the lone rectangular window along the back wall, boots skidding against the metallic tiled floor. She peeked beneath the black-out shade. She couldn't believe what she saw. She cupped a hand over her mouth as she gasped.

Fire erupted from the sky, raining beyond the forcefield. Red and orange streaks smoked and burned, smoldering in every which direction. The sky went as dark as night beyond the invisible barrier.

A transmission zipped through the room, emitting a high-pitched frequency. Everyone covered their ears screaming. Autumn closed her eyes, molars gritting together. How she hoped the sound would stop. The noise was unbearable.

The room went dark before a crackling image of the Grand Supreme rotated and glowed before her. His small child-like fingers gripped the silver arms of his seat. Horns twisted around his uneven skull. Stars raced by the windows outside of his ship. Everyone fell onto one knee except for her, Ronan, and Leyla, who stared silently in shock and disgust.

"Why hello, did you miss me?" his cracked lips and yellow jagged teeth curled into a smile. His voice faded in and out as he traveled at an incredible speed.

Autumn glowered, resting a hand against her hip. "What do you want?"

"And with that tone again," he lisped, lines crinkled at the corners of his eyes forming ridges through his sharp scaly skin. "Someone needs to teach you some respect. I should put you over my knee, Empress."

Her nose scrunched. *Eww gross,* her stomach churned. She'd gouge his eyes out if he so much as came near her.

Emperor Izzo continued, lacing his black taloned fingers in his lap. "If it isn't already apparent, I have your precious planet surrounded. And I know you're all by your lonesome."

The screen switched and her heart stopped, but she refused to let her resolve cave in front of him. He wasn't kidding. *Holy crap.* Thousands upon thousands of ships encompassed Surge. There was no hope for escape. Only death.

"Nobody gets hurt, you have my word, if you give me what I want."

"Where's my dad?" her voice jumped. Visions of him screaming threatened to surface in her mind again.

"He's fine and will continue to be if you comply," the Grand Supreme batted his golden cat-slit eyes. "But if you don't, I hate to break it to you—all bets are off."

Everyone fixated on her, waiting for an answer. After all, she was the empress of Universe 13. She should have all the answers, right?

She didn't want to ask but was left with no other choice. The words irked her as they left her mouth. "Okay, what do you want?"

He tilted his inhuman head to the side. "You have something that belongs to me."

She froze in place, heart accelerating. Her fingertips brushed against her pocket sliding against the scroll Dante had given her. She carried it with her at all times in case of an emergency like he asked. In her opinion, this definitely warranted an emergency.

She'd yet to open the scroll like she promised him, but somehow Izzo knew all about it.

The Grand Supreme's tail thrashed back and forth, through a hole in his chair, scraping against the metallic tiled floor. "If you come up to see me, we can have a little chat to discuss the terms. Let's say, tomorrow evening. My schedule is wide open for you."

"Autumn, don't do it," Leyla distracted her from making her decision. "He's a liar. I've seen him in action many times before. He's massacred—"

"Ah, Lady Leyla, so we meet again."

Leyla crossed her arms, her full pink lips twisted into a scowl and her dark-brown eyes thinned to slits.

"I'll never forget how your father expressed great disappointment that he had a baby girl instead of the second boy he was hoping for. He thought of leaving you for dead, casting your body into cold dark space, but it was I who convinced him of your worth, of your potential," he paused for a moment. "You could've been one of the greatest warriors the universes has ever seen if only you had applied yourself. It's in your pure blood."

"Shut up, nobody wants to hear the nonsense coming out

of your mouth," Leyla rolled her eyes. "And have you ever heard of a toothbrush? I'm guessing not. One would serve you well."

Izzo's wicked mouth fell into a tight flat line. "How dare you speak to me with such disrespect, I'm the Grand Supreme, Lord of the 24 Universes and all you see," he shouted, then exhaled. "I suppose it's no matter now, foolish girl. We'll meet in the flesh soon enough and I'll teach you a lesson then."

She crossed her arms. "I'd like to see you try," her voice jumped a bit. "But facts are facts, nobody has ever seen you fight."

His mouth moved as if he intended to speak, but his eyes drew to Ronan instead.

"Ah yes, the youngest of the Martynes. Don't think I've forgotten about you. I know you've never truly felt recognized. All the fame and glory always go to your older cousin. That can change in the blink of an eye if only you'll allow me to help. I'm known for making magic happen."

Ronan raised his head and folded his arms. "You're wasting your time. My family comes first, and there's nothing you can say or do to change my mind."

"Very well then. It was worth a try." His attention snapped back to Autumn. "Shall I schedule you for tomorrow evening, Empress?"

She hesitated. A lone bead of sweat dripped down her back.

"I—"

"If you refuse, here's what will happen. I have enough ammunition to last until the end of time. Eventually the force-field will wear out, and I'll swoop in and eradicate your planet. The Elattions will be but a memory, a fallen world. Plus, both you and I know your precious emperor is nowhere to be found. I mean, he's been gone so long—is he ever coming back?"

Everyone in the room stared at her.

Autumn's stomach twisted from the cold cruel facts. She had no idea but refused to admit the truth aloud. A sudden wave of anger coursed through her veins.

Her fists balled at her sides. "Dante is coming home. You don't scare me. I'll come see you tomorrow evening like you asked."

"A wise decision, Empress," his black forked tongue flickered, snapping back into his mouth before he grinned. "Perhaps you have more common sense than the others."

"No, Autumn, please don't," Leyla pleaded. "You can't trust him."

"No need to fret, Lady Leyla. I promise I'll take excellent care of her, and you as well. We'll all be acquainted soon enough."

Sixty-Four

DANTE RACED through time and space, sitting in the cockpit of his destroyer. Stars zipped by the windows in clumps and streaks. He had to get home. Everyone he knew and loved was in danger of being annihilated. His heart pounded in his chest.

Autumn—his hands grasped the control panel. He hoped she was safe. His wife, his mate, the love of his life.

He could only imagine how frightened she was if the Grand Supreme had gotten to her first. No, he couldn't let that happen. He'd torture her to the last thread of her life then kill her out of spite to get back at him.

It was all his fault.

He shouldn't have gotten distracted by Valdez, given into bloodlust and revenge like she wanted him to. Fallen for her perfect trap. Although revenge was sweet. He should've traveled straight to Universe 24 and made a deal with the Grand Supreme like he'd planned. Then maybe none of this would've happened.

His navy-gloved fist balled, bones cracking in his hand. Once again, he'd royally screwed up—

And he had no one to thank but himself.

No matter how hard he tried, he could never do right by Autumn. At least he had given her the scroll. Had she read the contents? His heart ached. He hoped not.

At least, not yet.

Dante entered Universe 15, traveling as fast as his spacecraft could go. His fleet of elite soldiers followed close behind at top speed. He had to get back home and work through the mess he'd created. He hoped upon hope his family was okay and his planet hadn't been erased from the map in his absence.

* * *

"AUTUMN, I hate to break it to you, but you are not going through with this," Leyla's silver go-go boots patted against the crimson carpeted floor.

Her sister followed close behind her through the hallway before she stopped at her bedroom door. Autumn punched her code into the side key panel before being granted access. The steel door slid open, and they walked inside her room.

While she appreciated Leyla's grave concern, there was no way out of this situation. At least no way she could see. The planet was surrounded by thousands upon thousands of spacecraft. The Grand Supreme was ready to start a war over her.

She was the empress, and it was her job to protect everyone, including Leyla, who refused to see her point of view.

"It's me he wants," she laced her fingers together. "Maybe if I go and speak to him, he'll leave everyone alone." She took a seat on the bed. Mr. Hiss yawned and stretched, climbing into her lap. He'd had a busy day as well playing with Kyo and Sean.

"Don't be naive," Leyla sat beside her, folding her hands in her lap. She turned her head examining her face with her large brown eyes. "He doesn't just let someone go unless it serves him. Those that get tangled in his web don't make it out alive."

Autumn rested her head on Mr. Hiss. He purred, nuzzling her. "What should we do then?"

"We should fight him, or at least try to hold him off until my brother gets back. I'm sure he's heard and he's on his way from wherever he is."

She wished she could talk to him. He would know what to do during an emergency like this one.

"How do you know he's coming back?" Autumn asked.

"Sometimes you have to believe in things you can't see," Leyla placed her hand over hers. "Sometimes you have to trust in the unknown."

BOOM. The entire room shook. Mr. Hiss sprang from her lap and ran underneath the bed. His sapphire eyes wavered with fear. Autumn rose, jogging over to the balcony. Leyla ran after her. They peered through the closed French doors. Another round of thunder rippled through the sky. Orange and blue flames crackled and roared.

Bzzzz. She heard. Her communicator rattled against the floor. Her heart leapt to her throat as she searched for the device. Maybe it was Dante, like Leyla had said. She knelt and found her communicator beneath her bed. It had fallen during the attack.

She slid the screen up with her fingertip and read the highlighted message inside:

"That was a reminder shot. Don't be late for our appointment tomorrow evening. There's much, much more where that came from. Be there or suffer the consequences."

"Who is it from?" Leyla peered over her shoulder and then gasped, cupping a palm over her mouth.

Autumn's hands slackened as the device slid from her grasp. The message was signed, The Grand Supreme.

PART SIX

Scarlet Lightning

Sixty-Five

AN UNFORTUNATE TASK had landed in Autumn's lap. *The perks of being empress,* she sighed, fidgeting her hands. Emblem and Allegoria fussed over her, making sure her hair and makeup were *perfect.* According to them.

But was anything ever really perfect, or was it all an illusion?

They combed the coiled strands of her hair into a high ponytail, fastening it tight to the top of her head. They glossed her lips with one of the only tokens she still had from Earth—her favorite watermelon lip gloss. She was lucky it hadn't disappeared with the rest of her belongings.

Golden glitter was sprayed over the strands of her hair. She wore a burgundy bodysuit with a gilded asymmetrical stripe.

Hours remained before she was scheduled to see the Grand Supreme, and she had to give a public statement.

Great. Her palms sweated in her lap. For whatever reason she was more nervous to formally break the news to the inhabitants than she was to meet with the Grand Supreme himself.

"You look gorgeous," Emblem and Allegoria each gave her a reassuring hug, then stepped away.

"Thanks," her cheeks warmed to the touch. She never knew how to handle a compliment.

Leyla and Ronan waved from across the throne room with their significant others. Too bad hers was somewhere in deep space and not with her when she needed him the most. She wished he was with her more than anything.

Isidora entered the room and waved as well. Worry lines graced her youthful blue brow.

"You're on in three, two, one, go," an advisor announced from the sidelines.

She stopped slouching and placed her hands into her lap. She tried to make a pleasant smile but for all she knew it looked like a frown. All eyes were on her.

The drones buzzed around her emitting a high-pitched tone. She was live in front of billions of viewers.

"Greetings, good inhabitants of Universe 13. I come to you with ill-fated news," her mouth grew dry, but she did her best to disguise her nerves. Her knee bounced slightly. It was an impossible task, but everyone was looking to her for guidance.

She continued. "We're facing an attack, and we are surrounded,as you've seen from beyond the forcefield. Negotiations for our freedom are currently under way. I will be going to speak directly to the Grand Supreme to see if we can reach an agreement. Please stay calm, and most of all don't lose hope. I will work tirelessly and do everything in my power to rectify the situation. Until then, be well."

The drones switched off, and her lap vibrated. She looked down and could barely catch her breath.

Not because of the speech she just gave, but because her communicator was buzzing with Dante's number.

Her heart accelerated. She stood up from the throne and ran out of the room to get some privacy.

"Autumn, where are you going?" She heard from Leyla and Ronan, but ignored the question.

She stopped at the end of the hallway, back pressed against the wall. She slid to the ground, fingers quaking as she answered her communicator.

"Hello, Dante, I'm so glad you're okay." She couldn't hide her smile. Tears streamed down her cheeks.

But the other side was silent. Heavy breathing crackled through the speaker. "Don't forget our agreement."

The Grand Supreme.

The device slid from her hand and hung up as it collided with the crimson carpeted floor. She burst into bitter tears, taking deep heaving breaths, then buried her face against her knees, sobbing her heart out.

Her communicator buzzed again. She stopped, staring down at the screen. Her vision grew blurry from crying so hard, but she could still make out Dante's number flashing. The Grand Supreme had somehow intercepted his call.

Autumn's teeth ground together in her mouth as she snatched up the communicator again. She answered the device, hands quaking.

"What do you want now?" she snapped.

"Autumn, it's me."

Sixty-Six

A WAVE of relief coursed through Autumn's body. Her limbs became as light as air. She couldn't believe Dante had finally reached out to her. She was beginning to wonder if he was still alive.

"I missed you," her cheeks warmed as she whispered into the speaker. Her entire body felt as if she was floating.

"I missed you too." She could tell he was smiling on the other end. She closed her eyes, processing his words.

"I can't talk long, and I need you to be careful what you say," his soothing voice crackled through the speaker. It sent shivers down her spine as always.

"He's been harassing me," her bottom lip quivered.

A long silence followed. He huffed. She could tell he was furious.

"I heard your broadcast," he changed the subject. "I think you did an amazing job smoothing out the situation. I knew I could count on you. You make me proud every day."

He continued. "Under no circumstances are you going to see him. Do you hear that, Izzo? This is between you and me."

A frequency hummed through her communicator, buzzing

against her ear. They weren't alone. As she was warned many times before, someone was always watching and listening.

"When I go, I need you to open what I gave you."

The scroll. Her lips moved as if she meant to speak but then she thought better of it. She didn't want to give the Grand Supreme what he was after.

"Are you sure?"

"I'm positive."

Buttons bleeped in the background.

"I love you, Autumn."

She pressed out a smile that burned her cheeks. "I love you t—"

The communicator cut off before she could finish her sentence. When she went to redial, the tone was dead. She sighed—another missed opportunity to tell him how much she cared.

Instead of dwelling on the situation, Autumn reached into her pocket, feeling around for the scroll.

She pulled the paper out, holding it in the palm of her hand, before slowly parting the pieces with her fingertips.

The golden paper sparkled in her palms. As she began to read the contents, she chewed a fingernail, and her entire body went numb.

* * *

AS DANTE ENTERED UNIVERSE 13, he blinked the fog away from his eyes, determined to stay focused on the task at hand. He couldn't allow himself to succumb to his emotions. *Not now.* He had to stay sharp and ready for any obstacle.

No matter how hard he tried, he couldn't shake the feeling of regret. Regret he couldn't talk to Autumn longer, regret that she wasn't with him, regret he couldn't hold her in his arms, and regret that he put her through this miserable scenario.

It was far from over. The fun was just beginning.

Most of all, he regretted that he'd never see her again.

He inhaled and exhaled slowly, navy-gloved hands sliding against the control panel as he rained fire on the ships surrounding his home world.

One thing was for sure, he'd make Emperor Izzo pay with his dying breath.

Sixty-Seven

AUTUMN SAT in silence as she read the handwritten note inside of the scroll:

Little Moonlight,

How I wish I could call you this name in person again. How I wish I could go back to the night we first met. I'll never forget the first time I saw you, and when you first saw me. Your smile, your eyes, and your kind heart are unmatched.

If you're reading this right now, it's because I'm not coming back. My only regret is that we didn't have longer together. I'm grateful for the time I was able to share with you as short as it was.

These last few years were the happiest in my life. I'm not sure I've ever felt happiness before you. I'm not sure I deserved to.

I wish I could do it all over again, except for maybe, the kidnapping, which I deeply regret.

I'm sorry for how that went down. I've since had time to reflect on my actions. I would've gone about things a little differently. I wouldn't have been so selfish. I should've given you more when I had the chance. I should've done what you asked. I shouldn't have forced you to put your dreams on hold for me, and for that I'm sorry. From the bottom of my heart, I hope you can forgive me. I'm far from perfect, but I think you knew that long before I did.

I'm going to find a way to make your dreams come true some-how. I swear it. Even if I can't be with you.

A lump formed in her throat. She could barely breathe as she continued. Salty tears streamed down her cheeks.

I need you to go behind the palace and into the great maze. At the center sits a fountain. At the bottom of the fountain, inside of the water, lies a silver orb. Once opened, it creates a passageway to the 25th Universe which exists beyond the map and only in legends. It's a place no one has ever ventured to. And the only place you will be safe from The Grand Supreme. He'll dedicate his life to hunting you down. He won't give you a moment's rest. And I can't allow that. I want you to be safe.

Please take care of everyone in my absence. And try to be happy. Live a fruitful life.

I love you, Autumn, always and forever.

Until the next life,

Dante

I'm sorry for everything I put you through.

She sat on the floor in pitch silence. *He wasn't coming back.* Her worst fear had been realized. She covered her mouth with her hand, releasing a quiet scream. How could he do this to her? All she wanted to do was be with him.

All she wanted to do was live happily ever after.

They were supposed to be together forever, like he'd promised. Her dreams of a happy life shattered before her eyes.

Autumn came to an unsteady stand. She didn't have time for self-pity. The entire planet was in danger of being extin-guished, and she was the only one with this information.

The key to the 25th Universe.

Sixty-Eight

STREAMS of static blue energy zipped and twirled through Dante's blaster cannons as he opened fire onto the gathering of ships blockading his home world. His teeth gritted, hands gripping the steering panel with intense ferocity. Of all the lousy ways to repay him for his endless years of loyal servitude. How dare Izzo challenge him. He glowered at all the commotion.

He wanted this entire situation to be done and over with. He wanted Izzo's head on a spike.

Spacecraft exploded, particles and debris collided with the glass windows surrounding the cockpit of his ship, skittering against the metal exterior. Enemy destroyers anticipated his attack, returning the favor.

He dodged their attempts, making his way through the legion of spacecraft, toward Izzo's slow-traveling pleasure cruiser. Everything Izzo did was a brute display of power and wealth. He couldn't be fuller of himself if he tried. He spit on the floor in disgust.

Arrogant ass, his mouth flattened. At one time he too believed that was the only way to survive and to gain respect.

He knew all the better avenues to take, and it was all thanks to Autumn. His sweet Little Moonlight. The love of his life.

He missed her more than anything and tried to cope with the cruel fact that he'd seen her for the last time. A heaviness settled in his chest as he cherished her memory.

Twisted horns sprouted in all directions of the octagon-shaped vessel. His heart pounded as he approached at an incredible speed.

His soldiers defended the planet, shooting their blasters and maneuvering through the vast sea of ships. Some made contact with the hostile spacecraft, causing them to lose control, while others weren't so lucky and exploded on the spot, forfeiting their lives for this miserable cause.

How many more would have to suffer at his hands if he couldn't stop him?

The elite soldiers on his squad were whittled down one by one before his eyes. There were too many enemy destroyers to fend off.

They were outnumbered by far and didn't stand a chance. The situation looked grim.

While he was a skilled warrior in his own right, one of the most fearsome the universes had ever seen, his fleet of two hundred men was no match for the Grand Supreme's legion. The ships were as numerous as the stars in the sky.

As he turned a corner, maneuvering through an opening in the spacecraft formation, one of his soldiers went to follow his lead and his ship was struck and exploded to pieces. Limbs and steel flew everywhere, suspended in the vastness of space. A helmet floated by his window, accompanied by a black-gloved hand. He shook his head, mouth twisting.

Another ship down. The breath caught in his throat. *All thanks to the Grand Supreme's cruelty.*

Would he make it to Izzo's pleasure cruiser? It seemed unlikely. Izzo was always two steps ahead of him.

In an instant, several enemy destroyers were hot on his

tail, and he couldn't seem to shake them no matter how hard he tried. Stars raced by his windows in a blur of pale light. They followed him through every roll and pass and turn. They out-maneuvered every move he could think of. It seemed he was cornered. It was only a matter of time until they made impact, causing him to crash. His heart raced, hands sweating within his navy-blue gloves. A swell of panic ripped through his limbs.

Just as he braced for the inevitable, four dozen sleek silver vessels came zipping through the gathering, taking out five enemy ships at a time. Explosions rattled through the surrounding planets and stars, sending debris crashing everywhere. His ship vibrated from their force. They stopped and waved at him as they continued forging a path. He caught a glimpse of Emperor Brumha with a navy helmet covering his silver face. His grand velvet white cape spilled over the back of his seat.

He'd come after all. Even after the terrible way he'd treated him. He didn't deserve his kindness.

"Fancy seeing you here," he received a transmission signal, crackling through his speaker.

All he could do was smile beneath the dark visor of his helmet. He was embarrassed he couldn't tackle the situation by himself like he'd intended to. He never wanted to ask for assistance from anyone.

"Thank you for coming," he finally muttered, shocked that the words came spilling out of his mouth. He seldom thanked anyone for anything, but this occasion seemed to be an appropriate one.

"Sometimes we could all use a little help," the emperor reminded him as he zoomed ahead, zapping the surrounding ships to dust. They exploded in red and orange streaks.

The Zambarian fleet massacred the enemy ships, forging a path for him to travel through. He raced against time and space to catch a small horizontal opening that formed at the base of Izzo's vessel. He would not miss this opportunity to confront him.

The desire to wrap his hands around his throat and strangle him to death was a lifetime in the making.

At the last second, as he went to enter, a blast rattled his destroyer, shocking his system. He shot forward in his seat, choked back by his harness, before slamming his helmeted head against the back of his chair. He inhaled, taking in the burning scent of metal. Flames flickered against the window. Black smoke churned.

Drat, he was losing control.

Using all his might, he guided his ship toward the sliver of an opening. He managed to slip inside the vessel as the entrance sealed airtight. A wave of relief rattled through him that he was able to make his way onboard, until the smoke intensified. It churned in thick black puffs. He unbuckled his harness and raced outside the vessel and onto the docking bay. He ran through the hallway and ducked for cover as his destroyer detonated into a million pieces, sending debris sputtering everywhere. Metal and smoke collided with the fleshy ceiling and floor.

He was trapped.

He inhaled and exhaled, covering his mouth with his hands. Izzo had to know he was on board. He made a far-from-graceful entrance.

His stomach twisted as he surveyed his surroundings. The walls breathed like they were alive. A pink fleshy substance decorated either side of the hallway—the skin of Izzo's enemies woven together in a quilt. Droplets of red dripped from the ceiling, pooling against his boots.

"Disgusting cannibals," he scrunched his nose. So many terrible memories flooded him of this place.

His communicator buzzed within the confines of his pocket.

He peeked. One new message from Emperor Brumha.

"Are you okay, Emperor? Do you need me to send rein-forcements?"

Dante shook his head then replied. *"No, this is where I leave you. Thank you for your kind offer—you've already done so much."*

As soon as he finished typing his sentence, he glanced up from his communicator to a blaster aimed straight at his face. Inky creatures only found in nightmares approached him. Their black scales glittered against the hall lights. Their fingers were sticky with death.

Sixty-Nine

AUTUMN DIDN'T HAVE time for self-pity.

Secretly she wanted to lie in a fetal position and cry. She had to be strong, not only for herself, but for the ones she loved. She shoved the handwritten scroll, with the neatest letters she'd ever seen, back inside of her pocket, and zipped it up for safe keeping.

Everyone was counting on her to succeed. Their lives depended on her next steps. Instead of going back into the throne room, where everyone was waiting with bated breath, she turned on her heel to go outside. Tears fogged in the corners of her eyes that she blinked away as the sunlight sparkled in the clear blue cloudless sky. The warmth of the suns grazed her skin.

Get it together Autumn, she scolded herself. She couldn't afford another emotional breakdown. *Not here, not now.*

She passed through the rear palace garden. The grounds were empty for the first time ever. Usually, the space was occupied by countless courtiers in ridiculous finery.

The long reflection pool glittered in silence. The cobalt blue grass swayed; not a giant butterfly or ladybug could be seen flitting anywhere.

She jumped as red and orange light erupted beyond the transparent forcefield. The sound of crashing spacecraft vibrated through the sky. A battle was ongoing. She had to hurry. Her heart pounded to her throat. From the looks of it, there wasn't much time.

She approached the Great Maze. The cobalt walls were dark and bushy, extending over eight feet high. Instead of traveling through the entrance of the maze, she flew into the air to access the center.

A shiver ran down her spine as she glanced and there was no fountain as Dante had indicated in his letter. She gasped. *Had there been a mistake after all this? How could he not have the correct facts?*

Her pocket vibrated and she reached to grab her communicator. Nobody was calling and there were no missed texts. When she went to put the device back into her pocket, she realized that the vibration was coming from where the scroll sat.

She pulled it out in a frenzy and unrolled it. The text had changed, her eyes widened as she scanned the golden contents.

"I'm sorry, I forgot to mention, you have to go through the maze the old-fashioned way. No cheating ;)"

Her forehead pulsated. Leave it to Dante to make light of such a serious situation. She wished he was with her so she could scream in his face for leaving her like this. She flew back down, landing on her feet before the entrance of the Great Maze. She tucked the scroll back into her pocket and rushed inside.

Long shadows trailed her as she raced down the aisle. The dirt floor beneath her feet kicked up in thick brown puffs.

She sprinted around the corner only to be confronted with a *dead end*. She didn't have time for this. *Crap.*

BOOM, the sky shook causing her to stumble over her own two feet. She braced her fall with her hands, covering her knees with dirt. She pushed herself to a shaking stand. The sky erupted with more vermillion and marmalade streaks from the battle. The sky went dark for a moment before going bright again.

She continued running to the uncertain center of the maze. All the while, she could feel prying eyes tracing her steps, peeling her to pieces. She had to hurry up and get out of here. Someone was monitoring her every movement. Her skin prickled with goosebumps.

After many missed corners and turns, she arrived at the dead center of the maze. Sweat-slicked and out of breath, she leaned over, palms resting on her knees, inhaling.

The structure had not been there before. The fountain was decorated with two pointy-eared cherubs, each standing on one foot with their hands joined above their heads in unity. Water trickled through the pearlescent fountain.

Autumn leaned over the edge, searching the contents for any sign of the orb Dante had described in his note. Offhand, she didn't see anything.

She removed her glove running her fingers through the cool crisp water in search of the sphere. *It had to be around here somewhere, it just had to be.* She panicked, waving her hands beneath the water.

As she was about to explore the possibility that the sphere had been removed and this entire ordeal was a hoax, her fingers collided with a metal ball. She pulled the sphere out of the flowing water, examining it. Her bright gray eyes stared back at her through the silver metallic finish. A crease lined the center of the orb. The ball was weighted in her palm and jingled like a bell as she shook it, although it was the size of a marble.

She couldn't believe she was holding the key to the 25th Universe in the palm of her hand. She had to rescue the others before it was too late.

* * *

DANTE STARED into the bloodshot slit eyes of a black-scaled creature holding a blaster against his forehead. The heat from the metallic weapon sizzled against his skin. The hideous monster cocked his head to the side. He wore an onyx bodysuit with the sigil of a decapitated man carrying his head in the crook of his arm. He was all too familiar with this barbaric clan.

His mouth twisted into a smile. "I know you. I never forget a face," he folded his arms, shifting his weight from side to side.

The creature didn't answer. Instead, he held the weapon closer to his skull. They stood at the same height. His scaled muscles bulged beneath his skin-tight spandex uniform.

"You were at my wedding—the ruby bearer, was it?" He turned to his lizard-like counterpart and chuckled before facing him again.

"Small talk won't save you, Emperor. Lord Izzo asked us to retrieve you at once; he'd like to have a word. On your knees and no funny business."

"You're more hideous than I remember though," he countered.

Dante bit his cheeks, stifling a smile, how dare these disgusting creatures order him around like some kind of slave. He was an emperor for heaven's sake. But for amusement, he decided to play along.

He fell to his knees, lowering his eyes in submission.

"Put your hands on your head."

He shrugged. "Sure, why not."

"Enough," the creature growled, aiming his gun. The other monster wrapped a pair of electric cuffs around his wrists. They shocked his skin through his indigo-gloved hands. The pain was nothing he couldn't handle. He'd been through so much worse.

He complied and the other lizard soldier roughly yanked him to his feet, holding him by the arm. His elongated talons scraped against his skin. The soldier's companion walked behind him, pressing his weapon to the back of his head.

Dante rolled his eyes. These idiots. *Who did they think he was?*

They walked through the long dark hallway and all he heard were screams. Screams of pain and desperation. Hopelessness. But nobody was around to end the pain.

The hairs on the back of his neck splintered. He didn't miss this miserable place. Not one bit. He couldn't believe how long it'd been since he'd come on board this ship. How he hoped the day would never come again.

As they went to turn the corner, he stopped dead in his tracks. The red fleshy walls pulsated like a heartbeat. His boots slipped against a small crimson puddle on the floor. His nose scrunched with disgust.

Disgusting cannibals.

"Move," the soldier ordered him, pressing the blaster between his shoulder blades, pinching a nerve. "If we're late, our master won't be pleased."

Dante turned around, grinning. "That's not my problem, now, is it?"

He tore his wrists from his constraints, and electricity shot up his arms. The scaly creatures took two steps in retreat, trembling with their guns in their hands. They opened fire, and he flicked the static energy away with his wrist.

Dante cracked his knuckles before crafting a ball of simmering orange and blue fire in his hand. He raised his palm and released the flame. In an instant their screams went silent, and the fire crashed against the opposite end of the corridor. Alarms sounded, indicating an emergency.

The passageway flooded with vile scaled creatures. Their tails whipped against the walls as they ran with their guns in hand.

He didn't allow them to get far. Instead, he raised a larger flame and sent the embers crashing through the hallway, taking Izzo's force out all at once. He inhaled, taking in the familiar scent of burning flesh. He ran a hand through his dark hair, tousling the strands.

Okay, now that he'd handled the situation, Lord Izzo had to be around here somewhere. He popped his knuckles, making his way through the ruined hallway in pursuit of his master.

Seventy

WHEN AUTUMN REENTERED the throne room, everyone was standing around watching and waiting for her. Leyla and the former empress, Isidora, approached her with slow, steady steps. Her hand shot into her pocket and a deep wave of relief flooded through her veins as her fingertips slid against the metal sphere. It was right where she left it.

Thank goodness.

"Where were you?" Leyla's deep brown eyes widened with concern. "Who were you talking to before?"

Isidora watched her, offering her a hopeful smile. Her graceful hands slid against the delicate tulle of her burgundy dress.

"You can tell her," Autumn said. Clearly Isidora was sifting through her thoughts whether she gave her permission to or not. She was careful not to think too much about the situation to keep them both calm, keeping hidden that the Grand Supreme had been the first one to call her.

"Dante."

Leyla gasped. "I knew it," tears welled along her lashes. "How is he? I know he's up there kicking Izzo's ass. Am I right?"

Autumn took a seat on the throne, staring at her hands. She wished it were true and he was coming home to her, but he wasn't. She fell into a regretful daze for a moment before saying, "I hope so." She lied through her teeth so as not to upset either of them.

"What's the matter? I thought you'd be happier than this to hear he's safe. Are you worried about your father? Did something happen to him?"

Panic ripped through her body. She should've asked Dante about her dad when she had the chance. It was too late. For all she knew—*no, she couldn't think that way*. There had to be a way out of this messy situation. There just had to be.

Isidora placed her hand on hers, squeezing them tight. "Dante is going to take care of everything. There's no need to worry. He always finds a way."

Autumn wasn't so sure. This time, everything was different. They were surrounded by an enemy force, protected by a mere invisible barrier.

Leyla turned toward her. "Are you still planning to go and see the Grand Supreme? He doesn't sound like he'll take no for answer—"

As she spoke, an advisor came sprinting over to them. He struggled to catch his breath, dry heaving. Sweat trickled down his blue temples and onto the collar of his black uniform. He fell into a deep bow.

"Your Imperial Majesty, there's something you have to see."

She sensed the seriousness of the situation and came to an abrupt stand. Leyla and Isidora followed her lead. He ushered them to the conference room, around the corner.

When they walked through the door, the room was pitch black.

The map of the 24 Universes was dark. All she could hear was the sound of her bated breath.

"What is it?" Autumn stared around the room. "What's wrong?" *And where were the other advisors?*

Leyla and Isidora glanced around as well. No answer came.

The projector flickered on, casting a pale glow throughout the room. 3D images swirled before focusing. She threw a hand over her mouth, her vision swirling.

Her dad sat in a clear confinement, trembling, surrounded by severed limbs and splintered bones, brown filthy rags draped over his bony shoulders. Breath passed through his mouth in white puffs. The hairs of his beard were coarse and stringy. She fell against the table as the image shifted to Dante who wandered through the halls of a ship. The deep-red walls pulsated around him. He was searching for something, or so it appeared. Her knees knocked together. She struggled to catch her breath.

She turned toward the advisor who melded with the shadows. His bloodshot slit-eyes glowed, wet black scales glittering in the passing streams of light.

She gasped, throwing a hand over her mouth. Goosebumps prickled along her skin.

"Lord Izzo is expecting you. Go to him, or they die along with the rest of your planet."

"I—"

"This is your final warning."

She blinked and he disappeared into thin air. The putrid smell of blood remained. Leyla caught her as her legs buckled. She helped her back to an unsteady stand.

"Autumn, what does he want with you?" Leyla's brown eyes widened. Isidora shook her head. Worry lines creased her delicate brow.

She remained quiet, too shocked to answer. She wished she could tell them.

* * *

DANTE SAUNTERED through the hallway of Emperor Izzo's slow-moving pleasure cruiser. Thick black smoke trailed him.

His master's soldiers were utterly pathetic once they were removed from the comfort of their destroyers. It was painfully obvious they were no match for him.

Weaklings.

An arrogant smile crashed across his lips for a moment, which he managed to suppress. He couldn't allow himself to be swept up in the moment, although it was tempting to gloat.

He had to stay focused and hold Izzo off long enough for Autumn and his loved ones to escape to the 25th Universe he'd read about in ancient texts. He'd never ventured there himself, but sometimes believing was seeing.

Apparently, his father had known about its existence as well, judging by the markings on the scroll and the notes he'd left. His father had planned to claim the territory for himself and escape from this situation until he met his untimely end.

On Varz, Dante had come to find his father had mined for more than crystals. The portal he'd discovered was his most valuable asset.

His wife's safety depended on his success.

When he turned the corner, a pang of anxiety coursed through him. Bad memories seeped into his subconscious. The misery and abuse he suffered here during his formative years. His family wasn't permitted to be present. The world was expected of him early on.

He'd seen too much too soon and had Izzo to thank for his distress.

Dante paused and closed his eyes, taking deep controlled breaths. He couldn't believe the time had finally come. He'd fantasized about fighting Izzo for years.

Smashing his fist into his ugly beady face was his deepest

darkest desire. He'd do anything to keep Autumn safe, even risk his own life.

His world stilled as he came upon Izzo's private quarters. Dante hesitated for a moment, so many emotions crippling his senses; fear included. His boots grew heavy, freezing in place. His hands perspired within the confines of his navy gloves, which Emperor Brumha had been kind enough to allow him to wear.

The Grand Supreme stood before him in complete silence. His back was turned as he stared out of a large circular window at the ensuing chaos. Ships exploded into fine space dust; others lit on fire from the inside. Streaks of destruction decorated the otherwise eerie dark landscape. Limbs and debris floated in the abyss. Everyone sacrificed their lives for this cause.

This was all because of him.

He swirled a goblet in his hand, long taloned fingers sliding against the metal before taking a lingering sip. The sound pierced his ears.

"Dante, I've been expecting you."

Seventy-One

AUTUMN RACED AROUND HER BEDROOM, tossing supplies into an open bag. An extra bodysuit in case she needed to change, a helmet, and a pair of warm socks. Space could be a miserable cold place, especially with an ongoing war. Firelight erupted beyond the forcefield and into the oncoming night. The dual suns set over the vast metropolis of Giarldinia, casting an orange pink glow. For the first time, the city was dark and quiet.

She had to get to her dad and Dante before it was too late. There was no telling what horrors the Grand Supreme was up to. All she could think about was her dad sitting alone in a cage, covered in filth with cracked glasses and rags for clothes, and Dante walking the halls of an enemy ship by himself.

As she pulled on a midnight-black bodysuit and a pair of boots, Mr. Hiss emerged from beneath the bed. He yawned and stretched before purring and rolling on the floor, exposing his soft underbelly. He blinked his innocent cerulean eyes. He wanted to play but she didn't have time. She ran her hands through his hot-pink fur, calming herself down. She would miss him too.

A knock came to the door, distracting her from her tortured thoughts.

"Come in," she yelled with a shaky voice. Her adrenaline spiked to an all-time high.

Emblem and Allegoria came sputtering through the door, out of breath. Emblem approached her, moonglow hair framing her delicate jaw.

"I'm sorry we're late. We're here to prepare you—"

"Don't worry about it," Autumn put the finishing touches on her plaited pigtail braids, pulling them through simple black hair ties. She smoothed her hands down the length of her thighs. "It doesn't matter where I'm going. Nothing matters anymore."

Leyla and Ronan followed, both dressed in onyx bodysuits as well. It was like a gathering for a funeral. They watched her quietly from the doorway. She walked over to them, folding her arms.

Ronan opened his mouth as if to speak. Worry lines flickered across his strong brow. "I don't think it's a good idea that you go."

"I don't either," Leyla added. Her brown eyes grew glassy as she pulled her in for a hug, sobbing bitter tears against her arm. Her blue cheeks slicked wet. "I think it's a trap."

Autumn's eyes wavered between them, sensing their sadness. "Then what do you propose we do?"

Ronan stepped forth, running a hand through his brown spiky hair. He stared at her with his emerald-green eyes. "I'll go. The Grand Supreme has always had a fondness for me, perhaps I can negotiate or distract him long enough so you can escape—"

She shook her head, *that wouldn't do.* "No, I can't drag you into this mess. This is my problem to solve."

Leyla glanced at her. "We're here to help you. You know that don't you?"

"Listen you guys, somebody has to stay here and take care

of everyone while I'm gone." For a split second she reminded herself of Dante who gave her the exact same lecture before he left. She blinked the oncoming fog from her eyes as she recalled the last conversation they had. "Sean needs you, and Kyo and his family need you. Stay here and take care of them. If the shit hits the fan, then you can leave, but I won't have you risk your lives for me."

She walked back into the room, grabbing the satchel from the floor, throwing it over her shoulder. She hugged Emblem and Allegoria for dear life. It was, more than likely, the last time she would ever see them.

As she went to pass through the doorway where Ronan and Leyla stood, Leyla pleaded with her large brown eyes. "You don't have to do this. There must be another way."

Autumn stared at them for a moment before speaking. "Sometimes, there is no other way. Sometimes you have to face your problems head on whether you're ready or not. That's life."

Leyla's mouth fell. Sometimes the truth hurt. They followed her down the hallway in silence as she made her way outside to the docks.

* * *

WHEN THEY ARRIVED at her destroyer on the palace roof, Isidora stood there wearing a long tulle gown, Sean wore his inline skates, and Kyo huddled with his family. The sky and the city were pitch dark. The sole sources of light came from beyond the forcefield in the form of cracking fire and liquid stars.

Kittlen ran over and gave her a warm hug, burying his face into her stomach. A red bandana remained tied across his brow and over his long, pointed ears. "Aww, do you really have to go?"

"Yes," she hugged him back as he rested his soft cheek

against her. "But I know you're going to be safe while I'm gone."

Treble walked over and hugged her as well. "Thank you again for everything, but most of all, thank you for your kindness."

She flashed her a small smile in return. Treble curtseyed as she joined Kittlen. Sean rolled up to her and kissed her cheek. Kyo placed his hand on her shoulder. His moonstone mohawk glowed beneath the night stars.

"Good luck," he said.

"Thank you."

Finally, she was met with the former empress.

"I wish we could talk you out of going," Isidora's dark-brown eyes flashed with grave concern. "I wish there was a better way. But with that being said, you're the empress. If you need anything, don't hesitate to contact us. We'll be there in a heartbeat."

"Thank you," she turned and waved one final time. Leyla buried her face in her hands and Ronan steadied her weight.

Autumn boarded the destroyer, closing the door. Her heart pounded so fast she could barely breathe. She took her seat, placing her bag on the floor beside her feet. She buckled her harness in place, closing her eyes, inhaling and exhaling. *Okay, she could do this. If she couldn't rescue her dad and Dante, nobody could.*

She reached for the control console. Hopefully she could figure this out. Maybe she should've asked for directions or something because the steering panel looked much different than her aircraft, divided into two pieces.

But she was a licensed driver, she reassured herself, *so it shouldn't be too hard. She had this under control.*

Autumn hit buttons and pulled gauges. The spacecraft rose in slow motion. Her body flooded with relief.

Okay, great, she was well on her way. She whipped out her communicator—she had to act as quickly as possible.

"Lower the forcefield for one minute," she texted Ronan.

"As you wish," he responded. The sky somehow became clearer as the twin crescent moons sparkled through the night.

The spacecraft soared into the air. When she glanced out the window, her newfound family became dark specks of dust, still gathered on top of the palace. The metropolis of Giarldinia disappeared into the night.

A chill skittered down the length of her spine. Perspiration pooled in her gloves. The next stop was the Grand Supreme.

PART SEVEN

When Darkness Falls

Seventy-Two

DANTE STOOD in the doorway of the Grand Supreme's private chambers. The time had finally arrived. He swirled a goblet of wine in his scaly hand as he stared out the window, talons scraping against the metal of his cup. Spacecraft zoomed by while others burned from the inside out. Debris floated, tumbling through space. Rubble drifted past the glass.

For whatever reason, he froze. An uneasiness overcame him every time he was in his master's presence. He was so utterly unpredictable, terrifying, and for whatever reason he felt small—

Like a child all over again in a room with a giant.

Izzo gulped the remainder of his blood-tinted wine before setting the goblet down on the ledge of the window. He slowly turned around, tilting his head to the side. He inwardly flinched, refusing to show any sign of fear. His first instinct was to fall on one knee in a submissive gesture, which he was more than accustomed to, but he willed himself to remain on his feet as a sign of disrespect.

It took every last bit of energy for him to remain standing. He inhaled.

Izzo scanned him with his golden slit eyes that always seemed to glow. A solemn expression graced his beady little face. Izzo stood approximately sixty centimeters shorter than Dante, which wasn't an intimidating height. The twisted crown of black horns on his head made him appear slightly taller but not by much. *Why was he so afraid?*

"So, it's come to this now, has it?" His master flashed a set of razor-sharp yellow teeth, for a moment, seeming welcoming. He licked a dribble of crimson wine from his chin with his black forked tongue. "Come sit with me, I'll pour you a cup."

Dante remained quiet, watching on in disgust, assessing his mood. He refused to fall for his fake kindness.

"No, thank you," he said abruptly.

"Suit yourself," the Grand Supreme shrugged. "You were always such a good boy and dare I say, my favorite subject. I considered you family at one time. You weren't self-centered like the others—you had something special about you, something they could never quite grasp no matter how hard they tried." Dante folded his arms, as he continued. "You were cold and ruthless. Obedient to a fault. You never questioned my orders no matter how much—"

Dante rolled his eyes then smirked. "Save me your pathetic tale. The others are dead. I killed them both with my bare hands. And now I'm here to claim your life."

Izzo stared on in silence before he shrugged. "I figured as much, especially after you led Valdez around the universes on a wild goose hunt instead of going straight to Keyserike's home world to interrogate his loved ones. It was the most obvious place he'd be. And Earth—"

A dizzying panic swelled through him. *Oh no, he couldn't possibly.* "What about Earth?" He managed to stay calm regardless.

His black forked tongue flickered through his cracked lips. "I know all about your haphazard plan and how you spared the planet for your human girl. Do you really think I'm that dense?" He paused for a moment. "Why do you think I sent you there in the first place?"

"Because I'm capable," Dante said matter-of-factly. "More capable than the others ever were."

"True, and you were the only one who could do what needed to be done."

Dante crossed his arms. "What's that supposed to mean? I purposefully failed. I made a laughingstock out of our operation."

Izzo remained quiet, mouth splitting into a wicked smile. "Just think about it. If you don't understand, you will."

"You fear humans more than anything, so the jest is on you," Dante spat back. For whatever reason he couldn't comprehend.

The Grand Supreme grew serious again, shaking his horned head. "I don't appreciate the insolent backtalk, nor do I appreciate being made a fool of. How dare you. When I'm done with you, and I finish scraping your remains from the bottom of my boots, and eradicating your home world, the very next place I'm heading is Earth. You and your entire race will be but a memory. A blip in time. A thousand years from now they'll say Emperor Dante II who?"

The breath swelled in Dante's throat. What had he gotten himself into? All he could do was hope Autumn had followed his directions and had gotten the hell off Surge. She should have been well on her way to Universe 25 if all had gone according to plan, where Izzo would never find her or his other loved ones.

How he hoped Izzo hadn't achieved immortality, or his efforts would be for naught.

The Grand Supreme cracked his knuckles, long heavy tail thrashing back and forth. "Shall we get down to business? You served your purpose well."

"I thought you'd never ask. This conversation has grown boresome."

His master's expression grew serious, hideous features straightening. His aura grew dark-purple, tiny fists trembling at his sides. Dante assumed a fighting stance. His heart raced as he anticipated his first move. Nobody had dared challenge the Grand Supreme in the last four hundred years.

He was the first. Perhaps he was a fool.

* * *

AUTUMN GRASPED the steering panel for dear life as she soared high into the sky, entering the rainbow atmosphere. The metropolis of Giarldinia and the palace of Sanguis had turned into tiny specks of dust far beneath her. The entire planet was cast in shadows thanks to the ongoing battle.

She had to be quick, only seconds remained until the forcefield reactivated. Then she'd be stuck and have to start the process all over again. Her heart slammed within her chest with anticipation. She closed her eyes for a moment as she continued up, up, up, sucking in a deep shuddering breath.

When she opened her eyes again, she was in the darkness of space. She gasped in disbelief at what she saw, cupping a black-gloved hand over her mouth. It was worse than she could've ever imagined.

Countless ships had been massacred. Too many to track. It was difficult to tell what side they were on. Steel and severed limbs floated through the black starry void of space; —a graveyard. Crimson blood pooled against the windows of her destroyer in splotches, dripping across the glass. Her stomach tied itself in knots. Thousands upon thousands of ships had been destroyed—

All because of the Grand Supreme's thirst for blood. How

many others would lose their lives because of his cruelty? Her fists trembled against the steering panel.

Beyond the devastation sat the most fearsome ship she had ever seen. It was the shape of an octagon with sharp angles and sprouting horns. Circular windows surrounded it in layers like a hive. Its obsidian steel glowed amidst the chaos. If she took a wild guess, it had to be where Emperor Izzo was located along with Dante and her dad. Goosebumps prickled over her skin.

As she stared in awe and horror at the massive spacecraft, a blue spark zapped across her line of sight. When she glanced, three destroyers headed her way at an impossible speed.

Holy crap, they were firing straight at her.

Autumn whipped her ship around in a one hundred and eighty degree turn and flew as fast as it would take her. She maneuvered around dead bodies and debris, twisting and turning through the battlefield.

Oh no, she panicked. If she got hit there would be no hope of her rescuing anyone. The key to the 25th Universe would be lost forever. The marble sized portal rolled around in her pocket. She had to keep it safe no matter the cost.

She approached the mothership at top speed when she heard the crunching of metal. She flew forward choking against her harness before slamming against the back of her seat. A burning smell filled her nostrils. One of the spacecraft had collided with her rear, knocking against her ship again and again. Her teeth gritted together as she spun out, screaming at the top of her lungs before steadying the direction of her destroyer.

Her adrenaline pulsated as she approached. She grew so close to the horizontal sliver of light peering out of the Grand Supreme's ship. It opened wider like a mouth that seemed to grin, creating an entrance.

Like he was expecting her.

When she slipped inside at the last possible moment, her ship came to a rocky landing. Autumn bounced around, finally steadying the destroyer. Her jaw fell to the ground. To her shock and horror, the other three ships had followed her inside. The door shut airtight behind them. The rear of her ship dented toward the control cabin.

She was trapped, unsure of whether she'd be able to fly again. A swell of panic raced through her body. Her senses went numb.

After her spacecraft had stilled, three of the most frightening lizard-like monsters she'd ever seen approached the outside of her destroyer wearing onyx uniforms. They put Valdez's scrawny Zexian soldiers to shame. Their bloodshot eyes appeared slit like a cat's. Their skin ranged from a translucent dark gray to the deepest shade of toxic obsidian. Their muscles were stacked. She hit the control panel, desperately making sure the entrance of her ship was locked.

Autumn didn't want them anywhere near her.

She unbuckled her harness, sliding down to the floor and into a fetal position. She removed her glove and threw a nail in her mouth. *Holy crap, what was she supposed to do?*

Sure, she'd been training for months and months, but suddenly she felt like she hadn't learned anything at all, like she was back at square one again.

Amidst her panic attack, she felt the hot pull of breath running across her hand. She glanced into her travel sack which sat beside her half-open. A long purr came followed by a wet pink nose. Mr. Hiss crawled out, rubbing his head against hers, licking her cheek with his rough tongue. He blinked his large indigo eyes, rolling on the cold metallic floor. His magenta and black striped tail swayed. His muzzle smiled at her.

"What are you doing here?" Her eyes widened. She had to protect him too.

KNOCK, KNOCK, KNOCK. Her stomach flipped. *Crap.* She looked at her pet before looking at the door.

"Come out, come out, little empress, wherever you are," a gruff voice said in Ivarkian. She could tell he was smiling like a fool by his tone.

"We know you're in there," a second high-pitched voice chimed in. When she glanced, a slit eye peered back at her through the window. She screamed, covering her mouth.

Cruel laughter erupted from outside.

"We can always smoke her out," she heard.

"I have a better idea."

Long talons scraped against the exterior of the door, creating a dent. She crawled back, holding Mr. Hiss in her lap as an eye peered through.

"There she is," a pair of inky upturned lips spoke through the hole in the door. Jagged teeth clicked, chattering together. She screamed.

The metal door dislodged, flying across the room, smacking into the wall at the opposite end. It crumpled, falling to the metallic-tiled ground.

She came to a shaky stand, resuming a fighting stance. She couldn't hide anymore.

A round of laughter erupted. "Come here, little empress. Let's make haste, our master is expecting you."

One of the creatures nudged the others with his spandex-covered elbow. "He was never specific about the state he expected you in. He left that open to interpretation."

Mr. Hiss rolled to his feet, stalking closer one paw at a time. His tail puffed, mouth curling in a snarl. He released a long angry hiss followed by a mini roar.

The three creatures glanced down, their red-slit eyes widening.

"It's our lucky day, boys. Not only have we captured the wanted empress of Universe 13, the pathetic specimen that she is, we're about to be rich beyond our wildest dreams," the monster knelt trying to lure Mr. Hiss to him, but he stayed put, claws scraping against the metallic floor.

"This baby ling will fetch a fortune," one of the soldiers rubbed his long taloned hands together in a greedy gesture.

"That is, if our master doesn't choose to keep him for himself."

"Who says we have to tell him?" the creature licked his scaly lips.

Mr. Hiss roared again, no louder than the last, but this time, he put more effort into it, opening his mouth to capacity.

They chuckled looking down at him. "Come here little guy, don't be fresh."

Suddenly, their wicked grins faded, and they stopped. Their eyes bulged in their heads as they jumped up and turned, pushing each other through the door, making a run for it.

Mr. Hiss's jewel-toned eyes glowed with a deep latent fury, lighting up the dark ship. A silver beam of light erupted from his mouth, zapping and twisting through the air. The energy swirled through the cabin and across the dock with such force that it turned the frightened soldiers to heaping piles of black dust upon impact. Their screams vanished into the void.

After vaporizing the intruders, her pet snapped out of his daze, yawning and stretching as if nothing had happened. He rolled over onto his side and entered a deep sleep, purring. His fluffy belly rose and fell as he entered a dream-like state. His tail rested against his leg.

Holy crap, Mr. Hiss.

Autumn walked over to him. Who would've thought a cub could possess such untapped power? She was beyond grateful for his help.

She knelt and kissed him on the cheek before coming to a

stand. His muzzle curved upward again. All she had to do was find Dante and her dad and get the heck off the ship.

Seventy-Three

DANTE LEANED hard into a fighting stance. His boots sat firm against the metallic tiled floor; his navy-gloved fingers twisted through the air. He stared down the Grand Supreme who stood before him with his arms folded. His crusty little mouth curved into an arrogant smirk, and his crown of horns sat askew on his tiny head.

An unsettling sensation rocked through his stomach. It was almost as if he was mocking his attempt. A ball of fire crackled through his palm, and he threw the flame straight at his beady little face. He stepped to the side easily deflecting his attempt. The flames sprayed along the wall, lighting his chair and surrounding furniture on fire.

"Okay, did you get that out of your system?" The Grand Supreme cocked his head to the side. His golden slit eyes grew wily with rage.

Before Dante could answer, Izzo leaped into the air, feet kicking, and kneed him in the gut with such force the wind knocked from his lungs. He gasped for air as his back slammed against the steel wall, forming an indentation. The impact created a crater he struggled to break free from. He peeled himself out and fell to his knees trying to catch his breath.

"Good, that's where you belong, on your knees like the meek slave that you are," the Grand Supreme took his teeny boot and kicked him in the back, causing him to fall on his stomach. He balled his fists with rage. *How dare he treat him with such disrespect.*

Dante rolled over and uppercut punched him in the jaw, sending him flying across the room and into the opposite wall. The flames widened for a moment with the passing wind before shrinking again. The room smelled of thick burning blood.

The Grand Supreme plopped himself out, landing onto his feet. He looked at him strangely. "I'm curious as to why you're wearing that uniform—it's not your house's crest or mine."

"Believe it or not, I have allies that aren't you," he said as a destroyer soared past the window, zapping one of Izzo's ships to fine space dust. The Zambarians had been most helpful, and Emperor Brumha's fleet was as impressive as he had hoped.

"Who would want to be your ally let alone your friend after the atrocities you committed?"

"You mean the ones you forced me to?"

Izzo slid his tongue over his yellow jagged teeth, grinning. "Believe me boy, you had a choice."

"I did—it was obey or die."

"Exactly," his master chuckled. "You were always a perceptive one, unlike your father."

"What about my father?" Goosebumps trickled down his spine. His fist trembled with fury.

"He was weak, greedy, and hard to control. I thought I was doing you a favor by getting rid of him. You were always so obedient, but little did I know, you'd turn out just like him. I wanted you to be the emperor I was hoping for."

Dante stared at him, unable to breathe. His father's death was no accident. As much as he despised him, he didn't deserve to meet his end the cruel way he did. The coward's way. Izzo was going to pay dearly.

Dante teleported behind him and cinched his short stubby arms against his back. Izzo released an inhuman scream, his long razor-sharp tail thrashed back and forth. Using the full force of his leg, he stomped the appendage out.

His vision flashed red. Every word out of his mouth was utterly infuriating since he had discovered he was behind his father's death. Something was strange about Izzo. They appeared to be neck to neck. He seemed no stronger than he was. His fighting skills were pathetic.

Could the rumors of his unfathomable strength be a myth?

"This is for my father," Dante flipped him around and took his boot, kicking Izzo square in the face. It was the only way to wipe off his self-satisfied smirk, forever imprinted in his memory. The force sent him toppling across the room once more and over his metal jug of blood-red wine. The container spilled, the contents running all over Izzo's body and between his boots, soaking the metallic tiled floor.

"For someone so strong, perhaps you should've seen that one coming. You fight like you haven't trained a day in your life."

"You dare disrespect me?" His eyes glowed golden yellow. A dark-red aura engulfed his whole body, piercing Dante to the core. Dante took two steps back as the floor trembled beneath them. His eyes widened as the Grand Supreme's legs and arms stretched a few feet and his face elongated, somehow becoming more hideous than before.

His heart pounded in his chest. *What on Earth did he get himself into?*

* * *

AUTUMN PLACED Mr. Hiss on the control seat of her damaged destroyer. He slept, hot pink and black striped belly rising and falling gently. She jumped as the floor vibrated beneath her feet like tremors from an earthquake. She had to hurry up and find Dante and her dad and get the heck out of here.

She pulled on her full-face helmet and activated the force-field on her spacecraft before she left Mr. Hiss, so he'd be safe while she was gone. Nobody would disturb him on her watch. Only a few hours of life remained on the destroyer after the scuffle she was in.

When she entered the dock, all that existed of the enemy soldiers were piles of fine black dust. She couldn't believe her sweet baby ling had so much power. She glanced back at him and smiled as he slept, purring in dreamland, before she advanced into the ship.

Autumn stopped dead in her tracks when she came to the hallway, unable to believe what she saw. A wave of sickness twisted through her stomach. Her nose scrunched from the rancid smell.

The ship was alive, she pushed a fingernail in her mouth, chewing the cuticle down to a nub.

A pink fleshy film resembling wet human skin coated the walls and ceiling. The sticky substance pulsated in rhythmic strides, loosening then firming again like a heartbeat. She cringed. By far the most unsettling detail was the dead alien bodies piled around the hall. Some appeared half eaten like they were mangled by wild animals while others were burnt to a blackened crisp. The lights above her head flickered wildly.

She closed her eyes for a moment taking deep controlled breaths. Dante had to have come this way, judging by the char marks on the walls and ceiling.

As she stepped over a faceless scaly alien body, the sight and smell of black blood became too much for her to bear. She knelt, tilting her helmet up, vomiting up her guts. *Gross.* She wiped her mouth against her arm before another round hit her more violently than the last.

When she reached the end of the hallway, a loud rattle came, and another tremor vibrated through the hollow interior of the ship, causing her to stumble a step. The lights dimmed, going dark for a moment. Her heart pounded in her ears, breath catching in her throat.

She looked both ways through the hallway. All was still and quiet. Another loud scraping sound came again, ricocheting down a flight of winding steps.

Autumn descended the stairs and onto the lower floor. She examined her surroundings. On either side were pulsating walls coated with containers of thick glass like a museum.

She ran her black-gloved fingers along the glass as she made her way deeper into the room. The containers were empty all except for one.

A wave of dizziness overtook her. Tears sprouted from her eyes, pouring down her cheeks. She choked from beneath her helmet. Her body grew as light as air. She ran over and pressed her palms against the enclosure, sliding down to the floor. She couldn't contain herself after seeing her dad.

Seventy-Four

DANTE QUIVERED; his eyes wide. Izzo had morphed into a monster. They stood eye to eye. His face grew long and lean like an insect's and his tail thrashed back and forth, whipping across the metallic tiles. His golden eyes thinned to slits, oversized head cocking to the side. He no longer appeared childlike in height but mature.

The Grand Supreme approached him one step at a time. Dante tried to size him up. He wasn't expecting him to transform. *Dammit,* he crossed his arms, doing his best to appear composed under the circumstances.

"You should be honored," he lisped, black forked tongue flicking through his dry lips. "Nobody has witnessed this form for the last four hundred years or so, since before the treaty was formed. Needless to say, the other party met their untimely end."

He rolled his eyes. Izzo's arrogance was sickening. How he wanted to wipe the smug smile off his face for good and avenge his father, who he hated but didn't deserve to die.

How he hoped Autumn had followed his directions and was safe in the secret 25th Universe. The very thought of protecting her kept him strong and focused.

"You're telling me like I care. Let's get down to business."

The Grand Supreme's eyes widened with rage like he had anticipated. He needed to see for himself what he was capable of. Curiosity got the best of him.

He charged over to him floating through the air, ready to strike. Izzo raised his foot to kick him, and he grabbed his scaly limb, swinging him around and around and around again, throwing him to the floor. He caught himself, landing back onto his feet. His reflexes had quickened, but he was still no match strength-wise.

Dante chuckled. "I'm rather unimpressed. Is this all the legendary Grand Supreme is capable of?"

Izzo stared at him strangely, then started laughing so loud his voice boomed through his chambers. He shook his elongated head, slapping his hand against his knee. His floor-length tail whipped across the metallic tiles.

Dante watched him. *What on Earth was so hilarious? It was like he was in on his own private joke.*

Finally, he stopped, straightening his features.

"Are you going to let me in on the big jest? Or are you laughing because you know you're about to die? It's a known fact that when we're faced with death, there's a tendency of succumbing to hysterics. So which is it? Spit it out, you disgusting bug."

"Neither," the Grand Supreme flashed a jagged yellow-toothed grin. "I have a funny little tale actually."

His eyes flickered to him as he continued. "You see, Armienti came to the Palace of Despair to see me. Your brother, isn't it?"

Dante's mouth fell wide open, almost hitting the floor. "How do you know he's my brother?"

"My dear Dante, everyone knows. You're the last to find out as usual. I thought it'd be more fun this way."

He could barely breathe; his vision flashed bright red.

What could he have possibly needed to speak to the Grand Supreme about? He was afraid to ask but needed to know.

He changed the subject, not feeding into his taunting nature. "What business did he have with you?"

"Wouldn't you like to know," the Grand Supreme chuckled. "Let's just say it has to do with someone near and dear to your heart. Someone you would kill for."

The anger swelled in Dante's chest. He was so furious he couldn't breathe.

Autumn.

Judging by Izzo's face it was exactly the response he anticipated. He wanted to infuriate him, to hear him beg for the information, but it mattered not.

"I don't care—keep it to yourself."

Izzo shrugged. "In case you're wondering, I gave him what he was looking for and so much more."

"Where is he? What are you talking about?" Dante's fists clenched, but he didn't answer. Unable to stand the self-satisfied look on Izzo's face, Dante leapt into the air, flying overhead. The Grand Supreme's eyes shot up at him, widening.

"You wasted your time with your little story, and I've since grown bored," he summoned a ball of fire in his hand so large the embers lit the entire room. Izzo's ink-black scales glittered in the firelight. He threw the flames at his elongated head, engulfing his body whole. Izzo screamed as the floor melted beneath his feet and he fell through multiple levels of the ship being guided by the fire Dante had created.

A *CRASH* came, shaking the entire ship, followed by pure silence. He took deep controlled breaths to compose himself. A few moments passed. Izzo didn't retaliate.

He suspected him to be dead after all his tough talk. Anyone else would be dead from a blast like he created. The force was enough to destroy a planet. To think he spent all the years of his life serving underneath his thumb. *Was he really that weak?* There was only one way to find out. He cracked his knuckles, flying down, down, down, through the layers of the ship, finally landing on the bottom floor. His boots slid across the cold steel floor.

His eyes widened in horror and disbelief at what he found.

* * *

AUTUMN'S BODY warmed with happiness as she moved closer to her dad, pressing her black-gloved fingers over the glass of his container. He sat in the corner staring at her, glasses cracked, sitting askew on his bearded face. His long, tangled whiskers covered his mouth and neck. The slash Izzo had given him remained on his cheek. He looked thinner than usual hunched over in threadbare rags.

"Dad, Dad, it's me," she smacked her palms against the glass, thrilled to see him. But he didn't budge from his seated position. Instead, he stared in silence. An indescribable sadness fell across his features.

"Dad," she said again. *Why wasn't he coming over to greet her?* And then she remembered her helmet. *Crap.* She removed her protective gear, placing it in the crook of her arm.

His large brown eyes wavered, turning glassy beneath his silver frames. He stood up and ran over to her.

"Autumn, I've been searching everywhere for you," he pressed his hands to the glass, his whiskered mouth curved into a shaky smile. "I'm so glad you're safe. How did you find me?"

A violent tremor rattled through the ship, causing them both to stumble to their knees. They stood up slowly as the vibration settled. They had to get out of here. Something wasn't right—she could feel it in her bones.

"I'm going to get you out of here," she reassured him. "We're going home."

His skin paled. "But how? I've tried everything. There's no way out," he lowered his voice to a whisper. "You have to be careful; this place is heavily guarded. They *eat* their prisoners alive. I'm the only one left."

A sick sensation rattled through her as she recollected the decaying alien bodies in the hallway upstairs. She didn't have time to dwell though, she had to act fast.

She drummed her black-gloved fingers, remembering how her friends from Earth reacted to her *change.* "Dad, I have something to tell you. Maybe it's easier to show you, but you have to promise that you won't freak out or think any differently of me."

"I love you no matter what, nothing could stop me," his whiskered mouth curved, eyes glimmering beneath the reflection of his cracked glasses.

She waved her hand, gesturing. "I need you to stand to the side."

He moved over at her request. She assumed a fighting stance as he watched her strangely, probably wondering what the heck she was doing.

Autumn tightened her fist as hard as she could, preparing to swing.

"Wait, don't do it. This enclosure is electrified. I tried—"

Her dad ducked down, covering his head. She swung with all her might, cracking the thick glass to the core. Stress fractures twisted and curled, coating its exterior. She raised her leg, taking her boot and slammed the bottom through, creating a passageway for her dad. She climbed inside and helped him through the hole. Waves of electricity sparked against her back as she covered him, but they barely phased her.

He placed his hands on her cheeks, staring into her eyes. "What did he do to you? When I get my hands on Dante—"

Autumn remained quiet for a moment as he hugged her with all his might, being an overprotective dad.

"Um, yeah, about that—"

He continued, appearing to not hear her. "I missed you so much. I thought I lost you forever like your mom."

Voices echoed in the background. The hair on the back of her neck stood at perfect attention. Her dad froze as well, hugging her still.

"Here they come. We have to get out of here," he whispered, but it was too late. Two scaly aliens approached them with bulging muscles and razor-sharp teeth. Their faces were far from human and deathly frightening. One chewed on an arm, sucking the contents clean before tossing the rubbery limb to the ground. Autumn covered her mouth with her hand and her dad quaked.

They spotted them together, and their expressions glowed.

Seventy-Five

AUTUMN WAS SO scared she couldn't breathe. Her dad's teeth chattered in his mouth and his eyes grew wide with terror. She had to be brave. There were no excuses, and there was nowhere to hide.

Nobody could protect her dad except for her. He was a helpless human, and she had special abilities.

Despite seeing her in action earlier, her dad threw himself in front of her to shield her with his body like only a dad would do. "Who's there?" he shouted, body shaking.

"Dad," she hissed, trying to move him aside.

He waved a hand. "Autumn, I got this."

No, he doesn't.

The two creatures stood there with their arms folded. They stared at him before glancing at the shattered hole in his container. They grinned wicked, yellow-toothed grins, speaking in their native language before advancing, despite his question.

"Stop right there," her dad shouted, raising his palms in the air. "Or else, I'll…"

Autumn sighed. *Crap.* She walked in front of her dad,

resting her hand on her hip, trying her hardest to look menacing. Her dad gasped, attempting to budge her, but he couldn't. She was too strong.

The monsters stopped dead in their tracks, their red-slit eyes bulged in their heads.

"Why if it isn't Empress Autumn Martyne," one of the creatures said in Ivarkian, licking his black tongue against his scaled lips. "How does it feel to be the ruler of a fallen empire?"

She cringed. "If you come any closer, I'll—"

"You'll what?" The other monster's mouth tilted on his frightening face. A dribble of blood ran down his chin from the arm he consumed, before he licked the droplets up greedily.

"I'll kill you both," she said. Her dad quaked beside her.

"What did you say?" he asked, and she shrugged.

She was glad he didn't understand her because he wasn't going to like what was going to happen next.

The aliens looked at each other and laughed. She was tired of being the butt of everyone's joke.

Instead of guns, the creatures unsheathed sabers from their thick black belts. They held the pommels, pointing the tip straight at her.

"Emperor Izzo is expecting her," one of the monsters whispered to the other loud enough for her to detect.

"She provoked us—we'll tell him she put up a fight. A few nicks won't make a difference." He charged straight at them swinging back his sword, high above his head. At the last moment, he lunged to strike her dad. She jumped into the air, bringing her knee to his solid gut, stopping him in his tracks. He flew through the air, smashing through another glass tank. Her dad gasped, covering his whiskered mouth. He stared at the creature and then at her.

She regarded the other monster whose knees knocked together, wobbling with each step.

"Well, what are you waiting for? There's plenty more where that came from," she taunted.

The second creature shrieked, dropping his saber on the ground with a *ping*. He attempted to make a run for it, boots skidding across the metallic tiled floor. Autumn flew after him. She couldn't allow him to escape, or else the Grand Supreme would figure out she was on board. She raised her fists high above her head, balling them with all her might, and smacked him in the back. He landed on his stomach, knocked out cold.

She knelt, catching her breath. Another wave of sickness rattled through her. These creatures sure stank. She rose to a trembling stand.

Her dad sprinted over to her. "Are you okay?" He hugged her again. She nodded slowly in his arms. "I don't understand any of this. We need to get out of here."

"No, not yet. We have to find Dante and bring him with us." She grabbed the saber out of the unconscious alien's hand. She passed it to her dad who fumbled it in his grasp. "Hold this. You need to be able to protect yourself just in case." *I can't*, she left unsaid.

He rolled his eyes. "What could you possibly want with him? He's a—"

"Murderer? Well, that makes two of us," she glanced down at her hands.

He gasped and she ignored his reaction and raced into the cage, grabbing the other saber for herself. She didn't have time to argue with her dad. She had to find Dante so they could get the heck out of there.

* * *

DANTE KNELT on the ground with his navy-gloved hand cupped over his mouth. He ran his fingers against what he thought was Izzo—only he wasn't there.

He picked up the pieces of shed skin in the silhouette of his body. A cool chill trickled down the length of his spine as he tossed the skin to the floor. The casing crunched and scraped across the ground. He surveyed his surroundings. He was on the lowermost level of Izzo's pleasure cruiser. Metal crates encircled him in stacks, piled high to the ceiling. Squealing chains swung overhead but he was nowhere to be found. The lights flickered and dimmed in a frenzy.

A throat cleared and he whipped around, but he couldn't see where the sound came from. His eyes shot over to the corner where a long shadow swayed ever so slightly.

His entire body trembled down to the depths of his toes. He glanced up slowly, tentatively. His eyes widened in horror. Izzo towered over him, head almost touching the high ceiling.

Izzo's muscles grew thick and bulging, his head rounded, free of horns and no longer elongated and cumbersome. His slit eyes ranged from yellow to a deep blood red, almost appearing purple. His teeth were sharp and jagged, and his tail slashed around, whipping through the air with cracks. As he walked toward him, his toenails scraped and clicked against the metallic tiled floor, dragging with fierce precision.

Oh please, no, he'd underestimated him. He transformed again.

Dante took two shocked steps in retreat before he froze in place. He struggled to move, struggled to think despite his attempts to break free. Izzo chuckled. His voice grew deep and raspy, and then his tail shot out, sending Dante hurtling into a pile of crates, smashing them to the floor. He groaned as Izzo's tail slithered over, coiling around his neck, then locking against his skin. He choked as he dragged him back over, suspending him in the air.

"Did you really think I'd be so easily defeated, foolish boy?"

Dante moved his lips to speak, but no words came out as

his windpipe was crushed by his master. He was in a world of trouble.

Izzo grazed his scaly taloned fingers against his ear, before chewing his lip into a smile. "What's that—no smart come back? Nothing about how you plan to kill me?"

Dante's eyes widened. All he saw was red followed by shooting stars.

"I didn't think so."

The Grand Supreme flipped Dante around and punched him in the back so many times he lost count. Fist collided with bone. No matter how hard he tried kicking and squirming, he couldn't break free. Izzo was too strong. Finally, after what seemed like forever, Izzo loosened his grasp from around his neck and let him fall to the floor in a weak slump. He rasped for breath, lying at his feet.

Izzo grabbed him by the hair, and he winced in agony. "What? Had enough already? I'm nowhere near done with you, slave."

He took his knee and brought the cap to Dante's face. His vision began to fade at the corners. Warm salty blood trickled down his nose and over his mouth. The Grand Supreme took his foot, raised it up, and with two stomps both of his thigh bones cracked. He groaned, lying on the ground.

Izzo then swept him into the air telepathically and tossed him into the wall. Dante slammed into the cold hard steel before falling on his back.

The Grand Supreme waved a long taloned finger. "What a shame. Things didn't have to end this way if only you had cooperated and given me what I wanted. It wouldn't have come to this. You could've been a living god."

Dante stared at him strangely before his eyes closed, and for a moment, he could've sworn he smelled Autumn, the love of his life. Her sweet floral scent permeated through his nose, warming his senses. He could leave this world knowing that she was safe, and at least he'd done one thing right. The jest was on his master.

A quiet buzz came, and he opened his eyes. A drone floated overhead.

"Now everyone can witness what happens to those who defy me. The end of a legend. Dante the Great Conqueror, do you have any last words?"

<h1 style="text-align:center">Seventy-Six</h1>

AUTUMN MADE her way with her dad through a long dark hallway. They each held a sharp saber in their hand. The fleshy walls pulsated. Droplets of water trickled down them like beads of sweat.

She led the way, and he followed close behind. She wondered where Dante was on the ship, and it surprised her she hadn't encountered him yet.

Suddenly, her dad stopped in his tracks. She turned around to see what was wrong.

He sighed. "Autumn, something is eating away at me. Something you said earlier."

A period of silence followed.

"What?" She couldn't think straight as adrenaline coursed through her veins. She had to find Dante. They had to get out of here. Her heart thundered in her ears. *What could she have possibly said that'd upset him in the short time they'd been reunited?*

He stuttered, bringing his dark-brown eyes to hers. "Well, you mentioned you murdered someone before. Is it true?"

Oh, that. She sighed. How she wished she hadn't brought it up at all. Guilt coursed through her body for worrying her dad after everything he'd been through. He didn't need this on top of everything else.

Her bottom lip quivered as her heart sank in her chest. Her stomach flip-flopped.

"If something happened out here in space, I just want to let you know that I don't blame you. These creatures are horrifying, unlike anything I've ever seen before. They're deadly and will stop at nothing to harm others. And if one of them tried to hurt you, then you made the right call. I would've done the same thing."

"No, it's not that," she glanced away, struggling to find the right words under the circumstances. She closed her eyes taking deep controlled breaths before finally admitting. "It's mom."

His thick brows furrowed. "Mom? What are you talking about?"

"It's all my fault," her voice skipped.

"What is?"

"That she's gone."

She paused for a moment; in disbelief she was about to tell him what happened. She'd been haunted for years by the last time they were together. She hadn't had a moment's rest. "She was hit by a guy from my school who was driving on his permit overnight. But it was my fault she was out," her throat went bone dry. "We chose not to tell you so you wouldn't get upset."

He threw a hand across his whiskered mouth, shaking his head. "How did you find out who hit her, or have you always known?"

"Dante."

His face hardened with anger. Lines crinkled across his brow. "I see. Somehow, I figured he was responsible for this."

She continued. "Caleb and I had a fight, and I smashed my phone out of anger. Mom found out, and she left the house to get me a new one during her morning jog so you wouldn't know. Dad, I'm so sorry," her chest grew heavy with pain.

His brows furrowed, before he hugged her again. "That was not your fault, none of this is. Her death was an accident. You're not to blame. Unfortunately, it's just one of those things that no matter how we look at it, couldn't have been changed. I'm glad you were honest with me though. Let's not keep anything from each other ever again. We used to tell each other everything, until—"

BANG, BANG, BANG, the sound rattled her to the core. She pulled away holding her saber. Her black-gloved palm slipped against the pommel.

"What was that?" Her Dad's eyes widened beneath his cracked silver frames.

"I don't know," she admitted, but there was only one way to find out. They had explored most of the ship except for the lowermost level.

They descended the final flight of steps. Autumn was sure to keep her eyes peeled and her wits about her. Her dad followed close behind.

Loud crashing continued as they advanced on the tips of their toes, trying their best to move as quietly as they could, so as not to be detected.

They arrived at an open doorway. She peeked around the corner to where the ruckus was coming from. *Oh my gosh.* Autumn's legs wobbled beneath her weight, and her dad caught her before she hit the ground, giving their position away. She was shocked and horrified and disgusted at what she saw. She cupped a hand over her mouth to prevent herself from screaming.

Seventy-Seven

THE INTERIOR of the room was dimly lit. Lights flickered on and off at a rapid pace. Heavy chains hung from the ceiling, swinging, and Autumn could've sworn a leg accompanied them as well as a severed head. Metal cargo boxes were stacked on all sides of the room, covered with Xs.

A monster towered at least fourteen feet tall, coated in sharp black iridescent scales, with his back turned to them. His floor-length tail thumped against the ground in rhythmic movements. Three toes scraped on either foot, nails clicking against the metallic tiles like a velociraptor.

Beneath him, Dante was on his knees being beaten senseless. His nose was bloody and deep purple bruises littered the flawless blue skin of his face. Drones buzzed overhead capturing the horrific scene.

She shuddered from head to toe — *the Grand Supreme.*

Autumn went back into the hallway hyperventilating with her hand over her mouth. She had to help him, but how? She'd never seen Dante suffer such defeat. Her dad's eyes grew wide with terror beneath his silver frames. The saber rocked in his hand.

"Autumn, I can't let you go in there. There's no way. There's nothing we can do—"

"Dad, I have to help him. I can't leave him like this. You have to stay here where it's safe," she reached for her pocket, unzipping the opening. The silver marble portal to the 25th Universe slid between her fingertips. She handed it to her dad, and he stared at her strangely. "If I don't come back, I need you to open this. It's the only way you'll be safe from him."

"Autumn," he went to grab her, but she brushed his hand away from her arm, ignoring his plea. He remained in the hallway like she requested, peeking through the doorway.

She took hold of her saber with both hands, tiptoeing against the floor. The drones buzzed all around her. Everyone could see what she was up to, whether she wanted them to or not. A lone drop of sweat rolled down her back. She had to stop him no matter the cost. Everyone in the universes and everyone back home was counting on her to succeed.

She got as close as two feet from his back, saber raised high above her head, ready to strike him square between the ribs. She inhaled. *What a mistake she made.*

In an instant, Emperor Izzo whirled around, and she went airborne, dropping the saber on the floor with a loud pang and crashing into a pile of steel crates. The boxes crumbled and exploded all over the floor in a heap.

The wind knocked from her lungs and dozens of stars crossed before her eyes. The Grand Supreme let Dante fall to the floor and he approached her. Her heart raced. Dante lay on his side, still conscious but barely.

"For an Imperial Guard, you sure have some nerve interrupting me."

Dante groaned in the background and Emperor Izzo turned around. "Don't go anywhere—I'll be with you in a moment." His yellow jagged teeth curled into a smile, dark-purple eyes lifting high on his face.

Autumn crawled backwards as he approached her.

* * *

DANTE LAY ON THE FLOOR, his vision fading at the corners. He blinked several times to keep himself from nodding off. Both of his legs were broken along with many of his ribs. Sharp pain shot through his torso. His temples throbbed with a migraine. He took his glove, wiping the fabric over his nose and lips to stop the bleeding. His mouth tasted of salty blood. Drones buzzed overhead adding to his humiliation. His beating was being broadcasted. Everyone would witness his end, including his own family. And worst of all, Autumn. She didn't need this on top of everything else.

He reached into his pocket to search for the metal vials gifted to him by Luz only to discover they had rolled out during the fight. A wave of panic washed through him until a glimmer of blue caught his eye against the wall. If only he could get closer to consume them, but he didn't want to risk drawing attention from the Grand Supreme. He'd surely destroy them.

He squinted, drawing his eyes back to the commotion. *Who was this foolish Imperial Guard wielding and outdated saber, and what the hell was he thinking?* Although he was grateful the pain had temporarily ceased, he would soon be among the dead. He was short and scrawny, much smaller than the others, reminiscent of the child who had sacrificed his life on Varz. He had no skill set whatsoever.

What a numbskull, he should've fled when he had the chance. There was nothing he could do to help him. He shook his head with what little strength he had left.

Then, his eyes connected with Autumn's father who peered around the corner before disappearing again. He too held an archaic saber. *Oh no, please no,* he begged the gods, although he doubted they'd listen to him. He didn't deserve their help, not after everything he'd done. It couldn't be, but nothing else made sense.

Autumn.

Seventy-Eight

AUTUMN GROANED beneath a pile of crates as a dark shadow loomed over her. A pair of deep purple eyes glowered in the flickering lights. She gulped. *Crap.* She'd royally messed up her rescue operation and she couldn't see any way out of the situation she'd created. She was screwed.

Before she could think, long taloned scaly fingers wrapped themselves around the collar of her uniform and slammed her against the wall back-first, holding her up with one hand. Pain rattled from her spine through her tailbone. She winced, biting back a scream.

The Grand Supreme breathed his blood-soaked breath against her neck, fogging the visor of her full-face helmet. Goose pimples prickled along her skin. She tried her best to conceal her fear, but it was so intense, she risked passing out.

"Something is different about you. You smell so much sweeter than the rest, and your inexperience is apparent," Emperor Izzo's black tongue flickered through his dry cracked lips.

"Oh gods, please no," Dante attempted to crawl toward her but fell onto his side, groaning.

The Grand Supreme whipped his head around and grinned. "My dear Elattion emperor, be patient—I'll be with you in a moment."

With his other hand, he removed her helmet, tossing it to the floor with a clunk. His smile widened.

"Why if it isn't Empress Autumn Martyne. How nice of you to join us, and right on time too." The drones swarmed around her face in a tornado before flying off to the center of the room.

Her eyes met Dante's before she looked back at the Grand Supreme in silence. She coughed and choked as he placed her onto her feet.

Emperor Izzo turned around and waved. "Dante, I hope you're paying close attention."

He leaned over and brought his sharp teeth to her neck, piercing her skin. His forked tongue licked up the droplets of blood before they hit the collar of her uniform. Her strength faded, her legs wobbling beneath her weight. He was draining her of her energy.

She twisted and squirmed, trying to escape, before taking her hand and smacking him clear across his scaly face, causing him to take a step back.

"Stay away from me," she shouted. "You creep."

He shook his head before his face contorted with rage. "How dare you lay your filthy hands on me, human. I should bite them off," his words echoed throughout the room, pounding against her eardrums.

Before she could think, his scaly palm connected with her cheek, and she fell onto the floor seeing stars. She sniffed, her nose trickling with thick blood. Dante punched the floor repeatedly, gritting his teeth, "Dammit."

Emperor Izzo grabbed her by the collar again, pulling her from the floor like a ragdoll.

The Grand Supreme cocked his head to the side. "I should

be more careful not to lose my temper, especially with someone in your delicate condition."

Her eyes thinned to slits, fists trembling at her sides. "What are you talking about?"

His flaking mouth curled at its corners. "The rumors are true. It's only taken four hundred years but it's finally time."

Emperor Izzo scanned her with his cat-slit eyes, and she remained quiet. Her mind raced a million miles an hour. "I can't believe you don't know. You're about to give me everything I've ever wanted. Everything I've ever dreamed of."

A wave of panic crashed through her body. *Could he know about the portal? Should she just give it to him? Maybe then he'd let everyone live. Maybe then he'd stop hurting Dante.*

"My dear, you're with child."

Her eyes widened, throat going bone dry. "No, I'm not. That's not true." She'd know something like that, wouldn't she? She looked at Dante with pleading eyes.

"Yes, you are—I can taste the innocence in your blood. You have a traitor among you watching your every move who has confirmed my suspicions," he cackled. "They report to me almost daily. The late night visits with your Emperor. The high fevers and nausea. The mood swings. All classic signs."

Dante dry-heaved and all she could do was stare on in horror. *Who?*

Emperor Izzo continued. "Your child belongs to me. To consume a single drop of their hybrid blood is priceless. The key to immortality. I'll raise them as my own to be the perfect warrior, the ultimate destroyer," he paused. "I could've sent anyone on my team to conquer Earth, what a weak and pitiful lower-life form species," he spat on the ground. "Why do you think I sent a pathetic heartbroken Elattion prince? I knew you'd do exactly what I needed you to do—fall in love with a human."

So many emotions swelled deep inside of her—shock,

hatred, disgust, and fear for her unborn child if what he claimed was true. There was no way she'd give him what he wanted. All she saw was red hot fury. Her energy spiked for a split second. She took her foot and kicked him in the gut, sending him hurling across the room into a pile of crates on the opposite side. Chains and limbs swung from the ceiling. He collided with a crash. The floating drones stopped and exploded in their places, pieces fluttering to the ground.

She went to go after him when a fist connected with her spine. He'd teleported behind her. The force knocked her to the center of the room where she landed flat on her face, feet bending over her head. Long, clicking toenails scraped against the silver tiles. Izzo's tail thrashed, thumping, causing the floor to shake.

DANTE GRITTED his teeth and punched the floor several times. He was beyond enraged that Izzo put his hands on his wife and there was nothing he could do to help her. His chest burned, sickness swelling inside of him. Their child was in danger. The child he'd always dreamed of.

He tried to stand up, but his legs crumpled to the ground. Sharp pain shot through his limbs. He was too weak, and his body had been badly damaged. He tried to fly, but he couldn't get up the strength. The vials were too far from him.

Izzo loomed over her with a sick smile on his face. It was the same expression he always had before he made a violent kill.

"Please, you don't have to do this. I'm the one you want. Take me instead. Just let her live," he pressed his palms together. He'd do anything to save her life. Tears streamed down his cheeks.

Izzo rolled his eyes. "Please, Dante, save your breath. You

sound pathetic. How many have begged you for their lives and you killed them regardless?"

Dante remained quiet and a deep painful sadness consumed him. A black hole.

He turned back to Autumn, ignoring him. "I'm not one to break my promises, little empress."

Seventy-Nine

AUTUMN LAID on the floor as Emperor Izzo crouched over her with a frightening grin. He held her arms above her head with one hand as she kicked her legs furiously, trying to land a hit on him, but it was no use; he was too strong.

She was way out of her league. She'd never stood a chance against him, despite her attempts.

He laughed in her face, sharp yellow teeth glinting. "You're a feisty one, aren't you, Empress Autumn? I'm going to enjoy making you scream. Nobody lays a hand or foot on me and lives to tell the tale."

In an instant, he took his elbow and crushed his limb against her left arm, causing the bone to snap. Her humerus cracked, still attached by dangling muscle and skin. Her scream echoed throughout the cabin as he pushed down harder and harder, digging his elbow in.

Dante tried once more to crawl over, but he couldn't make the trip. He was too weak. He stopped, punching the ground.

"I hope you're paying close attention, Emperor. I'm going to enjoy what happens next."

Suddenly, she couldn't move. Her body hovered inches above the floor. She twisted and tried to escape, but the

Grand Supreme's telepathic grasp was unfathomable, crushing her senses. Her broken arm throbbed. His forked tongue flickered against her lips and into her mouth, she gagged.

His long taloned nails ran over her stomach and her back, scraping against her bodysuit. A creepy sensation swept through her belly, and she gasped.

Autumn stared at Dante, her eyes bulging with terror. Finally, he managed to come to a stand, limping toward her one leg at a time, but his effort was in vain. Emperor Izzo laughed and suspended him telepathically in the air before thrusting him into a wall, leaving an indentation. He laid on the floor, trying to rise again but it was no use. He was too injured.

"Keep your filthy hands off of my wife, or I'll—" His hands slid against the floor.

"Or you'll what? What can you possibly do to stop me?"

He remained silent.

"That's what I thought. Settle down, your turn will come soon enough."

He shouted something else in his alien language that she couldn't understand, and red lights began to flash throughout the ship. The vessel rocked and revved.

"In an hour's time you'll be blown to space dust and so will your entire race. I can survive in the darkness of space, but you cannot. After I claim your mate's life, I'm heading straight to Surge to pay your family a long overdue visit. Ronan and Leyla are expecting me," he licked his lips. "And then, I'll embark on the long treacherous voyage to Earth. If only you had known your place and complied, none of this would've happened and you could've coexisted under my thumb."

The energy hemorrhaged from her body in sparks and waves. Her limbs grew weak and heavy. Her mouth dried out and her senses slowed to a crawl. She closed her eyes as they rolled back in her head, unable to bear this situation any longer. Instead, she focused on the pull of her breath. She tried to imagine what her life could've been like if everything had gone right. Her baby's smiling face, rosy cheeks, and bright eyes, being with the man she loved, helping others, and just being happy.

That's all she ever wanted.

As she faded into the darkness, a warm wet splash interrupted her fantasy. She spit the salty fluid out of her mouth. When she opened her eyes, thick black blood dripped over her stomach and pooled along the floor. She glanced up to find that the Grand Supreme had a saber piercing clear through the scales of his throat. He choked and struggled to remove the weapon, talons scraping in vain as he spun around in circles.

Her dad stood behind him, inhaling and exhaling, face shifting bright red. Dante grinned from the floor.

With adrenaline crashing through her veins, she came to a shaking stand. Her left arm fell limp at her side. She winced, grabbing hold of it. The pain shattered through her.

She heard a whisper of breath flow through her mind.

"Autumn, you must finish him off. There's a chance he might regenerate."

She frantically searched everywhere for her saber. She'd dropped her weapon during the struggle earlier.

She raced over to Dante. His handsome blue face was littered with purple bruises. His lip was busted and swollen. He could barely hold his head up. He pointed toward the weapon on the floor. She knelt and lifted her saber with her good hand and positioned it against her body.

Emperor Izzo fell against the wall choking on his own fluids, purple slit-eyes wide with terror. She hated to admit it, but something inside of her loved seeing him afraid. She held the weapon steady and focused.

"Here you go, Izzo. It's your worst fear realized," Dante's

voice was weak, his mouth curved. "Despite your tough talk, both you and I know there's nothing you're more afraid of than a human."

Autumn charged as fast as she could, sliding the blade through his scaly muscular stomach. Upon impact, she closed her eyes and turned around, covering her face with her hand. She heard his heavy body slump to the ground, struggling and gasping. Finally, he stopped moving all together. All went quiet.

Her dad rushed up to her and gave her a big hug. She winced as he touched her broken arm. It hung limp at her side.

"Are you okay?" he asked, his eyes wavered beneath his silver frames.

"Yes, I think so." The red lights continued to flash from the ceiling. They didn't have much time. The ship wouldn't last forever. She had to act fast.

She raced over to Dante, falling on her knees. She hugged him close.

"Come on, we have to get going," she kissed him, and he blinked slowly, amber eyes glowing. "We don't have a lot of time."

"Little Moonlight, you're hurt again and it's all because of me. I hurt you both," he brought his hand to her arm and then over her stomach, a tear rolled down his blue bruised cheek. "Here, let me help you."

Dante pointed to the corner of the room where a blue sparkle caught her eyes. Autumn raced over and discovered two clear blue vials rolling against the wall. She bent over and picked them up, staring at them strangely in the palm of her hand.

"Drink this for yourself and for our child and give the other one to your father."

"What is this?" She examined the containers.

"Instant rejuvenation from a friend I met along the way."

She popped the cork top open with her teeth and drank the bubbling blue liquid. The droplets tasted sweet against her tongue. Her energy returned and the bone of her arm shifted, knitting itself back together. She moved and stretched, the pain subsiding instantly. At his request, she tossed the second bottle to her dad.

"What about you?"

"I only have two and you both need it more than I do," his eyes closed.

"You and your father should get going. I'm just going to slow you down," he turned his head to the side, and his face fell. "I don't want to hurt you anymore. As long as we're together, you'll always be at risk."

"No, I'm not going without you," she rested her head on his chest, listening to his slow heartbeat. He ran his hand through the pigtail plaits of her braids catching his fingers in the loops. She brought her lips to his.

She sat up slowly, vision fogging. "Dad, you have to help me—it's the only way we can get him out of here."

Her dad hesitated before approaching them. He glowered at Dante, arms crossed. "I don't understand any of this. You've created a real mess for everyone. You kidnapped my little girl. You have a lot of explaining to do. After this is over, you and I are going to have a long talk and things are going to change."

Dante nodded slowly. "As you wish."

She sighed, throwing her hands up in the air. "Dad, we don't have time for this. The ship isn't going to last much longer."

She and her dad knelt, each taking one of Dante's arms and wrapping them over their shoulders. They helped him to a shaking stand. As they walked, he limped with each step. He hung his head forward, perspiration beaded across his brow. He'd taken a beating much worse than she had.

When they went to pass through the doorway, Autumn

stopped. Rage coursed through her as she looked at the dead tyrant. She reached and plucked the Grand Supreme's hideous inhuman head straight from his broken neck.

Dante turned, eyes widening. Her dad watched her in silence.

"What on Earth do you intend to do with that?" Dante asked.

She ripped a piece of his white velvet cape, creating a sack. "I'm taking it as proof. Nobody will believe he's dead."

"How very savage of you."

She shrugged. "I learned from the best."

The blinking red light quickened, snapping her out of her triumphant moment. They had to get out of here. Time was running out.

PART EIGHT

After Midnight

<h1 style="text-align:center;font-style:italic;">Eighty</h1>

AFTER MANY AGONIZING steps walking over dead alien bodies and through the disgusting pulsating halls of Emperor Izzo's ship, they arrived at the docking station. Only minutes remained before the ship self-destructed.

Izzo's parting gift.

The red lights frantically flashed and danced along the ceiling and the floor vibrated beneath her feet. Autumn's heart pounded in her ears.

She left Dante with her dad for a moment. They still hadn't spoken two words to each other. This promised to be a *fun* flight home.

She raced back onto her damaged destroyer and grabbed Mr. Hiss from the control seat. He was fast asleep, purring in dreamland, blissfully unaware of the battle for the universes that had taken place right onboard. He blinked his brilliant sapphire eyes at her before yawning and stretching. She picked him up, cradling him in her arms.

She rejoined them, Mr. Hiss in tow, purring. She led Dante and her dad onto one of the enemy ships of Emperor Izzo's alien soldiers that had chased and threatened her life when she had first arrived. She and her dad helped Dante onto one of the seats, clicking his harness in place. A total first for her. It was her turn to make sure he stayed safe. He leaned back, unable to support his own weight. His ink-black hair matted to his glistening blue brow.

Her dad took a seat as well. When she handed Mr. Hiss to him, all he could do was stare at her hot-pink baby ling as he nuzzled his ribs affectionately. She could only imagine what he thought of all this. Of course, Mr. Hiss chose that moment to relieve himself.

"I'm sorry, Dad," she shook her head and he sighed, rolling his eyes. Mr. Hiss's muzzle tilted up. He desperately needed to be trained. She'd add it to the long list of things she needed to do when they arrived back home.

Emperor Izzo's severed head sat in the makeshift sack, resting by her feet.

She hit a few buttons and the door sealed airtight. *Great,* she smiled. The destroyer itself was easy enough to start as well because the control panel mirrored what she was used to. *Thank goodness.*

After they had settled, panic rattled her to the core. *How the heck was she supposed to get off this ship?*

She began to sweat and twitch her fingers. She full-on hyperventilated, growing dizzier by the second. They were trapped and the ship was set to detonate any minute. Her shoulders ached from growing so tense. Perspiration crept across her brow.

"The exit of this ship is motion activated," Dante offered, probably sensing her out of control anxiety spiking to new levels. His head rolled to the side, midnight hair falling against his battered face.

She nodded. *Why didn't she think of that?*

The ship reversed. One minute remained. As they slipped outside of the horizontal entrance, her heart sped. Thousands upon thousands of destroyers had been massacred during the battle. Pieces of wreckage, along with carnage from the bodies of fallen soldiers, floated through the dark void of space. Countless warriors had lost their lives, all thanks to the Grand Supreme's reign of terror.

Autumn did a double take. She could've sworn she saw Emperor Brumha flying, accompanied by his impressive fleet. *What the heck? Why was he here?*

She glanced at Dante, who was suffering in his seat. She was sure he had something to do with it, but she didn't have time to dwell. She had to act quickly.

Upon first glance, Emperor Izzo's ship flew in close range to Surge. So close that the blast promised to take out the planet like he had intended. He would still win after death, and she refused to let that happen. Everyone was counting on her.

"What do we do?" Panic was apparent in her voice.

Dante looked at her, his navy-gloved hands falling at his sides. "Do you have it?"

"Have what?" she asked.

"The portal. Please tell me you do," he slumped over, too weak to sit up.

She searched her pockets with her good hand, unable to find the sphere. Her heart sped. Where the heck did she put it?

During her second panic attack, her dad tapped her shoulder and handed her the tiny silver orb she'd entrusted him with earlier. The ball sat in her palm the size of a marble.

"Open it," Dante instructed her, sounding like more of a demand than a request.

With her thumb and pointer finger, she popped open the pieces unsure of what to expect. At first nothing happened. She glanced at Dante. *Had they been duped?* He leaned over, joining his weak hand with hers, and his eyes fluttered closed. She watched for any developments. Inside, stars sparkled through the darkness followed by translucent purple rays spanning from inside the ship through the blackness of space.

A rumbling blast came from Emperor Izzo's ship, thrusting the destroyer forward, spinning it in a full circle, accompanied by hurtling debris. Rainbow colors swirled across her line of vision, and they disappeared through time and space. Her eyes fluttered closed from the overwhelming sensation of warmth, love, peace, and safety. There was no fear or pain where they were headed. No sadness or desperation. She could feel it deep in her bones.

When she opened her eyes again, all was quiet, like nothing had happened. No war. No death. No destruction. The wreckage had disappeared, and Emperor Brumha's fleet and the entire planet of Surge remained untouched. They floated through the peacefulness of space.

They were finally safe in the heart of the legendary 25th Universe.

Eighty-One

PLANET SURGE and the palace-top landing pad appeared as Autumn had remembered them. She lowered the destroyer onto X marks the spot. She took deep controlled breaths, calming herself down before unbuckling her harness. They'd been through so much, but she still had to focus on getting Dante immediate help. She and her dad pulled him out of his seat. He'd grown weaker since the flight through the portal. His teeth chattered in his mouth; his skin hot to the touch.

Mr. Hiss's soft pink paws padded along the floor after them. His tail swayed in the heated early morning breeze.

Giarldinia had emerged from its fearful coma. Ships zipped through the air and sped along the skyway in sparkling streaks. The lights from the city glittered through the golden rays of the sunrise. The most distinct difference, however, from Universe 13 had to be the sky. It was no longer blue but instead shone the rich hue of amethyst. Nearby, stars and planets peeked through the glittering milky galaxy.

Emperor Brumha and his massive fleet lingered in the air, high above the palace, watching over them. Autumn was beyond grateful for all their assistance. She signaled for them to land.

As they made their way inside of the palace, helping Dante along, gossiping courtiers stared and whispered at the disheveled state he had arrived home in. Some gasped in horror, others snickered. The deep bruises on his face, his busted lip, and broken legs as he limped along attracted more than his usual share of attention. It was far from a triumphant return.

If he had been well, they wouldn't dare open their mouths. They were unappreciative and two-faced.

Some things never changed.

They'd seen what Emperor Izzo had done to him. Humiliated him in front of all the universes over broadcast. It didn't matter though, what anyone said or what they thought they knew; she had an ace up her sleeve. She was glad she thought ahead. She bit her cheeks. Autumn loved him more than anything despite his many imperfections. He was perfectly imperfect, and she was determined to protect him as he had protected her.

Leyla and Isidora came racing through the crimson carpeted halls. Tears streamed down their blue cheeks when they saw Dante.

"Thank you for taking care of him and bringing him back to us." The former empress helped them hold him up, getting blood and sweat all over the delicate tulle of her dress.

"I'm so glad you're alive," Leyla threw her arms around her and her brother.

Her dad watched in silence. She'd introduce them later. There was plenty of time for introductions.

They walked him through the palace and downstairs to the medical bay, despite the many prying eyes.

* * *

AT THE MEDICAL BAY, Dante was stripped of his navy-blue Zambarian uniform, boots, gloves, and tattered white cape, and placed into a rejuvenation tank. A mask was strapped across his battered face. His eyes fluttered closed as blue liquid filled up the chamber. He fell into a deep restful sleep, bubbles consuming him.

She sighed, pressing her fingers to the glass, fogging it with her breath. She needed him to recover so she could hold him in her arms again and tell him how much she missed him.

She wanted nothing more than to wait with him until he woke up, but she couldn't. She smoothed her hands along her thighs, sucking in a deep shuddering breath. She knew what came next and it wasn't going to be easy.

It was time for damage control, yet again. She didn't have a moment to lose, everyone was waiting on her.

"It's okay Autumn, we'll watch over him," Leyla pressed out a small smile. "He seems to have calmed down a bit."

"Thank you."

Leyla and her mom sat by the tank, talking amongst themselves. Dante slept in silence.

When she went to turn, she bumped into her dad.

"I think you should stay here and get checked out," her dad suggested, glancing at Dante's family as they sat by the tank watching and waiting. "You may need medical attention for yourself and your baby. Who knows if the liquid healed everything. I can't believe you're having a baby and I'm going to be a grandfather."

Neither could she.

"Is that okay?" she asked tentatively, waiting for his reaction.

"Of course it is." The corners of his eyes crinkled beneath his cracked silver frames. "This is going to take me a bit of getting used to but I'm so happy. And I'm happy we're finally together. Nothing will ever separate us again." He kissed her forehead.

He paused for a moment, lowering his voice to a whisper. "I only wish the father was—"

"Human?" she blurted.

He shook his head. "Not Dante. He has a lot of explaining to do, and he's not off the hook after the stunt he pulled."

She sighed. Her husband and her dad were never going to get along at this rate, but she didn't have time to worry about the specifics of their relationship. She had to make a public statement and save face. The planet was in an uproar.

Autumn went to leave the room when she encountered Ronan who stood in the doorway, arms crossed, head resting against the frame. He ran a hand through his short spiky hair. His emerald-green eyes shifted with worry.

"Hey, I remember you," her dad glanced his way. "Ronan, right?"

"Yes, I'm glad you're okay and that you made it here safely. I'm sorry again for what happened," Ronan glanced at the floor. "I should've known better than to trust an imposter posing as my brother."

"Sometimes mistakes happen but all we can do is learn from them and life goes on."

His mouth curved. "Can I talk to you for a moment, Autumn—in private?"

"Yes," she rose and followed him into the hallway.

He lowered his voice, eyes wandering around to make sure nobody was listening or at least that's what she supposed. "What happened out there? I heard all about Dante's tragic state and I saw the horrific broadcast before it cut out. Things were looking bleak. Is the Grand Supreme—"

"Yes, he's dead."

Ronan placed a black-gloved hand over his mouth, his eyes widened. "I'm glad, this was a long time coming. Too many have suffered needlessly at his hands for centuries."

A long silence followed. He shifted his weight.

"Did you find Armienti?" Hope filled his eyes.

"No," her heart sank. "But I promise we won't stop searching for him. We'll bring him home and everything will work out, you'll see. I know we can overcome this misunderstanding somehow."

"Thanks Autumn," he hugged her, and she was on her way. She could sense his great sadness drifting through the room, but she meant every word of what she'd said. She would find Armienti and bring him home.

Eighty-Two

BY THE TIME Autumn arrived in the throne room, the area was packed to capacity. The air was so warm she could scarcely breathe. Daylight sparkled through the stained-glass skylight of twisting stars. Her heeled go-go boots slid along the crimson velvet floor.

All eyes followed her as she made her way through the center aisle, her head held high. She wore a scarlet bodysuit with a gilded asymmetrical stripe. Her hair was fastened in a high curly ponytail, flecked with gold. Emblem and Allegoria had worked a miracle on her in mere minutes.

A heavy white velvet sack swung from her right arm, containing her war prize.

She inhaled and took her seat, crossing her legs. Drones buzzed overhead capturing the public statement. For the first time she wasn't afraid to speak publicly, especially after what she'd lived through. She could do this with her hands tied behind her back. It was no big deal or at least she tried to convince herself. Deep down she knew Dante's reputation was on the line.

She waved. "Greetings everyone."

The room remained silent and serious except for Leyla who smiled at her from the sideline, resting her cheek on Kyo's tall shoulder. Autumn took her reaction as an indication that Dante was going to be okay. Relief flooded through her body. She missed him more than anything.

"I know a lot of rumors are floating around about the invasion and the state of the emperor, that somehow he's incapable of protecting us, but let me set one thing straight, the Grand Supreme is dead."

Skeptical whispers followed long blank stares. One advisor stepped forth with his arms folded. He cocked his blue head to the side, dark-brown hair fastened in a low ponytail. She could sense his attitude from across the room. It tempted her to roll her eyes.

"Permission to speak, Your Imperial Majesty," his voice fluttered with sarcasm.

"Go ahead," she sighed.

"Well, how can we be so sure what you say is true? We all saw what happened." Murmurs erupted from around the room.

The advisor continued. "Everyone saw what happened. You're not fooling anyone, the emperor arrived half-dead. I'm calling your bluff. The Grand Supreme is undefeated."

Everyone watched and waited for her reply with bated breath. Luckily, she'd thought ahead.

She reached into the sack, fingers sliding against dry ink-black plates and pulled out what remained of the tyrant who ruled over the universes for the last four hundred years with an iron fist. She held the scaly prize high for the drones to see.

Her mouth curved with satisfaction. "I present to you, his head."

Gasps erupted around the room and the advisor stepped back, falling into a deep bow. *Good.* That shut him the heck up.

"Does anyone else have anything to add? Anyone else doubt the emperor's capabilities?"

The room remained quiet, not a single breath left anyone's mouth. The drones bumbled around. She placed the head back into the sack.

"Good, we should all pray for the safe recovery of the new Grand Supreme who almost sacrificed his life to keep you safe."

As she went to stand, she suddenly grew warm and hesitated. Her eyes drew to the sack. Goosebumps prickled up along her skin. She could've sworn she saw the mouth on the severed head move, forming words with its loose tongue. She fixated on it for a moment too long, zoning out as if hypnotized.

"There's a traitor among you," he grinned.

She blinked hard before closing the sack as tight as she could. Her imagination was running away with itself. *Gross.* She came to a shaking stand. She smiled at everyone before leaving the room with the bag. Everyone remained behind in complete silence as she made a clear run for it. Nobody dared counter. Nobody challenged her.

Autumn needed some fresh air and quick. She couldn't tell if it was from the situation or her pregnancy.

She raced to the rooftop of the palace, up several flights of crimson winding steps, and over to the edge. She glanced down to the earth far below that disappeared in the shadows. She took one last look at the disgusting head of her husband's mortal enemy before throwing it over the edge. The sack disappeared into the darkness.

Her eyes shut tight as she took in the sounds of the city. The hum of the aircraft, the smell of floating lavender, and the heat of the dual suns shining through the newborn amethyst sky. The rays warmed her golden olive skin making her feel better, or at least a little bit better. There was no season more beautiful than eternal summer in deep space.

"It's a shame—I was going to mount that trophy on the wall."

She turned around, eyes fogging with tears. Dante.

Eighty-Three

HIS MOUTH TILTED to the side in an arrogant sort of way. His white teeth sparkled, but his amber eyes were fathomless, consuming her. Her chest grew tight. Autumn rushed over and jumped into his arms. Tears trickled down her face.

He cupped his hands on her cheeks, as he lowered her to her feet. He leaned down to kiss her. His lips were warm and soft and urgent against hers. He tasted like fresh cinnamon.

Dante was back to his old self again thanks to the rejuvenation tank. She felt safe in his strong arms and for the first time in a long time, she was at peace. They could disappear right then and there, and she would be happy.

"Don't you look lovely," the words played off his lips like a song. "You have a certain newfound glow about you."

She smiled so hard her cheeks hurt. "I'm so glad you're back. I thought you were—"

"Dead?" His midnight hair swayed in the heated afternoon breeze, grazing his sharp jawbone. His fresh crimson cape rested over his shoulders. The metropolis in the distance hummed and sparkled with life. Warmth consumed every pore in her body.

She remained quiet, running her fingers through the loose onyx strands of his hair.

"So did I," he gazed into her eyes. "You should've left when you had the chance. I gave you every opportunity to escape and stay safe. But still, you didn't listen. You're so stubborn, Autumn. You shouldn't have come for me. I'm not worth sacrificing your life for."

"Well, that wasn't your choice to make," she said. Her heart ached. "I'm tired of you making choices for me. I can think for myself."

He remained quiet, resting his chin on her head. She closed her eyes feeling safe in his strong arms. "That you can."

He sighed. "To think that monster put his hands on you and tried to steal the beautiful gift we created for his own selfish gain and there was nothing I could do to stop him," he gently placed his hand against her belly, choking up. "It makes me sick. I promise I won't fail you again. I'm far from perfect, but I can strive to be the best version of myself I can. I'll protect you and our family no matter what."

She listened to the sound of his accelerating heart, succumbing to his soft-spoken voice. She closed her eyes as he changed the subject. "I heard your speech before while I was healing. It was magnificent, but thank you, you don't have to worry about me. I don't care what anyone else thinks. I only care what you think. Your opinion is the only one that matters to me. It always has been."

"You mean everything to me," she murmured.

He brought his mouth to hers kissing her again and they walked along the rooftop, hand in hand. Her feet grew as light as air. She could fly—well, *literally*. She rested her head against his solid arm.

She did a double take as Emperor Brumha approached them. It wasn't her imagination after all. He commanded the massive fleet that rested in the air, glittering through the cloudless sky. His white velvet cape swayed over his shoulders. He removed his helmet, holding it in the crook of his arm and she prepared herself for the spray bath.

"Well, my friend, I must be going now," Emperor Brumha smiled between them. His silver skin sparkled in the sunlight. The wisps of his white hair curled along his scalp.

"Thank you again for all your help," Dante extended his hand shaking Emperor Brumha's.

"Don't be a stranger and don't be afraid to reach out if you ever need anything from me. I'll always be here even if it's just to talk."

"You as well," Dante waved as the ice emperor turned on his heel making his way back to his destroyer. Once he was safely onboard, Dante pulled the silver orb from his pocket and popped open the crack with his thumb. Purple light flashed, and in an instant, Emperor Brumha and his fleet were transported back to the lower universes. He closed the silver ball, placing it back into his pocket. She couldn't help but stare in wonderment.

She grinned. "Friends, did I hear you say friends? You made a friend while you were gone?"

"Yeah, I think so," the apples of his blue cheeks shifted to pink. He followed her over to the ledge where she had a seat. He sat beside her, holding her hand in his. "He's not so bad after I took the time to get to know him. He's actually kind."

"Well, I think that's wonderful."

"I think you're wonderful."

Her cheeks heated.

He glanced away before meeting her gaze. "You once accused me of not caring enough about what you want and your needs. You called me selfish. Well, I meant every word I wrote in the letter to you."

She stuttered. "I—"

"I have been selfish, and I'd like to change that. What is it that you'd find fulfilling? Just say the word and it's done. I want to make you happy more than anything."

She stared at him, thinking long and hard. She had her family, her dad, the man who she loved and adored, and a baby on the way. If she was honest, she no longer wanted to go back to Earth just yet. Eventually, she wanted to see her friends again, but she'd adjusted to her new life even if it took longer than expected.

Everything in her world for the first time seemed perfect. It was the oddest feeling.

She opened her mouth as if to speak, choosing her words carefully. She didn't want to jinx her current situation. She hadn't been this happy in years.

"I think I'd like to help people," she twisted her fingers in her lap. "I want to go back to school to be a doctor. The best in my field. I want to pick up where I left off on Earth."

His amber eyes lit up. "Then you start tomorrow," he paused. "I have something for you that will come in handy, something I should've returned a while ago."

She blinked and he disappeared for a moment before teleporting beside her. He held her cosmic backpack in his hands.

"I want to apologize for taking your belongings when you first arrived on Surge. It was so very wrong of me, but I just wanted to protect you from being mistaken as a hybrid and being hurt again. Now all that seems so trivial."

He handed her the bag.

She held her backpack in her lap. "Thank you for returning this to me. I thought it was gone forever."

"No, I kept it hidden in my closet for safekeeping."

She nodded, cheeks warming.

"Oh," his eyes lit up. He ruffled through the back pocket of his uniform and removed a book. He handed it to her as well. The copy of *Dracula* she'd failed to return to the library. The pages and cover were creased and fraying. It had a weathered smell. "I've carried this everywhere with me since

I brought you here from Earth. I read it to you many times during our first voyage together in the hope that I could somehow get closer to you. Somehow understand you better, somehow get you to forgive me."

She leaned over and kissed him, running her hand through the silken strands of his obsidian hair. "We understand each other perfectly. There's nobody I love, nobody I trust, and nobody I want to be with more than you."

He brought his lips to hers, running his fingers along her back. Goosebumps trickled down her spine. "*I love you more,*" his thoughts caressed her mind through their bond.

He pulled away, his mouth curling in a lazy grin. "I was thinking that maybe if you're up for it, I could use a long hot bath. The regeneration tank doesn't count," he nipped at her neck.

She chewed back a smile. "Sounds like a plan. In exchange, I'm making a second request."

Dante watched her, waiting. "Anything."

"You can start getting along with my dad. How's that?"

He snorted. "I'm sorry, that's one thing I can't promise."

Her forehead twitched. "I'm afraid it's non-negotiable." She remained determined to keep the peace in her family.

"I'll do my best," he offered, his long lashes grazing his prominent cheekbones.

By the time they left the palace rooftop and headed downstairs, the sky sparkled up with countless stars. Vibrant purple glimmered in the setting sun, casting rays over the never sleeping city of Giarldinia. Tomorrow promised to be a new day filled with love, hope, and endless possibilities. Finally, Autumn had gotten her wish because she wasn't afraid to ask for what she wanted.

Eighty-Four

SOMEWHERE DEEP IN the heart of Universe 24, Armienti stirred, haunted by the mistakes in his life. He was so tired, so very tired of nothing ever going his way. From losing the kingdom of his birthright, to never getting the girls he fell in love with, to always being "the friend," when he wanted so much more out of life. His family had lied about him and kept him like a dirty little secret to be discarded and ignored.

He deserved better, he finally realized.

He sat in the pitch darkness of the Palace of Despair wondering and waiting for far too long. He'd been duped. The palace was empty, and he wasn't worth anyone's time. What a fool he was to think the Grand Supreme could help him in his plight. What a fool he was to think he had all the answers he was searching for. They didn't exist, at least not for him. Nothing ever turned out the way it was supposed to.

A traitor they called him. Traitors never won in the end.

Shadows danced and swirled around the room. Disembodied voices whispered, chilling him to the bone. The voices wouldn't leave him alone no matter how hard he tried to ignore them. They crept into his subconscious, trailed him through every crevice of his mind. He was such a failure.

They told him to fight, told him to kill. They told him to take back everything that belonged to him. After all, it wasn't stealing when it always should've been his.

A series of gentle footsteps disrupted him from his tortured thoughts. Bare feet pattered against the carpeted floor outside of the closed door of Emperor Izzo's throne room he'd been locked inside of against his will.

His eyes drew to the door as it slid open slowly one centimeter at a time. A silhouette entered; a ghost long lost. His mouth fell open, curiosity getting the best of him as she approached.

Her silver eyes, dark curly hair, and rosy cheeks disarmed him. Maeve stood there smiling, chewing her bottom lip. She wore a pitch-black bodysuit. She stood on her tiptoes running her fingers through his hair.

His eyes flickered. "This is impossible. You're dead. You can't be here right now."

She tilted her head to the side, flashing a brilliant smile. Her lashes brushed against her rosy cheeks. "Am I?"

Acknowledgments

I want to thank my mom who was my first ever reader and who was the first person who was interested in what was going to happen next. Without your encouragement and feedback I never would have started writing to begin with and I never would have shared my stories and characters with anyone.

Thank you to my family for always being there for me.

Thank you to Mike for always supporting me no matter what.

Thank you to my friends who supported me throughout the years from our original WAT writing

group. Your friendship means the world to me: Cobie, Reina, Eric, Jessica, Tanya, Jess, and Reina Nyx.

Thank you to my editor friend B.K. Ntouris who helped me revise Foiled Stars while I was querying and thank you to my in-house editors Dannie and Chey.

Finally, I want to thank my publisher Stag Beetle Books for supporting me and my vision for my stories every step of the way. Without you none of this would be possible.